D1042380

MIDNIGHT BRIDE

By Susan Carroll:

WINTERBOURNE
THE PAINTED VEIL
THE BRIDE FINDER
THE NIGHT DRIFTER
MIDNIGHT BRIDE

MIDNIGHT BRIDE

SUSAN CARROLL

Ballantine Books • New York

A Ballantine Book
Published by The Ballantine Publishing Group

Copyright © 2001 by Susan Coppula

All rights reserved under International and Pan-American Copyright Conventions. Published in the
United States by The Ballantine Publishing Group, a division of Random House, Inc., New York,
and simultaneously in Canada by Random House of Canada Limited, Toronto.

www.randomhouse.com/BB/

Library of Congress Cataloging-in-Publication Data is available upon request.

ISBN 0-345-43397-1

Manufactured in the United States of America

First Edition: May 2001

10   9   8   7   6   5   4   3   2   1

This book is dedicated to two women of remarkable strength and courage:
My daughter, Serena, and my dear friend, Kim.
Ladies, out of the darkness, your light came shining through.

MIDNIGHT BRIDE

PROLOGUE

*T*he ship glided over the waves, the dark outline of the coast looming closer on the horizon. Passengers gathered on the deck, laughing and sharing the joy of imminent arrival, all except the man who had kept to himself for the entire voyage, so grim and unapproachable, no one had dared speak to him.

Raphael Mortmain stood alone at the deck rail, his profile averted from his fellow travelers. Even after an absence of five years, he had taken a great risk by returning to Cornwall, a man branded as a pirate, a thief, and a murderer with a large price on his head.

But illness had left his frame wasted to a skeletal thinness, his once trim dark hair lank and shaggy, his gaunt face lost beneath a layering of beard. Rafe doubted his own mother would have recognized him now. If she would have even bothered to try.

Evelyn Mortmain had abandoned him in Paris when he'd been no more than eight years old. He'd never heard tell of her again, except for the report of her death, her life flung away on the obsession that had consumed her, had meant more to her than her only son. The obsession that had tormented all the Mortmains for generations: the destruction of their enemies, the St. Leger family.

It was like a sickness in the blood, a madness that Rafe had never succumbed to in all his forty years—until recently. Now it was all that filled his thoughts both night and day. He shivered, taking a large quaff from a small silver flask. The whiskey burned his throat, but did nothing to warm the permanent chill that had settled in his bones. He wiped his mouth with a once strong hand that never seemed to be steady of late.

He squinted toward the distant outcropping of shore wreathed in mist. Cornwall, a land steeped in legends of romance and magic, fairy stories and hero tales, Rafe thought sardonically. It was nothing more than a bleak, isolated coast, the perfect place to exact his revenge, each swell of the ship drawing Rafe closer to *him*. The oh so noble Dr. Valentine St. Leger.

Hatred surged through Rafe, so virulent he shook with it as he remembered how hard he had once tried to lead a respectable life. His career as a customs officer had obliged him to return to that part of Cornwall where his ancestors had attained such infamy, but Rafe had sought desperately to put the taint of his heritage behind him. He'd managed to reach past the ancient Mortmain–St. Leger feud, find a friend in Lance St. Leger, perhaps the only true friend Rafe had ever known in his entire lonely life.

But Val St. Leger had put an end to all that. The stiff-necked doctor had made an extensive study of the misdeeds of the Mortmains, the injuries they had done to the St. Legers over the centuries. Val couldn't forget that Rafe was the last descendant of such a villainous line, nor would he allow anyone else to do so either, including his twin brother Lance.

And it hadn't helped that in his bitterness, Rafe had made mistakes. Terrible ones. He was willing to admit that, but he had been struggling hard to put everything right when Val St. Leger had interfered, cruelly exposing his sins, costing Rafe his friendship with Lance, costing him everything, obliging him to flee for his very life. No second chance for a damnable Mortmain.

"And now no second chance for a St. Leger either, doctor," Rafe whispered, taking another swallow of the whiskey. It caught in his throat, bringing on a coughing spasm, violent and painful. His entire body shook with the force of it, and this time when he wiped his mouth, his fingers came away bright with blood.

A consumption of the lungs, that was the verdict the doctor in Boston had pronounced about his condition. But Rafe felt that the illness wasting him was something far more insidious, more unnatural. Some darkness of the soul, years of suppressed rage, bitterness and despair, frustrated dreams and hopes eating away at him like acid, threatening his very reason.

Val St. Leger would pay for it. The mere thought of the St. Leger's solemn disapproving features caused Rafe to tense with longing to wrap his hands around the doctor's throat and—

It wasn't until his nails dug into his own palms that Rafe realized what he was doing, clawing his hands into fists. He forced himself to relax, released a jagged breath. No, killing the noble Valentine would be far too swift a vengeance, over far too soon. Rafe had something more subtle, more cruel in mind. And none of the doctor's unique heritage would be able to save him. All those romantic legends, tales of strange inherited powers, whispers of magic.

Indeed it was the fabled St. Leger magic that was going to prove the good doctor's undoing. Rafe reached beneath the flap of his greatcoat, drawing out the object concealed there, fastened by a tarnished chain around his neck. A small shard of crystal dangled from the end of the silver braid, looking so dull that for a moment the mists clouding Rafe's mind shifted, allowing him a brief glimpse of his own sanity.

There was something cursed about this crystal he had stolen from the St. Legers. It had done something to him dark, terrible, and strange. Even now he could put an end to this madness, if he would just . . . just . . .

The crystal caught the light, flashing in Rafe's eyes, and the thought was lost. His fingers closed over the shard, piercingly cold. It sent a shudder through him, a weakness so dizzying he was obliged to clutch the deck rail for support.

Ah, God! He didn't know how much longer he could conserve what remained of his strength. As soon as the boat docked, he needed to find a horse, ride as fast and hard as he could toward the village of Torrecombe, to Castle Leger perched high above the rugged cliffs. The risks of being seen and recognized no longer mattered. The threat of the gallows held no terror for him.

He was already a dying man and he knew it. And that made Rafe Mortmain more dangerous than he had ever been.

Chapter One

The wind rattled the cottage windowpanes, the pale sun presiding over a day that seemed endless to the young woman who writhed upon the bed. As the next contraction hit in a hard wave, Carrie Trewithan clutched her fingers across her distended belly and was unable to stifle a sharp cry.

The midwife hovered over her, patting a cool cloth to Carrie's perspiring brow. "There, there, dearie. Try to hold on. 'Twill all be over soon enough, I'll be bound." Sarah gave her a broad toothless smile, but the fear in the old woman's eyes was unmistakable.

Something was going terribly wrong this time. Carrie had labored hard for seventeen hours, all through last night, the morning and into the afternoon, longer than she'd ever done before, and still no babe. She sank back weakly against the pillows of the rough wooden bedstead, her lank brown hair tumbling about her. She couldn't endure much more of this. She could feel her strength fading with each fresh wave of pain.

I'm going to die, she thought, closing her eyes tight to stem the flood of tears. Not for herself but for the helpless little ones she'd be forced to leave behind. The new babe if it lived and her other children, Janey, Tom, Sam, and Aggie. What would become of them with no mother to look after them?

Lost in the haze of her own misery, Carrie was only vaguely aware of Sarah moving away from the bed to whisper fiercely to someone attempting to enter the room. No doubt little Tom, crying again, wanting his mama. Lord knows, Carrie didn't want any of her children seeing her this way. It took a great effort, but she turned her head to deliver a gentle admonishment, her eyes fluttering open. Her breath caught in her throat instead.

It wasn't Tom. A man filled her threshold, carrying with him the powerful scent of crisp autumn air. His broad shoulders were draped in a caped great-coat that fell to his knees, casting a dark presence like the specter of death itself.

Carrie stiffened in fear as the stranger stumped closer, his heavy boots ringing off the floor in an uneven gait. But before she could cry out, he stripped off his cloak and beaver hat, passing them to Sarah. The light filtering through the dirty windowpane fell full upon his face. No hideous spectral features but those of a mortal man. His wind-tossed black hair and heavy dark brows appeared too harsh for the pale hue of his countenance, the alarming lines of his hawklike nose at odds with the sensitive cast of his mouth. But one glance at him was enough for anyone to tell. This was a good man, a kind one, his strength tempered by gentleness.

Carrie's fear evaporated in an awed sigh of relief.

"Oh, Dr. St. Leger," she whispered. "You—you came."

"Aye, Carrie." He smiled down at her. He had a quiet smile, a mere half-quirking of the lips that marked him as a man who did not easily give way to mirth. He scolded gently, "Why on earth did you not send for me sooner?"

" I should not have sent for you at all. I—I have not much money—"

"Hush. That's not important."

As he drew up a chair close to her bedside, Carrie moistened her lips, rushing to finish her explanation before the next wave of pain robbed her of breath. " 'Tis only that it has gone on so long this time and—and it hurts so bad and I'm so tired—" Her voice broke on a dry sob. "You're the only one who can help me, Dr. St. Leger. The only one."

"And so I will, Carrie. Everything is going to be all right now." His voice was soothing, filled with such quiet conviction that she believed him, even though she knew that her husband, Reeve, would be mighty angry with her for daring to summon the local doctor.

She should have been frightened to have done so herself. He was the youngest son of the dread lord of Castle Leger, Anatole St. Leger, a man rumored to be descended from a sorcerer. It was whispered that all St. Legers had a bit of the demon in them.

But she saw no demons in Valentine St. Leger's solemn features. Rather he had the eyes of an angel, warm, compassionate, full of the knowledge of human suffering, because he knew what it was to suffer himself. She panicked a little as the next contraction started to build, but she felt his strong hand close over hers.

"Don't be afraid, Carrie. Just look at me and hold on tight," he said.

Her breath hitched in her throat, but she struggled to do as he asked. She gripped his hand and stared deep in his remarkable eyes, a rich velvety shade of brown. And at the touch of his palm against hers, something strange began to happen. First it was a mere tingling, then a warmth that slowly spread up her wrist like a golden liquid rushing through her veins. The terrible pain began to ebb.

She saw the doctor's mouth tighten as though all her suffering was being drained from her into him. It was what everyone in the village whispered he could do, work this inexplicable magic, but Carrie had never fully believed it until now.

She knew she was in the throes of another terrible contraction, but she felt nothing, her eyelids growing heavy, deliciously drowsy. She lost all track of the minutes that she had counted with such agonizing precision before. From some great distance, she thought she heard Dr. St. Leger's strained voice rapping out orders to Sarah, commanding Carrie herself to push. She felt a rush of warmth between her legs followed moments later by a tiny cry.

"God be praised," Sarah seemed to sing out from a hundred miles away.

Carrie merely smiled like one floating in the mists of a dream. When she finally felt able to open her eyes again, something nestled in the crook of her arm, something soft and wriggling. Still half-dazed, Carrie peeled back the blanket to see that it was a babe, a little girl.

Like a sleepwalker jerked awake, reality sank in. She had just been delivered of a daughter. She was worn to a thread; she already had four other children she scarce had the strength to care for. Ah, but this new little girl of hers was such a miracle, so healthy, so perfect, and Carrie was still here to cradle the babe in her arms. Tears of joy trickled down her cheeks.

She turned to thank the angel who had seen her through this ordeal. But like the mysterious St. Leger that he was, the good doctor had already disappeared.

The road leading to Castle Leger wound uphill, a narrow track half lost in the purple haze of twilight. But the roan gelding moved with a sure step, a fortunate thing for his master was scarce alert enough to guide him.

Barely able to remain upright in the saddle, Val St. Leger hunched over, his bleary eyes struggling to focus on the road ahead. Exhaustion melted into the very marrow of his bones. He felt as drained as if . . . as if he'd just endured three hours of agonizing labor to bring forth a child?

Val's mouth crooked in a tired smile. He'd wager there were few other men who could lay claim to such a feat. He would never make his mark in the world as a soldier, a brilliant artist, or a great statesman. But his strange St. Leger gift offered him at least one distinction. He knew firsthand how much pain had to be endured to give birth and he could only marvel at the strength of women to continue populating the world. Especially Carrie Trewithan.

The poor woman had been constantly with child these past seven years if one counted her miscarriages. Val had warned her oaf of a husband that Carrie's frail body needed time to recover. It had been a miracle that she had survived this last pregnancy, and while she had fought to bring their child into the world, Reeve Trewithan had been off drinking at the Dragon's Fire Inn, boasting about his potency. The man was notorious for neglecting his family, staggering home only when he felt the itch to drag his wife into bed.

Val would have to have another word with Trewithan tomorrow. A word! Val felt his hands tighten on the reins. He wanted to thrash Reeve Trewithan senseless. It was what his brother Lance would have done. But such behavior was not to be expected from the village doctor and a crippled one to boot.

An old injury had left Val with a permanent limp and his bad knee was flaring worse than usual tonight. Already tired from battling his own pain, it had not been the wisest thing, taking on Mrs. Trewithan's suffering as well. But what else could he have done? Val thought, remembering Carrie's hollow eyes, the desperation in her voice.

"You're the only one who can help me, Dr. St. Leger. The only one."

How often had he heard that plaintive refrain from too many suffering souls? The memory of pleading eyes, beseeching cries haunted him even in his sleep, pursued him in his waking hours. Unconsciously he attempted to spur Vulcan onward as though he would outride the persistent voices. He paid at once for the inadvertent movement. A stabbing pain shot through his knee.

Val gasped, drawing in several sharp breaths until the pain subsided to a dull ache. And it had made no difference to Vulcan. The horse continued to plod along at his own steady pace. There had been a time in his youth when Val had been able to spend a hard day in the saddle and then battle at swords with his brother half the night. A time when he had been able to handle the most spirited hunters in his father's stable.

But remembering could only stir up bitter thoughts and regrets. Grieving over all that he had lost was something Val never allowed himself to do. He kept such dark emotions tamped deep down in the secret corner of his soul where they belonged.

As Vulcan rounded the next bend, Val was heartened, some of his weariness dissolving at the sight of his destination. A thick line of oaks obscured the newer portion of Castle Leger, but the battlements of the old keep soared above the trees. Even after so many centuries, the main tower still pierced the sky. The chamber had been the private refuge of the first lord of the castle, Prospero St. Leger. In that weathered turret the wily sorcerer had worked his black spells, tampered with the strange alchemy that had eventually brought about his downfall, condemning him to be burned at the stake.

A fairy tale, some might scoff, but Val had researched enough of his family's past to know that it was all true. Both history and legend were mortared into the stone walls of Castle Leger, tales of valor and tales of magic.

How often his heart had swelled at the sight of those towering ramparts as he'd galloped home at twilight, Lance leading the way with Val following at a more sedate pace. He had always been the more cautious twin, the scholar, the dreamer. It was difficult to ride full tilt when his head was so stuffed full of books and romantic fantasies, imagining himself to be a bold knight returning to the castle astride his fiery steed to kneel at the feet of the beautiful lady who awaited him. He'd never been able to envision clearly her face, only the gentleness of her smile, the sweet glow of her eyes, her white slender arms reaching out to welcome him home.

That had been before he'd grown up enough to realize there were few professional prospects for a knight in the nineteenth century. Far more sensible to dream of becoming a doctor. And it was just as well, Val sighed, flexing his tired, aching muscles. He would have never been anyone's idea of a bold knight, Vulcan was no fiery steed, and as for the lady . . .

There would never be a lady. At least not for him.

And yet there was *someone* waiting at the crest of the hill. A woman. Her willowy figure was draped in a scarlet cloak, the hood flung back, her hair spilling like a rippling shadow over her shoulders. The dying rays of the sun framed her in a brilliant burst of gold, dazzling Val's eyes, stirring in him remembrance of the lady he'd conjured in his boyhood dreams.

He blinked hard, wondering if his exhausted eyes were playing tricks on him. Or perhaps his romantic imagination wasn't as dead as he thought it was. He leaned forward eagerly as he drew nearer, only to slump back, smiling at his own idiocy as he recognized who it was.

It was certainly no lady. It was only his young friend Kate, the adopted daughter of a distant relative of his, Elfreda Fitzleger. When she spied Val, the girl let out a loud whoop and came tearing down the hill, her skirts hiked up to a scandalous level.

"Blast it, Kate, slow down," Val roared out.

Either she didn't hear him or, far more likely, she paid him no heed. She only picked up momentum, her gypsy black hair streaming behind her. Val reined in Vulcan, fearful that in her recklessness, the girl would dart directly into the horse's path.

Val held his breath, expecting at any moment that she would lose her footing and come tumbling the rest of the way. He'd already lost track of the number of skinned knees he'd bandaged and the bones he'd reset for Miss Kate over the years.

But somehow the little hoyden made it down the steep track in one piece. Val let out a breath of relief as Kate fetched up beside the gelding's head, holding on to Vulcan's reins, panting and laughing from the sheer exhilaration of her mad dash. The horse gave a joyous whicker of recognition, nuzzling her ear.

Kate's laughter was pure silver, so infectious Val had trouble maintaining a stern façade as he frowned down at her. "Katherine Fitzleger. Have you quite taken leave of your senses?"

"Very—very likely," she gasped out. Fully recovering her breath, she marched around to stand by his boot. A rosy flush spread across cheeks that were still tanned from the summer. Kate found bonnets a great nuisance.

She smiled beguilingly up at him. "What have I done now to make you look so cross?"

"What have you done! Merely come plunging down that steep hill when it is already nearly dark. You could have fallen and broke your neck."

"But I didn't."

"What are you doing out here anyway?"

"Waiting for you."

"Alone? In the dark."

"In the *nearly dark*," she corrected him. "Besides, what could happen to me even if it were midnight? No one would dare trifle with me on St. Leger lands, not even an accursed Mortmain. And you drove off the last of those villains years ago."

So Kate persisted in believing, imagining Val to have performed some heroic action on that occasion. If Rafe Mortmain had been banished from Cornwall, it had been owing more to Lance, Val thought. Val had succeeded only in nearly getting himself killed.

"It doesn't matter how close we are to the castle," he continued to scold.

"You should not be wandering off alone anymore. You are a young lady—well, at least a young woman—now."

"You've finally noticed," Kate purred, fluttering her long thick lashes in a way that disconcerted him. If it had been anyone else but Kate, he might have imagined she was attempting to flirt with him.

"Yes, I've noticed, and no doubt so have many of the young lads hereabouts. If you persist in jaunting off alone . . ." Val paused, clearing his throat uncomfortably, trying to find some delicate way to explain his fear to the girl. "You could be—could be—"

"Raped?" Kate filled in bluntly.

"I was going to say subjected to some very unwelcome attentions."

"Pooh! I'd like to see any man try it. It would be the sorriest day of his life, especially when I have this." Kate groped beneath her cloak to the bulging inner pocket. With a triumphant flourish, she unsheathed a small flintlock pistol, which she brandished at Val.

Val jerked back involuntarily, startling Vulcan. "Sweet mother of God, Kate! Put that thing away before you hurt yourself."

"It hasn't been loaded . . . yet."

Val tightened his grip on the reins, leaning forward to give Vulcan's neck a soothing pat. As soon as the animal had quieted, Val extended his hand toward Kate. "Give me that infernal weapon. Right now."

All she gave him was a serene smile as she lifted up the flap of her cloak and tucked the pistol back in her hidden pocket. "You needn't fret, Val. I didn't steal it or anything. The pistol is mine. It was a present from Lance."

Val seldom swore, but he did so now, muttering under his breath. His brother had always been amused by Kate's wild ways, encouraging the chit to don breeches, climb trees, even learn how to fence. But giving Kate a pistol. Had Lance entirely lost his mind?

As soon as he reached Castle Leger, Val intended to seize his brother by the cravat and tell him—Tell him what? Val snorted. Lecturing his incorrigible twin was about as useful as lecturing the kitchen cat. Or Kate.

Unperturbed by his reaction to her *gift*, she struggled to mount in front of him, the perch she had claimed from the time she'd been a little girl. Val had no choice but to haul her up. Bracing against the inevitable pull on his knee, he hefted her into the saddle. Not a difficult task. She was still a slip of a thing. Sometimes, it seemed to Val, she had not grown much taller since the orphaned girl had first arrived in Torrecombe ten years ago, all knobby knees and wide, defiant eyes.

She settled against his thighs, wrapping her arms about him, causing him to flinch when she brushed her fingers against his neck. Her hands were ice cold. Kate had, as usual, seen fit to dispense with her gloves.

"Now, you were saying," she said, assuming a meek expression as though she meant to heed every word he had to say. But it didn't work with Kate. There was too much fire sparkling in her storm gray eyes, too much mischief lurking in her bow-shaped mouth, too much stubbornness stroked into her delicate chin.

Val gave over the scolding with a resigned laugh. "Ah, Kate, Kate, whatever am I to do with you? You worry the devil out of me, girl."

"You don't have any devil in you, Val St. Leger." She proceeded to rain enthusiastic kisses across his face, hitting his brows, his cheeks, his chin, and coming perilously close to the corner of his mouth.

"Stop that," he growled, struggling to get her to desist and still maintain his grip on Vulcan's reins. "When are you going to learn to behave yourself?"

"When are you going to stop fretting over me?" She subsided with a final peck on his nose. "I can take care of myself and you, too. If any villain ever threatens either one of us, I'll turn him into a warthog."

"Now, Kate, you promised me. No more of that kind of talk." Val pulled back enough to peer down at her anxiously. "Er, you haven't been meddling with any more of that—that—"

"Witchcraft," Kate filled in with a wicked waggling of her brows. "How could I after you took away that fascinating book I found?"

"And just as well I did, after what happened. You actually had old Ben Gurney believing that you could cast some sort of spell on his pig."

"A love spell. And what a charming couple they would have made." Kate chuckled but stopped immediately at Val's frown. She peeled one hand away from him long enough to raise it solemnly. "Val, I swear to you, since then I have not been attempting to practice any more magic upon the unfortunate people of Torrecombe."

"Good," he said, relieved by her earnest reassurance. It wasn't that he feared that Kate actually could instruct herself in the black arts. The book he had taken from Kate had been mere superstitious nonsense. Casting spells was not even an ability any of the St. Legers had ever possessed, unless one placed credence in all the old tales of Prospero's sorcery. Most of Kate's antics thus far had been harmless, but given the girl's penchant for making mischief, it was as well that she left dabbling in the occult alone.

She was looking deceptively angelic at the moment. Hugging him tightly, she nestled her head against his shoulder with a contented sigh. Val stiffened a little, knowing he ought to discourage this. Kate truly was too old to be fling-ing herself at him in this fashion, too old to be waiting for him at the roadside and running to be lifted onto his horse.

He could make her promise not to do it anymore. For all her madcap ways, Kate had a strong streak of honor. She'd keep her vow. But even knowing it would be for the best, he couldn't bring himself to extract such a pledge from her.

He was far too glad she'd come, too glad of the warm feel of her cuddled close, revealing that gentler side of her nature the restless Kate reserved for him alone. He deposited a brotherly kiss atop her curly dark head, some of his exhaustion seeming to evaporate merely with the fresh, sweet scent of her hair.

Arms stretched around Kate, he urged Vulcan into motion again, and the old horse set off at a very sedate walk as though aware of the precious burden he carried. Kate mumbled against Val's shoulder, "All right, I suppose I *should* have waited for you tamely by the parlor fireside. But you know how impatient I get and you were taking so long. Where have you been all this time, Val?"

"Tending to a patient, my dear."

"Old Mrs. McGinty?"

"No, Carrie Trewithan. I delivered her of her child, another daughter."

"But the Trewithans usually summon the midwife for that. Why did Carrie need to have you—"

Kate broke off, her head jerking up from his shoulder to study his face, her eyes far too keen and accusing. "Val! You used your power again, didn't you?"

He shrugged, but didn't attempt to deny it. Kate knew him too well for that, and no doubt the haggard set of his face spoke for itself.

"Damn it, Val. You know you—"

"Don't swear, Kate."

"—shouldn't have been messing about with your power again. It's wearing you to a shadow and—and it's dangerous!"

"Dangerous," Val scoffed. "My father's power to fling a man across the room with one flash of his eyes is *dangerous*. My brother's ability to separate his body from his soul and go drifting through the night is *dangerous*. My power to absorb pain is pretty tame by comparison."

"So tame that it already cost you the use of your leg."

Val flinched. The one time he'd lost control of his power had cost him more than his leg. It had nearly cost him his brother as well. He and Lance had been estranged for a long time after that grim day on the battlefield in Spain, a rift that had been mended only in recent years. Val didn't care to be reminded of that dark period in their lives and Kate knew that. But she never minded her tongue when she was angry or distressed, and she was clearly both at the moment. Val had assured her many times before that she did not need to worry so much over him, but he mustered his patience to do so again.

"Kate, I promise you I am very careful now about how and when I use my power. Today, I simply had no choice."

"That's what you always say."

He smiled at her and said, "This time it happens to be true. I verily believe Mrs. Trewithan might have died if I hadn't helped her. She simply had no endurance left. She was never that strong and her body is purely worn out from birthing children."

"Because that husband of hers is a disgusting lecher. Reeve Trewithan should be castrated, his pecker whacked off with a red hot knife."

"Kate!"

"I forgot. Innocent young ladies aren't supposed to be aware of such things. But you know I have never been all that innocent, Val," she added rather sadly.

Few details were known of Kate's childhood before her adoption, but it was obvious she had learned far too much too soon about the darker side of life. Whatever Kate remembered of those grim days, she had chosen to forget, but at times Val glimpsed a world-weariness in her young eyes that brought an ache to his heart. He tenderly eased her head to rest back against his shoulder.

They rode in silence, their bodies rocked together by the gentle pace of old Vulcan. But Kate could never allow any discussion to lapse until she had the final word.

"I'll tell you one thing, Valentine St. Leger. Whenever I am with child, I won't allow you to bear my pain. I'll be strong enough to handle it all myself."

Val was hard pressed not to laugh at that. The notion of his wild Kate becoming anyone's wife, anyone's mother was—was—

Not as absurd as he wanted to believe. Val felt his smile fade, knowing that time was approaching faster than he wished. Kate would sally out into the world and find herself a strapping young husband, begin a family of her own. It was only natural and right, yet it filled him with an inexplicable melancholy.

Val strained her close the rest of the ride home. Without any prompting from him, Vulcan carried them to the stable yard behind Castle Leger's newest wing, an imposing Georgian manor that seemed mismatched to the old fourteenth-century keep.

The quadrangular block of stables at Castle Leger was nearly as impressive as the house. On the ground floor were enough stalls to accommodate more than twenty hunters, mares, and carriage horses; the spacious tack room; and the coach house itself with its wide doors. Above were the hayloft and sleeping quarters for the army of grooms and stable hands.

The yard was quiet this time of evening, with Tobias, the plump head coachman, lolling on a bench, smoking his pipe. But at Val's approach, two of the burly young grooms darted out, nearly colliding in their efforts to help Kate down from the saddle. Val frowned, finding their overeagerness surprisingly annoying.

It scarce mattered in any case. Kate dismounted after her own fashion. Before Val could remonstrate, she had squirmed out of his arms and managed to slide to the ground in a flurry of skirts. Val suppressed a deep sigh. Just once, it might have been nice if he could have leapt down first and lifted her out of the saddle.

But his blasted leg was so stiff, he was fortunate he didn't disgrace himself by falling flat on his face in his struggles to alight. The impact of his boot striking the ground jarred his knee as he'd known it would. All he could do was grit his teeth and brace himself for the stab of pain.

He clung to the stirrup for a moment to steady himself. Kate unstrapped his ivory-handled cane from the saddle and handed it to him as practically as any medieval woman would have reminded her knight that he needed his sword.

But then Kate was well accustomed to his infirmity, Val reflected. She had never known him to be any different, had no recollection of when he'd been able to stand as steady and strong as any other man. That thought had never saddened him before, but tonight, for some odd reason, it did.

As Vulcan was led off to the stables, Val tried not to rely as heavily on the cane as he usually did. Ignoring the ache in his knee, he offered Kate his arm to escort her toward the house.

She seized hold of his hand instead, attempting to tug him in the opposite direction. "Please, Val. Must we go in just yet?"

Val regarded her in mild surprise. "I fear I am already overdue, and you know how my father is about dinner being served on time."

"It is not that late yet. Please, Val. We could go take a stroll in the garden."

"The garden." Val gave an incredulous laugh. "In the dark and the cold?"

"The moon is rising and it is only a wee bit chilly. And I have not seen you all day, nay scarce all week. I just want us to have some time alone. Oh, please, Val, *please.*"

She tugged more insistently at his hand, peering up at him through the thickness of her lashes. He was tired, his knee was aching like the very devil, but Val had never been proof against that look, perhaps because Kate rarely ever begged favors of anyone. She was far too proud.

It was no longer appropriate, their spending so much time alone with each other, but the truth was, he had greatly missed her company himself this past week. And their time together was growing so short. . . .

He acceded to her request, allowing her to lead him up the worn path that led to the gardens, a rustling wilderness of flowers and shrubs lit by the half-moon that hung like a broken locket in the dark night sky.

The current head gardener had labored all summer to lay out neat paths, rows of hedges that would border tidy flower beds. All to no avail. To Edmond's deep frustration, the plants rebelled against such man-made order, their tendrils shooting out, growing sweet and wild to reclaim the walkways.

Perhaps, like so much else at Castle Leger, the garden possessed its own kind of magic. It had been planted during the time of Cromwell by Deidre St. Leger, a young enchantress who had possessed the startling power to coax seeds out of the ground, their flowers blossoming almost overnight. Her life had been cut tragically short, and to Val the garden still whispered of her sorrow, the last roses of the season dropping their petals along the path like a carpet of velvet tears.

The winters were so mild in Cornwall, even along this rugged section of coast, that something always remained in bloom. But the crowning glory of Deidre's garden, the magnificent arbor of rhododendron trees, would not begin to bud again until February. The barren branches made the garden seem to Val a rather bleak place for a stroll on such a raw autumn eve.

He compelled Kate to don her gloves, while he himself tugged up the hood of her cloak as he had done from the time she had been a little girl.

"This is hardly romantic, Valentine," she complained.

Romantic? Val's eyes widened in surprise. There had been a time when his Kate would have never thought of such things. Whenever he'd read aloud to her from the King Arthur tales, she always insisted he skip over those "sticky sweet" love passages between Guinevere and Lancelot, and go straight on to the exciting parts where heads were being lopped off with swords.

At times she still appeared the same madcap hoyden she'd always been. At others, Kate seemed to be changing too much, too fast. She peered up at him now with a look of such melting softness, Val felt a faint stirring of unease. Perhaps this moonlit walk was not such a good notion after all.

But there was no resisting Kate as she tugged him over to the nearest stone bench and insisted that she needed to sit down for a while. He wasn't fooled. Kate had the stamina of a young colt. The knowledge that she proposed this rest out of consideration for him was both painful and sweet.

He wished it hadn't been necessary, but he was too grateful to get his weight off his throbbing knee to refuse. He settled on the stone bench with a wearied sigh, propping his cane in front of him. Kate nestled beside him, wrapping her gloved hands about his arm.

They sat in that kind of companionable silence only longtime friends could share. He and Kate had often done this, sat in the garden together, staring up at the night sky, identifying the constellations, weaving fantastical stories about the far-off world of the stars. Why then did this particular evening keep weighing him down with sadness?

Of a sudden he felt so old, far older than his two and thirty years, as though the entire world were passing him by. Was it the dying leaves, the fallen rose petals making him so conscious of the relentless march of time? Or was it the budding young woman pressed so close to his side?

"Val," Kate said at last.

"Hmm?"

"Have you completely forgotten what day it is?"

Val was forced to bite back a smile. "St. Swithin's Day?"

"No!" Kate straightened to peer reproachfully at him.

Val frowned, pretending to wrack his brain. "Well, it cannot be Michaelmas. I am sure we are past that."

Her head drooped, her eyes so downcast with disappointment, Val could not bear to tease her any longer. Crooking his fingers beneath her chin, he forced her to look up at him.

"Of course I recall what day it is, child. Many happy returns."

Her face lit up with a radiant smile. He tenderly smoothed back one of her stray curls. "How could you possibly think I would forget your birth date? After all, it was I who gave it to you."

Val could still remember clearly when he had discovered that the orphaned Kate had no idea when she was born, neither the date nor the year. It had not been many months after she had arrived in Torrecombe. February 14, the date of his own birth, as usual had been an embarrassment of riches of festivities, presents, and congratulations from his affectionate family.

When Kate had been prodded forward, nudged by Effie to wish him many happy returns, the child had shocked everyone by declaring fiercely, "I hate birthdays!" Only Val had seen the wistfulness beneath her gruff façade and guessed the reason for it. He had set about remedying the situation at once.

Kate murmured, "Val, do you remember why you chose this particular day in October to be my birthday?"

"Certainly. Because it is the anniversary of the day you arrived in Torrecombe."

"And also the anniversary of the day we first met."

"Yes, that, too," he agreed. He hadn't intended to give her his gift until after supper, but suddenly *now*, when they were alone, seemed like a very good time. Very likely this would be the last of Kate's birthdays they would ever share this way.

He tried not to think about that as he fumbled beneath his cloak until he produced a small brown wrapped parcel that he presented to her with a solemn smile.

"For you, milady."

Kate let out a delighted cry. She pounced on the package with a greed that both amused and tugged at his heart, as though even after all this time his wild girl feared any gift, any happiness would be snatched away from her in a puff of smoke.

As she tore away the wrapping, he watched her, his pulse quickening with anticipation of her reaction. For all her hoyden's ways, Kate harbored a secret delight in pretty trinkets, especially anything that glittered or sparkled.

When the small jewel case was revealed, Kate lifted the lid and gave a purely feminine shriek of joy at the contents. With quivering fingers, she lifted out the delicate gold necklace. Dangling from the end of the chain blazed a magnificent bloodred ruby. Pearls might have been a more suitable gift for a young girl, but not for his gypsy Kate.

"Do you like it?" he asked.

"Like it?" she breathed. "Oh, Val, I adore it. Thank you a million times." Box and wrappings flew to the ground. Still clutching the necklace in her hand, she flung her arms about him in an impulsive hug that nearly sent them both tumbling off the bench.

Val chuckled softly, patting her shoulder, but like the quicksilver creature she was, Kate peeled herself out of his arms. She pressed the ruby into his hand and demanded, "Fasten it on me. Please."

"Here? Now?" he protested, laughing. "It would be better if you waited until we went back to the house."

But Kate leapt up from the bench, eagerly undoing the fastenings of her cloak.

"You'll catch your death—" Val's words died on his lips as the cloak fell away, revealing the gown she wore. For a moment all Val could do was stare, unable to speak another word, the necklace nearly slipping between his fingers.

He firmly believed Kate would have strutted around in breeches the rest of her life if it had been possible. It was a rare thing to see her attired as elegantly as she was tonight. The white silk crepe gown adorned with chenille embroidery fit her to perfection, the short puffed sleeves emphasizing the gracefulness of her arms.

The night breeze tugged at the folds of the dress, molding the fabric to Kate's slender frame, revealing a hint of her supple limbs, soft hips, and narrow waist. The close-fitting bodice displayed *more* than a hint of her high, rounded bosom.

Val blinked, dazed. With her dramatic dark hair spilling about her shoulders, it was as though she had been transformed into a young goddess before his very eyes. He stared for so long, even Kate noticed.

Holding out the folds of the gown, she twirled around in front of him. "This is the new frock Effie had made for my birthday. Don't you like it?"

"It—it's very nice," Val said. "But it does not quite look like the design you showed me. The fashion plate was—was—"

Decidedly different. Sweet and demure, whereas this gown . . . well!

Kate shrugged. "Oh, I did have Mrs. Bell attempt to copy that design, but she put too much lace on it. I had to take all that trim right back off again. You know I can't abide frills."

But the frills had been very necessary, Val thought with dismay. Especially about the neckline. Without the trim, Kate's décolletage plunged to a daring level, displaying far too much of her to the chance eye of any wandering rogue.

That lace had to be sewn back on at once. But when he opened his mouth to tell her so, he found himself averting his eyes instead. Good lord, he was almost blushing. He thought that he'd always be able to talk to Kate about anything, but this was clearly a subject his mother was going to have to broach with the girl. The best he could do was fasten the necklace on her and get Kate covered up again as quickly as possible.

He struggled painfully to his feet, balancing his weight upon his good leg. An awkward position. Likely that was what made his hands so unsteady as he draped the chain around Kate's neck.

He was so much taller than she was. It was far too easy to see over her shoulder, to notice the way the moonlight played over the creamy expanse of her skin, dipping down to form an intriguing shadow between her breasts. He fumbled with the clasp, trying to touch her as little as possible, and still he felt how warm she was, her flesh seeming to pulse with all the vibrant energy and passion that was Kate.

Gritting his teeth, Val forced himself to focus on the necklace. As soon as he had it fastened, he all but snatched his hands away. For once, he scarce felt the wrench in his knee as he bent down to retrieve Kate's cloak.

He straightened, shaking out the scarlet folds, frowning as he felt the weight of that blasted pistol knock against him. He was tempted to slip his fingers into the hidden pocket and confiscate the thing. But he had never behaved in such high-handed fashion with Kate before and he wasn't about to start now. He merely held out the cloak to her instead.

Despite the gooseflesh parading along her arms, Kate seemed in no hurry to be bundled back up again. She fingered the fragile chain, peering dreamily down at the ruby nestled against the swell of her breasts in brilliant contrast to the ivory of her skin.

"Val, how old do you think I really am?"

"Fifteen. Sixteen at most," he said promptly.

She shot him a wry smile. "You can be so exasperating sometimes, Valentine. I think I must be nearly one and twenty."

Val merely grunted by way of response, determinedly swirling the cloak back around her shoulders. As he worked to redo the fastenings, Kate slanted a glance up at him.

"I must certainly be old enough to be kissed by you."

Val deposited a brusque kiss upon her forehead as he did up the next button.

"No." Kate pouted. "I mean a *real* kiss."

Val drew in a sharp breath. The invitation in her eyes was as dangerous as the full, tempting curve of her lips.

"That wouldn't be wise, Kate." He secured the last button and prepared to retreat, but Kate slipped her arms about his neck.

"Why not? I have to get the hang of kissing sometime and you've already taught me everything else—my sums, my Latin, my copperplate."

Val attempted to disengage her. "This would be a little different. You need to wait until you are properly betrothed to some nice young man—"

"Oh, Val, do you really want my first kiss to come from some callow boy who will slobber all over me and ruin the magic of it all?"

No, he didn't. In fact he was surprised how much he was disturbed by the image of some oafish lad crushing his mouth against Kate's tender lips.

She stood on tiptoe, straining toward him, tipping back her head. Her eyes were soft, dark, and vulnerable. "Please, Val," she whispered.

Oh, God, not that *look*. Val tried to steel himself against it. And yet . . . one little kiss. What harm could it do? Kate had always had a boundless curiosity about everything, and it might be the surest way to end any further desire on her part to experiment. After all, kissing him could hardly prove to be that great of a thrill.

He bent toward her, intending to do no more than touch his mouth to hers, a mere whispering of lips. But he reckoned without Kate. She yanked him forward so that their lips met in a collision of warmth that sent a jolt through his entire system. She buried her fingers in his hair, her mouth exploring his with an eager innocence that touched him deeply. It was wrong, but he couldn't stop his arms from stealing around her, holding her fast as he savored the fresh sweet taste of her lips.

He sighed, his heated breath mingling with hers. Tentatively Kate's tongue crept forward to flicker against his, stirring in him desires he'd long denied, desires he could not allow himself to feel for any woman, let alone Kate. He started to deepen the kiss, only to snap sharply back to his senses.

What the devil was he doing? This was Kate, his young friend, his wild girl. He wrenched his mouth free, thrusting her away from him, appalled and repulsed by his own ungentlemanly behavior.

He staggered away from her, his bad knee threatening to give out beneath him. Where had he left his infernal cane? He limped painfully back toward the bench and located the walking stick, his fingers for once closing gratefully over the worn ivory handle.

The cane returned to him some measure of control, and he needed it, for Kate showed no signs of displaying any. Her face flushed, her breasts rising and falling too quickly, she attempted to pounce on him again. Somehow he managed to hold her at arm's length.

"That will do, young lady," he said as sternly as he could manage. "No more kissing lessons. You learn far too quickly."

"That is because I have been practicing with you every night in my dreams." She added almost shyly, "I love you, Val."

"I know you do, my dear. I have been like your older brother forever, but—"

"No, not like a brother! I never thought of you that way. Even when I was a little girl, I always knew I would belong to you one day."

Oh, lord. Val suppressed a groan. He had realized that Kate had once harbored such nonsensical notions, but he had hoped, nay believed, she would outgrow them. Clearly she had not. He longed to swear, to call himself every kind of fool imaginable. Stupid! Stupid to have allowed that kiss, this stroll in the moonlight.

He should have seen this coming, but perhaps he hadn't wanted to, knowing Kate's feelings would threaten their friendship.

He touched his hand to her cheek, attempting to reason with her. "Kate, I know you believe yourself to be in love with me, but you have met few other men. In time you will forget—"

"Why would I want to forget the best thing that has ever happened to me?" She caught hold of his hand and pressed her lips against the palm. "Marry me, Val. Please."

She gazed up at him, her eyes shining with such naked trust and adoration, it was enough to unman him. He tugged his hand from her grasp.

"I can't, Kate," he said as gently as possible. It was not often Kate wore her heart on her sleeve. The last thing he wanted to do was trample all over the love she so innocently offered, but he could already see the hurt beginning to well in her eyes.

"Why not?" she cried. "Because you're the son of a great lord and I am the bastard daughter of no one knows who?"

"Don't be ridiculous, child. I couldn't marry you even if you were the queen of England. I can never marry anyone."

"Because of the legend. The stupid legend!"

"Aye, the legend," Val said. A painful fact of his existence, as much as his crippled leg. "Perhaps you have forgotten all the details of it."

"I have certainly tried to," Kate snapped.

"Then I need to remind you. Once upon a time—"

"Oh, Val," she groaned, rolling her eyes.

He offered a sad smile, realizing he was treating her like a little girl. But it seemed by far the safest way to diffuse this situation. He began again, spinning out for her the story as he had done so many winter nights, while sipping cider, and huddled by the fireside.

"Once upon a time there was a family named St. Leger who lived in a magnificent castle high atop the rugged cliffs of Cornwall. They were a strange breed, in many ways as wild and mysterious as the land itself, perhaps because they lived in such splendid isolation, but mostly because they were the descendants of Lord Prospero, a man who had been a great knight, but was an even greater sorcerer."

Kate folded her arms rebelliously across her breasts, impatiently tapping her foot.

"Through Prospero, the St. Legers all inherited vastly differing powers, gifts that were both blessing and curse. Some could predict the future, some could read the hearts of other men, some could separate body from soul to go drifting through the night."

"And some could nearly kill themselves trying to absorb the pain of everyone they touched," Kate put in tartly.

Val frowned, but chose to ignore the interruption.

"Along with these strange gifts came an even more powerful legacy, the legend of the chosen bride."

Kate gave a very unladylike snort.

"According to the tradition, each St. Leger was promised a perfect mate, a love that would last forever, through death and beyond, shining as long as the stars. But there was a condition to this great gift."

"Isn't there always in these silly stories," Kate muttered.

"St. Legers are forbidden to seek their own mates. If they do so, only death and tragedy will follow. They are forced to rely upon the services of the Bride Finder, a being born in each generation with mystical powers to find for each St. Leger his perfect bride—"

"Oh, for mercy's sake, Val!" Kate cut him off, clearly unable to endure any more. "I know the damned story."

"Don't swear, Kate."

She glared at him. "You told it to me at least a hundred times."

"I thought you loved hearing it."

"Well, I didn't. I *hated* it."

Val stared at her, stunned. "Then why did you always let me—"

"Because I hoped you would finally outgrow it."

His mouth fell open. He might have been tempted to laugh at the notion of Kate standing there sounding so pompous, scolding him like someone's elderly aunt. Except—Val winced. Except she sounded too much like him.

"Kate, I realize I have always presented the legend to you in the form of a fairy story. But every word of it is true."

"Piffle!" Her mouth set in a mulish line. "I don't know how an educated man like you can continue believing such nonsense."

"It isn't nonsense. You have practically grown up in my family. You have witnessed the strange powers—"

"The powers are one thing, but this chosen bride legend is pure foolishness. I happen to be the adopted daughter of your supposedly wise and wonderful Bride Finder, remember?" Kate gave a contemptuous shrug. "I am very fond of Effie, but I assure you, there is nothing magical about her. She still dresses like a woman half her age and she hung fuchsia curtains in our drawing room. Fuchsia, for mercy's sake!"

"I admit that Effie's judgement may err in some respects, but as our Bride Finder, she has always been impeccable. She matched up my brother and his wife."

"Lance and Rosalind were simply right for each other. Effie made a lucky guess, as she always does." Kate took to pacing along the garden path, waving her arms in such an agitated fashion, Val was obliged to step out of her way. "Ask Victor St. Leger how clever he thinks Effie is. I happen to know he is very unhappy with Effie's choice of Mollie Grey for him."

"That is because Victor is an ungrateful idiot. But he'll come around in time."

"And what about you, Val?" she demanded. "Where is your chosen bride?"

Val stiffened. It was a painful question, the answer equally as painful.

"I don't have one," he said quietly. "Effie—the Bride Finder has decreed that there will never be a bride for me."

"Because she won't bestir herself to find you one! And if she refuses to find you a wife, why can't you choose your own?"

"You know it doesn't work that way, Kate. Any St. Leger who acts on his own in this matter is cursed."

"Ohhh!" Kate stamped her foot, venting a low growl of frustration.

"It is true. My own grandmother . . . she died long before I was born." Val paused, his gaze drifting toward the skeletal arbor of trees that sloped down the hill. Somewhere out there in the darkness, the beautiful wild garden ended abruptly at the edge of the towering cliffs. Even from this safe distance, one could hear the dull roar of the sea as it crashed against the treacherous rocks below.

"My father never spoke of it, but I stumbled across the story myself when I was researching our family history. Cecily St. Leger was not a chosen bride. She was terrified when she realized what manner of family she had married into. Even though she loved my grandfather, she eventually went mad, and one dark night she fled the castle, heading for the cliffs. No one seems to have been entirely sure if she slipped and fell or if she flung herself to her death."

Kate shivered a little at the grim tale, but she said, "Your grandmother was obviously very fragile. I am not, Val. Even if there really is a curse, I am perfectly willing to take the risk."

"But I am not!" Val said vehemently. "Not with your life."

Kate shot him an exasperated look. "So you intend to live out the rest of your life alone?"

"I have no choice. It is something I have had to learn to accept."

"Oh, Val!" She melted past his guard, coming close enough to cup his face with her hands, forcing him to look at her.

"How can you always be so resigned about everything? You're far too patient and good. Why should you be condemned to such a loveless existence?"

"I don't know. Perhaps because I am only a simple country doctor, hardly the stuff legends are made of."

"Yes, you are. You have always been my hero." Her eyes fluttered closed and he saw she meant to kiss him again. Val managed to prevent that, pulling away, putting the stone bench between them.

"Someday you'll find your hero, Kate. A real one. You are so beautiful, you'll have plenty of dashing admirers."

"I don't want them! I'll use the fools for target practice," she said, pursuing him determinedly around the bench.

"I think it is time we returned to the house," Val said hastily. He started to turn away, but Kate rushed after him.

"No, Val, wait." She appeared to struggle with herself for a moment then conceded, "All right. I understand. I cannot be your wife."

Val heaved a great sigh of relief. He reached for her hand to give it a comforting pat.

"I'll have to be your mistress instead."

Val froze in absolute horror.

"Oh, don't look so shocked. I have never been all that respectable. After all, I am only a bastard."

"Kate—"

"I realize I am not what a man would envision in a mistress, but I am sure I could learn to be more charming and seductive."

"Kate, stop—"

"I'd try to be more ladylike, wear elegant gowns for you, and even if eventually you grew tired of me—"

"Kate!" He seized hold of her shoulders. "How can you believe that I ever would— That I would for one moment consider— Damn it, girl. I don't ever want to hear you talk like this again."

He had never spoken to her so harshly before. She flinched as though he'd struck her, her fierce gray eyes gazing up at him wide and wounded.

"So even if I were to change," she said in a small voice, "you don't think you could love me—just a little?"

Love her? He felt as though she were tearing his heart out. He drifted the back of his fingers down the soft curve of her cheek.

"Kate," he said hoarsely. "I am so sorry."

She stared at him for a long painful moment, then backed away. Being Kate, she didn't burst into tears. She merely whirled around and with a savage oath smashed her fist against the nearest tree with a force that made him wince. She cupped the hand to her, smothering a soft cry.

There was nothing he could do about a bruised heart, but bruised knuckles were another matter. At least being a St. Leger made him good for something. Val limped to her side, reaching for her hand, preparing to do what he'd often done for her as child. Open his mind, open his power, and absorb her aches into himself.

But before he could even start to focus, Kate snatched her hand away.

"Oh, no, you don't," she choked. Even though her eyes blazed with unshed tears, she raised her chin proudly. "This is my pain, Val St. Leger. Not yours! Just—just leave me alone."

She spun away from him and tore off running, but not in the direction of the house. Off through the trees, heading toward those treacherous paths that plunged down to the sea.

"Kate!" Val roared out her name and started to run after her. He took a few halting steps only to have his knee give out. He stumbled, would have fallen if he had not managed to catch at a low-hanging branch.

Sharp pain pierced his leg, but he set his jaw, trying to ignore it. Steadying himself with his cane, he hobbled forward only to realize how useless it was. Kate had already vanished into the darkness. She was as fleet as a young deer. He'd never be able to catch up to her.

A rare surge of anger churned through him, fury at his own blasted helplessness. He longed to slash out with his cane, striking out at the trees, the flowers, anything in his path. But he forced himself to take a deep breath until he mastered the dark impulse. Losing his temper would help nothing. He would still be just as crippled and Kate would be just as gone.

Coming about, he limped back toward the house as fast as he was able, grinding his teeth against the throb in his knee. Kate would be all right, he reassured himself. Even in the dark, she knew that rugged path down to the sea better than any St. Leger, and he would find someone else to go after the girl, soothe her.

That in itself was a bitter thought. He had always been Kate's comforter. When angry or distressed by anything from skinned elbows to when the village brats taunted her for being a foundling, she had ever run to him.

But she wouldn't want him now. Things could never be the same between them ever again. Not after tonight, he thought bleakly.

She was young, he tried to tell himself. She would get over this infatuation she felt for him. It was only that Kate was so passionate, flinging herself at life so hard, yet beneath that tough façade, so vulnerable. It had almost been inevitable that at some point some man would break her heart.

Val had simply never realized that he was going to be the one.

CHAPTER TWO

The tide was in, foam-crested waves breaking against the shore, dashing against the jagged rocks. Moonlight cut a bright streak across the water, shimmering far out to where the sea became no more than a restless shadow on the horizon.

Otherwise the beach was dark, lonely, and cold, a place where few would have ventured after the sun had gone down. Kate trudged along the water's edge, oblivious to the pebbles poking at her delicate kid shoes. The wind pierced through the folds of her cloak, tangling her hair about her face.

It had been a miracle that she'd managed to race down the path from the steep cliffs above without breaking her neck. But Val had always told her that there were fairies hereabouts that looked after little children and fools.

And she was certainly that, Kate thought, savagely dashing the tears from her eyes. The greatest fool in the entire world to ever think that Val St. Leger could love her. Oh, there had never been any doubt that he cared about her in that gentle brotherly way of his, but that was not at all what she wanted from him.

Even now he was likely distressed because she'd run off and headed down here alone in the dark. But besides Val's arms, the sea was the only place she'd ever been able to find comfort, perhaps because the relentless roar of the waves moved in time with the restless rhythms of her own heart. The sea was so vast, it made her own problems dwindle in significance, and if anyone ever caught her crying, she could always blame it on the salt spray stinging her eyes.

Of course Val had ventured his own reason for why she was so drawn to the shore's edge. In one of her more bitter moments, she'd shocked him by declaring that her mother must have been some hardened trollop who would just as soon have aborted Kate as given birth to her. It would explain her own fierce temper, the ability to lie, cheat, and steal that had helped her survive her early years in London. No doubt she had bad blood in her, and it had to have come from somewhere.

But Val had draped his arm about her shoulders and woven her one of his stories about how he was certain she must be the daughter of a selkie or a mermaid. That was the only thing that could possibly account for how beautiful and brave she was and her fascination with the sea.

Although she had laughed, she had been half inclined to believe him. She'd always believed everything Val told her. So why then did she doubt him when he'd insisted that he could never marry?

Kate felt fresh tears start to her eyes and she rubbed them away. Huddling in her cloak, she blinked hard, trying to focus on the way the waves battered that distant piling of rocks. But it reminded her too much of how all her hopes for this evening had been dashed.

She'd taken such care when she'd readied herself, bathing in rose water, brushing out her hair a hundred strokes. She'd gone after that sweet, childish frock Effie had given her with a pair of scissors, cutting down the neckline until Kate herself had almost blushed. And that was something she never did.

She had been so determined to force Val to see her for what she was, no longer a silly girl, but a woman full grown. For added measure, she'd had her love charm as well, the amulet she'd fashioned herself according to local folklore. Carefully, by the light of a full moon, she'd worked the clay, mingling it with dried heather that grew near the mystical old standing stone and a few drops of her own blood. Before she'd left the house, she'd tucked the small amulet between her breasts near the region of her heart.

For a while everything had seemed to be going according to her plan. She remembered the way Val had stared at her in her daring dress and the gift he had given her. That beautiful necklace. It was not the sort of thing a man would give to someone he thought a child.

Then their lips had met in that kiss. It had been every wonderful thing she had ever expected Val's kiss to be, sweet, warm, tender. Her heart had soared. Something had seemed to be working, either the dress or the love charm . . .

until he had wrenched himself away and immediately begun treating her like a child again. Keeping her at bay, once more spinning out for her that all too familiar St. Leger fairy tale about the chosen bride.

Kate plunged her hand down her bodice and dragged out the small lump of clay, which had started to make her itch. It was clear all the cursed charm had done was give her a rash. Climbing on top of a flattened rock, she hurled the amulet as hard as she could into the dark, churning waters of the sea. She didn't know how she could have been stupid enough to ever believe such a thing would work.

But she had been that desperate. Not only was she fighting the fact that he refused to see her as a woman, she was fighting that damned legend as well. As much as she had scoffed, she had feared the legend from the first time Val had ever told it to her. She had lived in dread of the day when Effie would find Val a bride, fearing it might happen before she was old enough to have the chance to secure him for herself. If a bride was chosen, Kate had been miserably certain of one thing. It surely wouldn't be her, not little Katie Fitzleger, the wretched foundling brat who swore too much, fought too much, and still found a good pair of breeches preferable to a silk gown.

It shamed Kate to admit it, but she had been so relieved the day Effie had announced she could never find a wife for Val. No simpering chosen bride could ever love Val the way Kate did. Merely being with Val had always *gentled* her, made her acutely aware of her softer, more feminine side. He brought out the best in her. He was her rock, her anchor, and she could never give him up. She just couldn't.

But she was going to have to, she thought with a hollow ache, remembering too clearly the regret in his eyes, the finality in his touch.

Kate, I am so sorry.

Some might confuse Val's gentleness with weakness, but Kate had never made that mistake. Beneath that kind, patient exterior, the man had a core of steel when he believed himself in the right. Even if she could get him to stop viewing her as a child, there was no getting around that legend. Val would never risk invoking the curse by flouting his family's most cherished tradition. It would be like expecting Sir Galahad to betray his oath to the Round Table. He was too good, too unselfish, too frustratingly noble.

"Damn the man," Kate muttered. "I wish I had never met him."

She regretted the words the instant they were out of her mouth. She'd lived among the St. Legers and their strange magic for far too long to discount the power even of stray wishes.

"I didn't mean it. I didn't mean it," she whispered, peering anxiously up at the relentless night sky. Leaping down from the rock, she walked backward in a tight circle three times.

"Undo, undo, undo," she muttered.

Sinking down behind the rock, she hugged her knees to her chest, clutching the precious memory close to her heart as though malevolent fairies would try to steal it from her. She closed her eyes, willing herself to remember every detail of the day she had come to Torrecombe ten years ago, the first time she had ever clapped eyes on Valentine St. Leger . . . .

Kate huddled down on the floor of the still carriage, tired, battered, and miserable from the endless days of journeying. Occasionally she dared to peek beneath the shade drawn down over the window to shut out the world. A world that she did not like the look of at all in the deepening twilight. Too much open space, and the cluster of stone cottages that comprised the village seemed grim, unwelcoming shadows. And the land that stretched beyond seemed frighteningly vast, dropping off into nothing.

Kate already missed the bustle of London. Life in the foundling home had been bad, too little food, too many beatings. But at least the hardship and dangers had been familiar and understood, while this place, this—this *Cornwall*, with its rocks, pounding sea, and strangers, was—was—

Kate compressed her lips together, stifling the thought, refusing to admit that anything could frighten her. Craning her neck, she stole another wary glance beneath the shade she'd pulled down over the coach window. A curious crowd appeared to be gathering outside. She caught glimpses of hard chiseled faces as rough as the land, heard the mutterings of disapproval.

"What the devil is going on?"

"The girl won't get out of the coach."

"Oughta haul her out and give her a good switchin'."

"Girl? What girl?"

"Some orphan Miss Effie's taken a notion to adopt."

"A foundling brat? Oh, that will prove to be a great mistake."

Kate's lip quivered and she bit it hard to make it stop. She didn't give a damn what those fools said. It was not the first time she had ever heard herself described as a "mistake." From her earliest years, she had known what being born a bastard meant. No name, no father, no home. A child to be hidden away and ashamed of.

She slunk away from the window, shrinking deeper down between the seats, more determined than ever not to be hauled from the carriage. She'd already driven off the postilion with a hard punch to his nose and bitten through that great dolt of a coachman's hand.

That woman with the silly brassy curls who had adopted her, that Effie Fitzleger who cooed too much and expected Kate to call her "Mama," had attempted to coax her out with a box of sweetmeats. Kate had sworn and flung the tin out into the road. Effie had retreated in terror and now the foolish woman stood just outside the coach loudly weeping.

Kate rubbed her eyes. She was tired, cold, and hungry. Her knuckles were bruised and sore from hitting the postboy. She felt a little like weeping herself, but she would have bitten out her own tongue first. Her back pressed to the bottom of the seat, she waited, bracing herself for the next assault.

When the coach door opened again, it was neither that silly Effie nor the fat bear of a coachman. A strange young man with dark strands of hair falling across his pale brow peered inside.

"Miss Katherine?" he called.

Kate glanced about her to see who the devil he could be talking to. When she realized he had to be addressing her, she scowled. She hated to be mocked and that was what he had to be doing, wasn't he?

"Get away," she growled, brandishing her sore fist. "Before I give you a bunch of fives. No one's dragging me out of here."

"I wasn't going to try. I was going to ask your permission to come inside."

The respectful tone and unexpected request caught her off guard. No one had ever asked her leave to do anything. She stared at him, torn between astonishment and suspicion. He must have taken her silence for consent because, thrusting an ivory-topped cane inside, he prepared to mount the carriage.

Kate flinched back, baring her nails, preparing to claw his face if need be. But his attention seemed completely fixed on his struggles to climb inside. He appeared to be a vigorous enough young man, but it was obvious that simple movement didn't come easy to him. It occurred to Kate he wasn't like the other dandies she glimpsed swaggering about the streets of London, flashing those walking sticks for show.

He really needed his, his one leg appearing stiff and awkward. His mouth tightened with pain, and when he eased himself down on the seat, he breathed a deep sigh of relief.

Kate was intrigued for a moment, wondering what he'd done to injure his leg so badly. She stiffened, reminding herself it was none of her concern. And what was more, she didn't give a fig. When the coach door was closed, shutting him in with her, her initial alarm returned. She braced herself, fearing the coach would set into motion at any minute.

"Say," she cried, "what are you planning to do? Run off with me or something?"

His lips curled. He had an odd kind of smile that touched only half his mouth and looked a little sad.

"No, I only wanted to talk to you."

Talk to her? No one ever talked to her. They either shouted or hit. She particularly did not trust men. She'd seen enough of what was done late at night to the older girls at the orphanage by some of the matron's gentlemen friends. She had been made frightened and uncomfortable by the speculative looks that had been cast in her direction, teaching her quickly that it was in her best interest to appear younger than she was.

Pressing her knees to her chest, Kate curled away from the stranger, trying to look as small as possible. Behind the veil of her snarled hair, she studied him, attempting to figure him out. She'd picked enough pockets in her time to know the difference between a rich man and a poor one.

This fellow wasn't poor by any means. His frock coat and waistcoat were cut of a good cloth but rumpled, as though he'd slept in them. His cravat appeared about to come undone and his sleeve had an ink stain on it.

He was no dandy, that was for certain, but no clerk either or a tradesman's son. So who and what the devil was he? Kate brushed several strands of hair out of her face to get a better look at him. It interested her to note that he had to do likewise. Brushing back his own hair, his gesture was almost a mirror image of hers.

He smiled again and she was caught and held by his eyes. A warm, deep brown, they reminded her of the melting chocolate she'd once pinched from a confectioner's shop. Oddly, she found herself wanting to smile back at him.

She scowled instead. "So who the devil are you, anyway?"

"I'm a friend of your adopted mama's."

A friend? Kate crinkled her nose skeptically. She'd seen enough to know that men and women were never friends. Still, this one looked too young to be that ridiculous Effie's lover. Too young and, at the same time, strangely too old and wise.

"Well, whoever you are, go away," she said. "I don't want to talk. I have nothing to say to a great fool like you."

That should have made him angry, but he merely looked so disappointed, Kate squirmed. But why the blazes should she care?

She fretted her lip for several moments and at last said grudgingly, "What the deuce did you want to talk about?"

"I only wanted to welcome you to your new home."

"It's not my home and I'm not staying here. I'll run away as soon as I can and no one will be able to stop me."

She tipped her chin to a defiant angle, waiting for him to challenge her. He only appeared exceedingly grave.

"I don't suppose that I can prevent you, if you are truly determined to run off. But I shall be very sad if that were to happen."

"Why should you care? Most folks are quite glad to be rid of me. Old Crockett at the foundling home had an extra tote of rum to celebrate. She said she was getting rid of the devil incarnate."

His mouth twitched, but he said solemnly, "This Crockett person was quite mistaken. I daresay she didn't know you as well as I would like to do. You strike me as an intelligent and interesting girl."

Kate frowned uncertainly. If he had told her she was sweet and charming, she would never have believed him. But she knew she was clever, and as for interesting, well—she supposed there was a chance she might be.

She wriggled, beginning to find her position on the floor cramped and uncomfortable. With another wary glance at her companion, she trusted him enough to creep up onto the seat.

He made no move to touch her, his hands resting on top of his cane. There was a calmness about him that she had never known in anyone before. She felt soothed in spite of herself just being near him. She leaned back against the squabs with a tiny sigh.

"You must be feeling very tired after your long journey," he said.

She was, but she wasn't about to admit that to him. She shrugged. "It wasn't so bad. It was even kind of amusing seeing the looks on those other fools at the orphanage when I rattled off in such a fine coach pulled by a grand team of horses."

"Aye, poor fellows."

"Poor fellows," she exclaimed indignantly. "They're the best damn horses you'll ever see."

"Perhaps they are. But it is not good for them to be kept standing about in the night air when they are all lathered and sweating from a long journey. They could get very ill, perhaps even contract pneumonia."

"Horses don't get pneumonia," Kate said scornfully. What kind of fool did he take her for? But she shifted, seized by an uncomfortable memory of one of her many attempts to run off from Mrs. Crockett. She'd fetched up at the Bell and Crown and one of the stable lads there, Tom, had been quite nice to her. Seeing her interest in the horses, he'd let her help water them. And Tom had told her pretty much the same thing as this man. It was bad for the horses to be kept standing.

Pricked by a twinge of guilt, she said, "Then that damn fool of a coachman should get them unhitched and rubbed down."

"Aye, but that would leave the carriage here blocking the lane."

"Then move the whole blasted thing," Kate said irritably.

"With you still inside?" the man countered. "I am afraid you would find being shut up in the carriage house very cold and dark."

"That wouldn't scare me. I'm used to it."

"No doubt you are," the young man agreed softly, though why that should make him appear so sad was beyond Kate. "But you would also be locked in and *that* I don't believe you would tolerate so well."

Kate flinched in spite of herself. He was right. She hated the sensation of being trapped, locked away. It made her chest feel all tight as though her lungs were being squeezed too hard. But how could this stranger know that?

It was as though he'd climbed inside her head and walked around, understood her as no one else had ever done. It was an uncomfortable sensation and she hugged her arms protectively about herself. The movement caused her sore hand to throb and she winced.

"What's wrong?" he asked. "Are you hurt?" For all of his gentleness, those great brown eyes of his were far too keen, missing nothing.

Kate tried to shrug it off. "It's nothing. I just banged my hand when I hit that blockhead of a postboy."

"Let me see." The young man leaned closer and Kate scooted away, bristling.

"It's all right," he said. "I am training to be a doctor."

Kate wanted to twist away from him, tell him to go straight to the devil. But she couldn't. It was those blasted eyes of his. So warm and beckoning like the flicker of firelight on a cold winter night. She surprised herself by extending her hand toward him, although she kept her fingers tightly curled in a fist.

He took hold of her hand, lightly touching her knuckles until he got her fingers to relax. Then he enfolded her smaller hand entirely in the strength of his own. Kate cocked her head to one side, frowning. What kind of doctoring was this? He was doing nothing but holding her hand.

She should have jerked free, but she found herself lost in the dark light of his eyes, pulled in deeper and deeper until something strange began to happen. The ache in her knuckles began to fade, replaced by a rush of warmth that spread through her veins.

When he finally released her, her knuckles still looked raw, but the pain was gone. He rubbed his own hand and winced as though he were the one who'd struck the postboy.

Kate cradled her fingers and gaped at him. "How did you do that?"

"Magic," he said with a mysterious arch of his brows.

She half believed him and she had never believed in any sort of magic her entire life. "Are you some sort of conjurer or wizard?"

"No, only the great-great-great-grandson of one." His brown eyes twinkled. He had to be teasing her, but somehow she didn't mind. She came very close to smiling. This time when he leaned forward to touch her hand, she didn't try to pull away.

"Miss Katherine, this may be impertinent of me upon such short acquaintance, but I hope you will permit me to offer you some advice. You may well not like it here in Torrecombe and wish to run away. But it is never good to make such a weighty decision when one is exhausted. I know Effie's cook has prepared a fine roast beef dinner. I would be greatly honored if you would come into the house and share it with me."

The mention of food made Kate's stomach rumble in spite of herself. "Will there be a pudding, too?" she asked reluctantly.

"I daresay."

"And some cake?"

"If there is not, I vow I will don an apron and bake you one myself."

Kate felt the dimple quiver in her cheek and she could no longer contain it. She smiled. But it was never her way to surrender without driving a hard bargain. Her gaze fell upon his cane with its fancy handle, which had fascinated her from the first.

"Will you allow me to try that out?" she asked, pointing to the walking stick.

Her request appeared to surprise him, but he nodded. "If you wish, although I doubt you'll find it very amusing."

Because he didn't, no matter how he might conceal how much his infirmity bothered him, Kate realized with a startling flash of insight, perhaps because she too understood about putting a brave face on things.

She was on the verge of relenting, but she cast an anxious glance toward the coach window, fully aware of the interested crowd still gathered outside.

He appeared to comprehend her look at once for he said, "Don't worry. I'll get rid of them. No one will bother you. And if you are very tired, I will carry you straight into the house so you won't so much as have to look at a soul."

Kate was astonished at how welcome the offer was. She was bone tired, but she cast a doubtful look from him to his cane. "How can you do that when you can hardly walk your—" Horrified, she checked her blunt words for perhaps the first time in her life, conscious of not wanting to hurt someone else's feelings.

To her relief, he merely winked at her. "You will be very surprised what I can manage to do when I put my mind to it, Miss Katherine." Gripping his cane, he started to reach for the coach door when she stopped him, clutching at his sleeve. Her heart sank, but she knew there was something she had to make clear to him, something he had to understand.

It was even harder to speak when he glanced down at her with those wonderful honest eyes of his. She swallowed thickly. "I—I'm not Miss Katherine. I'm only Kate." Before he could even ask, she added fiercely, "I don't have any other name because I'm a bastard."

She hung her head, waiting for him to scorn her, reject her as so many others had done. Instead he crooked his fingers beneath her chin, obliging her to look up at him.

"That is hardly any fault or shame of yours, my dear." His dark eyes softened, his mouth curving into that lopsided smile that ever seemed to have a tinge of melancholy. "You have been adopted. You will be Miss Kate Fitzleger now."

She hardly cared about that, only how warm his hand felt as he patted her cheek. Then he turned away, struggling to alight from the coach. He was half out the door when he turned to look back at her.

"By the by, my name is Val St. Leger."

"Val St. Leger," she repeated. She thought it the most grand name she had ever heard. As the door closed behind him, Kate let out a long tremulous breath, cupping her own cheek in an effort to imprint the feel of his touch there forever.

Scooting to the window, she lifted the shade and flattened her nose against the glass to see what he would do next. That nebulous sea of strange faces had already begun to disperse, but she was mystified how Val had brought this about. He didn't shout. He didn't threaten. He merely spoke in that calm, quiet voice of his. Maybe he was a wizard's grandson after all or—

Kate's breath snagged in her throat as she realized exactly who and what Val St. Leger was. He was a gentleman, a *real* gentleman, the kind she had stopped believing existed. When he returned to the coach and opened the door, there was no one left but him and a night scattered with stars. He had handed off his cane to the postboy and stood balanced on his good leg, waiting for her to alight.

Although she inched closer, Kate still hesitated. She had never been able to trust anyone before. What if he just carried her into Effie's house and abandoned her? What if she never saw him again?

"You are truly going to stay and share dinner with me?" she asked.

"Of course."

"And your cane?"

"I promised, did I not?"

A wonderful thought struck her. She released her breath, forming the most daring request of all. "I don't want to be Kate Fitzleger. Would you share your last name with me?"

He only laughed. "Well, Miss Kate, we'll have to see about that."

He stretched his hands up to her with that crooked smile she was already learning to adore. Kate was seized by a peculiar giddy feeling that she would have jumped off a cliff if he had told her it was safe to do so. It took no effort at all to leap down from the carriage and into his arms.

His arms closed around her, far stronger than she would have expected. He cradled her high against him, moving away from the carriage with an awkward, dragging step. But Kate didn't care about that. Nor did she particularly care where he was taking her, to the house that loomed ahead. Pressed so close, she had eyes for nothing but him, his face a mixture of strength and gentleness, the hawklike nose, the sensitive mouth, the thick mane of black hair, the soft gleam of his eyes.

Wrapping her arms tight about his neck, she dared to rest her wearied head upon his shoulder. She had never given much thought to her future before, but she suddenly knew irrevocably what it would be.

She was going to love Val St. Leger forever and ever. . . .

Forever and ever, the wind seemed to whisper with a sad echo. The tide lapped closer to the base of her rock, the cold dark water threatening to intrude on Kate's memories. She scrambled to her feet, trudging back toward the safety of the cliffs. Remembering the day she and Val had met usually afforded her so much comfort, but now it only added to the weight of her misery.

He had kept all his promises to her. He had taken dinner with her, allowed her to play with his cane, stayed until she had drifted off to sleep in the unfamiliar surroundings of her new home. And over the years as she had grown, he had shared so much more, his books, his learning, his remarkable family, and his friendship.

There was only one thing he had ever refused to share: his name. And tonight he had made it perfectly clear he never would.

"Never is an infernally long time, Val St. Leger," Kate murmured, setting her jaw and fighting off a fresh wave of despair. Damn both the legend and the curse. She would not give up that easily. She might have her faults aplenty, a bad temper, no patience, and a complete want of any feminine graces. But no one had ever accused her of a lack of courage and determination.

She would be Val's bride before the year was out, she vowed, though she did not have the slightest notion how she would bring this miracle about. Certainly not through the use of any more silly love charms. The legend of the chosen bride was too powerful for such superstitious nonsense. It would take a far stronger magic to break the legend's hold on Val, the kind of magic no man living possessed.

Then perhaps she needed to seek her answer among the dead.

Kate's breath caught in her throat. She could scarce have said where the notion came from that whispered across her mind. Perhaps it was carried to her by the seductive call of the wind, borne to her on the siren rush of the waves.

Or perhaps it was merely the sight of Castle Leger perched high atop the cliffs behind her. From this distance, the vast manor appeared no more than a looming shadow except for the one tall tower etched stark against the face of the moon, the place where a dreaded sorcerer had once practiced his infamous magic until he met his untimely end. His restless spirit was rumored to have drifted through the old keep for centuries after.

But it was a long time since any terrified servant had reported sighting a spectral presence stalking the ramparts at midnight. Either Lord Prospero had been exorcised at last or he had simply lost interest in haunting Castle Leger. Nothing remained of the once mighty wizard except for his collection of books stored in the tower chamber, ancient tomes filled with such strange and forbidden knowledge, no one had ever been tempted to make use of them.

Until now.

Kate's heart beat more quickly, her hands actually trembling a little at the thought seizing hold of her. She could well imagine how horrified Val would be if he knew what she was contemplating, what he would say to her. He would tell her she needed to forget such a dangerous notion at once and try to forget about him as well.

Forget about Val St. Leger? Oh, no, Kate thought, a tremulous smile curving her lips. All she needed was a stronger spell.

CHAPTER THREE

$\mathscr{T}$he narrow stone stairs wound upward into impenetrable darkness, the wind whistling through the arrow slits producing a mournful sound that pierced one to the soul. The ancient tower seemed far removed from the bustling new wing of Castle Leger and the warmth of any human contact.

Heart thudding uncomfortably, Kate crept forward, shielding the candle she carried from the cold drafts of air, trying not to think of all the ghost tales Lance St. Leger had told her. Chilling stories of how he had often encountered Lord Prospero in this very tower, the ancient sorcerer appearing in a burst of lightning, demonic eyes blazing in his hideous countenance.

All more of Lance's teasing nonsense, of course. Now, if Val had been the one to tell her such things, she would have believed him. Her hero never lied and he assured her that *he* had never seen any ghost.

Val . . . His dark eyes and melancholy smile seemed to swim before her eyes, haunting Kate more than any phantom ever could. It wasn't the fear of a long-dead sorcerer that caused her footsteps to lag so much as an unexpected attack of conscience.

She felt as though she was about to betray him and his family as well. The St. Legers had all been very kind to her in their different ways. And how was she going to repay them? By plotting to steal their ancient secrets, flout their tradition of the Bride Finder, and practice black arts against the man who had ever been her truest friend.

But she had been left no choice, Kate assured herself. What was the alternative? To dwindle into a foolish spinster like her adopted mother, Effie? To stand aside and watch while Val also lived out his days alone, sacrificing himself to both that infernal legend and his strange power, absorbing the suffering of everyone he met until his very compassion proved the death of him?

If there had ever been a man who needed a woman to love and look out for him, it was Valentine St. Leger. She might not make him the best wife, no perfect chosen bride, but Kate was certain she would be better than no bride at all.

Strengthening her resolve, she continued doggedly onward, taking care not to lose her footing on steps that had been worn smooth by centuries. The stair seemed to spiral upward forever, and just as she began to despair of reaching the end of it, she suddenly emerged into the tower chamber itself. Despite all of Val's assurances, she stiffened, half closing her eyes, bracing herself for an alarming burst of light, a hobgoblin face leering out of the darkness, a dead sorcerer snatching at her with skeletal fingers.

When seconds ticked by and nothing happened, Kate dared to hold up the candle and take stock of her surroundings. She released a long breath, feeling like she had surfaced in another century. The feeble light flickered over a massive bed hung with rich brocade curtains, the dark wood intricately carved with ancient Celtic symbols that appeared as mysterious as the collection of bottles and vials adorning a nearby shelf.

Kate's wondering eyes took in a small writing desk, a heavy oak chest, and a bookcase filled with ponderous-looking tomes, all appearing perfectly preserved, untouched by the passage of time.

She had expected a cobweb or two, at least a little dust. But every piece of furniture gleamed with polish, the bedcover turned partly down as though awaiting the return of the master whose life had ended in fire over five centuries ago.

An unnerving thought, that, and Kate was quick to shrug it off, focusing her attention on what she had come to find, Prospero's store of forbidden knowledge, the sorcerer's collection of spells.

She rushed over to the bookcase and, heedless of any damage to her gown, knelt down on the cold stone floor. Setting the brass candlestick on the floor beside her, she began to wrench one book after another down from the case.

Manuscripts bound long before the age of the printing press, they were all beautifully copied out in flowing scripts, apparently collected from many lands. None of them was written in English, but Kate was not daunted by that fact. Val had a penchant for foreign languages, a fascination he had shared with her over the years. Thanks to his excellent tutelage, she was fairly fluent in French and Spanish, possessed a working knowledge of Latin and Greek, even knew a smattering of Italian, German, and Gaelic.

But translations would take time and she feared she might have little of that. It must be nearly an hour since she'd run off from Val. He would be worried, might even have roused half the estate to go in search of her.

She would simply have to select the most promising-looking text and take it with her. Wiping her moist palms on her cloak, she scanned the row of books again, one of them drawing her attention from the others. Small, slim, so ancient, it appeared likely to crumble at the merest touch.

Kate took hold of the volume gingerly and drew it out into the flickering light. The binding was crude, the leather cracked. It bore no title, only an emblem burned deeply into the cover, the symbol of a ferocious dragon rising up out of a lamp of knowledge, and beneath it a faded inscription in Latin.

"He . . . he who possesses great power must use it wisely," Kate translated in an awed whisper, the words not unfamiliar to her.

It was the St. Leger family motto, first adopted by the man who had more reason than any other to know the truth of those words. This had to have been Prospero's particular book, the words no doubt penned by the sorcerer's own hand. Kate quivered with excitement, certain she'd stumbled upon the very thing she sought, the wizard's spell book. Her fingers trembling with eagerness, she started to lift the cover.

"Put that down!"

The voice was chillingly soft, seeming to whisper against the nape of her neck, sending an icy shiver down her spine. Kate gave a startled squeak, clutching the book. Her gaze darted fearfully about the chamber, but there was nothing there. Only sinister shadows conjured out of her overwrought imagination. She released a long, unsteady breath, disgusted with herself.

"You are such a goose," she muttered. All the same, she would be better off gathering up the book and getting out of here. Tucking the volume under her arm, she reached for her candle, struggling to her feet.

"Are you hard of hearing, mistress? I *said* put the book down."

"Oh!" Kate gasped. She hadn't imagined that! The voice slashed at her like the steely blade of a sword. In her fright, she fell back to her knees, dropping both book and candle. The taper rolled away from her, snuffing itself out against the stonework, leaving her in darkness except for what meager moonlight penetrated the arrow slits. Heart banging against her rib cage, she froze, for a moment too terrified even to breathe.

A sharp wind tore through the room. The pages of the book fluttered. The ancient torches set into the wall exploded into flame, sending out a shower of sparks. Kate shrieked, snatching up the book and using it to shield her eyes from the sudden blaze of light.

An eternity passed before she dared lower it and peer up at the alarming specter that now loomed over her. Tall and powerful, he seemed to fill the chamber, his imposing frame clad in a black tunic shot through with golden thread. A scarlet mantle swirled off his shoulders, providing a brilliant foil for his lustrous mane of hair, as black as his finely trimmed mustache and beard. Far from being any hideous demon, he was almost wickedly handsome with his hawklike nose, aristocratic cheekbones, and sensual lips. Just like in the portrait that had hung below in the great hall for centuries.

"Prospero?" Kate croaked as soon as she was able to find her voice.

"You appear to have the advantage of me, milady." The sorcerer gazed at her from his lordly height, his eyes rather exotic, slightly tilted at the corners, dark, compelling. Drifting closer, he extended one hand toward her from his long, flowing sleeve.

His skin was strangely bronzed for a phantom, almost swarthy, his fingers appearing long and elegant. Although she trembled, Kate reached up instinctively to accept his hand, quite forgetting he was a ghost until her own hand passed through him. It sent an odd tingle through her, the sensation unnerving, like being struck by lightning that chilled instead of burned.

Kate snatched her fingers away, shrinking back. The gesture had obviously not been a chivalrous one meant to help her to her feet. Prospero presented his hand again, more imperiously this time.

"My book, if you please," he demanded in a tone that brooked no argument.

Kate clutched the precious volume to her chest, vigorously shaking her head. She didn't know exactly what she had done to conjure this alarming phantom back from the grave, but it must have something to do with the book. If it truly contained that much power, she was not about to surrender it without a fight.

The contest was short-lived. With one languid wave of his hand, the sorcerer wrested the volume from her grasp. Kate emitted a faint cry of protest as she felt the book wrench free, watched it float across the room. Prospero settled the volume atop the writing desk, well out of her reach. Then he turned back to deal with her. His eyes didn't burn with demonic fire as Lance had said, but his narrowed gaze certainly looked capable of reducing a full-grown man to ash. Or one diminutive young woman.

But Kate had never cowered before anyone, not even old Crockett when that redoubtable madam had taken a whip to her. She wasn't about to start now. Heart hammering, she struggled to her feet and declared with all the defiance she could muster, "I am not the least afraid of you."

"No?" He arched one brow in a taunting fashion, stalking closer.

Kate stumbled back a step. "I don't care if you are a dreadful sorcerer," she bluffed. "I happen to be something of a witch myself."

"One who needs to borrow her spells?" he mocked.

"Well, it is not as if you were using that book for anything. It has been years since Lance St. Leger reported seeing you here in the tower."

He continued to move closer, forcing her to retreat until her back was nearly against the wall. But her words appeared to give him pause. "Years?" he murmured. "I thought it more like decades." An odd expression filtered through his dark eyes, something a little pensive, a little sad. But in a flash it was gone, his fierce scrutiny once more trained upon her.

"Now that I bethink me, I do recall seeing you somewhere before. And don't try to convince me it was dancing naked about the fire at some Black Sabbath."

Kate flinched at his sarcasm.

"All right," she muttered. "I'm not a witch. My name is Kate Fitzleger and I am from the village."

"Little Katherine Fitzleger? The young hoyden who used to tromp about here wearing breeches? Playing at swords in the great hall?"

"Aye," Kate replied, unsettled that he should know so much about her, especially since before this night, she had not been entirely convinced of his existence.

Prospero stepped back, his eyes raking over her in a leisurely fashion that brought the blood surging to her cheeks.

"You've grown some," he said appreciatively.

Kate was annoyed to feel herself blush, something she never did. She fumbled, tugging her cloak more tightly about her, only wishing that Val would look at her that way. She was convinced that she could get him to do so, fall in love with her enough to forget everything, his family traditions, the legend, and the curse. If only she could lay her hands on that book. Her gaze traveled to where the volume rested on the corner of the desk.

As though he could read her mind, Prospero shifted to block her view. "And so, milady," he purred. "Lance St. Leger told you all about his encounters with me and yet you were still foolish enough to invade my tower?"

"Because I never believed him. I thought he was just making up tales to scare me. Fortunately, I don't frighten easily."

"So I have observed." Prospero's mouth crooked in a faint smile.

"You are not nearly as hideous as Lance said you were."

"Hideous? By St. George! I'll have the young whelp know I was accounted one of the handsomest men of my day."

And not just a touch vain, Kate thought as she watched Prospero smooth the ends of his beard. An entirely human failing that somehow rendered the great sorcerer far less formidable. She felt the last of her tension ease.

"I am sure Lance didn't mean to insult you. He only described you thus to tease me, something he is very good at."

"Aye, I recall," Prospero said dryly. After a brief hesitation, he asked, "How fares the rogue and his pretty bride?"

"Lance and Rosalind are both well, as much in love as ever. They have a son now, three years old. He was christened John, but everyone calls him Jack."

"How drearily unimaginative," Prospero said, but Kate detected a certain softening in his haughty features. He drifted away from her to pace about the chamber, rustling the curtains of his bed, lifting the lid of his chest as though seeking to reacquaint himself with his surroundings, resurrect old memories. Something any ordinary man might have done after an absence of so many years.

Except that Kate doubted Prospero could ever have been termed ordinary even when he had been alive. An aura of mystery clung to him, his every movement fraught with the arrogance of a conquering emperor. Now that she was no longer afraid, Kate watched him with awe and fascination, wondering where he had been all these years, what dark netherworld he might have inhabited.

There had to be great power in that book of his to bring him storming back here when all she'd done was touch it. If only she could steal one small peek at the contents.

As Prospero inspected his trunk, he fired off questions regarding the fate of the other St. Legers. Kate did her best to answer him in a calm voice, all the while inching away from the wall, nearer to the desk.

". . . and Dr. Marius St. Leger moved away from the village last summer. He's taken a teaching position at the medical college in Edinburgh. Lord Anatole's daughters are all gone, too, Leonie and Phoebe both married. And the youngest, Mariah, wed a Scottish laird. The only one left unmarried now is Val."

But not for much longer if she could help it, Kate vowed. Keeping a wary eye on Prospero, she reached for the book.

He moved so quickly her eye scarce registered the fact. She could not have said whether he stalked or flew. One minute he was bending over the trunk, the next he lounged in front of her, resting one hand atop her prize.

Blast him! Kate seethed with frustration. He was only a ghost after all. Surely if she tugged at the book, it would pass right through him. She grasped hold of the binding and pulled. But for a hand that was not corporeal, Prospero's fingers seemed to possess the weight of iron. The book was held fast.

Rather than angered by her audacity, the sorcerer appeared amused. He endured her efforts to pry the book free for several moments until he seemed to grow bored of the game. He made a careless gesture and Kate felt herself lifted off her feet as though plucked about the waist by two strong hands.

She gave a startled gasp as she was propelled backward, then plunked down upon the edge of the bed. Although the sensation of flying had left her a little giddy, she immediately attempted to rise.

One steely glance from Prospero warned her that would be most unwise. She subsided, feet dangling over the side of the bed, glaring at him.

"You appear to be a most single-minded young woman, Mistress Kate," he said. "What is it you think to find in this old book that you want so badly?"

"A spell. Just one little spell."

"What kind of spell?"

She found it difficult to meet his eyes, certain that he would mock her.

"A love charm," she mumbled.

Prospero didn't laugh, but his dark brows shot upward in surprise. "I would hardly think a young lady possessed of your obvious assets would have need of such a thing."

"Well, I do," Kate said miserably. "I've already tried everything else. I even asked him to marry me."

"*You* actually proposed to this reluctant beau of yours?"

"Yes, and he rejected me."

"I shouldn't wonder, if you looked that fierce. Why didn't you just whip out a pistol and march the poor fellow to the altar?"

"I might have done, but he would probably have just let me shoot him."

Prospero stroked his beard, gravely considering her words, but there was an irrepressible twinkle in his eye. "Granted, the fashions of the world have changed much since my day, but this does not seem to be the best way to go about charming a man."

"Then help me!" Kate cried. "Why can't you open that book and give me a spell to win his love?"

"Because it is always dangerous to use magic to trifle with the human heart."

"You did it. The tales are legion about how many women you seduced using the black arts."

Prospero's brows knit together in a mighty scowl. "It is hardly fitting that a chit like you should know of my liaisons."

"Then you should have been more discreet," Kate retorted. But she mollified her tone, realizing this was not the best way to secure his aid. For all his mockery and hauteur, the sorcerer did not seem entirely unsympathetic to her cause.

"Please help me. You are such a powerful wizard, I am sure it would pose no difficulty for you at all," she said, flattering him shamelessly, shooting him a melting glance from beneath her lashes.

Prospero merely looked amused. "And just who is this young swain of yours?"

"Well—ah," Kate faltered. It would hardly do to explain to Prospero it was his own descendant whom she hoped to bewitch. Far from helping her, the sorcerer would be more apt to send her flying down the tower stairs. "Er, he is no one you would have heard of. Only a gentleman residing here in Cornwall."

"Of good family?"

"Oh, yes." Kate smiled serenely. "Quite as noble as your own."

"Well-to-do?"

"Moderately so. I don't love him for his wealth."

"Ah, a handsome fellow then."

"I think so," Kate said softly. "And brave, kind, clever, generous. He's a perfect gentleman, so noble and—and—"

"Enough," Prospero protested, rolling his eyes. "Please spare me the entire list of this paragon's attributes. I concede that he sounds like a good match."

"You will help me then?" Kate slipped off the bed, daring to approach him again. She abandoned all attempts at guile as she peered up at him, for once allowing her heart to surface in her eyes.

"Please," she whispered.

Prospero stared down at her for a long time, his expression so inscrutable Kate had no notion what he might be thinking. But she remained hopeful until he slowly shook his head.

"No."

"But—"

He silenced her with an imperious wave of his hand. "I make it my policy never to meddle in human concerns."

"That's a stupid policy," Kate said. "I don't see why—"

"However, I will offer you some advice."

"Oh, thank you so much!" She shot him a reproachful look before asking grudgingly, "What advice?"

"You have no need of magic to win this young clod. You simply need to make better use of your own natural charms. Brush the tangles from your hair, mend your manner of walking."

Kate bristled. "What is wrong with the way I walk?"

"Nothing, if you were a captain leading a regiment into battle."

"I walk to get where I'm going. I am not going to mince about like some die-away ninny."

"I never told you to do so. Simply learn to adopt a more elegant manner, carry yourself like a queen."

Kate compressed her mouth in a stubborn line before snapping, "Fine. Then show me."

"Me? I have no time to be giving deportment lessons to saucy wenches."

"You have nothing *but* time."

His eyes darkened so ominously that Kate feared she had carried her impertinence too far. But his face suddenly relaxed, a silken laugh escaping him.

"You are right about that, my dear. I do have time, all eternity in fact, the devil take me.

"Because heaven never will," he added, a fleeting look of sadness stealing into his eyes, which he veiled at once behind his sardonic expression.

"Very well." He beckoned to her. "Come here."

Kate gaped at him, taken aback. She had only flung the challenge out to him in a fit of pique. She had never expected him to take her up on her angry words. When she hung back, she felt her shoulders seized in the icy grip of invisible hands.

She could not restrain a startled cry as she felt herself marched forward while Prospero barked out commands.

"Straighten your spine. Hold your head up. And take daintier steps! Remember you are a lady, not a squire in training for knighthood."

Kate stiffened, attempting to resist. But as she marched about the room, an idea came to her. A desperate and brilliant idea.

When Prospero snapped at her once more to keep her head up, she cried, "Wait, I know something that might help."

He allowed her to pause and she moved toward the bookcase. Hoping he would not notice the tremor of excitement in her, she snatched up a book of Celtic folklore and balanced it atop her head.

Prospero chuckled, but he nodded in approval.

Back across the room Kate glided, keeping a smile fixed on her face while her heart missed a beat.

The sorcerer tipped his head to one side, scrutinizing her every movement.

"That is better," he said. "You have a natural grace, milady. You could have been born to be a duchess."

Kate pulled a wry face at that, certain she had been born for a far different fate. The gallows most likely. But she rather fancied the idea of being a duchess. She turned, sashaying back over the stone floor, imitating Prospero's own imperious manner, which caused him to laugh.

Kate giggled as well, nearly toppling the book from her head. She was enjoying herself, so much so that she was nearly beguiled into forgetting her purpose. She came to an abrupt halt, reaching up to pluck the volume from her head.

"What's amiss?" he demanded. "You were doing quite well. Why did you stop?"

Kate released an unsteady breath, avoiding his eyes. "It must be getting very late, Effie, my—my mama, will be worried about me. I should go."

She almost imagined the great sorcerer appeared disappointed, but he shrugged, saying smoothly, "Then I expect you had best be gone."

Kate clutched her cloak about her and dipped in a nervous curtsy. "Thank you for my lesson."

"The pleasure was all mine, milady." Prospero swept her a magnificent bow. "Come again sometime and we'll work upon your curtsy."

Kate nodded and sidled toward the door. She held her breath, expecting at any moment to see his eyes narrow with thunderous displeasure. But when nothing happened, she slipped into the passage leading down the tower stairs.

And ran for her very life.

She no longer had her candle; the stairway was all but pitch black. Somehow she stumbled her way to the bottom without tumbling headlong. As she emerged into the cavernous recesses of the great hall itself, her heart banged against her ribs like a blacksmith's hammer against an anvil.

She paused and waited. Still nothing. No roar of outrage, no lightning bolt hurled to reduce her to ashes.

He hadn't noticed.

Trembling, she dared to remove the book she had secreted beneath her cloak, tracing her fingers over the dragon emblem burned into the cover. During her London days when she had often been obliged to steal to survive, she'd become quite a bold and accomplished thief, frequently robbing old Crockett herself. But she had never imagined that one day she would possess the skill to dupe a five-hundred-year-old sorcerer.

She was good. She was still damned good, Kate thought, suppressing a chortle of triumph. She didn't delude herself she would be able to fool Prospero for long, but she had hopefully bought herself enough time to find the spell she needed and memorize it.

Gleefully clutching the book to her chest, Kate rushed off into the darkness.

Prospero stared down at the book that now rested upon the corner of his desk, a harmless volume of Celtic folklore. His mouth crooked into a smile of wry amusement. The little minx! She was as bold a piece as he'd ever encountered. Did she truly think he, Prospero, would be that easy to trick?

Still, the switching of those books was as pretty a bit of sleight of hand as he'd ever witnessed, and he'd performed many himself in his day. Mistress Kate was quite remarkable. The only thing remaining to consider was how far to allow her to go before he stopped her. And what illusion should he use? A sudden burst of light, a chilling wind, perhaps even a fire-breathing dragon? That might be enough to daunt Kate, teach her both some wisdom and some manners.

But even as he started to raise his hands, Prospero paused, rethinking the matter. Why not just let her keep the book for a while? It was filled with some of his most dangerous secrets, that was true, but he'd penned it in the alphabet of a long-dead language no mortal could hope to decipher.

He smiled to himself, imagining Kate's chagrin when she opened the volume and realized she could not read a word of the book she'd fought so hard to obtain. Likely she'd storm back up to the tower and be impertinent enough to hurl the useless text at his head.

And he was not averse to having her return, he was surprised to realize. She had been like a wild, sweet wind invading his tower chamber, reminding him of things that he'd almost forgot. Of what it had been like to be that young and so passionately alive.

The reminder was both poignant and painful. He was quick to shrug it off, preparing to extinguish the torches and vanish back into the night. He could not imagine what had drawn him back here in the first place.

Not the problems of one lovelorn young woman, that was for certain. He'd never liked haunting Castle Leger. The place was too filled with memories of the folly of his mortal days. More often than not the blasted castle ended up haunting him.

Yet over the centuries he'd frequently been drawn back against his will, usually when great disaster loomed over these reckless descendants of his. Times such as when Cromwell's Roundheads had threatened the castle with destruction or those grim days in the eighteenth century when Tyrus Mortmain had been hell-bent upon murdering St. Legers. Or when Anatole St. Leger had been left orphaned and disillusioned at far too young an age. Or more recently when his rogue of a son, Lance, had permitted the St. Legers' most cherished sword to be stolen, the weapon Prospero had fashioned himself, imbedding a magic crystal in the hilt.

So what the devil was amiss now? Prospero's gaze swept the tower chamber as though the stones of the castle itself might provide his answer. He felt nothing but a troubling silence.

Drifting through the walls, he paced along the tower parapet, staring far out across the night-swept panorama. Even after so many centuries, the rugged beauty of this land, the rocky stretch of coast, the towering cliffs, the sea surging against the shore in all its white-crested mystery was still able to move him.

Search the night though he would, he could find no answer to the unease that had drawn him back. His powers of prognostication no longer seemed what they once had been. Mayhap even a ghost could grow old, Prospero thought wryly.

Although he could not put a name to it, he could still feel it, like a dark ripple in the fabric of the night itself. There was something out there that threatened Castle Leger, this family of his.

Something evil.

CHAPTER FOUR

*T*he demons lurked in the darkness. Rafe could feel their hot breath, hear the suppressed sounds of their cruel laughter. Heart pounding, he hurled himself after the tall woman who threatened to disappear down the narrow mist-bound street.

"Maman! Maman! Ne me laissez pas," *he cried, catching at her stiff silk skirts.* "S'il vous plaît."

Evelyn Mortmain spun around to glare at him, her eyes already cold and distant. Rafe shrank back, remembering that she did not like him to speak French.

"Please, Mama," he faltered, struggling for the right words. "Do not . . . leave me."

She drew back her hand and dealt him a sharp cuff to the ear that caused his eyes to water. "Don't whine like that, Raphael. You know I have no patience for it." She bent down to his level, seizing him by the shoulders.

"I am returning to Cornwall to destroy the St. Legers and reclaim your birthright, you foolish boy. Now dry your eyes, you will be safe enough here at the monastery with the holy brothers."

She brushed her lips fiercely against his brow and turned to leave, oblivious to his panic. Didn't she understand? He didn't care about Cornwall, St. Legers, or birthrights. He only wanted his mother. No one was safe here. Not even the holy monks. The demons were everywhere, red caps tipped over their hideous grinning faces, knives clutched in their hands, waiting.

"Mama. Please, come back."

"Don't . . . don't go." The words rasped through Rafe's throat, stirring a violent coughing spasm that jolted him awake. His eyes flew open as he struggled for breath, gazing about him in wild confusion at the rough-hewn planks of the barn. The fogbound streets with all their hidden terrors faded. He was no longer a terrified boy abandoned in the vast city of Paris, but a dying man flat on his back. His bed was a heap of straw somewhere in a barn near the portside town where he had docked just yesterday.

But even as he recollected where he was, Rafe felt just as frightened, just as lost. He dragged one shaking hand over the sweat-soaked mat of his beard. It was only that cursed dream again. How he despised it and himself for having it. At least this one had not been as bad as some of his other nightmares when those faceless demons actually emerged from the shadows. . . .

He rolled onto his side with a pain-filled groan. He half expected to see night pressing against the barn doorway, but the pale light of early evening still glimmered. He could not have been out that long, although he was not quite sure if he had fallen asleep or lapsed into unconsciousness. He felt so blasted weak, his chest and throat so raw with coughing, he might as well have been on fire.

He dragged himself to his knees, a task that required all his strength. It was the fault of the crystal. The shard seemed to have grown stronger, rendering him even weaker. He longed with all his soul to be rid of the cursed thing.

Soon . . . soon. Then the nightmare would be all Val St. Leger's, not his. That thought gave Rafe the will to rise to his feet. He staggered into the next stall to complete the task he'd abandoned when he had become too exhausted.

The saddle he'd been forced to drop lay tumbled on its side, the stolid gray gelding munching placidly from a bucket of oats. It twitched its ears, barely troubling to give him a glance as he strained to heft the saddle on its back. He succeeded this time, but the effort left him so spent, he was obliged to lean against the side of the stall, suppressing another coughing spell. The spasm passed. He wiped his brow and turned wearily back to the task of fastening the girth.

"I could help you with that, mister."

The piping child's voice startled him, fraying at his taut nerves. He jerked about to glower at the small figure in the doorway, a delicate-looking boy, no more than eight. Rafe wondered how long the little wretch had stood there watching him. He had small patience for children, even less for being spied upon.

"What the deuce do you want?" Rafe growled.

The child flinched at his tone, but crept a step closer. Earnest blue eyes peered up at Rafe from beneath a mop of unruly white-blond hair.

"I only wanted to help you with the saddle."

"I don't need any help!" Rafe turned back to the horse, assuming the boy would take to his heels. Such a frail-looking whelp. He should have been easily frightened.

To Rafe's surprise and annoyance, the boy lingered, shuffling his feet on the straw-covered floor.

"Rufus is a real good horse," he ventured.

Rafe said nothing, struggling to tighten the cinch. To him, horses had never been anything more than an inconvenient necessity when obliged to travel on dry land.

"You are going to take good care of him now that you bought him, aren't you, mister?" the boy asked with a tiny catch in his voice.

Take good care of it? Aye, until the horse carried Rafe to his destination. After that, the wretched brute could be claimed by the knackers or whoever else happened to stumble across it.

When he didn't answer, the child plucked timidly at his sleeve to gain his attention. "He likes to have a carrot with his oats and—"

"Damnation!" Rafe snapped. "Leave me alone. Can you not see I'm busy? Shouldn't you be in bed or something?"

The boy stumbled back, paling, the freckles standing out on the bridge of his nose. For one moment Rafe thought he saw his own reflection in the child's wounded eyes, the frightened lad he'd once been. He half reached out to the boy, only to check the gesture, subsiding into one of his hacking coughs.

Rafe pressed his hand to his mouth while the boy continued to retreat. The lad stumbled against a woman entering the barn, her black dress and faded apron as homespun as her face. She took in the situation with one thoughtful glance, her gaze traveling from Rafe to her quivering son.

"There you are, Charley," she said, stroking her work-worn fingers through the boy's uneven lengths of hair. "You should be washing up for supper. Get along with you now."

The boy stole one more uneasy glance at Rafe before heeding her gentle command. She watched as the boy vanished across the chicken yard before turning back to Rafe. He braced himself, belligerently awaiting the farmwife's sharp rebuke for his treatment of her son. He was nowise prepared for her quiet apology.

"I am sorry if Charles was bothering you about the horse, Mr. Moore."

Rafe started a little at the name until he recollected that it was the one he had given her when she'd caught him prowling about her farm like an injured wolf. He muttered some vague reply, waiting impatiently for her, like her son, to be gone.

Instead she actually gave him a sad smile. "You see, poor Rufus there belonged to my late husband. He was one of the few possessions my son had left of his father."

And this touching bit of information was supposed to mean something to him? Rafe shrugged, pretending to be inspecting the girth, wishing she would just go away. He tensed when she came closer, easing into the stall to pat the old brute's neck as tenderly as she had touched her son. The stupid creature actually responded to her, lifting its head to nuzzle her arm. The widow . . . what had she said her name was? Corinne Brewster . . . Brewer, something like that. Rafe couldn't recall, but it was of no importance.

She was one of those foolish sentimental women he'd never been able to abide. All soft eyes and soft mouth, her unremarkable brown hair bundled beneath a plain linen cap, untidy wisps escaping to straggle about her ruddy cheeks.

"I want to thank you," she said shyly, peeking at him around the horse. "For making such a generous offer for our old Rufus. I know he is not worth such a sum. I feel quite guilty for accepting that much money, but Charley and I do need it rather desperately."

"And I need the horse. The amount is of no consequence to me," Rafe said. Money matters were of little concern to a dying man. He would have stolen the horse if she had not stumbled across him first. It would have been much simpler. But he couldn't afford to raise a hue and cry, risk being captured and arrested. Not when he had so little time left, not when he was drawing this close to exacting his revenge upon Val St. Leger.

"All the same, your generosity is much appreciated," the widow continued. Couldn't the woman shut her mouth and simply go away? Apparently not.

"The farm has to be sold to pay my late husband's debts," she said earnestly, as though she truly expected Rafe to care. "My poor George was never much of a farmer. He was a seafaring man like yourself."

"How the devil did you know that?" Rafe snarled, drilling her with his gaze. Was it possible she had somehow recognized the infamous Captain Mortmain even beneath his shaggy coat of hair and straggling beard? He tensed like a wolf about to spring, his hands clenching.

Although she appeared both bewildered and taken aback by his ferocity, she replied calmly, "It is the way you walk, your rolling gait, like a man who has spent much time at sea. I am sorry if I offended you."

Rafe expelled a deep breath, forcing himself to relax. He was far too edgy. He needed to get out of here.

"I have to be going," he muttered, reaching for the gelding's reins.

"Can I not at least persuade you to stay to supper?"

Supper? Was this woman completely mad? Did she have the least inkling of the danger she'd been in but a heartbeat ago? That if she had recognized him, he'd been fully prepared to throttle her to insure her silence?

"Are you always like this?" he demanded.

"Like what?"

"So damn trusting of any stranger that happens by."

She flushed at his sarcasm, but she replied with quiet dignity. "No, I am not. I am usually most cautious."

"Then why did you abandon that caution for me?" he jeered, brushing back his tangle of black hair. "Because of my charming appearance?"

"I don't know why I did," she faltered. "Perhaps it had something to do with your eyes. You looked like a man who needed to—to be trusted."

That had to be about the stupidest thing Rafe had ever heard of. She was obviously quite mad or one of those women pathetically hungry for the attention of any man no matter how disreputable. Either way, he had no time for this.

Tugging on the reins, he guided the horse through the barn door when another of his infernal spasms seized him. This one left him doubled over, clutching his chest, coughing, struggling to breathe.

As he shuddered with the pain, he felt a hand both gentle and unexpectedly strong take hold of his elbow, supporting him.

"Mr. Moore, you really are not well," she said. "You should rest tonight, set out in the morning. I could make you up a bed in the tack room."

Rafe shrugged her off, forcing himself to straighten. He closed his eyes for a moment, able to will the pain away, but it left him weakened. He would never be able to travel hard. Even if he set out now, he'd be fortunate to reach Castle Leger by this time tomorrow eve. Yet he had no choice. His time was running out.

"My business brooks no delay. I must be gone," he said through clenched teeth.

As he struggled to get his foot in the stirrup, she irritated him by hovering near him as though she expected him to fall flat on his face. He half expected it himself. Panting, he managed to lever his body up into the saddle.

Rafe swayed, overcome by a dizziness, which he fought to shrug off. When he was able to focus, he saw the widow staring up at him with worried eyes.

"I do not know what business makes you so desperate to be gone, but I wish you would reconsider, sir." Their eyes met, hers so open and honest, his so guarded, and yet Rafe still experienced a strange feeling she could see straight to his soul, read all the dark purpose there. And she pitied him.

Though it cost him great effort, Rafe straightened, thrusting back his shoulders. He had no need of her pity. If there was one thing he'd inherited from his mother, it was her infernal Mortmain pride. He touched the crystal shard outlined beneath his shirt. Now it seemed he had inherited her madness as well.

He dug in his knees, setting the gelding into motion, taking little heed of Corinne's gentle, "Godspeed."

As he galloped off into the twilight, Rafe knew it would not be God speeding him toward Castle Leger. He was completely in the devil's hands now.

CHAPTER FIVE

$\mathcal{T}$he ring of flames leapt higher, showering the black curtain of night with fiery sparks, bathing the ancient standing stone in an unearthly glow. No bonfire had been lit upon the old druid's hill for centuries, not since during the reign of Cromwell when it had been rumored a coven of witches had practiced their hellish rituals before the base of the mysterious monolith.

Only one woman crept about in the flickering shadows tonight, enveloped in a flowing black cape like a slender young sorceress. The wind made a tangle of her gypsylike hair, the heat of the flames painting color in her pale cheeks, reflecting firelight in her intent eyes. Any passerby stumbling upon the scene would have thought he *had* encountered a witch of olden days and fled for his life.

But as she tossed more twigs into the flames, Kate had never felt less like a terrifying sorceress, more like a trembling child playing with fire. The wind wrestled her for possession of the crackling branches, sending smoke whipping into her face.

Kate choked and backed away toward the shelter of the gigantic stone that towered above her. She wiped her stinging eyes and peered nervously about her, trying to calm herself. The hill provided a breathtaking view, a magnificent vista of the rugged St. Leger lands. But tonight the slope was lost in darkness, the sea far below like some invisible beast, roaring out as it clawed at the land.

Despite the warm folds of her cloak and the blazing fire, Kate shivered. She had never been particularly afraid of the dark before, but it promised to be a wild night. All Hallows' Eve was said to be that time when the veil between this world and the next thinned and disappeared, allowing unquiet spirits to walk abroad.

The night did seem to be alive, the wind moaning through the trees, the clouds streaking eerie shadows across the face of the moon. Something rustled through the heather. A stoat or a badger no doubt, Kate sought to reassure herself. But no matter how quickly she whipped about, heart thudding, she never caught sight of anything.

Any person of good sense would be keeping close to the bonfires of the village tonight. Kate almost wished she had, too, merrily dancing with the others to keep demons and curses at bay for another year.

Instead she was preparing to cast some dark magic of her own. Kate delved beneath her cloak and produced the purloined spell book, half dreading that at any moment Prospero would rise before her in a dark cloud of smoke, wrathfully snatching back his stolen treasure.

It both puzzled and worried her that he had not done so already. She'd had the worn volume in her possession for two days now. Surely he must have noticed the trick she had played upon him. If he'd made no move to reclaim the book, it must be for some mischievous reason of his own.

Perhaps the great wizard had been merely toying with her, allowing her to think she'd carried off something special when she had pilfered nothing more than an ordinary book full of nonsense.

No, Kate couldn't believe that. Stroking her fingers over the dragon emblem burned into the leather cover, she thought she could feel the power that thrummed between the brittle pages, sensed the magic in the strange writings inked out in Prospero's arrogant hand, writings that should have been a complete mystery to Kate.

But she had recognized immediately what they were. The cunning Prospero had chosen to write out his spells in the ancient alphabet of Egypt, hieroglyphics. Kate had Val to thank that she was able to decipher them at all.

She remembered all those long ago rainy afternoons, curled up beside Val near the library fire while he had shared with her his latest course of study. He had peered quizzically at her over the ponderous tome that detailed the discovery of the Rosetta Stone, the tablet that had finally unlocked for scholars the mystery of Egyptian writing.

"I am sorry, my dear," he had said. "I ofttimes get carried away in my enthusiasms. This must all be incredibly boring to you."

"Oh, no," she had cried. How could she possibly make Val understand that although she had spent her youth in the vast city of London, it was not until she had met him that she had realized how narrow those streets were? That it had been his patient teaching and love of books that had opened her eyes to far off times and places, entire worlds she had never dreamed existed.

"I like learning about the pyramids, and the pharaohs, and the hy-hyroglips."

"Hieroglyphics," he had corrected her gently.

"Yes! 'Tis like learning a special language only you and I understand. As though you trust me enough to share a great secret with me."

"I would trust you enough for anything, my Kate."

How his words had warmed her, she who had been reviled as a thief and a liar from her earliest years, she who had never been valued or trusted by anyone.

Aye, Val trusts you. To be his true and honorable friend. To respect his family and their customs. To never do anything that might bring him harm.

Kate flinched from the sudden sharp prick of her own conscience.

"But I'm not trying to hurt him," she murmured. What she was about to do was not so very terrible. No different from the other village lasses who sought to work their love charms upon the young men they desired.

What a dreadful liar you are, Kate Fitzleger, she told herself. It was very different and she well knew it. All the difference between tossing a pinch of salt over one's shoulder to ward off the devil and seeking to meddle with the darkest kind of sorcery, summoning up powers that might be too terrible for her to control. If something should go wrong . . .

Kate glanced at the dancing flames and for one awful moment fancied she saw Prospero's exotic slanted eyes glaring back at her, heard the fearsome whisper of the great wizard's voice.

"It is always dangerous to use magic to trifle with the human heart."

Kate gave a frightened squeak and leapt back. She stared into the fire for long seconds before she was able to reassure herself she had seen nothing more than a falling log, heard nothing beyond the hiss of the flames. It was only her overwrought imagination and her too vivid memory of some idle remark Prospero had made.

And yet she couldn't help wondering, as she sought to still her racing heart, exactly what had Prospero meant by that? What was so dangerous about casting a love spell? Kate wished she had pressed him for more information, but it was too late now.

Except that it wasn't. She could abandon her desperate course, let the bonfire die out, scurry back to the village. She could run to Val's doorstep and beg to be let in, like a bedraggled kitten seeking shelter from a freezing storm. Val would see at once that she was distressed, even frightened, but he would not torment her with questions.

He'd merely pull her into the strength of his embrace, tuck her head against his comforting shoulder, and hold her fast.

No, Kate was forced to remind herself. That was not what would happen. After the way she had thrown herself at him the other night, Val would be too wary even to touch her. He'd be kind, gentle with her as always, but he would insist that she go home to Effie.

If she didn't find the courage to go through with this tonight, she would never feel his arms around her again. Tightening her grip on the book, Kate resumed her place before the standing stone like a priestess taking up her position at the altar.

A low rumble sounded through the night as though the sky itself had cracked open to issue her a warning. Kate turned her frightened gaze heavenward, seeing a flash of light upon the far horizon.

It was only a bit of thunder, a distant blaze of lightning, heralds of an approaching storm. She was able to breathe a little easier, although she realized she had not much time before the rains would come, dousing her fire.

"Oh, Val," she whispered. "Please forgive me for this. But you've left me no other choice."

Steeling herself, Kate opened the book.

The taproom at the Dragon's Fire Inn, usually bustling on such a raw autumn eve, was all but deserted. Reeve Trewithan slouched over the worn oak table, nursing the last tankard of ale he had enough coin to purchase. Flecks of foam clung to his grizzled chin, the greasy strands of his unwashed hair slicked back from his broad forehead.

His once stalwart frame showed signs of turning prematurely soft. The paunch of his stomach brushed against the edge of the table as Trewithan swiveled to glance out the window and watch the antics of his neighbors.

Bonfires blazed on the village green, the shadows of dancers silhouetted against the flames as skirts swirled and heavy country boots stomped in time to the fiddles. The music, shouts, and laughter carried even through the walls of the inn. All that capering about merely to drive the devil away from the village tonight, Reeve thought with scorn.

"Parcel of superstitious fools," he muttered, turning back to his drink. He appeared to be the only man in Torrecombe with enough sense to ignore this All

Hallows' Eve nonsense. Well, him and the young fellow sprawled across the armchair in the taproom's darkest corner, staring glumly into his whiskey glass.

He was the sort of strapping lad who'd no doubt set the village lasses' hearts aflutter, Trewithan thought sourly. The youth had the kind of heavy, sulky mouth that seemed to make the silly chits all fit to swoon. His coal black hair waved back from his forehead in a widow's peak, his dark eyes fringed with thick black lashes that would have looked better on a wench.

There was no mistaking that prominent hawk's nose or the elegant cut of his clothes. The youth had to be one of those damned St. Legers, though Reeve was hanged if he could remember which one. Not one of the main branch of the family; a distant cousin most likely.

It didn't matter to Trewithan. The rest of Torrecombe might still worship the mysterious family with all their peculiar ways, but Reeve had little use for any of them, especially Dr. Valentine St. Leger. Interfering bastard. Lecturing Reeve, telling him to go gentle with his wife, that bearing another babe too soon might be enough to kill her. Encouraging Carrie to shirk her wifely duties by avoiding Reeve's bed.

That kind of celibacy might do well enough for Val St. Leger. The doctor was practically a monk. But Reeve was a real man and a real man had *needs*.

He took a deep swallow of his ale and nearly drained the tankard, stopping himself just in time. He was all too aware the landlord's beady eyes were fixed upon him. Mr. Wentworth would be ready to hustle him out the door as soon as his last drop was gone.

The innkeeper moved leisurely toward Reeve's table, the portly man's silk striped waistcoat and glossy boots making him look more like some city merchant than the keeper of a country inn.

"Well, Mr. Trewithan, I trust the ale was to your satisfaction," Wentworth remarked.

"I paid for it, didn't I?"

Wentworth rested his well-manicured hands on the back of an empty chair, seemingly oblivious to Reeve's surly reception.

"I was very surprised to see you in here this evening. I thought you'd be out with the rest of the village, joining in the fun."

"If you call that fun, wearing out your boot leather and getting your arse singed dancing around a fire."

Wentworth merely smiled. He nodded toward the gloom-ridden youth in the corner. "It seems that young gentleman shares your views."

"Bah, him." Reeve shot the lad a contemptuous glance. "Foolish whelp. Look at him, gaping into his glass. Who the deuce is he, anyway?"

"Master Victor St. Leger, grandson of the late Captain Hadrian St. Leger."

"Aye, I remember him, a hard-drinking old cove. You'd think he'd have taught his grandson better—that good whiskey like that is for swilling, not just looking at."

"I think Master Victor is only trying to work up his courage."

"For what? Drinking?" Reeve sneered.

"No, for marrying. Do you not pay any heed to the village gossip, Mr. Trewithan? The Bride Finder, Miss Effie Fitzleger, has selected Mollie Grey to be Master Victor's chosen bride. The lad is expected to go propose to the young lady tonight. Unfortunately, I don't think Master Victor is enthusiastic about Miss Effie's choice."

"Can't blame him. Mistress Grey is a scrawny wench. No bosom at all to speak of."

"Large bosoms are not the only thing to be valued in the selection of a wife, Mr. Trewithan," Wentworth reproved him mildly.

No, Reeve thought. There was also stamina to be considered. He hunched his shoulders in a heavy shrug. It was only more superstitious nonsense anyway, this business of the St. Legers and their chosen brides.

All the same, he wished he could have had a Bride Finder to choose his wife for him. Maybe even that silly Miss Effie could have done better than he'd done for himself. Carrie had seemed a good enough choice, a pretty buxom lass. Who'd have ever guessed she'd end up too sickly to perform a woman's most basic functions, birthing babes and pleasuring her man?

Reeve raised his tankard again only to peer with bitter disappointment into the mug. Not even a decent mouthful left. He fingered his empty purse and cast a speculative glance at Mr. Wentworth, but he knew there was no use expecting credit from that quarter. Not like in the old days.

The former landlord of the Dragon's Fire, Silas Braggs, had been a regular scoundrel, a smuggler and thief; some even said a murderer. He had mysteriously disappeared five years ago around the same time as that arrogant customs officer, Captain Mortmain. But for all his wicked ways, old Braggs had been willing to treat a regular customer to a drink.

Mr. Wentworth, who gave himself such gentlemanly airs, was downright mean in that regard. He'd been known to refuse to serve Reeve even when he had the money. "No more tonight, Mr. Trewithan. You've had enough," the sanctimonious bastard would proclaim. "You'd best be saving some of that coin to feed your family, sir."

If he'd wanted homilies, Reeve thought, he'd have taken himself off to the vicar. Swirling the dregs in his glass, he glanced around, wondering if there was any chance that Victor St. Leger might be persuaded to— No, the young man had finally tossed down his whiskey and was stumbling toward the door like a fellow marching off to his own execution.

Reeve sighed. If there was no prospect of another drink, he might as well go, too. As he lurched to his feet and shuffled toward the door, Wentworth cleared his empty tankard from the table.

"Good night, Mr. Trewithan," he called. "Oh, and do give my congratulations to your wife on the birth of her new daughter."

Congratulations to Carrie. *Her* daughter. As though the blasted woman had done it all herself. Reeve glowered at Wentworth, then let himself out. Grimacing at the bite of the wind, he headed for home. Home to a cottage full of brats, a wailing babe, a sickly wife, and a cold bed.

Feeling much put upon and sorry for himself, Reeve took great care to avoid his merrymaking neighbors and kept to the dark path that skirted around the village. He barreled straight into another person who also seemed bent on avoiding the bonfires, a tall man cloaked all in black, the hood pulled far forward, concealing his features.

Reeve snarled, "Damn you, man. Why don't you push back that hood and watch where you're going?"

He attempted to shove his way past, but the stranger's hand shot out, detaining him.

"Your pardon, friend," a voice rasped from the depths of the hood. "Perhaps you may be of use to me."

Trewithan started to growl that it wasn't his way to be of use to anyone, but something in the stranger's aspect gave him pause. That and the hand that was now clamped about his wrist. The fingers were of an appalling thinness, almost skeletal, yet the man's grip was like iron and just as cold. An inexplicable shudder sluiced through Reeve.

"What—what d'you want?"

"Merely some information."

To Reeve's considerable relief, the man released him. He took a wary step back, rubbing his wrist.

"I am told that Dr. Valentine St. Leger no longer resides at the castle upon the hill."

"Aye, that's right. He's taken lease on a cottage closer to the village. The better, I suppose, to be able to meddle with the marriage beds of honest—"

Reeve checked himself, nervously licking his lips. For all he knew, this unnerving stranger might be an old friend of the doctor's.

"And where would this cottage be?" the stranger asked.

" 'Tis just down this lane about half a mile, close to the shore's edge. Slate House, 'tis called and—"

"Never mind. I remember the place."

"You've been to these parts before?" Curiosity overcame Reeve's unease. He leaned closer to squint beneath that cowl and wished he hadn't.

Soulless dark eyes glinted feverishly, set in a death-white face all but swallowed by a wild matting of beard. Reeve jerked back and stumbled over a rock, falling hard.

He couldn't have said why, but he was seized by a sudden panic. Thrashing about in the underbrush, he scraped and cut his hands. By the time he regained his feet, he was ready to bolt.

But there was no one to run from. He was entirely alone. Reeve glanced about wildly but saw no sign of the hooded stranger. He'd melted away into the darkness as though he'd never been. *Perhaps he hadn't.*

"Damn," Reeve whispered. He realized he was trembling, hairs prickling at the back of his neck. Lord knows, he'd never been a superstitious man. But if his neighbors were trying to keep the devil out of Torrecombe tonight, they had better dance a little harder.

Slate House perched near the edge of the sea, the weathered two-story gray cottage melancholy in its isolation, its nearest neighbors the shifting dunes of sand, tufts of sea grass, and gulls that emitted their strident cries. The only light that flickered came from the tiny library at the back of the house, the walls so crammed with shelves, the chamber resembled a small dark cavern constructed of books.

Jem Sparkins lit a few more of the candles, then paraded about the room, making sure the shutters were secured against the blasts of damp salt air.

"I don't much like the notion of leaving you alone tonight, sir," Jem said, stealing a worried glance toward his master seated in the wingback chair before the fire.

Val St. Leger leaned against the cushions, his bad leg propped on a footstool, his cane near to hand. A worn brown shawl lay draped across his lap, warding off the evening's chill, and a book was held open in his hands.

But for the past half hour Val had made little sense of the treatise on herbal medicine. He stared into the hearth, not seeing the warm crackle of flames but instead a wild, moonlit garden, a young girl's desperate eyes as she wrenched away from him.

"This is my pain, Val St. Leger. Not yours!"

Ah, Kate. Val suppressed a heavy sigh. He knew full well how the girl behaved when she was hurting. She was like some wounded wild creature, striking out, driving everyone away. But she had never run from *him* before. It was that thought that cut Val more deeply than anything else.

Kate had been avoiding him ever since the disastrous night of her birthday. Two days. Two whole days. When he had stopped by Effie's cottage to inquire after her, Kate had dispatched a maid to inform him that the young lady was not receiving callers. She had a headache.

A headache! Val would have laughed at the ridiculousness of it if he had not been so worried about the girl. His Kate had never suffered from a headache in her entire life, although . . . Val rubbed his brow. She was certainly adept at inflicting them upon other people.

"Sir? Dr. St. Leger?"

It took a moment for Jem's voice to recall Val back to his surroundings, away from his brooding about Kate. He glanced up at his lanky manservant.

"Mmm? Did you say something, Jem?"

"Aye, sir. I *said* I don't much like leaving you alone tonight, especially not on All Hallows' Eve."

"Why? Are you afraid that some hobgoblin is going to come down the chimney and whisk me away?"

Jem's craggy face eased into a grin. "No, sir. I doubt even a ghost would dare trifle with any of you St. Legers. But you've already given Sallie and Lucas leave to attend the bonfires and—and—"

Jem broke off, looking uncomfortable. But it was unnecessary for him to finish. Val understood him well enough.

Someone needed to stay behind and look after the poor crippled doctor.

It was an unusually bitter thought for Val and he was quick to suppress it. Lord knows, he should have been accustomed to the solicitude his lame leg inspired from his servants, his family, even total strangers. But it still chafed him. The only one who had ever fully understood and had given him no quarter was Kate.

"I think I can manage on my own for a few hours, Jem," he said. "Now you had better be off or you'll miss the bonfires yourself."

Jem opened his mouth to speak again, but Val cut him off, "Thank you, Jem. Good night."

Although Val was the kindest and most patient of masters, his servants knew when he would brook no further argument. Especially a retainer who had been in his employ as long as Jem.

"G'night, sir." Jem shuffled over to the door and let himself out, although he looked mighty unhappy about it.

Val heard the outer door slam, and a heavy silence settled over the library, broken only by the crackle of the fire and the wind rattling the panes of glass, causing the shutters to creak.

Val shifted in his chair. He'd spent an exhausting afternoon tending to patients scattered all along the coast. He had longed for this moment when he would find himself left alone with the solitary comforts of his hearth, his books, a glass of brandy.

But now that he had achieved his goal, he felt strangely restless. He donned his spectacles, attempted to read, only to close the book up again.

The house was perhaps too quiet and empty. Although it was termed a cottage, Slate House was a large, rambling structure, meant for half-a-dozen urchins sliding up and down the stair banister, a cheerful wife bustling about to serve the evening tea. The family that he would never have, Val thought, his mouth twisting ruefully.

Fortunately he didn't own the place. He'd only leased it from his second cousin, Dr. Marius St. Leger. A generation older than Val, Marius had been his tutor, his mentor, like a second father to him. But this past summer, Marius had taken up a teaching position at the medical college in Edinburgh, much to the chagrin of Val's own father.

Lord Anatole had always considered Marius his closest friend and he'd been both hurt and angered by the doctor's decision.

"Cornwall is your home," Anatole St. Leger had raged. "Why the devil would you ever want to leave it and go haring off to Scotland?"

Marius had smiled and given some vague answer, but Val had understood why well enough. The reason still rested perched on the mantel above the fireplace—the objects that practically constituted a shrine to Marius's lost love. A pair of dainty yellowed gloves, a faded hair ribbon, and a fan were positioned reverently before a miniature portrait of a sweet-faced young lady. Anne Syler, the woman who should have been Marius's chosen bride. But he'd defied the St. Leger family tradition, delayed claiming her for far too long. Marius had finally sought Anne out only to have her die in his arms.

Val had no difficulty in understanding why Marius had felt compelled to move away. Too many years of being haunted by Anne's memory, of bearing silent witness to the daily joy of men like Val's father, Anatole, or his brother, Lance, both contentedly wedded to their destined brides, of knowing that such happiness would never touch Marius's own lonely life.

Sometimes Val didn't know what was worse, to have had a chance at true love like Marius and lost it, or to have never had a chance at all like Val himself.

Perhaps one day he, too, would be driven to flee Cornwall, when he was an old man and no longer—

When? Val peered wryly at the spectacles slipping off his nose, the brown shawl tucked across his lap. In a fit of self-disgust, he flung off the garment and set his spectacles aside.

Reaching for his cane, he levered himself to his feet, only to sink back with a sharp gasp at the stabbing pain in his knee. Sucking in his breath, he bent to massage his leg, which throbbed at this touch. He could feel the rock-hard tension in the muscle below the knee and his heart sank, recognizing the familiar warning sign. He was in for another devil of a night. By the wee hours of the morning, he'd be grinding his teeth down to the roots at the pain, tempted to take the laudanum again, a weakness he despised.

Forcing himself to his feet, he limped about the library, trying to work some of the stiffness out. He heard a low rumble in the distance, but he scarce needed that to tell him a storm was imminent. How bloody wonderful to have a knee that acted like a blasted weather predictor.

Val hobbled to the window, opened the shutters, and peered at the gloom-ridden night, the moon but a pale crescent shadowed by the eerie shapes of the shifting clouds. No doubt the villagers would be dancing up a frenzy, waving their pitchforks to chase off any stray witches that might happen to fly past Torrecombe.

He wondered wistfully if Kate was at the bonfires tonight. He hoped that she was instead of moping in her room. She'd always loved the celebration of All Hallows' Eve, wild gypsy that she was, dancing around the flames, her dark eyes flashing, her silken black hair in mad disarray.

Val would have been content to have watched her, delighting in the sheer abandoned joy of her graceful movements. But Kate would never have any of that. She had always tugged at his hands, ignoring his stern protests, insisting that he dance with her.

Pure folly, but he'd never been able to resist the plea on her smiling lips, the firelight shining in her eyes. Somehow she'd been able to make him forget everything, his dignity, his pain, his limp and he'd capered with her about the fire until they'd both been left laughing and breathless.

Over the years they had danced away a lot of demons together, he and Kate. But no more. Never again, Val thought bleakly.

He could accept with resignation the injury to his leg, the fact that for some unknown whim of fate, he was destined to never have a bride of his own. But at least he'd always had the consolation of Kate's friendship.

If he was obliged to surrender that, too, then he might as well be dead.

It was a wild, bitter thought, and Val was quick to swallow it. He refastened the shutters, closing out the night, and turned to limp his weary way up to bed. But as he crossed the entrance hall, the bell mounted outside the front door jangled loudly.

Kate.

Val gripped his cane and felt his pulse quicken eagerly. She often stole from her home to visit him at all unseemly hours despite how he lectured her about the impropriety or the dangers of it.

But the swift hope faded as quickly as it had come. Kate would never have paused to ring the bell. She would have slipped around the house to the library where she knew he'd be and banged at the windows until he let her in.

The only people who ever used that bell were his patients or their distressed relatives seeking his aid.

"Oh, Dr. St. Leger. You must come at once. You are the only one who can help. The only one."

"Dear God, not tonight," he murmured. He was so worn down, the pain in his leg flaring in intensity.

When the bell jangled again, Val closed his eyes, wondering what would happen if he ignored the summons. Why could he not do so just this once?

Because of who and what he was. A doctor, a healer, a man uniquely qualified to heal another's pain. Anyone else's but his own.

Leaning hard on his cane, he trudged across the hall and tugged open the thick oak door, letting in the wind and the night.

The hard bulk of a shadowy form hurtled at him out of the darkness. Val emitted a gasp of surprise and alarm, staggering painfully back. The heavy weight all but dragged him to the floor, nearly causing him to lose his grip on his cane. Just as he was in danger of toppling over, the burden shifted, collapsing at his feet.

Heart pounding, Val struggled to recover his balance, slamming the door closed before the wind extinguished the hall lamp. Only then was he able to focus on who had stumbled across his threshold. A man lay sprawled facedown on the oak floor.

His initial shock wearing off, Val felt the familiar surge of energy he always experienced when he was needed. All exhaustion and pain faded. He hunkered down beside the unconscious man. Keeping his weight balanced to his good leg, Val struggled to turn the body over. The hood fell back from a gaunt face obscured by a growth of beard.

Val detected no sign of any wound or injury, but this stranger was clearly in a bad way, his breathing labored, his skin burning. He needed to get the poor wretch into his surgery where he could perform a more complete examination. But how the devil was he to do so? Even on one of his best days, he could never have hefted the man over his shoulder. Despite the stranger's emaciated condition, he was still a tall man, large boned.

He'd be obliged to treat the unfortunate stranger right here on the cold hard floor. Val swore softly, regretting he'd been so insistent about sending Jem Sparkins off.

At that instant the stranger jerked violently, his gaze darting wildly about the unfamiliar surroundings until his burning eyes came to rest upon Val's face.

"Easy now," Val soothed, resting his hand on the stranger's shoulder. "Everything's going to be all right. I'm a doctor. I'm here to help you."

"St. Leger? Val St. Leger," the man rasped.

"You know me?" Val asked in surprise. He peered more intently at the stranger's face, trying to delve past the layer of straggling beard and the changes illness must have wrought in those thin features. There was something about the man's voice, weak as it was, that stirred a chord of memory and rendered Val uneasy.

The man's mouth snaked back into a familiar mocking smile. The chill of recognition pierced Val like an icy blade being thrust into his spine.

"Rafe," he whispered in horror and disbelief.

"Rafe Mortmain!"

The storm moved in from the sea. Kate had never seen clouds advance at such a rate, like a black stain spreading across the sky, blotting out all traces of the moon.

The wind threatened to tear the page of the book from her hands. Heart pounding, she struggled to hurry, using the red glow of the firelight to pore over the strange symbols. She had studied Prospero's writings for the past two days, but the translating still did not come easy to her.

"Come you at night to—to a place of high magic—" she intoned.

She stole a glance behind her at the standing stone, stark and massive in all its mystery. Surely she could not have found a place of higher magic than this, nor a better time for casting her spell . . . All Hallows' Eve.

The wind flipped the page from her grasp and she had to flatten it back into place before she could continue.

"Place upon the flames the symbol of your heart's desire, the initials of your passion carved upon solid black fire."

It had taken her some effort to figure out what that meant. Solid black fire? Prospero must have been talking about coal; and the initials of your passion— it had to mean the initials of Val's name. Or so Kate hoped.

Groping in her cloak pocket, she pulled forth a lump of coal on which she had shakily scratched out a "V.S." She hesitated for a long moment, then drawing in a deep breath, flung the coal into the bonfire.

It struck up against a burning branch, sending out a hot shower of sparks. Kate flinched back, clutching the book. The wind whistled in her ears, the flames danced before her eyes. The coal had vanished.

No, there it was, in the very center, the hottest blue-white core of the fire. The flames licked against the glistening chunk of coal. Kate watched for a moment, mesmerized, breathlessly waiting for something to happen. Then she remembered she had not finished the spell. She wrenched her gaze back to the book and continued.

"Now speak the proper words."

This was the difficult part. It was one thing to decipher the words to a spell, quite another to figure out how they should be pronounced. One syllable out of place, one misspoken vowel, might well mean disaster.

A loud rumble of thunder sounded overhead, closer now, the wind tugging hard at the book as though the night itself warned her to stop.

"Courage, girl," Kate murmured, fighting to still her unsteady hands. She moistened her lips and closed her eyes.

"M-mithcaril bocurum epps," she whispered.

A clap of thunder shook the cottage windows, the light from the hall lamp flickering over the wan face of the man sprawled in front of Val.

"Rafe Mortmain," he repeated again, still unable to credit his eyes. He snatched his hand from Rafe's shoulder as though he'd reached out to a savage wolf.

A strangled laugh escaped Rafe only to break off into a fit of coughing that shook his entire frame.

"Not—not here to hurt you," he said hoarsely as soon as he could speak again. "You should . . . see clearly . . . in no condition to kill anyone, not even myself. No reason to be afraid."

No reason? Val thought. None except that the last time he and Rafe Mortmain had met, they had been locked in a life or death struggle at the Dragon's Fire Inn, the combat coming to an abrupt end when Rafe had flung him down the stairs. And what Rafe had started, his confederate had finished, shooting Val in the back.

If he had been anyone else but a St. Leger and possessed of such unusual healing abilities, Val would have moldered to dust in the family crypt beneath St. Gothian's Church long ago. He had survived, but with no thanks due to Raphael Mortmain.

Rafe might appear weak and helpless, but Val had enough experience to know a wounded wolf could prove more dangerous than any other creature. He felt himself involuntarily begin to retreat.

"Please . . . Can't hurt you now. Took all of my strength . . . just to find you. Only came to give you this." Rafe reached beneath his cloak, groping for something.

Val tensed, bracing himself for anything, a pistol, a knife. He was too slow to defend himself when Rafe lurched upward to a half-sitting position and seized his arm with surprising strength.

"Here. Take this!"

Before Val could wrench free, Rafe pressed the weight of something against his palm. Rafe collapsed back, the effort appearing to have drained what little strength remained to him.

"There. 'Tis done," he murmured, an odd look of satisfaction stealing over his grim features.

Val took a moment to steady himself, unnerved by Rafe's assault. Then he slowly uncurled his fingers to see what Rafe had given him.

He froze, his lips parting in awe. Resting in the palm of his hand was a silver braided chain with a small stone attached, a piece of crystal of such unsurpassed beauty, it robbed Val of breath. The shard had been stolen years before, chipped away from the fabulous stone imbedded in the pommel of the St. Leger ancestral sword.

Val dangled the chain, holding the crystal up to the light. It was but a tiny fragment of the original stone, but it glittered with all the cold clarity of an icicle struck by sunlight, sparking a rainbow array of colors off the walls and the rafters of the silent hall.

Stunning, beautiful, mesmerizing.

"Put—put that damned thing away," Rafe croaked, twisting his head to one side as though the glitter of the crystal hurt his eyes.

With great difficulty, Val tore his gaze away from the crystal shard. Reluctantly he fastened the chain about his neck, tucking the stone out of sight. His mind reeled with questions. Rafe had had the stolen fragment in his possession all this time. Why had he now risked coming back to Cornwall to return it? And why to Val? The St. Leger sword belonged to his brother, Lance, as eldest son and heir to Castle Leger. By rights, the stolen fragment did, too. And where the blazes had Rafe been hiding these past five years? What had reduced him to this terrible state?

But one glance at Rafe told Val he would gain no answers to these troubling questions. His eyes closed, Rafe appeared to be sinking into unconsciousness. It didn't take Val's instincts as a doctor or a St. Leger to realize beyond all doubt:

Rafe Mortmain was dying.

Val expected he ought to feel a sense of triumph to see his old enemy brought so low. Instead his heart twisted with an unexpected pity for such a waste of a life. Rafe had once been a vigorous man, intelligent, a commanding presence. If he had not also been a cursed Mortmain, who knows what he might have achieved?

Val reached for his wrist. Rafe's pulse was very faint. His chest rose and fell with a stifled wheeze as though it tortured him to continue breathing. Val noted the tightness about Rafe's mouth, the tension near the eyes, signs of pain all too familiar to Val. He'd experienced them often enough himself.

"Please," Rafe mumbled, the rest of his words incoherent. Val had to lean closer in order to hear him.

"I . . . I beg you, St. Leger," Rafe's cracked lips whispered close to Val's ear. *"Kill me."*

Val jerked back in shock. It was not the first time that a patient in such misery had begged Val to end his life. But he'd never have expected such a request to come from the proud Raphael, the last of the once powerful and arrogant Mortmains. It was obvious he was dying in terrible agony, and there was nothing Val could do about it.

Nothing except ease the man's last hours by . . . Val felt the familiar tingle in his fingers, but he recoiled at the thought.

No! He almost cried aloud. By God, that was too much to ask of any man, even one named for a martyr and a saint, that he should employ his power at all tonight when he was so drained and hurting himself, and that he should aid one who had been his mortal enemy. A Mortmain.

He couldn't do it. But even as Val hovered over Rafe Mortmain, the man writhed. A sob rattled his chest, a single tear escaping the corner of his sealed eye to leak down his beard-roughened cheek.

Val doubted Rafe Mortmain had ever wept in his entire life. Almost involuntarily, his hand closed over Rafe's.

Surely he could do that much for Rafe Mortmain, absorb just a fraction of his pain. Val forced himself to concentrate, blocking out all other sensation except for the pressure of his own hand clutching Rafe's, delving beyond the mere physical contact. He focused harder, mentally dissolving his own flesh, muscle, bone, twisting his thoughts until they nicked like sharp razors at his veins, opening them to let his own strength flow out.

Nothing had happened.

Kate opened one eye and felt the first splash of rain on her cheek. The bonfire seemed in danger of dying, the stubborn lump of coal, immutable in the center of the flames, not even starting to glow.

Kate wasn't exactly sure what she had expected to happen, but certainly a little more than this. She gazed desperately back at the book. Was she mispronouncing the words or merely not saying them with enough conviction?

"Mithcaril bocurum epps," she repeated a little more loudly.

Still nothing. Kate swallowed hard and summoned up all her courage. She flung back her head and shouted into the wind.

"Mithcaril bocurum epps!"

There was a brief ominous silence. Then flames shot up, flaring into the night with an angry roar. Kate gave a startled cry and leapt back. A savage clap of thunder rocked the entire hillside, shaking the ground beneath her feet. A jagged streak of lightning rent the darkness, striking at the standing stone in a sizzle of sparks and smoke.

Kate screamed and dove for cover.

Val steeled his spine, braced to receive Rafe's pain, to control the transference.

"Ah, dear God!" Val's eyes flew wide at the unexpected intensity of the sensation. Not a trickle of pain, but a crushing wave of agony rolled through him. Not physical. He might have endured that. But this was different, something ugly and terrifying.

A flash flood of unbearable emotion, rage, bitterness, and despair coursed through him. Gasping, Val fought to regain control and stop the transference. But he couldn't get his hand free. Rafe latched on to him like a drowning man, threatening to drag Val under with him into his own river of darkness.

His breath coming in labored pants, Val's head swam. He yanked harder, striking out at the joining of their hands in an effort to release himself. The crystal fastened about his neck swayed with the violence of his efforts, casting off sparks of light.

A red haze descended over his eyes. He realized he was in danger of losing consciousness and fought harder. He grew weaker by the moment, so weak. He made one last futile effort.

A deafening explosion sounded in his ears, accompanied by a blinding flash. Rafe's grip loosened and Val fell back, surrendering himself to the darkness.

The rain pelted down in icy sheets, consuming the last of the flames in a soft, angry hiss. Kate emerged from her hiding place in the heather, soaked to the skin and trembling. She staggered a few steps forward, feeling bruised and battered.

With dazed eyes, she stared at the ruin of her bonfire, nothing left but a blackened ring of scorched earth. The sky overhead roiled with dark clouds, but the thunder and the flares of lightning seemed to have retreated to a distance.

Kate shivered, turning her gaze skyward. What had she done? She had no idea, only this terrified feeling that she had just loosed something dark and dangerous into the night.

Clutching the sodden remains of Prospero's spell book to her breast, Kate turned and fled for home.

Jem Sparkins managed to reach Slate House just before the rains broke. He bolted into the entrance hall only to find his master sprawled on the floor just inside the front door. A horrified cry breached his lips. His pulse thumping with fear, he bent down by the doctor, shaking his shoulder.

"Dr. St. Leger? Master Val. Master Val!"

There was no response, the doctor's features frozen in an expression so cold and still, Jem thought his own heart would stop. He stroked back the black strands that had tumbled across his master's eyes. His complexion was ice white. He looked . . . he felt dead.

A blind panic seized Jem, and he fought to control it and remember what little he'd learned while in the doctor's employ. What should he do? Fetch water, brandy? Chafe the master's wrist? No, the pulse. That was it. He ought to check for a pulse.

He reached for the master's hand and pressed his fingers tight to Val's wrist, fearing his worst dread would be confirmed. He would feel nothing. To his astonishment, the doctor's pulse gave a powerful throb, strong and steady.

Then why did Master Val lie there, so stiff and cold? Had he fallen? Fainted?

Been attacked by some intruder that had broken into the house? There was no sign that anyone else had been here. Perhaps Master Val's bad leg had given out and he'd stumbled and cracked his head.

Damnation. Somehow Jem had just known that something terrible was going to happen tonight. Perhaps during all of his years working for the St. Legers, some of their peculiar ways had begun to rub off on him.

He raked his hands back through his hair, trying to decide what to do next, when the doctor's eyes fluttered open. His pupils were so enlarged, his eyes seemed almost black, but startlingly clear.

Jem bent anxiously over him.

"Dr. Val? Can you hear me? How badly are you hurt? What happened? Did you fall?"

The doctor shifted his head to stare blankly at Jem. For one awful moment, it was as though Master Val didn't even remember who he was.

Then he murmured, "No, I didn't fall. I was struck by lightning."

Jem's mouth fell open. "Here? In the house, sir? But you are lying in the front hall."

"Aye, so I am," the doctor murmured. "How extraordinary."

Jem studied him with new anxiety as a terrible thought struck him. Perhaps the doctor had had a fit of some kind. After Mr. Peters had had that stroke of apoplexy, the poor old man had never been quite right in the head again.

Even as Jem worried over this grim possibility, the doctor calmly shifted to a sitting position.

"No, sir, please. You had better remain lying still until—"

The master ignored him, bent on getting to his feet. Jem hastened to fetch the doctor's cane. The ivory-handled walking stick was lying but a few yards away. But by the time Jem's hand closed over the cane, Dr. Val was already standing.

"Y-your cane, sir," Jem faltered.

The doctor cast him an odd look and took a few steps, his legs strong and steady beneath him. *Both* of them.

Jem gaped at him. "Sir. You . . . your leg. You're not limping. What—what's happened?"

"I don't know. I can't remember. A miracle perhaps." The doctor whipped about, staring at his own reflection in the hall's gilt-edged mirror as though he'd never seen himself before.

"A bloody damned miracle!" the doctor said, flinging back his head.

Jem flinched from his master's sudden burst of laughter. If Dr. Val had indeed experienced some miraculous recovery, Jem knew he should be rejoicing, too. Instead he felt as though he'd stumbled headlong into the middle of a bizarre dream.

The doctor paced the room, his strides growing longer, more confident, until he fetched back up in front of the mirror. Jem thought he caught the flash of something silver dangling from Master Val's neck, but before he could see what it was, the doctor tucked it out of sight.

The doctor raised his bad leg and deliberately stomped his foot against the floor with as much force as he could manage.

"What do you think of this? Eh, Jem?" Dr. Val demanded with another ringing laugh.

"It—it's wonderful, sir," Jem stammered. "But perhaps you should take it a little easy, sit down for a spell. You don't seem quite yourself, sir."

"No, I don't, do I?"

The doctor leaned closer to the mirror, studying his own image with great intensity. His lips snaked back in a way that left Jem chilled.

The expression was far different from Dr. Val's usual gentle smile.

CHAPTER SIX

The village was on fire.

Thatched roofs crackled and blazed, the stonework of cottages crumbling to cinders, the spire of St. Gothian's Church caving in with a mighty roar. Kate clutched the spell book to her chest as the skies rained down fiery bursts of hail. She tugged at the cover of the book, trying to find a spell to undo this dark magic of destruction, but the pages were stuck fast.

All she could do was run. The lane was so heavy with smoke, she could scarce see where she was going, could only hear the shouts from the angry mob of villagers thundering after her.

"There she goes!"

"She's the one who did this to us."

"Witch! Sorceress!"

"Hang her! Burn her at the stake."

Kate glanced wildly about her for a way to escape, a place to hide, but there was none. Her pursuers pounded closer. She could see the gleam of their eyes through the thick billows of smoke.

Kate stumbled and fell, snatching at the folds of someone's cloak. She gazed up to find Prospero looming over her. The mob overtook her, rough hands gripping her by the arms to drag her away.

"Prospero!" she cried.

The great sorcerer merely stood by and scowled at her. "You should have heeded my warning, milady. It is always dangerous to use magic to meddle with—"

"No!"

Kate struck out at the hands that seized her, fighting and kicking for her very life. But all she succeeded in doing was tangle herself in the bedcovers. Her eyes flew open and she blinked, a few moments passing before she realized it was no longer smoke, fire, and night weighing against her eyelids, only the calm flood of sunlight that penetrated the confines of her small bedchamber, playing over the rose-patterned wallpaper.

Kate rolled onto her back, giving her heart a chance to steady itself before releasing a deep sigh. A dream. Only another stupid bad dream like the ones that had tormented her since falling asleep. The twisted sheets bore mute testimony to the many demons and angry villagers she had fended off last night. She struggled free of the bed linens and swung her legs over the side.

Her entire body groaned in protest, her head throbbing. She felt as bruised and battered as though—as though she'd been—

Nearly struck by lightning? Tumbled down a hillside to escape? Ridden home through the cold pouring rain?

Kate grimaced and forced herself to stand. She stepped over the pile of sodden clothes she'd stripped off and left in a heap, her bare feet padding across the carpet, her white nightgown swirling about her ankles. Rubbing her bleary eyes, she stumbled to the window and hesitated before peering out, half dreading that she would find the village in ruins.

But Torrecombe spread out below her, dozing in the autumn sunshine. The pale light touched the thatched roofs of the cottages, snug as ever. The only traces remaining of yesterday's storm were a few broken branches and the puddles that muddied the lanes. The dancing shadows, the bonfires, and the pitchforks to ward off flying witches were all gone.

It was as though the madness of All Hallows' Eve had never been.

The village was still standing, the countryside had not been rent asunder by lightning bolts. Kate rested her aching brow against the windowpane, her relief crowded out by more anxious emotions. She'd had difficulty in deciphering all of Prospero's notes on the subject of love spells, but what little she'd read had led to her believe that if the spell worked at all, it would be swift and sure, exactly like a bolt of lightning.

Yet there was no sign of Val galloping toward Rosebriar Cottage, so overcome with love and passion for her, he'd break down the door to take her in his arms. The lane below remained peaceful and empty no matter how long she stood and stared.

Perhaps she had misread Prospero's notes. Perhaps the spell did not work that quickly. And perhaps it hadn't worked at all. Kate drew back from the window, seeking out the book she had left perched on the corner of her dressing table. In the calm light of day, the sorcerer's book of spells looked far tamer than she remembered, like a quaint old volume of folklore.

Kate touched the leather cover still damp from the storm. She tried to summon up the mysterious tingles, the anticipation, and even the shivers of dread she'd experienced last night. But she felt nothing.

It was as though the same chilling rain that had doused her bonfire had extinguished any enchantment. She ruefully examined the pages of the book, water-stained, the ink blurring in many places. Prospero would make her nightmare a reality when he saw what she had done to his book. He'd roast her alive, but that hardly mattered.

She had failed. Somehow she knew that. She doubted that she had managed to conjure up anything more serious than—Kate stifled a quick sneeze—a head cold.

After the fright she'd given herself last night, she knew she would never find the courage to tamper with such dark magic again. Who was she to think she could ever have pulled off such a feat of sorcery anyway? Nobody, only a stupid lovelorn girl.

So what was she going to do now? Kate slumped down on the stool by her dressing table, resting her aching head upon her arms, too tired and disheartened even to think.

A sharp rap sounded on her bedchamber door. She tried to summon the energy to bellow at whoever it was to leave her alone but it was too late. The door swung open and Kate retained just enough presence of mind to jerk upright and hide Prospero's book beneath a fichu draped across her dressing table.

But her bedchamber could have been overflowing with spell books and wizards. Kate doubted that the housemaid who burst into the room would have noticed. Nan's starched cap was knocked askew, her placid features extremely harried.

"Oh, Miss Kate. You are awake at last, thank God! You must come down to the parlor at once. Miss Effie is asking for you and she is in one of her terrible states."

Oh, dear God, Effie! Kate thought, holding her head. *Please. Not now.*

"Whatever is the matter?" Kate asked.

"That Mrs. Bell has already been here to call, demanding to see Miss Effie before poor mistress was even out of bed and finished with her chocolate."

Kate tensed, her stomach curling with dread at mention of the local seamstress and dressmaker. Alice Bell was the village's most notorious gossip.

"The woman squeaked on you, Miss Kate," Nan went on indignantly. "She told Miss Effie how you were seen sneaking out last night and getting your horse from the stables."

"Oh, damnation!"

"Indeed, miss," Nan agreed with a sympathetic nod, although she flinched at Kate's language.

Kate had to restrain herself from letting fly a string of epithets that would have turned the little housemaid's ears blue. With the commotion of All Hallows' Eve, Kate had hoped that her absence from the village would go unnoticed, especially by Effie who had a marked tendency to lapse into hysterics over the least little thing. Effie had long ago given up efforts to control Kate, preferring to remain blissfully deaf and blind to whatever Kate might be doing.

Damn Alice Bell. Kate would have loved to strangle the woman. If Mrs. Bell had plied her needle with the same skill she did her tongue, Torrecombe would have replaced Paris as the hub of the fashionable world. The woman seemed positively to enjoy distressing poor Effie with reports of Kate's escapades.

As exhausted as Kate felt and after everything that had gone wrong last night, she didn't need this to deal with as well. Her gaze strayed to the window and she felt a strong urge to climb down the old oak tree and escape as she had often done as a child when Effie had nearly driven her to distraction. Plying Kate with dolls, hair ribbons, and dress fittings. Fixing Kate with large sad eyes and bursting into tears whenever Kate had tried to explain she didn't want another blasted doll or new frock. All she had ever wanted was to be left free to run to Val.

Kate winced at the memory. Effie could be rather foolish at times, but she was unfailingly kind and generous. Kate feared she had caused the poor woman more than enough grief over the years. She stole one last longing glance at the window before turning back to the anxious Nan.

"Tell Effie that I will be down directly," she said with a wearied sigh.

Fifteen minutes later Kate descended to the lower hall clad in a plain gray dress that matched her mood. Gone was any hint of the wild gypsy who had danced about the bonfire last night, muttering incantations. She had twisted her unruly black hair up into a haphazard chignon, which she feared gave her the look of an absentminded spinster. But why not? Kate thought bleakly. That seemed destined to be her fate.

She crossed over to the parlor door and braced herself. If only Effie would rant and rail at her, even box her ears. Blows and harsh words Kate could have endured. It was the tears and lamentations she found unbearable.

Gritting her teeth, she turned the knob and crept into the strange world that comprised Elfreda Fitzleger's favorite sitting room. A roaring fire blazed on the hearth and Kate cringed. Effie already had it hot enough in here to roast chestnuts. She could have raised tropical plants if one could have found room for them in the amazing jumble of furniture. Chinese, French Empire, Egyptian, and Hepplewhite pieces all butted against each other like warring nations.

And then there was Effie's collection of clocks, dozens of them mounted upon the wall, crammed upon the mantel, perched upon the étagère. When Kate had first come to Rosebriar Cottage, she had thought the incessant ticking would drive her mad, but she had finally grown so accustomed to it, she barely noticed except when they all chimed the hour in one deafening din.

Some of the timepieces had actually been gifts from grateful St. Legers acknowledging Effie's services as their matchmaker. As incredible as it often seemed to Kate, the flighty Effie was considered to be blessed with mystical powers, the supernatural gift to find each St. Leger his one true love.

But at the moment the Bride Finder lay prostrate on a chaise longue, still clad in her nightgown and wrapper. Effie lolled against the bolster, a tripod table near at hand containing her sal volatile and a crumpled mound of handkerchiefs.

But for all her tragic pose, Kate noted that the parlor curtains had been left open, the better to observe who might be passing by in the lane. Beneath her lace cap, Effie's profusion of golden ringlets was as carefully arranged as always. For someone who had turned forty, Effie's hair showed a remarkable lack of gray, and Kate suspected it was because Effie removed these unwanted strands. She feared that someday Effie was going to pluck herself bald.

For as long as Kate could remember, Effie had refused to acknowledge the passing of years, adopting a youthful style from her gowns to those absurd ringlets. This morning the sunlight pouring through the windows was almost cruel, emphasizing the inroads that time had made in the lines that bracketed Effie's mouth and eyes.

As Kate eased the door closed, Effie shifted toward her with a deep mournful sigh.

"Oh, Kate. Kate," she quavered, stretching out her hand.

Kate had learned a long time ago that the best way to deal with Effie's megrims was to maintain an attitude of determined cheerfulness. She threaded her way through the furniture, snatching up a pillow as she went. Plumping it, she eased it beneath Effie's head.

"Now, Effie, whatever is this all about?" she asked.

"Oh, Kate. Mrs. Bell has been here this morning and she has been telling me the most dreadful things about you."

"Mrs. Bell is a damn— I mean a wicked gossip. You should know better than to listen to her."

"Aye, but she had her information from Mr. Wentworth. Such a fine gentleman, even if he is only an innkeeper. And he s-said—" Effie's lip quivered.

Kate hastily handed her another handkerchief. Effie blew her nose with a loud sniff before continuing, "He said that you s-saddled up Willow and rode away in the middle of the night."

"It wasn't the middle of the night. It was much earlier."

"But you were still gone after dark. How could you, Kate? Running about the countryside unchaperoned at night? Not only was it improper, it was highly dangerous. *Anything* could have happened to you."

"But it didn't," Kate pointed out quite reasonably. Drawing up a tapestry-covered footstool, she settled herself beside the chaise longue. "You see me here before you quite safe."

But Effie was not to be so easily mollified. "It was bad enough to behave thus when you were still a child," she said, fluttering her handkerchief for emphasis. "But you are a young lady now. Think of your reputation."

"What reputation?" Kate demanded wryly. "Most of the village believe that I must be the devil child of some wandering gypsies."

"Only because you do your best to convince them it's true. If you won't think of your reputation, think of mine." Effie had recourse to her handkerchief again. "E-everyone thinks that I am a t-terrible mother."

"Oh, Effie, no one thinks that. Only that you made a terrible choice of a daughter. I can't think why you ever adopted me."

"Because you were the prettiest, sweetest little girl I'd ever clapped eyes upon."

"Effie!" Kate rolled her eyes. "I was a mother's worst nightmare. I still am."

"No, no dearest." Effie stretched out her fragile fingers to pat Kate's cheek. "It is only that at times you are a little more *lively* than one could wish."

Kate bit back a smile and gave Effie's hand a comforting squeeze. "I am truly sorry if I have distressed you again. But I had to go out last night. It was necessary."

"Necessary? Child, what could you possibly have had to do in the dark of night that was that important?"

Kate evaded Effie's sad, bewildered eyes. From her earliest years, Kate had been an accomplished liar and Effie was as trusting as a child, far too easy to deceive. Was that what often made it so uncomfortable to do so? Yet telling her the truth in this instance was out of the question. Not unless she really did want to send her gentle guardian off into a fit of apoplexy.

Kate forced herself to give an airy shrug. "You know how I am, Effie. I can't abide just sitting about all the time like a proper little miss, tending my stitching. Sometimes the devil just gets into me and I have to tear off on my horse and be alone."

"Were you alone, Kate?" Effie asked in a small voice.

"Why, yes," Kate said, astonished by the question. "Who else would have been mad enough to go traipsing the countryside with me after dark on All Hallows' Eve?"

Effie ducked her head, fidgeting with the lace on her handkerchief. "Well, you are a young woman now and—and a moonlit ride along the beach can be quite romantic. I used to think so. I was young and rather headstrong once myself you know. I understand how a girl can sometimes be tempted to—to—"

Kate stared at her, for a moment unable to make sense of this halting speech. Then comprehension dawned and she gave an incredulous laugh.

"Dear lord, Effie! You can't possibly be worrying that I had an assignation with someone last night, can you? There is only one man I would ever want to seduce me by moonlight, and unfortunately he is far too honorable to do so. You know that I have always been in love with—"

"No, don't say it," Effie shrieked, sitting bolt upright. She actually clapped her hand over Kate's mouth to still her.

Gently, but firmly Kate eased Effie's hand aside. "My not saying it won't change anything. I love Val St. Leger and I always will."

"Oh, dear God." Effie paled, groping for her bottle of smelling salts. "I prayed you had gotten over that. You never mentioned it anymore."

Kate had stopped mentioning it because the subject always produced precisely this reaction from Effie. Her hands trembled so badly that Kate had to uncork the bottle for her. Effie took a fortifying sniff before fixing Kate with large, pleading eyes.

"This feeling you have for Valentine is just a passing infatuation, Kate. You will get over it. *You must.*"

"So everyone keeps telling me. All because of that stupid legend." Kate forced a smile to her lips, half-wry, half-wistful. "You are the great and wise Bride Finder, Effie. Couldn't you overlook the rules just this once and choose me to be Val's bride?"

Effie looked so stricken at the mere suggestion of such a thing, Kate made haste to disclaim, "I was only teasing. I don't even believe in the legend. And even if it were true, such fairy tales were only meant for golden-haired princesses like Rosalind St. Leger, not for some unwanted nuisance of a foundling brat like me."

"Oh, K-kate. Please d-don't talk that way." Effie's face crumpled and she dissolved in a flood of tears, making Kate wish she had curbed her tongue. She knew the tenderhearted Effie couldn't bear any reference to Kate's past, the grim foundling home where she'd first clapped eyes on Kate. Sometimes she thought that Effie preferred to believe that she had found Kate drifting in a reed basket like Moses or else tucked beneath a rosebush like a fairy child. Kate wished she could have dismissed all dark memories of her early childhood so easily.

Effie burrowed her face in her handkerchief, weeping softly. Kate watched her in dismal silence for a moment. This was one of those rare mornings when Kate felt like weeping herself, her heart heavy with thoughts of Val, the hopelessness of her love for him. She'd wondered what it would be like to have a real mother to pour out her woes to, to feel wise and loving hands stroke her hair, somehow making everything all better.

But Kate had realized and accepted certain facts about Effie Fitzleger a long time ago. That no matter how many frocks and hair ribbons Effie might shower her with, there were other things that Effie was simply incapable of giving. Kate would always be the stronger of the two. She wrapped her arms about Effie, cradling the older woman against her shoulder, Kate's own eyes dry and tired.

Effie's sniffles subsided and she raised her tear-streaked face, attempting to smile. "I know what is wrong. You simply have not seen enough of the world. We ought to get away from here. We could go to London."

"London?" Kate released Effie, staring incredulously at her guardian. Horrible images tumbled through Kate's mind of dirty streets, rat-infested hallways, and starving children, their faces hopeless and hardened well beyond their years.

"Effie! London is the last place I'd ever want to go."

"I don't mean back to—to that dreadful—" Effie couldn't even bring herself to mention the foundling home. "We would go to the pretty part of the city where my cousin lives. A baronet's wife. She moves in the best of society."

Effie brightened, clapping her hands together. "Oh, do but imagine it, Kate. The theatres, the balls, scores of admirers. A London season, just like we've always dreamed of."

"Your dream, Effie," Kate said gently. "Not mine."

"We cannot always have our dreams, Kate." An odd look flashed over Effie's face, a sad kind of wisdom that Kate had never expected to see in Elfreda Fitzleger's eyes. But it was gone in a heartbeat, replaced by Effie's usual vacant and amiable expression. She chattered on about all the wonderful things that she and Kate would do when they arrived in London.

Kate had no intention of going anywhere that would take her so far away from Val. But she made no effort to interrupt. At least Effie had stopped crying and she was distracted from making any more inquiries about Kate's activities on All Hallows' Eve.

"Kate, you must go and tell John I'll have a letter for him to post this afternoon. And I should go consult with Mrs. Bell. We'll need some new traveling clothes." Effie swung her legs over the side of the chaise longue, looking ready to bolt off at once.

"Perhaps you had better get dressed first," Kate suggested.

Effie glanced down at her wrapper and tittered. "Oh, yes. Silly me. But first be a dear, Kate, and instruct Nan to fetch me some toast and tea. I need a little nourishment. It has been such a trying morning with Mrs. Bell bearing dire tales about my darling girl and that Victor St. Leger."

"Victor?" Kate asked in surprise. "What's he done?"

"Oh, that wicked boy," Effie sniffed. "He'll be the death of me yet."

"But he should have left off plaguing you. You found him his chosen bride."

"Aye, but the ungrateful wretch is not satisfied with my choice. He was supposed to have proposed to Mollie Grey last night. Everyone was expecting him to do so. And what do you think, Kate? The dratted boy never turned up, left the poor girl waiting all night. Mollie was completely mortified. Mrs. Bell told me."

"Mrs. Bell obviously had a very busy morning," Kate muttered, then shrugged. "You shouldn't worry about it, Effie. You found Victor a bride. If he won't have her, it's not your problem. I am sure Mollie will be much better off."

Kate had never had a high opinion of Victor St. Leger. He was nothing but a callow boy, not in the least like his grandfather or his father, both magnificent, hardy sailing men with salt water in their veins and a hundred adventures to their credit. Victor turned green and swooned like a girl if he had to so much as set foot in a rowboat.

But Effie continued to lament, "Sometimes I don't know why I try so hard. I wear myself half to death seeking out the perfect mates for these St. Legers, and they never appreciate my efforts."

"Then don't do it anymore."

"My dear, you simply have never understood. I don't have a choice. I was born to be the St. Leger Bride Finder, just as my grandfather before me," Effie said forlornly. "Destined to find love for others, attend their weddings, while all I ever wanted was one of my own."

"Then why didn't you ever marry, Effie? I am sure you were a pretty young woman." Kate amended quickly, "I mean you still are. You must have had plenty of offers."

"Aye, so I did." Effie preened, reaching up to pat her curls. "I had my share of admirers. But none of them ever captured my heart. If only I could have gone to live with my cousin in London after Grandpapa died. I am sure I would have found someone quite handsome and dashing there."

Effie's face clouded over. "But of course I could not abandon my bride-finding duties here. And now it is far too late."

"You still have a suitor," Kate reminded her. "Reverend Trimble quite adores you. He calls here all the time and I am sure it is not because he entertains any hope of salvaging my soul."

"Oh, that rogue. Such a silly man." Effie turned pink to the root of her curls, a warmth stealing into her eyes. Yet she stubbornly shook her head. "He wouldn't be suitable. A simple country vicar."

"But, Effie, you were a country vicar's granddaughter yourself."

"Aye, but we Fitzlegers are descended from noble blood, the same family tree as the St. Legers."

An illegitimate branch of that tree. The Fitzlegers had been spawned from one of Prospero's numerous indiscreet liaisons. But there was little to be gained from pointing that out to Effie or trying to persuade her of Mr. Trimble's merits.

"No, dearest," Effie insisted a little too brightly. "It doesn't matter anymore. I have learned to be quite content with my life as it is."

That was utter rubbish, Kate thought. Effie still cried her eyes out at every wedding she attended, and not out of joy for the bride and groom. She should have been married a long time ago to some cheery, sensible man like the vicar, with a house full of docile golden-haired daughters to fuss over, the kind that didn't climb out bedchamber windows in the dark of night.

Kate had never realized it before, but in some measure Effie's dreams had been blighted by that infernal St. Leger legend as much as her own. The thought made Kate a little sad, a little angry, and strangely frightened. Gazing at Effie's fading beauty was suddenly like catching a discomfiting glimpse of her own fate.

Perhaps she, too, was destined to spend her life like Effie, alone and unwed here in this cottage while all these blasted clocks ticked off the minutes of her youth. Maybe if she were fortunate Val would call upon her occasionally like the vicar did Effie. It was too depressing a vision of the future even to contemplate.

Suddenly Kate's need to escape the stifling parlor was overwhelming. She wrenched to her feet. Bending down, she planted a swift kiss on Effie's cheek, clearly surprising the older woman with the unusual display of affection.

"I'll tell Nan to fetch your tea," Kate said gruffly, backing away.

"Won't you stay and have a cup with me?"

"No, I need to get out for a walk."

"Unchaperoned?" Effie cried, her face tensing with fresh alarm. "Oh, Kate. After all we just discussed."

"It is broad daylight, Effie. I'll be fine."

"But wherever will you go, dearest?"

Where? At one time, there would have been only one answer to that question, but now—

"I don't know," Kate said, slipping out the door before Effie could protest further.

Effie clutched her hands to her bosom in pure panic, her heart constricting with an age-old fear. Perhaps Kate truly didn't know where she was going, but Effie did. And she could no longer pretend the situation away or continue to ignore it.

"Oh, she'll end up going straight to *him*," Effie moaned. "She still believes she's in love with him."

Just as Kate had done from the time she'd been a little girl. Only Kate was not so very little anymore, and the attraction had finally grown dangerous.

"You are the Bride Finder, Effie. Couldn't you forget the rules for once and simply choose me to be Val's bride?"

Kate's lips had been curved in a teasing smile when she'd spoken those words, but oh, the expression in the poor girl's eyes, that sad, wistful look. It was quite enough to break Effie's heart.

"Whatever am I going to do?" she whispered. If only . . .

But any marriage between Kate and Valentine St. Leger was quite impossible and no one knew why better than Effie.

She buried her face in her hands, realizing she was going to have to find a way to whisk Kate away from Torrecombe and Val St. Leger. Before it was entirely too late.

Kate drew up the hood of her cloak to shield her face from the brisk nip of the breeze. After all the rage of last night's storm, the sea lapped peacefully over the shingle, rendering the coarse pebbles slick and shining. The sun glinted off the water, giving the glassy waves an appearance of deceptive warmth, but Kate knew better.

She kept well back from the water's edge, her eyes trained unhappily on the distant house. Even the sunlight failed to soften the stark lines of Slate House. Surrounded by a low stone fence, it resembled a small fortress, lonely and abandoned by the edge of the sea, the only sign of habitation the smoke curling lazily from the chimney tops.

But the gate had been left open, the worn path leading to the front door beckoning to Kate. She gripped her gloved hands together beneath her cloak, remaining where she was. She hadn't meant to come here. Truly she hadn't. She could not see what good could come of it.

Nothing had changed. She still loved Val to distraction; he could never love her. And not all her wishing, praying, or dabbling in sorcery had altered that fact. But dear lord, how she missed him, the quiet sound of his voice, the calm light of his eyes. Missed him so badly it hurt.

Kate bit down on her lip as she reached a desperate decision. She could never have Val, never be his wife or his lover. Then she would do whatever she had to merely to be with him, to put everything back as it had been before she had kissed him and begged him to marry her.

She would tell Val it had all been a mistake. Everyone was right. What she had felt was only a schoolgirl infatuation, but she had come to her senses. She was over it and they could go back to being friends again.

She was a good liar. Surely she could get Val to believe it. And maybe she could even manage to convince herself.

But before she could put this grim resolution into action, Kate became aware of a horse and rider coming from the beach in the opposite direction. She turned to look, using one hand to shield her eyes from the sun, and her breath snagged in her throat.

Coming from the beach? No, the stallion looked as though it had sprung straight from the depths of the breaking waves and blazing sunlight, its glistening coat the color of sea foam, its flowing mane a silvery gray. As the massive horse churned through the edge of the surf, its powerful forelegs flung up a glistening spray.

Kate squinted hard, but the glare of the sun refused to allow her to make out the details of the rider other than the mad tangle of his black hair. Yet there was only one man hereabouts capable of riding in that reckless neck-or-nothing fashion. Lance St. Leger.

Val's twin brother had always felt very much like Kate's own. Lance had taught her to ride, to fence, often encouraging her more outrageous behavior, much to Val's dismay. One minute stuffing sweetmeats into her pockets, the next teasing and tormenting her by tweaking her curls.

As fond as she was of Lance, Kate felt in no humor to bandy words with him right now. Yet there was no place to duck out of sight on this flat, open stretch of shore. As he thundered closer, Kate raised one hand in halfhearted greeting, only to freeze.

Lance had angled his horse away from the water's edge and he—he—

He was galloping straight for her.

Had Lance entirely lost his mind? Shock kept her immobilized for a moment. Then with a startled cry, she whirled to flee, hitching up her skirts to leap out of the way.

But she was too late. She could hear the horse hard upon her, felt flying pebbles strike at her cloak. Heart pounding, she tried for one last burst of speed, bracing herself to be trampled.

Instead there was a wild blur of movement. The horse surged past and Kate felt herself seized about the waist and plucked roughly off her feet like a hapless maiden snatched up by some marauding Celtic warrior.

Lance hauled her up in front of him. Kate clutched wildly for purchase, seizing handfuls of his cape, expecting at any minute to tumble back to the ground.

But Lance's arm banded her to him like a manacle of steel. With his other hand, he reined in sharply. The white demon of a horse objected, threatening to buck and rear. But somehow Lance brought the stallion under control.

As soon as she felt it was safe to draw breath, Kate whipped her head up to glare at him.

"Damn you, Lance St. Leger. You could have killed me. What do you think you're—"

The angry words died in her throat. It wasn't Lance's devil-may-care grin she found herself confronting, but another man's entirely. Rich brown eyes were set beneath heavy black brows and above a half-crooked smile that should have been so familiar to her, yet somehow wasn't.

Kate's mouth fell open, her voice cracking in a quaver of disbelief. "*Val?*"

CHAPTER SEVEN

*V*al flung back his head and laughed in a way that startled both Kate and the horse. The stallion plunged to the right, on the verge of bolting. Val let go of Kate, reaching both arms around her to grip the reins while she clung to his shoulders, heart thudding.

He steadied the restive brute, although Kate couldn't begin to imagine how. Val would have had to use both his knees, and the impact on his bad leg must be excruciating. Yet she saw no sign of pain tightening his features. He was actually smiling.

"Well, Miss Kate, my long-lost friend," he drawled. "So you thought I was my brother, Lance. Apart only three days and you've already forgotten me."

"N-no, of course not. I was just coming to see you."

"Then why did you try to run away?"

"Why?" Kate bristled with indignation at the question. "Because I thought you were going to gallop straight over me, that's why!"

"You should know better than that. Haven't we always played this game? You rushing to greet me, me scooping you up on my horse."

"Yes, but this isn't Vulcan."

"How perceptive of you, my dear."

Kate's eyes widened. Was Val actually *mocking* her? No, he would never.

"Where did you get this devil of a horse?" she asked.

"Bought him this morning. From my cousin Caleb. Don't you like him?"

"He's magnificent, but, Val, you shouldn't have."

"Why not?"

Why not? Kate gaped at him, scarce able to believe that she should have to explain such a thing to him. Val had always been so patient and reasonable about his limitations.

"You don't believe I can manage this great brute, do you?" he demanded. "You think the only one who can ride such a spirited animal is my brother."

"Well, I—"

"Let me tell you something, my dear. I was once able to ride as well as Lance. Even better."

There was a bitter edge to Val's voice that Kate had rarely heard, and it took her aback as much as the powerful horse shifting beneath them.

"Perhaps you require a demonstration?" he asked, his mouth thinning.

"No, of course not, Val. You don't have to prove anything to—" But the rest of Kate's words were lost as Val kicked the stallion hard in the flanks. The horse plunged forward, needing little encouragement to tear off into a full gallop.

All Kate could do was hang on, clutching desperately at Val as they headed for Slate House at a breakneck pace. The stallion *was* magnificent. She might have found the wild ride exhilarating if she hadn't been so afraid for Val, alarmed that he would do further damage to his leg.

Her fear escalated into full-blown panic when she realized the horse's thundering course veered away from the open gate, taking them straight toward the low stone wall. They would never make the jump. Val's knee was too weak, the stallion too damned skittish, herself an added awkward weight.

"Val! Noooo," she cried, but he didn't seem to hear her. He leaned forward like a man possessed, a hard glint in his eyes. The stone wall rushed at them in a dizzying blur.

Kate flung her arms about Val's neck and braced herself. Her stomach lurched as she felt the terrifying lift, the giddy second of weightlessness, and then the awful rush back to the ground.

The stallion's hooves struck the earth hard, jarring every bone in her body. The great white horse stumbled, nearly sending Kate flying from the saddle. For a sickening instant she expected them all to go down in a horrible tangle of breaking limbs and snapping necks.

But somehow Val steadied the horse, holding her fast. The next Kate knew they were halted calmly in the middle of the yard, and it was over. Except for the mad thudding of her own heart.

"How was that?" Val whispered into her ear. "Would you like to have an-other go?"

"No!" Kate choked. She loosened her death grip on his neck and jerked upright to glare at him. "Damn it, Val! What the blazes has gotten into you? How could you— We almost— You could have—"

But she had never had to scold Val for recklessness before. Usually it was the other way around. Kate spluttered into incoherence, unable even to find the words. She thumped her fist against his chest in sheer frustration.

"Just put me down. Put me down right now!"

Val's brows arched in amusement, but he hunched his shoulders in a lazy shrug and lowered her from the saddle. Kate breathed a sigh of relief as her feet struck solid ground. She felt bruised and shaken all over, not so much from the wild ride or that mad jump, but more from Val's unaccountable behavior. It was like someone had turned the entire world upside down.

She hugged her arms tight against herself to still her trembling. Val leapt down from the saddle and strode over to her. He crooked his fingers beneath her chin and forced her to look at him. At least when he spoke, it was in his familiar gentle tone, his dark eyes warm.

"Forgive me, Kate. I didn't mean to frighten you that badly, although I admit I find a certain poetic justice in it. You have scared the devil out of me often enough, my wild girl."

"Yes, but—" Kate stopped as fresh realization washed over her like a dash of cold water. She stumbled, nearly tripping over her own two feet in her haste to back away from him.

"Now whatever is amiss?"

Kate stared down at his mud-spattered boots. "Your—your leg—" she faltered.

"Aye, I have two of them. A handsome pair, aren't they?"

Kate pressed her hand to her mouth, scarce crediting what she thought she had seen only moments ago.

"W-walk toward me again," she said. "Please."

Val smiled but complied, marching toward her until he towered over her once more, standing nearly toe to toe. Far from having sustained any harm from their wild ride, his gait was even, steady, and strong.

Kate raised dazed eyes to his face. "Val, you—you are not—"

"Not limping like an old bear with its paw caught in a trap? No, it would seem I've been cured."

"But how?"

"Damned if I know, and I don't really care. It happened during the storm last night. As near as I can recall, there was a violent surge of lightning. I think it must have startled me. I fell, hit my head, and blacked out for a bit. And when I came to, this was the result."

Val stepped back and executed a few playful steps of a quick jig.

"Maybe the fairies did it," he said with an exuberant laugh.

Kate fought to contain the sudden tremor that coursed through her at Val's words.

"It happened during the storm . . . a violent surge of lightning."

No, not fairies, Kate thought, with a quiver of excitement. *She* had done this. She, with all her wild dancing about the bonfire, her clumsy efforts at witchcraft. There could not be any other possible explanation. She had been trying to cast a love spell on him and she had accomplished something far more incredible instead. She had cured him.

"Oh, Val!" Her breath came out in a joyous sob. She flung her arms about his neck in an impulsive hug. Laughing, he lifted her off her feet and swung her about in giddy circles. She clung to him, half weeping, half laughing, until they were both so dizzy, she was certain they'd end up tumbling to the ground.

Val came to an abrupt halt, holding her high against him so that her face was level with his.

"Don't cry, my wild girl," he murmured. "You don't ever have to weep over me again."

"It's just that I am so happy for you." Kate smiled mistily at him.

His arms tightened, holding her even closer, her breasts crushed against him. Val's smile slowly faded. Kate peered at him through the sheen of her tears and her heart suddenly missed a beat.

She'd studied his face so often over the years, thought she knew every expression of those well-loved features. But the look that crept into Val's eyes was new to her. White hot, so hard and intense, it left her feeling breathless and . . . strangely a little frightened.

But the look vanished so quickly, she thought she must have imagined it. Val lowered her to her feet, his attention pulled elsewhere.

Val's stable hand had come into the yard and attempted to take charge of the white stallion. A slender lad of fourteen, Lucas looked half-afraid of the massive beast. Sensing his timidity, the stallion pulled back, resisting Lucas's nervous clasp on the reins.

A flicker of annoyance crossed Val's face and he strode over to intervene. "Not like that, boy. This is a full-bred stallion, not an old nag like Vulcan. You have to get a firm grip here, show him who's master. And stop acting so scared to death of him."

Val seized the bridle, murmuring in firm tones to the horse. When Lucas still hung back, Val snapped, "Damn it, lad. Come on. Take charge of him."

Lucas crept forward, looking almost as wary of his master as the horse, much to Kate's surprise. She had never heard Val speak so sharply to any of his servants before. He seemed to realize himself how abrupt he'd been. He forced a smile to his lips and tousled the boy's hair.

"If you have trouble handling this great demon, get Jem to help you."

The boy nodded, still looking less than happy with the situation. But soothed by Val's touch, the horse reluctantly permitted Lucas to lead it toward the small stable behind the house.

Val frowned after the boy, then turned back to Kate. He must have read the troubled look in her eyes for he lightened his expression, becoming almost apologetic.

"I suppose I shouldn't have been so short with the lad. The truth is I didn't get much sleep last night. All the excitement, I suppose. And when I realized my leg truly was mended, I was up at dawn, my first thought to roust out Caleb and secure that horse."

Kate managed to nod and smile, concealing an inexplicable stab of hurt. This wonderful thing had happened to Val and his first thought had been to go buy a horse? It was understandable, she supposed. He had borne bravely and patiently with his affliction for years, tolerated plodding along on stolid mounts like old Vulcan.

But she and Val had been friends for a long time, despite the recent awkwardness between them. He might have spared a moment to come and share his good tidings with her.

Yet she couldn't bring herself to reproach him. This was hardly the time to nurse wounded feelings. Not when Val looked so incredibly happy, all traces of that melancholy that had once haunted his eyes completely gone. He stood facing seaward, his legs braced wide apart, reveling in the breeze that teased unruly dark strands of hair across his brow.

"Ah, Kate," he said. "You can't begin to imagine how it feels. To be free of that infernal limp, to be able to walk like a normal man. To be strong and whole again.

"I am fairly bursting with this need to rush out and do all the things I haven't been able to do for years. To ride, to run, to fence again. I used to be good with the foils, Kate. Damned good."

He spun toward her, impulsively seizing her hand. "I simply want to do everything before this miracle up and disappears."

"It won't," she started to say, only to check herself. How could she promise him that? She had no idea of the nature of the spell she had cast on him, let alone how permanent it might be.

Perhaps she ought to tell him exactly what she'd done. But Kate recoiled from the notion. Even if he was a St. Leger, she knew Val would never approve of meddling with dark magic, the use of witchcraft. He'd likely be angry with her and it might completely shatter their newly mended friendship. Val was so infernally noble he might even insist the spell be undone no matter the cost to himself.

And Kate could not bear that. She had never seen Val look so feverish with excitement, his dark eyes aglow. It was as though years had fallen away from him, allowing him to be the kind of wild, impulsive young man that he had never been.

He tugged her along after him, pulling her toward the house. "You and I, Kate. We have got to do something to celebrate."

"Like what?" she asked, struggling to keep up with him.

"I don't know." He came to a sudden halt, looking as though a wondrous realization had just struck him. "Waltzing. I could squire you to a ball, dance with you now."

Kate laughed. "You know I never paid much heed to that dancing master Effie engaged for me."

There had never seemed much point in learning all those intricate steps. Not when she had known she would never be able to dance with the one man she most desired.

"I'll teach you myself," Val said. He stole his arm around her waist and spun her a slow circle that left her feeling strangely lightheaded. Perhaps it was more owing to the nearness of him, the sudden blaze of tenderness in his eyes.

"You remember those fairies I once told you about? That is what we'll do, Kate. We'll go waltzing with the fairies in the moonlight. And we'll drink champagne."

"Champagne." She gave a breathless laugh. "Oh, no. Remember the effect it had on me when I sneaked a few glassfuls at your sister Mariah's betrothal two summers ago?"

"You got a little tipsy, my dear," Val said, playfully waltzing her toward the house. "You were going to regale the company with one of those bawdy sea chanteys my wicked old uncle Hadrian had taught you."

"Don't remind me." Kate groaned. "Fortunately you stopped me from making a fool of myself. Then I think I got sick all over your shoes and you weren't even angry with me."

"How could I ever be angry with you, my Kate? I simply whisked you off home, carried you upstairs and tucked you up safe in—" Val hesitated. His footsteps faltered, his grip on her waist tightening.

"Safe in your *bed*," he finished in a strangely altered tone. All gentleness melted from his features and there was no mistaking the intensity of his eyes. But his thick black lashes swept down, veiling the look.

He released her so abruptly, Kate stumbled back a pace. Spinning away from her, he said, "Perhaps you are right. No champagne. Tea would be safer."

He stalked off into the house, not even glancing back to see if Kate followed. She stared after him, confused by his quicksilver change of mood, shaken by her first ripple of doubt.

What if her dark spell had done something else to Val other than transform his leg? Something else like what? Render him madly in love with her? She saw no sign that that had happened, but spells could be highly unpredictable things, working in ways no mortal could understand. She was afraid to guess all she might have done to Val, and she hardly dared hope. All she could do was anxiously follow him inside the house.

After the bright flood of sunlight, the interior of Slate House appeared dark and gloom-ridden. Kate had far preferred calling upon Val at Castle Leger. She had never cared for this isolated house by the edge of the sea, even in the days when Dr. Marius St. Leger had lived here.

The very walls seemed saturated with a pervading loneliness and melancholy, shadows creeping across the floor although it was not that late in the afternoon. She wished that she and Val had remained outside in the sunlight, laughing and talking about waltzing with fairies. Everything felt so wrong, so out of kilter, since they had entered the house. Or had her entire world begun to feel unsettled from the moment Val had first swept her up onto that mad white stallion?

Kate trailed after Val into the library and he closed the door behind them with a soft click. She crept across the carpet, trying to draw reassurance from her surroundings, breathing in the soothing scent of leather and old books. Whether at Castle Leger or at this lonely house, the library was that special place she and Val had always shared, warm, familiar, and comfortable.

Then why was she standing like she'd been turned into a stick of wood? Val strode forward to help her off with her cloak as he'd done from the time she'd been a little girl.

But even that felt disturbingly different. His fingers lingered over the fastenings and he peeled her cloak away slowly, easing it off her shoulders almost like a man undressing his lover.

The image brought a surge of heat to her cheeks. Val folded her cloak and tossed it carelessly across the back of a chair. It was incredible, but she imagined that he'd been able to read her embarrassing thought and was amused by it. His mouth curled back in a faint, almost predatory smile, rather like a wolf regarding his prey.

Val, a wolf? Kate brought herself up short, appalled at the notion. Val St. Leger was the last man in the world who could be thought of in such terms. He had always reminded her of Chaucer's description of the squire in *The Canterbury Tales*—"a gentle, perfect knight."

That was who Val was and ever would be, and no power on earth, no dark magic, no spell could ever change that. These looks she kept imagining in his eyes were all the product of shadows and her own absurd fancies.

Rustling about the room, Kate struggled for some return to normalcy. The fire in the grate had nearly burnt itself out and she bent down to remedy that, tossing on a few more logs. Val made no move to help her. He strode over to a small cabinet, pulling out a decanter of whiskey.

Kate paused in the act of applying the bellows to stare at him. Val had ever been a temperate man, not much given to drinking strong spirits, especially at this hour of the day. When he caught Kate looking at him, he paused and inquired pleasantly, "Shall I pour you a glass as well, my dear?"

Kate's jaw fell open and she nearly tumbled over into the fire irons. After the champagne incident, Val had vowed he'd never allow her to touch anything but lemonade for the rest of her life, and now he was offering her whiskey?

Numbly, she shook her head.

Val shrugged and returned to filling his own glass. "Would you care to propose a toast for me then?"

"A toast?" Still reeling from this fresh shock, Kate felt unable to think.

"Bad 'cess to all Mortmains?" she suggested weakly. It had been the traditional toast of the St. Legers for generations, the rallying cry against the family who had long been their most deadly enemies.

Val had been the one to teach Kate that toast. Despite his gentle nature, Val had always despised the Mortmains as much as the rest of the St. Legers, perhaps even more so because he had made a study of the family history. He'd recorded every dark incident, every vengeful act of the Mortmains against the St. Legers, including the black career of the last surviving member of the breed, Captain Raphael Mortmain.

"There appears to be a madness, an evil in their very blood, Kate," Val had once told her gravely. "And I doubt that Rafe can overcome that, no matter how much my brother wants to call him friend. Lance's trusting nature makes me afraid for his very life."

Val had been right, of course. Rafe had nearly succeeded in destroying

Lance and her beloved Val, too. She could hardly bear to think back to that dark time when she had actually believed Val was dead. Ever since then, she had taken a grim satisfaction herself in hefting her lemonade and drinking to the destruction of all Mortmains.

Yet instead of seconding her toast as he always did, Val seemed reluctant. He frowned into his glass. "That is a rather foolish tradition now, isn't it, Kate? The Mortmains are no longer enough of a threat to waste a good glass of whiskey on. Think of something else."

"Very well," Kate said, a little bewildered by the curt command. "To your miraculous cure then, and to our friendship."

"To our friendship," he repeated, but he didn't seem to like her second toast any better. He pulled a bitter face as he tossed down the whiskey, then promptly poured himself another.

Kate watched him with troubled eyes. She turned back to the fire, using the poker to stir the embers beneath the new logs. Flames licked up, reminding her disturbingly of the bonfire on the hill last night. Despite Val's cure, she was almost starting to wish she'd never laid eyes on that spell book of Prospero's.

"Why did you come to see me today, Kate?"

Val's soft voice sounded directly in her ear. She started, nearly dropping the poker as she whipped around. She was amazed to discover he'd managed to steal up behind her, with her not hearing a sound. She was going to have to grow accustomed to his new quiet way of moving without his cane. Accustomed to other changes as well.

He stepped beside her, leaning one arm along the mantel, looming above her. There was already a difference in the way he carried himself now that he no longer had to rely on his cane. Vigorous, confident, almost overpowering. She felt suddenly shy of him. Shy of Val, her dearest friend, a man she had known for so much of her life. Although she had the fire crackling nicely again, she continued to fidget with the poker.

"Well, Kate?" Val prompted, reminding her of his question.

Why had she come to see him? Now was the time to trot out her lies, stammer out her apologies for the way she'd thrown herself at him the other night, try to convince him that she could be content just to be his friend.

Kate opened her mouth, but the words simply wouldn't come.

"I just needed to be with you," she confessed at last. "I missed you."

"You would have been wiser to stay away."

Kate gave a shaky laugh. "When have you ever known me to be wise? And we are still friends, are we not?"

When he didn't answer, she glanced up at him. A dark brooding look had settled over Val's face, so foreign to his usual steady expression. He toyed with the faded glove, the old fan resting atop the mantelpiece, and the ivory miniature of Dr. Marius St. Leger's long-lost love.

Kate put away the poker. "Val?"

He didn't even seem to hear her at first. When she repeated his name again, he snapped out of his frowning abstraction, a taut smile touching his lips.

"Sorry. I was just thinking I should gather up all this rubbish and send it to Marius since he seems unlikely to return anytime soon." Val flicked one finger contemptuously against the portrait of Anne Syler. "Or maybe I should just chuck it all into the fire."

Kate's eyes flew wide. He couldn't be serious. "But those are Marius's most cherished mementos. All that he has left of—"

"Of a woman who died over thirty years ago. Marius should forget her, find himself some nice little Scottish widow up there in Edinburgh."

"But you always told me that he can't. Anne was his chosen bride. The legend—"

"Damn the legend!" Val slammed his fist with such force against the mantel, Kate leapt back, startled by the sudden flare of anger in his eyes.

He raked his hand back through his hair as though making some effort to contain himself. He stalked away from her, prowling about the room.

"All my life I have submitted to the dictates of that legend, even though it condemned me to an eternity of being alone. I've always had such pathetically simple dreams, to be a doctor, have a wife, children. I could have waited forever for the Fates to tell me who my chosen bride was to be.

"But, oh no," he said with savage sarcasm. "The great Bride Finder decrees that Val St. Leger is never to have a love of his own, never to wed. If he does, there will be the devil to pay. The St. Leger curse will come crashing down on him and his bride's head. Well, I am sick to death of such nonsense!"

Kate clutched her hands together, frozen with shock. She had long wanted Val to repudiate the legend, but not quite like this. Not with such rage and bitterness.

She shrank back as he paced furiously past her again. "I'm sick of all of it, the legend, my stupid family tradition, the cursed power I inherited, even my bloody name."

"I adore your name," she murmured, but he paid her no heed.

"Valentine," he sneered, flinging up his hands. "What the devil kind of name is that for a man? A saint, a martyr surrendering his own life, his own happiness to every other idiot in the world."

Val paused, whipping around to glare at her. "Do you know what I am like, Kate?"

At one time she could have readily answered that question. She was no longer so sure. "N-no," she said.

He stalked across the room and snatched up a piece from the carved ivory chessboard. "I am like this ridiculous little pawn, allowing myself to be manipulated by everyone, this village, my family, a God-cursed fairy tale. Do you know what piece I'd like to be?"

"N-no."

"This one." Val flung the pawn aside, picking up one of the intricately carved horse's heads.

"The black knight?" Kate asked in bewilderment. "But that is hardly the most powerful piece on the board."

"Powerful enough to destroy all opposition until—" Val used the knight to plow through the white pieces, his lips snaking back in a hard smile. "Until I capture the queen."

Kate swallowed, watching in dismay as the hapless chessmen tumbled to the carpet. She was no longer left in any doubt. The change that had come over Val went far deeper than his leg. What exactly had she done to the man?

Val dropped the knight as well, raising his eyes from the board to settle on her face.

"Come here," he said quietly.

When she didn't move, he held out his hand. "Come here!"

Kate hung back, almost afraid to obey him. Afraid of Val? That was surely ridiculous. Forcing her feet into motion, she crept forward until she placed her fingers within his outstretched hand.

He drew her closer and scowled, reaching up to touch one stray tendril that curled by her cheek. "What the devil possessed you to put your hair up that way?"

Kate lifted up one hand herself, self-consciously patting the chignon that she realized was half tumbling down. "It was somewhat tidy before the wind got at it. I thought putting my hair up might make me look older."

"Well, it doesn't. Only more vulnerable." Val trailed his knuckles along the exposed column of her neck, sending a shiver through her. His fingers moved through her hair, plucking out the rest of the hairpins, discarding them until her hair cascaded down over her shoulders.

He eased one hand beneath the wild tangle, cupping the nape of her neck, forcing her nearer until all she could see was the dark glitter of his eyes. Her heart pounded so wildly, she felt unable to breathe. His mouth closed fiercely over hers. Kate's eyes widened, stunned by the heated contact.

It must have worked after all. Her love spell had worked.

That was her last coherent thought before Val dragged her closer, deepening the embrace. With a muffled sigh, Kate closed her eyes, surrendering to Val's ruthless kiss, his lips tasting of whiskey and heat.

She had begged him to teach her how to kiss on the night of her birthday and he was doing it now with a vengeance, his mouth moving masterfully over hers, tasting, demanding, devouring. With a low growl, he breached the seal of her lips. She was startled by the first feel of his tongue brushing against hers, then strangely excited.

Always quick to learn anything that Val cared to teach, Kate responded, clinging to his shoulders, engaging his mouth in a sweet wild mating. Her heart was pounding so hard, her head swimming. She had never been the sort of woman to swoon, but Kate almost feared she was going to.

Panting, Val drew back long enough to allow her to catch her breath before continuing his passionate assault. He rained kisses across her temple, her eyelids, her cheeks, her chin, as though he could not get enough of her.

"Kate, Kate. My wild girl," he groaned. "I have been such a bloody fool, resisting you for so long."

"T-there is nothing to forgive," Kate managed to stammer out before he crushed her in his arms, molding her body to the hard length of his.

He buried his face in her hair, his breath hot against her ear. "I love you," he rasped. "I have always loved you and now nothing shall stand between us. I swear it."

Kate's heart constricted with joy at the words she'd been waiting half her life to hear.

"Oh, Val, I love y—" But her own declaration was smothered by his mouth. He claimed her lips in another long feverish kiss that left her weak, melting in his arms. Her spell had worked with a passionate fury that even she had never dared imagine.

Never breaking contact, his lips locked to hers, Val swept her off her feet. He carried her over to the settee and plunked her down upon the cushions. He drew away only long enough to strip off his coat and waistcoat. His chest rising and falling with short quick breaths, his face a dark mask of desire, he wrenched off his cravat as well.

Kate watched him in a daze, experiencing a tiny flicker of alarm. But it was quickly forgotten as Val fell upon her, kissing her until her pulse pounded, her blood surged through her veins. His mouth traveled down the column of her throat, and Kate's breath escaped in a blissful sigh. This was all she had ever hoped for, more than she ever dreamed of.

She was hardly aware that he had undone the buttons of her gown until he shoved open the front of her bodice. Kate never wore stays and it was an easy matter for him to unlace the ribbons of her loose-fitting chemise as well, baring her breasts.

A hot blush seared her cheeks and she moved instinctively to cover herself, but Val refused to allow it. He pinned her hands to her sides.

"No, Kate. Let me look at you," he said, raking her with a hot, greedy stare. "You're so beautiful and I want you so damned bad I am like to die from it."

His dark head swooped down, his lips abrading the tender flesh of her breasts, his mouth fastening hungrily over her nipple.

"Oh, m-my," Kate gasped at the lick of heat that rushed through her. She had thought that she knew and understood all about that passion that could flare between men and women, but she had never imagined anything like this. She buried her fingers in his hair, swept away by these new feelings he aroused, the aching need for him to touch her, to keep on touching her in even more intimate ways.

Part of her realized that things were moving much too fast, spiraling out of control. Val had her pinned under his weight, his hand beginning to ease up her skirt. Kate felt a fleeting sense of panic, wondering if she would be able to stop him, even if she wanted to.

But she didn't want to. Especially when his lips found hers again, offering her no mercy, kissing her to the brink of delirium. She could no more have resisted him than she could have flown to the moon. This was her Val, the friend she trusted, the man she adored and had wanted forever.

Trembling at her own daring, Kate eased her hand between them and fumbled with the topmost button of his shirt. But Val's hand closed over hers, forcing her to stop. Levering himself up onto one arm, he stared at her, almost as though he was really seeing her for the first time.

The light burning in his eyes flickered and died.

"Oh, my God," he said hoarsely.

"Val?" Kate quavered, fearing that in her inexperience she must have done something truly wrong. She reached up to touch his cheek, but he recoiled from her in horror. Dragging himself off her, he staggered across the room in his haste to get away. He fetched up against the fireplace, gripping the edge of the mantel so hard, his arms trembled from the force of it.

Her mouth yet warm from his kiss, her skin still quivering from his touch, Kate sat up more slowly, feeling both bewildered and strangely bereft.

She regarded him anxiously. "Val, are you—"

"Get out!"

The harsh words cracked through Kate like the bite of a whip. "W-what?"

"Get dressed and get out of here," Val snapped. He twisted around to glare at her, his hard dark eyes like those of a stranger.

"B-but," Kate stammered, more astonished and confused than ever by the quick shift of his mood.

"Are you hard of hearing, girl? I *said* fix your gown and get the devil out of here. Now! Before I—" He left the angry threat unfinished, turning his back on her, his hands balling into fists.

Kate flinched, feeling as though he'd just slapped her. She cast him a look rife with all of her feelings of hurt and bewilderment, but she scrambled to obey, the flush of her own passion receding. As she fumbled with the lacing of her chemise and refastened her gown, her cheeks burned. She suddenly felt foolish, embarrassed, and ashamed. As cheap as any London doxy, like the kind of trollop her mother must have been. Spell or no spell, Val St. Leger was still a gentleman. Small wonder that he was disgusted with her reckless and wanton behavior.

Kate did up her last button and said in a small voice, "I—I am sorry, Val."

"*You* are sorry?" Val turned just enough to frown at her.

"Yes, what just happened was all my fault and—" She broke off, both wounded and appalled when he laughed at her.

A rich booming sound of mirth, but when he finished, it was suddenly her Val looking down at her again. He dropped to one knee beside her, gathering her hands into his own.

"My wild Kate," he murmured. "You are such a little fool. How could you possibly think you are responsible for what happened between us?"

"Because I am." Kate's chin came up, recognizing that indulgent tone of his all too well. "You cannot possibly still be thinking of me as this ignorant girl who doesn't know anything. I have told you many times before, I am far from innocent."

"You are as naïve as a newborn babe." Val brushed a kiss against her fingertips. "You don't even understand how close I came to dishonoring you."

"You could never dishonor me, Val," Kate said.

"Yes, I could. I am just beginning to understand myself what I might be capable of." His expression turned dark and somber. He stood up, and tugged her to her feet.

"Please go now," he said quietly.

She had no choice but to obey when he asked her that way, even though all she wanted to do was stroke his hair, smooth back the troubled look from his brow. When she had been weaving her magic over the bonfire last night, she had pictured only happiness and joy, an end to Val's loneliness and her longing. She had never thought to unleash this turmoil in him, never thought to hurt him. But as usual, Kate reflected, she hadn't *thought* at all.

Her heart heavy with self-reproach and chagrin, she skirted past Val, trudging toward the door.

"You don't have to leave quite that way," he murmured. "Without a word of farewell or even a kiss good-bye."

Kate's spirits lifted, her head coming up at once. She moved toward him, only too ready to comply. But Val caught her by the shoulders, maintaining a chaste distance between them. He deposited a soft kiss on her brow, then one on her nose, then touched his lips lightly to hers.

His mouth was warm and tender. Kate sighed, straining toward him, and the next she knew she was back in his arms, trading desperate kisses while he held her as though he'd never let her go.

"No!" Val pulled back with a ragged laugh, thrusting her away. "Dear God, Kate, this is pure madness."

"No, Val. It's wonderful," Kate pleaded, trying to cling to him. "I have always loved you and now you love me. What could be wrong with that?"

"Nothing. Everything." He caught both of her hands to hold her back from him. "This has all come over me too sudden. All these changes. I—I need time to think."

When she started to protest, he silenced her by placing his hand to her lips. He ended by tracing the outline of her mouth, the feel of his fingers warm and tantalizing. Kate sighed when he jerked his hand away.

"I will come to you soon, my angel," he said. "I promise."

Before Kate could even catch her breath, Val shoved her cloak at her and thrust her out into the hall. Kate blinked as the door was slammed in her face. As she stood there, dazed, she heard the key turn in the lock.

Merciful heavens. Did Val actually believe it was necessary to lock her out? Maybe it was, Kate thought in dismay. Her skin still tingled with the memory of Val's heated embrace. Even with all her dreams of him, she had never imagined him capable of kissing that way. The man was incredible, and she longed to fling herself back into his arms and finish what they had started upon the settee. Never mind the risk they might run of being discovered by any of Val's servants, creating the most dreadful scandal for both of them.

It was fortunate that even under the influence of a spell, Val was possessed of better sense than she was. At least now she understood what was wrong with him, the reason for his edginess, the unlikely outbursts of temper and the abrupt shifts of mood. Her magic was working on him, but he was nobly resisting with all his strength, still clinging to his scruples and his misguided notions about her innocence.

But she doubted that it was a battle that Val would win.

The poor man had to be already far gone if he was starting to call *her* an angel. There was nothing the least bit divine about her. In fact, at the moment, she was feeling more like the devil's own daughter.

"I have always loved you," Val had whispered. *"And now nothing shall stand between us. I swear it."*

Wonderful passionate words, but had that really been her Val talking or only the spell? How could she have done this to him, worked black magic on her dear friend, depriving him of his will, tricking him, trapping him?

No, Kate reassured herself desperately. It wasn't like that at all. She hadn't trapped Val. She had *freed* him from his crippling pain, from the terrible restrictions of that legend, from a lifetime of being alone.

Everything was going to be all right as soon as Val surrendered and stopped fighting the magic she had wrought. Perhaps all he did need was a little more time to grow accustomed to all these incredible changes. After all, he had promised . . .

I will come to you soon, my angel.

"Don't make it too long, my dearest friend," Kate whispered. Swirling her cloak about her shoulders, she touched her hand to her lips, then pressed it against the sealed door, leaving a parting kiss.

By the time Kate returned to the village, she had managed to quell any further misgivings. Fairly tripping along the lane, she lost herself in rose colored visions of her future with Val. The St. Legers would all object at first, but their resistance would be gradually overcome when they saw how happy she and Val were, how devoted to each other. They would realize that a legend could sometimes be wrong.

Even Effie would beam with pride the day that Kate stood up with Val in St. Gothian's Church. Between her wifely duties, she would find time to do a little matchmaking herself, pairing Effie up with her adoring vicar so that Effie would not be lonely when Kate moved to Slate House.

What a change Kate would make in that dismal place. Throwing open the shutters, clearing out the cobwebs of the past, painting and repapering all the rooms in bright, cheery colors. She would learn to help Val in his medical practice, prevent him from wearing himself out, overusing his power, and working too hard.

On sunny days, she and Val would race magnificent horses down the beach or polish the dust off his foils and practice dueling. On rainy afternoons, she would serve him tea in the library while they pored over some intriguing new volume together. Or spent long leisurely hours making love on that settee.

She was already tenderly presenting him with their firstborn son by the time she reached the bend in the lane leading to Rosebriar Cottage. Kate's footsteps faltered, her fantasies coming to an abrupt end.

A gleaming new curricle hitched to a pair of grays had drawn up before the cottage gate. Both the elegant equipage and the livery-clad tiger who tended the horses looked ridiculously out of place in Torrecombe. Kate bit back a dismayed curse. Her head was far too full of Val at the moment to help Effie entertain any caller, especially this one.

Victor St. Leger picked his way toward the path leading to Rosebriar, taking great care to avoid getting any mud on the toes of his well-polished Hessians. Kate knew the other girls in the village accounted him devastatingly handsome. The fools went on and on about his dark-fringed melting eyes and the sensual curves of his full lower lip. But Kate had always found his perfect features a little too smooth for her taste. Next to Val, he was nothing but a callow boy.

Victor appeared to catch sight of his own reflection in one of the rain puddles and paused to adjust the angle of his high-crowned beaver hat, smooth down the multiple capes of his driving coat. Kate's lip curled in contempt. Poor Mollie Grey. She doubted that Victor would ever propose to the girl until he fell out of love with his own reflection. He was the most idle, useless young man, living off the fortune acquired by his seafaring grandfather and father, usually squandering all his time in the larger towns like Penzance and Plymouth, attending assemblies, balls, and horse races and flirting with silly women.

So what the devil was he doing back here at Rosebriar? No doubt he'd returned to torment poor Effie with more complaints about her plain choice of a bride for him.

"Be damned if he will," Kate muttered. Bristling like a protective terrier, she hitched up her skirts and tore off running. She easily overtook Victor, getting between him and the cottage door.

He muttered an angry imprecation at being jostled, only to check himself.

"Kate," he exclaimed.

If she hadn't known better, she would have thought he sounded glad to see her. But that was most unlikely. They had barely spoken to each other since the fête day held on the St. Leger estate over a year ago. For once Kate had been trying to act like a lady for Val's sake.

Victor had eyed her through some ridiculous quizzing glass and commented that her new frock had too many ribbons. Some of them might have been better employed tying up her wild mop of hair. Kate had sweetly suggested that he'd better loosen his collar. No doubt that was why his head was so swollen. He'd replied that she still possessed all the charming manners of a foundling brat. It shouldn't have bothered Kate to have her hateful background flung in her face by a dolt like Victor. But somehow it had. She had brought an abrupt end to the exchange of insults by cracking the nearest object over his thick head.

At least after that, Effie had stopped insisting Kate carry a parasol.

Positioning herself in front of the cottage door, Kate planted her hands on her hips and blocked Victor's path.

"What are you doing here?" she demanded without any attempt at civility.

One hand tucked behind his back, Victor used the other to tip his hat in greeting. It was an unusually gallant courtesy, at least for Victor to pay her.

"I came to see—"

"Effie's not at home," Kate snapped.

"But—"

"At least not to you. She's already done enough, just by finding you a bride. Mollie's a sweet girl, far too good for a conceited fool like you. You should consider yourself lucky."

"But I am—"

"And even if you don't have the wit to be grateful, you ought to know how your own family legend works. Once Effie declares her choice, it cannot be altered, no matter how much you coax and bully, so you might as well turn right around—"

"Kate, Kate," Victor interrupted at last with a laughing protest. "I have not come to plague Effie, I assure you. I came to see you."

"Me?"

He whipped his hand from behind his back, producing a nosegay of delicate pink rosebuds. He extended it toward her with a small flourish.

Kate stared at the flowers as though he'd just offered her a snake.

"What are those for?" she asked suspiciously.

"For you. Take them." He flashed her that smile that usually had all the silly local girls swooning in the hedgerows.

Kate was momentarily nonplussed by the gesture until she realized what Victor had to be up to. She shook her head at him with an incredulous laugh.

"If you think you can turn me up sweet and get me on your side, you really do have maggots in your head. I may believe the St. Leger legend is pure nonsense, but Mollie doesn't. You had that poor girl waiting half the night, expecting that you were coming to propose."

Victor winced, at least having the grace to show some guilt. "I didn't mean to hurt her, Kate. I might not have been happy about it, but I was fully prepared to do my duty as a St. Leger. I was actually within view of her house when I realized I could never ask Molly to marry me, not when I was already in love with another woman."

"And just who is the unfortunate creature?"

"You."

"What!"

Victor caught hold of her hand and Kate was far too surprised to prevent him. "I am in love with you, Kate. I should have realized it a long time ago."

"Oh, yes, of course. It must have come over you when I whacked you with my parasol. I daresay I hit you harder than I thought."

Victor made no response to this scornful remark. He tried to carry her hand to his lips.

"Stop that!" Kate said, snatching her fingers away. "Have you entirely lost your mind?"

"No, only my heart. But I hardly meant to declare myself on your doorstep. May I come inside?"

"No!"

Victor sighed. "Then you leave me no choice."

To Kate's consternation, he dropped down on one knee, right there on the cottage path for all the village to see. He laid the nosegay before her for all the world like some ancient Roman making a burnt offering to a goddess. Whipping off his hat and holding it over the region of his heart, he beamed up at her.

"Kate Fitzleger, will you do me the honor of becoming my wife?"

"No, certainly not," Kate said, seizing him by the front of his driving cape and trying to haul him back on his feet. "Do get up before you make a complete ass of yourself and get the knee of your breeches dirty."

"I don't care about that."

He didn't care. Was this Victor St. Leger talking?

Kate glared at him. "If this is your idea of a jest, I don't find it the least—"

"I am totally serious, Kate," he declared in injured tones. But at least she managed to get the fool up off his knee.

"Victor, maybe you need to go somewhere and lie down. You've obviously been out in the fresh air and sun too long. You're not accustomed to it."

"It's not the sun, my dearest heart. It was that storm last night reminding me of your magnificent flashing eyes. That was when I first knew I adored you. It came over me like—like a bolt of lightning."

"That is the most ridiculous—" Kate began, only to falter as the full import of his words struck her. *Like a bolt of lightning?* Oh, no, surely not. It could not possibly be that—that—

She anxiously scanned his features for some sign that he was teasing, mocking her as he always did. Although his face was filled with his customary arrogance, there was also a sincerity in his eyes that disconcerted her.

Kate was so stunned, she couldn't think, couldn't move. Victor took full advantage of the moment, stealing his arms about her waist. Damnation! He was actually preparing to kiss her right here on the doorstep.

Kate snapped back to her senses, barely managing to get her arms between them in time. "Victor, stop it. Right now."

He paid no heed, straining to draw her closer. "My dearest, darling girl," he breathed. "Say you will be mine."

"No. Are you insane?" Kate cried, struggling to thrust him away, rather surprised to find Victor that strong.

"What about your chosen bride? Mollie, the legend," she went on desperately, trying to bring him to his senses. "If you don't marry her, you—you'll be cursed."

"I would risk anything for one kiss from you." He swooped down, his mouth but a breath from her own. Kate twisted her head to one side and he grazed her cheek instead.

She fought to push him away, but he practically had her pinned to the cottage door.

"Victor, if you don't let me go right now," Kate said through clenched teeth, "you are going to be really sorry."

"Kate," he moaned, pressing clumsy kisses to her temple. "You are breaking my heart."

"No, I am going to break your head!" She gave a violent twist, managed to get one fist up to clip his jaw. Not a hard blow, but enough to make him back off. She then slammed both fists against his chest to shove him the rest of the way. Whirling, Kate bolted for the safety of the cottage.

She slammed the door closed and leaned panting up against it. To her consternation, Victor immediately began knocking and pleading with her through the keyhole.

"Oh, Kate, I am sorry. I didn't mean to pounce on you that way. It is just that I adore you so much. Please let me in so that I can beg your forgiveness."

Kate suppressed a groan. "I forgive you, Victor. Now just go away."

"But I cannot until you allow me to convince you that I will love and cherish you forever. Kate?" When she did not respond, he only hammered louder. "Kate, please open the door."

Kate grimaced, her gaze darting about the empty hall. If Victor didn't stop this infernal racket, he was going to bring the servants running, maybe even Effie. And if her guardian discovered what was going on, poor Effie would likely collapse down dead on the spot.

Kate turned around and cried through the door. "Go away, Victor. Or I—I swear I'll send for your cousin Anatole."

It was a hollow threat. The dread lord of Castle Leger had left Torrecombe only that morning, heading north to visit Dr. Marius. But Victor apparently didn't know that. The knocking ceased. Kate held her breath. After long moments of silence ensued, Kate darted into the parlor and raced for the front window.

Keeping herself well concealed behind the curtains, she peeked out at the young man trudging toward the curricle waiting in the lane.

Oh, please, Kate prayed, let Victor be laughing and nudging his manservant, telling his groom what a grand joke he had just played on Miss Fitzleger. But there was no sign of mirth in Victor's downcast features. His step had lost its swagger as he mounted into the curricle and gathered up the reins from his tiger. She had never seen the arrogant young man look so crestfallen. He cast a wistful glance toward the cottage before driving away. It was as if she had really broken his heart.

Kate closed the curtain and drew back from the window. Oh, God. What had she done now?

Nothing, *nothing*, she told herself fiercely. What she feared had happened to Victor could not possibly be true, no matter if he did talk about bolts of lightning. It was purely a coincidence.

Her spell had been aimed at Val, not him. It had been Val's initials she had carved on that piece of coal. "V.S." for Valentine St. Leger.

And also for Victor.

No! Kate squeezed her eyes shut tight to quell her rising dread. It was still impossible. She had been thinking only of Val when she had woven her magic. Surely one love spell could not work on two different men, could it?

She was certain it couldn't, but all the same, she had better go have another look at that book. Fleeing from the parlor, she rushed upstairs, nearly colliding with Nan in the process.

"Oh, Miss Kate. Did I just hear someone at the door?"

"No!" Ignoring the housemaid's startled look, Kate bolted past and headed for her bedchamber. Slamming the door behind her, she all but hurled herself at her dressing table, snatching up the fichu under which she had concealed Prospero's spell book.

Or at least she thought she had. Kate frowned, straining to remember, then yanked open the topmost drawer. And then the next one. And the next. From there, she pounced upon her dresser, her wardrobe, her small writing table, her search growing more frantic with every passing minute.

A half hour later and she had torn her bedchamber apart to no avail. Kate sagged down weakly upon the corner of her bed, her stomach sinking. She could hardly believe it.

The infernal book was gone.

Val flung back the shutters. From his library window he watched the sun set over the sea in a fiery blaze, sending out red gold ripples of light like fingers of blood stretching across the waters. He released a shuddering breath and wondered what was happening to him.

He didn't know, only that it seemed to be getting worse with night coming on. His servants had long ceased trying to rouse him from his self-imposed prison. Even Jem seemed afraid to bother him again, and Val could not blame him. All afternoon he had been snapping and snarling at everyone who'd come near the library, ordering them to get the devil away and leave him alone.

No, he didn't want any tea. He didn't want supper. All he wanted was . . .

Kate.

You bloody fool. Why did you ever let her go?

Val gripped the edge of the windowsill hard, even now fighting the overwhelming urge to go track her down, carry her back here, straight up to his bed. And why the blazes shouldn't he? It wasn't as though Kate would resist. She'd already shown herself to be more than willing, so eager, so trusting and . . . God! What the devil was he thinking?

He pressed his hands hard against his brow, wishing he could as easily crush these persistent dark desires. This was Kate he was lusting after, his wild girl, his dearest friend. It was bad enough that he'd already come close to ravishing her this afternoon. Seducing her right there on the settee, nearly robbing her of her innocence, ruining a young woman he would have ordinarily given his life to protect.

The truly hellish thing was that he *still* wanted her, all consequences and decency be damned. He'd oft heard tell of the other part of the family legend, that a St. Leger male knew when his time had come to mate. It was supposed to be a like a fever in the blood, an ache of the soul. Val doubted it could be any worse than the agony he was going through right now, his hunger for Kate, savage in its intensity. And she wasn't even his chosen bride.

There was only one thing he could do. No matter what he'd promised Kate, he had to stay away from her. Val slammed the shutters back into place, as though closing out the night would aid his resolution.

It didn't. He paced toward the door, only to check himself at the last minute, dragging trembling fingers through his hair. What was wrong with him? It was as though his clarity of thought was blurring, every scruple, every sense of right and wrong he cherished starting to erode away. Every raw emotion, every dark desire or thought he'd ever suppressed seethed far too near the surface.

He had no idea what had triggered this descent into madness. It was all tangled up somehow with the miraculous cure he'd experienced last night. Last night . . . Val dragged his hand wearily across his eyes. He would sell his soul to be able to remember exactly what had happened last night.

He gave a mirthless laugh. For all he knew, maybe he already had traded his soul away for *this*. His fingers crept across his chest, feeling the outline of the chain and shard of stone hidden beneath his shirt. He hadn't even dared to look at the thing all day. But now, with unsteady fingers, he drew the crystal out into the candlelight.

It was only one stolen piece of the magnificent magic stone imbedded in the St. Leger sword. And yet the fragment sparkled with such hypnotic beauty Val couldn't tear his eyes away from it.

How had he come to be in possession of the long missing crystal? Try as he might, he couldn't recall. There could be only one answer. Rafe Mortmain. Yet that seemed impossible. If Rafe had returned to Torrecombe after so many years, he'd left no more trace of himself than if he'd been a ghost.

Did it really matter anyway where the crystal had come from? It was his now. Val caressed the sparkling icicle of stone. It was as though everything he'd ever wanted, ever desired, shimmered in this one small piece of—

No. Val blinked hard, shaken by the direction of his thoughts. His hand closed over the fragment, shutting its mesmerizing glitter away from his sight. The crystal seemed to be exerting some sort of strange hold over him and it didn't even belong to him. By rights, it should be returned to his brother, Lance, the present owner of the St. Leger sword.

Val removed the chain from his neck, surprised and disturbed by how hard it felt to do so. Gripping the crystal tight in his hand, his gaze roved about the library, seeking something to do with it until the morrow. He marched over to his desk and retrieved the small worn purse he kept there. At the moment it was empty of coin, and the chain and crystal fit perfectly inside.

Val yanked the drawstring closed and shoved the leather pouch inside his desk drawer. He'd no sooner done so when it struck him.

The pain. Returning to his leg with a vengeance. A horrible stabbing agony unlike any he'd ever felt, making him grind his teeth to keep from crying out. He gasped, managing to stagger over to the settee before he collapsed. It seemed that his miracle was over.

Yet as he clutched at his throbbing knee, Val suddenly understood. His cure was bound up in that crystal somehow. He needed to get the thing and put it back on. But even as he started to struggle upward, some instinct restrained him. No, touching that crystal again was the last thing he should do.

He fell back onto the cushions, trying to massage his pulsing knee, ease the spiraling pain. My God, it felt as bad as it had done when the injury was fresh, that terrible day he'd found Lance lying wounded on the battlefield in Spain. His reckless brother had finally tested his foolhardy courage once too often.

"Hold on, Lance. I'm coming," Val cried, trying to make his voice heard above the blaze of cannonfire, the groans of dying men. He fought his way through the acrid haze of smoke to where Lance writhed on the ground, blood spilling from the shattered mass of bone that had once been his right knee.

His heart constricting with fear, Val bent down beside him, fumbling for his medical kit.

"It's all right, Lance," he soothed. "I'm here."

"N-no." Lance was already so out of his mind with pain, he tried to twist away from him. Val reached instinctively for his hand.

"Leave me alone, damn it." Lance fought to pull away, even in his agony sensing what Val was about to do.

But Val hadn't even hesitated. He'd focused quick and hard, mentally dissolving his own flesh, slicing open his own veins for this brother he loved so well, bracing himself to share his twin's pain.

"No, damn you, Val. Don't do it. Let me go."

"It's all right, Lance. I can take it," Val said, although he had to grit his teeth. *"Just hold on."*

And that was when everything had gone horribly wrong. Val's head pounded, beads of sweat gathering on his brow, the remembrance of past pain mingling with present agony. He'd never understood quite how, but he'd absorbed far more from Lance that day than his pain. Val had taken on the injury itself, transferring his brother's crippling wound to his own leg.

It was the only time in his life Val had ever lost control of his power that way. At least until last night. Val took deep breaths, suddenly experiencing a flash of memory.

He was kneeling on the hall floor of Slate House, bending over someone, trying to help. A man . . . a man who was dying in terrible agony. Val closed his eyes, straining to remember. A storm. There had been a storm, thunder and lightning. The shard of crystal was swaying, glittering around his neck. Someone was gripping his hand, so hard Val couldn't pull free, couldn't stop the—

God! Why couldn't he remember? The memory dimmed and vanished, the effort to recall hurting him as much as the ache in his leg. Yet it seemed desperately important that he keep trying, as though his sanity, nay, his very life depended upon it.

What had happened to him last night? Something dark and terrible. Something that seemed bound up in the storm, the crystal, and his age-old enemy.

Rafe Mortmain.

CHAPTER EIGHT

*T*he harbor bustled with activity, dockhands hauling crates and barrels up gangplanks, rugged seamen in search of employment toting their canvas bags. A queue of carriages drew as close to the wharf as possible, passengers supervising the unloading of their trunks.

Even in the midst of such a busy crowd, the gentleman in the navy colored greatcoat drew a stir of attention, especially from the ladies. Possessed of a tall military bearing, he carried himself with a quiet dignity. Wings of silver threaded through his dark hair cropped with a neat precision that became the fine chiseled lines of his face. He looked far too pale to be a seaman, but every lady who saw him was convinced he had to be the captain of one of the vessels. He had that aura of command.

And yet Rafe Mortmain had never felt more uncertain in his life. He wound his way past the line of coaches, his portmanteau clutched in his hand. He kept his gaze fixed forward, avoiding any eye contact and not merely because he was conscious of still being a wanted man.

He felt so damned odd, different and unsure of himself. Like a man who had somehow stumbled from the other side of the grave and found himself thrust back into the land of the living. Which was perhaps exactly what had happened to him.

By all rights, he should have been dead. Why wasn't he? As he pressed closer to the waterfront, Rafe inhaled deeply, filling his lungs with the fresh sea air, feeling the strength surge through his limbs. It was a bloody miracle.

He should have been wildly rejoicing. Part of him was, the other part felt unnerved.

Something very strange had happened to him on All Hallows' Eve.

How long ago had that been? One day? Two or three? His recollection on that score was extremely vague. He could not even remember how he'd fled the village of Torrecombe or managed to return to Falmouth and retrieve his hidden cache of money and clothes.

His loss of memory should have alarmed him. Yet when he'd awakened this morning at the Red Lion Inn, his chief concern had been the disheveled reflection that had peered back at him from the looking glass. Rafe had never been a particularly vain man, but he had maintained a standard of Spartan neatness about his physical appearance.

Summoning a barber, he had set about remedying the situation at once. At least now he felt almost human again, and better still . . . Rafe's hand flew to his throat, groping for the familiar chain that should have been there, but wasn't.

The crystal was gone. He had managed to rid himself of the cursed thing, although he was damned if he remembered how. Fragments of memory flashed through his mind of the isolated house by the edge of the sea, Val St. Leger catching him as he fell over the threshold, the doctor bending over him, the deadly gleam of the crystal.

And then nothing. He couldn't remember anything more until his return to Falmouth. Was it possible that with the transfer of the crystal, Dr. St. Leger had perished in his stead? Somehow Rafe didn't believe that, although if he wasn't dead, the doctor would very soon wish he was.

But perhaps the dark magic would not work on him as it had on Rafe. After all, the fragment had come from the St. Leger sword and Val was a St. Leger, an insufferably noble one at that. What was it his friend Lance had always teasingly called his solemn brother? *Saint* Valentine.

Perhaps evil could never touch such a man. Rafe frowned at his own thoughts. It was as though he was actually hoping the crystal wouldn't harm Val, and that was absurd. He'd plotted this revenge for months. Val St. Leger had always been his enemy and he hated the man, didn't he?

Rafe rubbed his temple, trying to summon up the old rage, envy, and bitterness. But it was as though those dark emotions that had sustained him for years had simply vanished. Just like the crystal. It made him feel like a slate that had been wiped clean. The sensation was eerie, even frightening.

Rafe shrugged off his disturbing reflections, focusing his mind on the present. Shielding his eyes from the glare of the sun upon the water, he scanned the forest of masts silhouetted against the jewel blue sky until he sighted *The Venturer*, the merchant ship on which he'd booked passage to the East Indies.

He didn't particularly care where he went as long as he could feel the roll of a ship beneath his feet again, hear the lash of the waves. The seductive lap of the water against the quay seemed to whisper of far-off places, freedom, and adventure, the kind of tug at his soul he had not experienced since he'd been a very young man.

There was nothing to hold him here any longer. Cornwall had never meant anything to him. The inhospitable shore had proved as much of a disaster to him as to all the Mortmains before him, including his own mother. A land of wrecked hopes and disappointed dreams.

This time when he set sail, he would do no looking back. But he was in no haste to embark. *The Venturer* was not due to set sail until the evening's tide. He had time now. All the time in the world.

Strolling to a small inn near the waterfront, he bought himself a light repast of bread and cheese. He would have been wiser to remain in some cool dark corner of the inn until it was time to sail, but he was tired of lurking in shadows. Unable to resist the lure of the sun, he stepped back into the daylight, reveling in the nip of the sea breeze as it fanned his hair.

Ambling down the narrow cobblestone street, he devoured the bread and cheese, a little surprised at himself. He hadn't had much appetite these last months, but nothing had ever tasted so good to him as this simple meal.

He savored the coarse texture of the bread against his tongue, the mellow taste of the cheese as though it were some delicately seasoned French dish. He could never recall his senses being so keen, so attuned to every pleasure. So conscious of simply being alive.

When he'd finished the cheese, he paused by a barrel that some housewife had left out to collect rainwater. As he washed his hands, Rafe was startled by his own reflection shimmering in the water. After his visit to the barber, he'd had no desire to inspect his naked face, but he studied his image now.

When had he gotten so gray? His once rich black hair was now flecked with silver. Hardly surprising, he supposed, for a man past forty. He was getting older. Except he didn't look it. The removal of that heavy beard had left his face seeming younger, more vulnerable.

"Mama! Mama, please don't leave me."

The child's cry cut through Rafe like the cold blade of a knife. He jerked back from the barrel, half fearing he had imagined it, a nightmare echo from the mists of his own worst memories.

"Mama, please!"

When the cry sounded again, he whipped about, looking for the source of it. Only yards away, in front of one of those snug row houses that faced the waterfront, a woman in brown shawl and bonnet was trying to pull away from a small thin boy.

The mother's distress and the boy's grief drew little attention from passersby in the street. Rafe scarce knew why he stopped to stare. He had long ago schooled himself in the art of indifference, especially to the plight of strangers.

Except they weren't strangers. Rafe's eyes narrowed. As unlikely as it seemed, he knew that unremarkable little brown wren of a woman and the fragile boy with the white-blond hair. He'd met them only recently, or had it been a lifetime ago?

In a barn on an old rundown farm just outside of Falmouth. He had a sudden clear image of Corinne Brewer looking up at him with soft, concerned eyes as he struggled to remain upright on that old gray gelding.

"Godspeed, Mr. Moore."

Aye, *Corinne Brewer.* That was who the woman was. That foolish trusting widow who'd let him sleep in her barn and sold him her only horse. The frail looking boy was her son. Chad? No, *Charley.*

So what were they doing here in Falmouth, obviously faced with separation? Corinne had a small traveling bag clutched in her hand. Not that it was any of his concern. Rafe half turned to go when he became aware of the other woman.

She hovered in the doorway of the house, an older female somewhat better dressed than Corinne, her tall thin frame clad in black silk. Her peppery hair was swept back beneath her white cap in a style as severe as her face.

Corinne hunkered down by her weeping son, trying to dry his tears, but to little avail.

"D-don't go, Mama." The boy's voice broke on a sob. "P-please don't go."

Corinne brushed her fingers through the child's hair, murmuring something. From his position in the street, Rafe couldn't catch what she said, only the tone, sweet and soothing.

"Oh, for heaven's sake, Corinne!" the older woman snapped. She swooped down from the doorway. "Let us have an end to this nonsense. Just give me the money and go."

Corinne straightened sorrowfully, Charley still clinging to the folds of her shawl. Corinne handed over what appeared to be a thin purse of coins. Rafe frowned. What the deuce was going on here?

Corinne bent to give her son a parting kiss, but the older woman appeared to have lost all patience. She seized hold of Charley, wrenching the boy from his mother's arms. Corinne's faint protest was lost in Charley's cry. He strained frantic arms toward his mother as he was hauled away from her.

"No! I want to stay with my mama."

Corinne pressed a trembling hand to her lips and Rafe felt himself tense. That black-clad harpy was dragging away her son. Why didn't Corinne do something? What was wrong with the woman?

"What's wrong with *you*, Mortmain?" Rafe muttered. "This is none of your affair."

He was astonished he even had to remind himself of that fact. He should retreat, head back to the wharf, but he couldn't seem to do it, his gaze riveted. Corinne stared after her son, looking as if her heart was breaking.

But it was the boy's expression Rafe found unbearable as Charley was dragged toward the house. Scared, hurt, and abandoned. The boy's sobs tore at raw places in Rafe that he had thought long ago toughened over.

He felt a strange tightness in his chest and it was as though time itself spun and fell away from him. He was back in that cold street in Paris, small, frightened, and helpless. Brother Jerome's strong hands restrained him as Evelyn Mortmain's coach vanished into the night.

"Maman! Maman!"

"You must let her go, mon fils."

No! Something seemed to snap in Rafe. Before he even considered what he was about to do, he charged forward. Brushing past Corinne, he headed straight for the other woman and the struggling child.

"Release that boy. Now!"

His ringing command caused both women to freeze in astonishment. Even Charley ceased his frantic struggles to peer fearfully up at Rafe.

"What?" the older woman asked.

"I *said* let him go."

She stared at him. Rafe discovered that her appearance didn't improve upon closer inspection. At one time, she might have been a handsome woman, but Rafe doubted it. Her eyes were cold, hard, and merciless, an expression Rafe knew well. It was far too like the one he saw in his own mirror.

Quickly recovering herself, the woman subjected Rafe to an icy glare. "Have you entirely run mad, sir?"

Very likely he had. That seemed the only possible explanation for this strange impulse. He certainly couldn't blame his behavior on the crystal. That was gone.

"Release the child," Rafe repeated. "Let him return to his mother."

"Of all the impertinent—" the woman spluttered. "Be gone, sir. Before I summon a constable."

Now there was a threat that should have brought him to his senses. If he still had any. But by this time Corinne had rushed forward to intervene.

She laid a hand on Rafe's sleeve. "Oh, please, sir. I thank you for your concern, but you don't understand. This lady isn't stealing my son or anything like that. She—"

"Good God, Corinne," the woman said scornfully. "There is hardly any need to explain your affairs to *him*. He's a complete stranger."

"No, he's not, " Charley quavered, wriggling free of the older woman's grasp. He scrambled for the safety of his mother's skirts, raising his tear-stained face to whisper to Corinne. "It is Mr. Moore, Mama."

Rafe started at the sound of the assumed name he had given the Brewers. With his appearance so altered, he had never thought the boy would recognize him. But then he hadn't thought much at all when he had come blundering into the middle of this situation.

He was already regretting it, especially when Corinne regarded him with wide, wondering eyes. "Mr. Moore?"

He was loathe to admit that he had been that filthy, unkempt creature who'd slept in her barn, but there seemed little point in trying to deny it. Rafe nodded curtly.

In spite of her distress, Corinne managed a shy smile. "I am glad to see you looking well, sir. You were so ill when you left our farm. I was worried about you."

She had worried about *him*? Rafe's brows arched in surprise and some discomfort. He had never given her a second thought.

"And who pray tell is this Mr. Moore?" the other woman demanded, her cold eyes darting suspiciously from Corinne to Rafe.

"He is the gentleman who bought our old gray gelding."

"He seems to take a rather tender interest in your affairs for such a casual acquaintance, Corinne."

"Which appears to be far more than you are doing," Rafe replied coolly. "Just who the deuce are you, madam?"

The woman gave an affronted gasp, but Corinne spoke up hastily. "This is my cousin, Mrs. Olivia Macauley. I have accepted a position as nursemaid to a merchant's family here in Falmouth. Naturally they will not allow me to have Charley with me. Olivia has consented to my son's living with her. I am sure she will be very kind to him."

"The devil she will. I've seen kinder faces on carrion crows."

Mrs. Macauley looked about to choke. "How—how dare you, sir!"

"And if this cousin of yours is so blasted *kind*," Rafe continued, "why did she take your money to look after the boy?" He gestured contemptuously toward the purse that Mrs. Macauley still clutched in her hand.

"Well, I—I could not expect—" Corinne faltered.

"Why not? She is clearly far better off than you."

Mrs. Macauley bristled. "I am not wealthy enough to offer charity to any indigent relative that comes a-begging! Small boys can prove to be very expensive."

"Not in my experience," Rafe said. "In fact, they must come rather cheap. They so often seem to be considered disposable."

Rafe immediately regretted his bitter words because it was Corinne who flinched and not the harpy.

Corinne hung her head. "I don't want to give up my son, Mr. Moore. I simply have no choice."

"Oh, enough, Corinne," Mrs. Macauley said sharply. "I don't have all day to stand here while you chat with this Moore person. Now, do you want me to take the boy or don't you?"

"Yes," Corinne whispered miserably.

"No," Rafe said.

Corinne's eyes flashed to his, clearly bewildered by his persistent intervention. Rafe couldn't blame her. He was damn confounded by it himself.

Mrs. Macauley folded her arms across her thin bosom, her pinched features settling into a dark scowl. "Now I begin to see how the matter stands, Corinne. Bad enough you made such a wretched marriage, eloping with that sailor. You have obviously found yourself another man, equally as low."

"N-no," Corinne stammered, a hint of pink stealing into her cheeks. "I assure you—Mr. Moore isn't—"

"Well, this time I completely wash my hands of you."

"Just as long as you wash your hands of her money as well," Rafe said, snatching Corinne's purse from the woman's grasp. He supposed he should try to set matters straight, point out the truth of his interference in Corinne's affairs. But damned if he knew what it was himself.

As if any explanation would help. The Macauley woman's mind was clearly as narrow as her small, mean eyes. She shot Rafe a killing glare, gave a mighty huff, then stormed into her house, slamming the door behind her.

Any satisfaction Rafe felt in routing the old harridan vanished the moment he saw Corinne's face. She looked pale enough to faint.

"Oh, Mr. Moore," she said. "What have you done to me?"

Rafe flinched from the stricken expression in her eyes.

"Nothing," he said gruffly. "Merely saved you from making a terrible mistake."

"But Olivia is my only relative, my only hope. Whom can I leave Charley with now?"

Rafe had no answer for that. He was distracted by a peculiar sensation, a small warm hand being slipped into his. He glanced down, astonished to find Charley pressed close to his side. He'd all but forgotten the boy and wondered how much he had understood of what had just taken place. Apparently enough to realize he wasn't being left with Mrs. Macauley.

The boy smiled up at Rafe as though Charley thought him some kind of blasted hero.

"How is Rufus, Mr. Moore?" the child asked, dashing away the last trace of tears from his freckled cheeks.

Rufus? What in blazes was Charley talking about? Then Rafe remembered. That wretched horse. Unfortunately he could not recall what he'd done with the beast. Sold it off to some knacker most likely.

"Uh, Rufus is fine. He's in the stable at—at—" Rafe floundered. Disengaging himself from the child's hand, he all but thrust the boy at Corinne. "Here. Take your son."

"Take him where?" Corinne gave a laugh that bordered dangerously on the edge of hysteria.

"Well, er, back to your farm."

"We no longer have a farm! It went to my husband's creditors."

Rafe winced at his own stupidity. Of course, he should have realized that. Why else would Corinne be seeking employment?

"I had it all arranged," she went on. "Charley was to live with Olivia. Perhaps she is not the gentlest of women, but she has a fine house. The position I found pays remarkably well and I require very little. I could have sent money. Saved for Charley's education so he could attend a good school. Become a fine gentleman someday. Maybe even a doctor or a solicitor."

"And you shall live in a castle, Raphael. Castle Leger, your birthright. I vow you shall have it after I have waded through the blood of those usurping St. Legers." The memory of his mother's fierce voice sliced through Rafe's mind.

He glowered at Corinne. "Do you think your boy cares about any of that? A fine house, a good school, all your blasted ambitions for him? Do you really believe any of that could make up to him for—"

Rafe checked his angry outburst, forced to remind himself this wasn't Evelyn Mortmain he was addressing. All he was doing was frightening Charley and pushing Corinne to the brink of tears.

He lowered his voice. "All your son wants is to be with you."

"W-where? In a workhouse or a d-debtor's prison?" Corinne sank down on the front stoop of the house and ducked her head, but not before Rafe saw the first tear track down her cheek. He sensed that she was not the sort of woman to weep before strangers or her young son. Her shoulders shook with her effort to contain it, a hoarse sob breaking past her control.

Rafe flinched at the sound and Charley looked absolutely horrified. He flung himself at Corinne, wrapping his thin arms about her neck.

"Don't cry, Mama. Everything will be all right. I'll take care of you. I can work real hard."

The boy's words only made Corinne cry harder and soon Charley was weeping again as well. Tunneling into his mother's arms, he buried his face against her shoulder.

Rafe took a hasty step back, thoroughly discomfited. He had never known what to do with a weeping woman except to coldly order her out of the room until she managed to compose herself.

But he clearly was the one who should go. He had done more than enough damage already with his misplaced interference. He couldn't imagine what the blazes had come over him. Since when had Rafe Mortmain ever constituted himself the champion of the small and helpless?

He'd always left that sort of noble folly to heroic idiots like Val St. Leger. Aye, this was exactly the sort of situation Saint Valentine would have gotten involved in, only he wouldn't have made such a mess of it. St. Leger was the sort of man who would even try to help his worst enemy.

Rafe's breath stilled at an unexpected flash of memory. He was collapsed on the floor at Slate House in terrible agony. Dr. St. Leger bent over him. Doing what?

Rafe frowned hard, remembering Val's hand closing over his, then a glowing warmth. Rafe had always heard tell the St. Legers possessed strange powers, Val's being an unusual gift for healing. It was almost as if Val had somehow drained him of the anger and bitterness that had long been Rafe's shield. His armor against such things as sad-eyed widows and weeping children.

"Damn you, St. Leger," he muttered. "What the devil did you do to me?"

Shaken by the memory, Rafe felt an urgent need to put as much distance as possible between himself and Corinne and her son. He backed away, mumbling an apology, but Corinne was so lost in her own misery, Rafe doubted she even heard him.

He all but bolted for the street, to the spot where he had dropped his portmanteau when this bout of madness had first overtaken him. He was damned lucky the bag was still there. Scooping it up, Rafe stalked away as fast as he could. Back to the harbor, to the sea and sanity.

Corinne and her son would be fine. She would bring them both about somehow. Perhaps she could even knock at Mrs. Macauley's door and beg that old trout to relent, take Charley in after all, although Rafe felt sickened at the prospect. But it didn't matter. There was nothing more he could do.

Rafe walked faster. He might have been all right if he hadn't felt compelled to pause and look back. Just one quick glance toward Corinne and her son.

Damnation. They were just sitting there on that blasted cousin's doorstep, looking like two castaways cut adrift in a cold, uncaring world. If only Rafe didn't know exactly how cruel that world could be.

His footsteps faltered. He cast a desperate glance at the harbor, all those ships at anchor, the beckoning masts, and the open sea. The only kind of peace and freedom he'd ever known or understood.

He couldn't possibly think of surrendering that, risking his very neck to stay here in Falmouth, to go back and help that woman and her child. Rafe Mortmain had never been that big of a fool.

He took another hesitant step, then came to a complete halt.

"Oh, bloody hell," he groaned. He must truly be mad. Or else possessed by some infernal St. Leger magic.

He gave one last longing look toward the distant ships, then came slowly about. Gripping his valise, he trudged back to where Corinne and the boy sat huddled together.

"Stop crying," Rafe said in that brisk tone he'd always used when rapping out orders on the deck of a ship. "All this caterwauling is not going to help anything."

Corinne seemed to have come to that conclusion herself. She lifted her head, obviously much surprised by Rafe's return. One arm draped about Charley, she used the end of her shawl in an effort to dry her eyes.

Why did weeping women never seem to have handkerchiefs? Pulling a disgruntled face, Rafe fished out his own and handed it to her. Corinne hastily applied the white linen to her own eyes and then her son's.

Rafe picked up her traveling bag with his free hand. "All right. Let's go."

"G-go?" Corinne faltered.

"Aye, you can hardly sit about here forever on the old bit—" With a glance at the boy, Rafe quickly amended his choice of words. "You can't stay on your cousin's doorstep."

He turned back toward the street, not even waiting to see if she would follow. But he soon heard her coming after him, leading the boy by the hand.

"Mr. Moore, please wait. I don't quite understand what you are doing."

"How astonishing. Neither do I."

"But where are you taking us?"

"Damned if I know."

"And Charley's things. They are still back at Olivia's house."

"We'll send for them."

"And I was supposed to report to Mr. Robbin's house today to take up my duties."

"Forget about that. It was never a good idea, leaving your son to go care for someone else's grubby brats. We will have to think of something else for you to do."

"Something like what?"

"I don't know. Stop asking me so many irritating questions." Rafe halted long enough to glare at her in frustration. He noticed that she was barely able to keep up. It was because of the boy.

Charley dragged his feet, beginning to look worn down by all this excess of emotion and upheaval. Rafe understood exactly how the boy felt. He stared at him for a long moment. He had never attempted to pick up a child before, had never felt the least impulse to do so.

After a brief hesitation, he balanced both valises with one arm and awkwardly lifted Charley with the other. He was astonished by how light the child was, even more astonished when Charley melted against him. He wrapped his arms about Rafe, burrowing his face against Rafe's neck. So warm and completely trusting.

Rafe experienced an odd stirring of emotion, all the more disconcerting when he realized Corinne was staring at him.

"Mr. Moore," she said. "You must allow me to ask you at least one more question." She regarded him gravely. The woman was no beauty by any means, but her eyes were not entirely unremarkable. Clear, honest, and genuine. They were quite her finest feature. Rafe grimaced. Which was a damned odd thought for him to be having at such a moment.

He sighed. "What the deuce else do you want to ask me?"

"It is extraordinarily kind of you to want to help Charley and me. But I don't understand why you are doing it. Why did you feel compelled to intervene in the first place?"

Why? How the devil should he know? Rafe rolled his eyes in exasperation, but Corinne stood waiting, requiring an answer.

"Well, because—because— Damn it." He took a deep breath. "Because a boy should never be abandoned by his mother. No matter what the reason!"

Rafe was immediately appalled. It was the last thing in the world he'd meant to blurt out. With those few simple words, he felt as though he'd revealed more of himself to Corinne Brewer than he ever had to anyone in the entire course of his life.

Her eyes widened with sudden understanding, then softened with compassion. She reached out her hand to him, but after all the other unsettling experiences Rafe had recently endured, that gentle touch promised to be one thing too much.

He turned his back on her and strode off down the street with Charley in his arms, leaving Corinne no choice but to follow.

$\mathcal{V}$al climbed slowly out of the curricle, leaning hard on his cane to steady himself. One of the Castle Leger grooms hurried forward to take charge of his winded horse. Poor Vulcan was not accustomed to being hitched in the traces, but this morning Val had felt unable to ride even his steady old mount.

It was a most painful contrast to yesterday when he had thundered along the beach on the back of that glorious stallion. But Val didn't suppose he would ever be riding Storm again.

Miracle over. Magic ended. He had brought himself to accept that during the long desperate hours last night. But the most difficult part still remained . . . telling Kate. He blamed himself bitterly for all that he had allowed to happen yesterday, all those long passionate kisses, those fiercely whispered words of love. Now he was going to have to break her heart all over again.

But why? You know it doesn't have to be that way. You know how easily all the magic can be restored. Just put the crystal back on.

The voice seemed to whisper so softly and persuasively in his head. Val felt his fingers creeping toward the buttons of his greatcoat. The crystal rested snug in the small pouch, tucked deep in his waistcoat pocket where his watch should have been. It would be so easy to—

No. Val drew his hand back, resisting the lure of the fragment as he'd been forced to do all last night. It was a little easier in the cold, misty light of morning, but not much. Val didn't begin to understand the peculiar properties of that small fragment of glittering stone, only its effect on him. Mesmerizing, seductive, in some odd way as addictive as opium. The sooner he handed the crystal over to his brother, to be placed in the St. Leger coffers, the better it would be.

Val limped toward the new wing of house, but it was the older portion of the castle that seemed to shadow his every step, the ancient stone keep with its battlements and high towers. His heart had always swelled at the sight of it before, Castle Leger, his birthplace, his home. Over five centuries of tradition and legend.

But this morning he felt overwhelmed, almost crushed by his heritage. He hastened his steps as best he was able, heading up the worn path that led through the gardens. He was not the only one up and stirring this early. They kept country hours at Castle Leger and Val spied his mother already hard at work among the flower beds.

Madeline St. Leger had never been the sort of fashionable lady to languish upon a settee while her servants took care of everything. His mother had often reminded Val more of a medieval chatelaine, busily attending to all the domestic arrangements of her lord's castle, but most particularly her well-loved garden.

She was bundled up in the sensible worn blue coat she reserved for her gardening on chilly days, a simple straw hat tied in place over her head with a scarf. Her hair had once been so fiery red, she'd been known as the lady of flame, but the color had softened with the passing years to a regal shade of silver.

Yet Madeline St. Leger was one of those women whose serene beauty could never fade, her eyes as brilliantly clear and green as they had ever been. Her face lit up with joy as Val approached and she straightened to greet him.

"Valentine!"

Though it cost him a sharp twinge in his knee, Val forced his leg into an elegant bow. It was a courtly ritual observed since the days of his boyhood, when he and his brother had played at being Round Table knights and his mother had been his only lady, the queen of Castle Leger.

"Good morrow, Your Highness," he murmured.

"Good morrow, Sir Galahad." Madeline St. Leger dipped into a playful curtsy. But when Val reached for her hand to carry it respectfully to his lips, his mother snatched her fingers away, scrubbing them against her old coat.

"Oh, no, my dear, you don't want to be doing that. As you can see, I have been busy grubbing in the dirt, as your father calls it."

She stretched up on tiptoe to deposit a kiss on his cheek instead. Although she continued to smile, she studied his face and Val shifted, uncomfortable. His father was the true St. Leger, the one possessed of supernatural gifts of perception, but it was his mother's gentle probing gaze Val often feared, her eyes that saw too much he wished to conceal. He knew she had to be observing the signs of his sleepless night, perhaps even more. All the ragged edges left by whatever had happened to him on All Hallows' Eve, the frayed ends of memory that he still did not seem able to knit back together.

He avoided her gaze by bending down to retrieve her basket for her. And sucked in his breath at the sharp stab of pain. Damnation, his leg had gotten worse. Or did it only seem that way after yesterday, that all too brief taste of freedom?

Gritting his teeth, he handed his mother her basket. If she noticed anything amiss, she was wise enough not to comment on it.

"It is so good to see you, Valentine," she said. "Your father was complaining only the other day that you do not come home often enough now that you have moved so far away."

Val sighed. He was tired. He was hurting. That made it difficult to respond with his customary patience. "So far away, Mama? I have moved only to the other end of the village."

"But you know how your father is, my dear."

"Aye, I verily believe if he could have, Father would have kept his entire family at Castle Leger forever with the door nailed shut while he guarded us like a fierce old dragon."

His mother chuckled. "I never thought of your father that way. But I suppose he is very dragonlike."

"No doubt that is why he has gone north. To roar and breathe fire at poor Marius until he agrees to return to the safe folds of Torrecombe."

"I fear so. Your father and Marius have always been more like brothers than cousins. I daresay Marius will be glad to see your papa even if he does roar a trifle." His mother smiled, but her eyes were rather wistful. "It is quite absurd, I know. Your papa has been gone only one day and the man frequently drives me to distraction. Yet I do miss my dragon most terribly whenever he is gone."

Of course she did, Val thought. Even after thirty-three years of marriage, Anatole and Madeline St. Leger remained devoted to each other, as passionately in love as ever, the embodiment of the St. Leger legend. No, they *were* the legend, matched through the offices of that wisest of Bride Finders, Septimus Fitzleger, Effie's grandfather.

Two hearts brought together in a moment, two souls united for an eternity. Just like Val's brother, Lance, and his bride, Rosalind. His cousin Caleb and his wife. All his sisters and their husbands and a score of other St. Legers.

Aye, all of them so happy, so content. And where is your share of this lovely fairy tale? Do you think any of them even notice how lonely and miserable you are? You might as well be invisible to your own family.

The reflection was bitter, disturbing, and Val rubbed his hand wearily across his eyes, fighting against it.

"Valentine?"

He lowered his hand to discover his mother peering up at him, for once unable to hide her concern. "My dearest, I keep getting this odd feeling. Is something wrong?"

"No, nothing," Val said. Too quickly, he realized. He forced a smile to his lips. "I am merely a little tired this morning. Not quite myself."

What a lie that is. The problem is you are far too much yourself. Too patient, too resigned, too crippled. By both your blasted leg and that cursed legend.

The thought was so dark with anger, Val was shaken. It was almost as though he could feel the crystal pulse through his pocket, piercing him with suppressed rage. He had to get rid of that cursed thing. *Now.*

"Mama, is Lance anywhere about this morning?"

"Why, yes. I believe he is in the study."

"Good. I have something particular I need to speak to him about." Val bent stiffly to brush a kiss against his mother's brow. Then he stumped quickly away before she could ask any of the anxious questions he saw clouding her eyes.

Madeline watched Val's retreat, feeling deeply troubled. A mother was not supposed to have favorites and she adored all her children, her roguish son Lance, her three very different daughters.

But she had always reserved a special corner of her heart for this quiet son of hers, her Valentine, who from his earliest years had shared her passion for books, her love of learning. She'd watched him grow from a sweet-tempered boy to a man remarkable for his gentle strength and courage, his boundless compassion.

She and Val had always been so close. This was the first time he'd ever lied to her, Madeline thought with dismay. No matter how he sought to deny it, she knew there was something very wrong with her son.

*   *   *

Val handed off his greatcoat to one of the footmen and made his own way toward the familiar study at the back of the house. Gripping the handle of his cane, he moved with even greater difficulty, the mere effort of getting down the hall exhausting him.

It was as though the crystal grew heavier with every step he took, the closer he came to surrendering it. How ridiculous, Val thought. He was surely starting to let his wearied imagination get the better of him. It was only a stone, a tiny fragment of stone.

All the same, he felt obliged to rest a moment, leaning against the study door. His knock was feeble at best, and when he received no response, he simply turned the knob and eased it open.

The study was a darkly masculine chamber paneled with sturdy English oak, the walls lined with hunting prints. Lance sat hunched over the desk at the far end of the room. Stripped down to his waistcoat, shirtsleeves thrust up out of the way, he looked slightly harried this morning. Perhaps because he was laboring over a letter, never one of his favorite tasks. He'd always preferred conducting estate business from the back of a horse.

He was so absorbed by his work, he didn't even glance up, affording Val a rare opportunity to study his brother. Lance rarely stayed put in any one place that long, even to have his portrait painted.

He'd once been a wild rogue, a restless soldier, a notorious rakehell, although marriage and fatherhood had done a great deal to tame him. The smile that had devastated so many women was entirely reserved these days for Lance's much adored wife, Rosalind.

But other than that, Val could only marvel at how little Lance seemed to have changed. Val might be feeling every one of his thirty-two years and then some, but Lance appeared as young and vigorous as ever. The pale light streaming through the long windows outlined his broad shoulders, the muscular strength of his bared forearms.

It made it difficult for Val to remember they were twins. Although not identical, they shared the same dark hair, dark eyes, and the infamous St. Leger hawk's nose. Lance was the elder of the two, born near midnight on the thirteenth of a cold dark February while Val had made his appearance during the early hours of the next day, trailing after his lusty brother even then.

Had he ever been anything more than a pale copy of Lance St. Leger? Val wondered. His brother was the very picture of a hale and hearty man in his prime, which was what Val should have been, too. If things had been different . . .

Val fingered the outline of the crystal hidden beneath his waistcoat.

If Lance hadn't been so reckless that day in Spain, so careless of his own life, you would never have had to use your power to save him. He's the one who should have ended up lame, not you.

But Lance had never asked for such a sacrifice from him, hadn't wanted it. It had been Val's own choice and he'd never regretted it, would do it all again in a heartbeat, anything for the brother he'd always loved and admired . . . wouldn't he?

Disturbed that he could even question such a thing, Val rapped again on the open study door, a little harder this time.

"Lance?"

His brother looked up at last, a broad grin creasing his handsome features.

"Val! This is an agreeable surprise."

"Is it?" Val murmured, and flinched as Lance leapt up and bounded across the room. He wrung Val's fingers in a hearty handshake, followed by a brisk clap to the shoulder.

He was fond of his brother, Val told himself, damned fond. But there were days when Lance's exuberance exhausted him, made him all the more aware of his own affliction. Days like this one.

"You are the very man I've been needing to talk—" Lance broke off, frowning as his gaze raked over Val. Never as tactful as their mother, he blurted out, "Damnation, Val. What have you been doing with yourself? You look like the very devil."

"Thank you," Val muttered. "It's good to see you, too."

He eased away from his brother, hobbling toward the nearest chair, a stiff upright wingback. Suppressing a grimace of pain, he lowered himself onto the cushion.

Lance trailed after him. "Blast it all, Val. You've been up again all night, tending to patients, haven't you? No doubt using your power—"

"No, I bloody well haven't." Val cut him off before he could launch into the familiar lecture Val too often received from members of his family, even from Kate. He was tired of it.

No one knew better than he how dangerous the excessive use of his power could be. But he had not used his unusual St. Leger gift since—since—

Like a flash of lightning, the memory cut through his mind. Rafe Mortmain's desperate eyes, the man's fingers crushed around his.

And like a flash of lightning, it was gone.

"I was not attending any patients. I merely . . ."

I was merely in pure torment last night, fighting off the urge to seduce my dearest friend.

Now there was a confession that would astound his brother and the entire village, Val thought wryly. Their noble doctor, their Saint Valentine lusting after a woman.

"I merely had one of my bad nights," he finished. Usually Val made a great effort to conceal any painful episodes from his family, especially Lance. Lance had experienced enough guilt over the injury to Val's knee and that was the last thing Val had ever wanted.

But he was feeling too raw, too exhausted this morning to spare his brother's feelings. Lance perched on the corner of the desk, peering down at him with a worried frown.

"I have been hearing some unusual reports about you, *Saint* Valentine."

"Oh?" Val forced himself to smile, to respond in the manner they'd always adopted from the time they were boys, teasing and tormenting each other over their unusual names.

"And just what have you heard, *Sir* Lancelot?"

"Caleb told me you bought his white stallion."

"Aye, so I did. What of it?"

"What of it? Val, that horse is pure demon."

"And you don't think I can handle him."

"Well, it's not that exactly," Lance hedged.

But that was precisely what it was, Val thought, feeling the more irritated because he knew his brother was right. He couldn't handle the stallion, not in his present state.

"You don't have to worry," he said. "I have quite come to my senses and mean to be rid of the brute. Would you care to take him off my hands?"

Val was surprised at how grudgingly he made the offer. In fact, he almost choked on it.

Because Lance already had everything. He was oldest son, heir to Castle Leger, married to a beautiful woman, father to a handsome little boy. He didn't need that incredible horse as well. Val's horse . . .

Val pressed his hand over the region of his waistcoat pocket. It was almost as though he could feel the crystal pulse beneath his hand, and he sought to crush the dark sensation. He'd never envied Lance before, never allowed himself to do so. All the same, he felt relieved when Lance rejected his offer.

"You probably should just return the stallion to Caleb," he said, "I have more than enough horses and my lady would not welcome such a wild addition to my stables. Rosalind strongly objects to me risking my neck, especially now when we've had such good tidings."

When Val regarded his brother questioningly, a smile spread across Lance's face, a tender light springing to his eyes.

"Rosalind is increasing again."

"Oh. Congratulations." Val was dismayed that he couldn't manage to infuse more warmth into his voice. He was genuinely pleased for both Rosalind and his brother and yet . . .

He supposed he would be obliged to attend her as he had done at the birth of young Jack, absorb Rosalind's pain. When her labor was done, Val would feel battered, exhausted, but Lance would proudly lift his new offspring into his arms.

The son or daughter Val would never know, the joy he would never feel. As Lance and Rosalind gazed adoringly at each other and their babe, he would just limp from the room, forgotten.

The stab of resentment came sharper this time, harder to quell. Val ground his fingertips against his eyes. He needed to hand the crystal over to his brother and get the devil out of here.

Reluctantly he eased the pouch from his pocket. He managed to spill the chain into the palm of his hand, quickly closing his fingers to avoid looking at the crystal. Even doing that much required great effort from him. He actually felt beads of perspiration gather on his brow.

Surrendering the stone to Lance was more difficult than he'd ever imagined. How could he hand over the long-missing crystal without offering awkward explanations, without bringing up the name that had ever created friction between him and his brother?

Rafe Mortmain. The man Lance no doubt still persisted in regarding as a friend. The man Val had always recognized as an enemy. What good would it do to stir up all that old hostility when Val couldn't even recall what had happened on All Hallows' Eve?

Perhaps if he waited until he could more clearly remember—

And perhaps he was only manufacturing an excuse to hang on to this damnable stone a little longer.

Val took a deep breath, steeling himself. "Lance, there is something urgent I have to tell you, something I have to give . . ."

But to his intense frustration, he realized his brother wasn't even listening.

Lance had leapt up, settling briskly behind the desk once more, reaching for his unfinished letter.

"There is another reason I am glad you called today, something else I have to discuss with you."

"That's fine, Lance, but first, if you will allow me a moment—"

"Victor has already been here to call upon me this morning."

Val expelled an impatient sigh. Giving up the crystal was already hard enough and Lance certainly wasn't making it any easier. He didn't have the slightest interest in Victor St. Leger, but he knew how single-minded Lance could be.

"So what did the boy want?" Val asked wearily.

"You're not going to believe this. He wants to marry Kate."

"What!" Val stared at his brother, certain he could not have heard him right. "You have to be jesting."

"I wish I was."

"But he's supposed to marry Mollie Grey. She is his chosen bride."

"Something that Victor has apparently forgotten, but it is not entirely surprising. Mollie is a sweet but rather plain girl. And in case you haven't noticed, our little hoyden Kate has grown to be an astonishingly beautiful young woman."

Oh, aye, he'd noticed all right, Val thought grimly. That was both his joy and his torment.

"Victor was here on the doorstep at the crack of dawn," Lance continued with a grimace. "Literally throwing down the gauntlet. He came to inform me as head of the family in Father's absence that as far as Victor is concerned, the legend can be damned. He is completely besotted with Kate and will have no other woman but her."

Val sagged back against the chair, his mind reeling at Lance's words. Under other circumstances, he might have admired Victor's foolhardy courage. The lad was certainly showing more spirit than he had ever done, Val reflected bitterly. But this was Kate that the stupid boy was talking about. *His* Kate.

Val clutched the crystal hidden in his fist, overcome by a savage stirring of jealousy, the like of which he had never known. He drew in a deep breath, struggling to fight against it, to remind himself that Kate wasn't his. She didn't belong to him and she never could.

But for damn sure she didn't belong to Victor either. Although Val didn't know what he was so worried about. He forced himself to relax, saying with a shrug, "It hardly matters whether Victor fancies himself in love with Kate or not. She'll send him packing fast enough."

He expected Lance to agree heartily with him. When his brother merely looked grave, Val exclaimed, "Good God, Lance. You cannot possibly imagine that Kate would ever encourage that conceited puppy?"

Lance frowned. "Frankly, I don't know."

"But Kate despises Victor. She always used to threaten that she would march him onto one of his grandfather's ships one day and force him to walk the plank."

"And Kate also used to say she was going to marry you. Fortunately she appears to have outgrown both foolish notions."

A foolish notion? That Kate would ever want to marry Val, would ever love him that much? And yet Lance didn't seem to have much trouble imagining that Kate could fall for that young dolt Victor.

Val swallowed hard, barely managing to suppress his bitter thoughts as Lance continued, "Victor is very handsome and quite charming with the ladies. He has already made an alarming number of conquests among the village lasses."

"But not Kate. Never Kate," Val said fiercely.

"I hope you are right." Lance reached for the quill to finish his letter. "In the meantime, it seems prudent to send Kate away, out of the path of temptation."

"Temptation? What temptation?" Val began contemptuously only to check himself as the full import of Lance's words sank in.

"Send Kate away? Where?"

He waited with strained patience while Lance inked out another line on his letter before answering. "To London. You know Effie has always wanted to take Kate there. She has a cousin in Mayfair who she hopes can introduce the girl into society."

"That's only Effie's damn fool notion. Kate has never wanted a London season, and it is not as if Effie could even afford such a thing."

"She can't. That is why I am writing this letter of credit. To place the funds at her disposal."

Val stared at his brother. Lance could not possibly be serious. Ignoring the sharp protest from his knee, Val shoved to his feet. Bending over the desk, he watched anxiously as his brother scrawled his signature across the bottom of a very official-looking letter. A letter that threatened to sweep Kate out of his life forever.

"Damn it, Lance," he said. "You can't do that. You can't help Effie to take Kate away from—from—"

From me, Val nearly blurted out.

He gripped his cane, striving to contain himself. "From Torrecombe. Kate would be miserable in London. You don't know how she feels about that place, what it was like for her there."

"No one is talking about returning the girl to the foundling home. She'd be lodged in the finest part of town, attend balls, dinners, the theatre."

"As if Kate would care for any of those things. All she would feel is exiled, driven out of her own home, cast aside as though she was unwanted again. And all because some damn fool boy fancies himself in love with her."

Lance glanced up, his brows arching in mild surprise at the vehemence of Val's protest. Val lowered his eyes, unable to meet Lance's gaze, feeling a little ashamed as he realized it wasn't Kate's welfare he was considering at all, but his own.

He couldn't bear to lose her . . . even though he had no right to keep her either.

Lance regarded Val gravely. "It is not merely because of Victor that the girl should go. There is Kate's own future to be considered as well. There is little for her here in Torrecombe. London would be the best place for her to make a good marriage, which is something you yourself have always wanted for her, isn't it?"

"Of course," Val mumbled. Aye, back when he had been a noble and self-sacrificing idiot. Before yesterday when he'd known what it was like to hold Kate in his arms, feel her sweet breath mingle with his as he'd claimed her lips in kiss after kiss.

Ignoring the pain to his leg, he paced off several agitated steps, clutching the crystal so hard, the fragment bit into his palm. He'd had to give up everything else that had ever mattered to him in his life. But damn it, he wasn't giving up Kate. He loved her and—and— No! It was only the crystal clouding his mind, confusing him.

He forced his hand to relax so the shard stopped pressing against his flesh. But it made little difference. It was as though the crystal had already done its work, breaking down his defenses, cracking the shield that he'd placed around his heart to keep him from ever facing the truth. That he wanted Kate, needed her, and loved her beyond all reason, beyond fear of any curse or legend.

It was all he could do not to reach down and snatch the letter from his brother, shred it to bits, fling the pieces into Lance's face.

The urge was so intense he had to turn away until he regained command of himself. Putting the distance of the room between them, Val limped over to the fireplace. He leaned up against the mantel for support, fretting the crystal between his fingers.

He was only dimly aware when a knock sounded at the door, a footman arriving with a message for Lance. When the servant departed, Lance stood up, rolling down his sleeves and shrugging into the frock coat he'd left draped over a chair.

"I am sorry, Val. I forgot that I promised Father's steward that I would ride out with him this morning to look at some storm damage done to the tenants' cottages."

Val tensed, not trusting himself to look around as Lance came up to stand behind him.

"Look, old fellow," he said. "Don't worry about our little Kate. I am sure Victor will come to his senses soon enough and Kate will do just fine in London. But there is one thing you could do to help."

"And what is that?"

"You could talk to Kate yourself. Persuade her that it would be in her best interest to go. She always listens to you."

Val stiffened, completely incredulous. Bad enough that Lance proposed to send away the only woman Val had ever cared about, the only one he would ever love. But on top of all that, Lance actually expected Val to help him do it. Lance with his perfect marriage, perfect love, perfect life.

In that moment Val almost felt like he hated his brother, but he gritted his teeth and nodded. "I'll do what I can."

"Good man." Lance patted his shoulder.

Val clenched the crystal, barely able to stop himself from whirling around and smashing his fist into his brother's face. He felt relieved when he heard Lance retreat, only wanting him to be gone.

But Lance hesitated on the threshold. "Oh, lord, Val. I am sorry. I almost forgot to ask. Was there something particular you wanted to see me about?"

Val nearly choked on a bitter laugh. Wasn't that just like his brother? To finally pluck his head out of his own blasted affairs long enough to notice that Val might need something. And always when it was too damned late.

Because . . . Val suddenly realized, staring down at his tightly clenched fist . . . he could no more have surrendered that crystal now than he could have cut off his own arm.

"No, there's nothing," he said hoarsely.

He waited until the door closed behind his brother, until he was quite certain Lance had gone, before he unfurled his trembling fingers and allowed himself to look at the crystal.

The shard sparkled against his palm, its mesmerizing beauty seeming to pierce his very soul, refracting images deep in his mind. Terrifying images of Kate mounting into a carriage, vanishing down the road, not even pausing to say good-bye.

Or worse still, Kate melting into Victor's arms.

No, she would never do that, Val told himself fiercely. She loved him. She always had. Only yesterday she had clung to him, scarce able to get enough of his kisses. She would have allowed him to make love to her right there on the library settee.

Yesterday he had been very much Victor's equal and more. Young, strong, vigorous. Today he was hunched over his cane again, more pathetic than ever. But he had the power to change all that resting right here in his own hand.

Val caressed the crystal fragment, wondering why he continued to resist its magic. True, it had a strange effect on him, but it waxed worse only at night. Why shouldn't he wear the thing, take advantage of the relief it would offer, at least during the day?

He dangled the chain, the crystal twisting, turning, and glittering before his eyes. In that instant, he experienced a flicker of sanity, a realization that if he ever put the thing on again, he wouldn't be able to take it off. That he would prove a danger not only to Kate, but also to everyone else around him.

And yet if he didn't use the crystal, he was going to lose Kate. Forever.

The crystal flashed, dazzling his eyes, and the brief glimmer of sanity faded and was gone.

Val eased the chain over his head, thrusting the crystal beneath his shirt until the fragment rested over the region of his heart. Ice hot. The crystal froze. It burned. Like lightning, striking off a shower of sparks.

Val gasped, doubling over at the sudden force that rushed through him, nearly bringing him to his knees. He clutched at both his cane and the mantel for support, his vision blurring.

The entire room seemed to spin around him and he closed his eyes, feeling as though he was about to faint. And then just as suddenly it all stopped. Expelling an unsteady breath, he opened his eyes. And straightened, feeling the unearthly surge of power beating through his veins, his leg once more strong and sturdy beneath him.

Val glared at the useless cane clutched in his hand. With slow deliberation he raised it then cracked it against the stone of the fireplace. Again and again, taking a vicious satisfaction when the cane finally splintered in two.

He flung the pieces to the carpet, then whirled about, storming over to the desk. He snatched up the letter Lance had written and rent that apart as well.

No one was taking Kate away from him, he vowed. Not Effie or his brother. And as for this so-called rival of his . . . Val's lips snaked back in a savage smile.

He would deal with Victor himself. One way or another.

CHAPTER TEN

$\mathcal{B}$undled in her cloak, Kate slipped out the kitchen door of Rosebriar Cottage. With a wary glance back at the house, she scurried through the garden. Unlike the lovely wilderness of blossoms at Castle Leger, the much smaller gardens at Rosebriar were confined behind a high stone wall and consisted of tidy flower beds bordered by neat walkways and a small pond stocked with bright-colored carp.

It offered few opportunities for concealment other than the ancient apple tree and the summerhouse at the back of the property. Kate slunk behind the tree. With another nervous glance behind her, she produced the object she had kept hidden beneath her cloak.

Yet another floral offering from that lunatic Victor. Kate grimaced at the bouquet, then hurled it with all her might over the stone wall. She was gratified to hear the light tap of hooves, followed by a bleat.

What a blessing it was that their nearest neighbor, the Widow Thomas, kept a goat that would eat anything. But all the same, Kate thought with a deep sigh, she could not keep this up much longer.

Victor appeared to have made a remarkable recovery from her rejection of him yesterday and he had been driving her to distraction ever since, deluging her with embarrassing love letters, bad poetry, and flowers left deposited on her doorstep. Kate had managed to burn the letters and poems before anyone saw them. The flowers she had been tossing over the fence. But if she didn't find a way to discourage Victor soon, the entire village would become aware of his pursuit of her.

Kate found it a bitter irony that the man she didn't want couldn't seem to leave her alone while the one she did appeared to be successfully resisting her magic. Val had not kept his promise. He had not come anywhere near her either last evening or this morning. But until she found someway to—to unbewitch Victor, perhaps it was just as well.

But how the devil was she going to do that without the book? Kate wondered, stepping out from behind the tree. She had spent most of last night searching to no avail, her alarm waxing stronger by the minute. She had experienced that book's terrible power firsthand. It was far too dangerous to be left floating around where it might fall into the wrong hands.

Maybe it already had.

Kate went cold at the thought, but she soothed herself with the reminder that the book would be useless unless one knew how to decipher ancient Egyptian. And even if a thief was that clever and realized she possessed such a wondrous book, no outsider could have slipped in and out of her bedchamber undetected in broad daylight.

Nor could she believe that anyone in the household would have taken it. The retainers at Rosebriar were all innately honest. Kate had closely questioned all the servants, but none of them had seen the book she described, let alone touched it. As for Effie, Kate hadn't bothered asking her. The only books Effie ever noticed were the ones containing plates of the latest fashions.

But if the book hadn't been stolen, moved, or borrowed, what did that leave? It couldn't have just sprouted legs and walked away, could it? Considering that it was a magic book, perhaps it could.

Kate almost wished she could believe that. It would be so much better than the prospect that faced her. If she couldn't find the book, she felt obliged to seek out Prospero and tell him the truth. Not only had she stolen his spell book, she had lost it as well.

What would the outraged sorcerer do to her? Suspend her headfirst over the moat, chain her up in the oubliette, turn her into a toad? Maybe that would be a blessing considering the shambles that she had made of everything, casting a love spell on not one but two men.

She trudged back toward the house, head bent low, peering behind every rosebush, hoping that she might have just dropped the book, that it would somehow miraculously reappear.

Absorbed by her search, she paid no heed to the low thud of something dropping to the ground, the rush of footsteps behind her, until two hands circled her from behind, covering her eyes. She gave a startled gasp.

"Guess who?" a masculine voice murmured in her ear.

She didn't have to guess.

"Victor!" Kate said through clenched teeth. Recovering from the fright he'd given her, she struck his hands away, whirling angrily about to face him. "What the blazes are you doing here?"

Victor's high-crowned beaver hat had nearly tumbled off in his climb over the wall. It sat at a crooked angle over his brow. He swept the hat off the rest of the way, flourishing it in a magnificent bow.

"I have come to prostrate myself at your feet again, my princess," he announced grandly.

Kate's anxious gaze trained back on the house, fearing at any moment one of the servants or even Effie herself might walk out into the garden.

She seized Victor by one of the multiple capes on his driving cape and dragged him in the direction of the summerhouse. The folly was constructed after the fashion of a Grecian temple and was more open than Kate could have desired. But at least the mock pillars offered some concealment.

Unfortunately, Victor drew entirely the wrong inference from her actions.

"Kate," he said huskily, stealing his arms about her waist, his lips straining toward hers.

With a frustrated growl, Kate gave him a mighty shove, sending him staggering back. "If you ever try to kiss me again, I swear I'll—"

"But, my dearest Kate—"

"I am not your dearest Kate, so you just keep your distance. For mercy's sake, don't you realize that my guardian sometimes uses the sitting room at the back of the house? She could look out the window at any moment and see us."

Victor sighed, but gave up his efforts to embrace her. He tossed his hat down on a stone bench, then leaned back against one of the pillars, folding his arms.

"I appreciate your scruples, my love. But I daresay Effie will know all about us very soon anyway."

"What do you mean?"

"Only that I have already been to call upon Lance St. Leger this morning and I told him that I intend to marry you."

"You what!"

"I thought it for the best to declare my intentions at once and quite openly."

"You bloody idiot!" she snarled, advancing on him. Victor abandoned his nonchalant pose, retreating a few steps.

"But, my love, after what you said to me yesterday about my cousin Anatole, I could not have you thinking that I am a coward, that I am afraid to inform my own family of my adoration for you."

"It's *me* you should be afraid of," Kate said, clenching her fists.

Although Victor flinched in anticipation, he did not even attempt to raise his hands to ward off a possible blow. "Go ahead. Strike me then," he murmured. "Any touch from my Kate is better than none at all."

Kate raised her fist, longing to take him up on his offer. She had hoped to cure Victor before anyone found out about his ridiculous infatuation for her. And now he had gone and told Lance. What a disaster.

But she realized that hitting Victor would be like hitting the village idiot. The man was completely moon mad and it was all her fault. Kate lowered her hand, her anger fading.

"Please, Victor," she said. "Just go home and give me a few days. I promise you that somehow I will make everything all right by then."

"You'll marry me?" he asked, his dark eyes lighting up.

"No!" Kate stormed away from him, heading back to the house. No doubt Lance would be descending upon Rosebriar Cottage soon after Victor's extraordinary pronouncement. Kate needed to get to Effie first, find some way to explain things so her poor guardian did not go off into complete hysterics.

But Kate did not get very far before she felt Victor's hand upon her arm, holding her back. "No, Kate, please don't go."

She tried to shake him off, but he clung firmly. Kate came to an abrupt halt, twisting around to scowl at him.

But it was not Victor, the arrogant rake, the elegant dandy, facing her. Rather it was a young man looking as shy and uncertain as any boy experiencing his first love. And that somehow made all of this so much worse.

"Please," he said. "I know I have begun badly. If you would just allow me to speak with you. Only for a few moments."

Kate squirmed. Talking to Victor, offering him any sort of encouragement at all, was the last thing she wanted to do. But she was the one who had inflicted this torment upon him. She supposed she owed him something.

Reluctantly she followed him back into the summerhouse. At least he kept a respectful distance this time. Clearing his throat, he offered her a diffident smile very different from that blinding flash of teeth he aimed at most women. "Kate, I know you have every reason to despise me. In the past, I have never been particularly kind to you."

"Oh, well." Kate shrugged. "As to that, I suppose I haven't been exactly—"

"No, please. Let me finish. It was very wrong of me to tease you about being a foundling, even cruel. I don't know what caused me to behave so ungentlemanly. Perhaps it is the way you always looked at me with such complete contempt."

"Victor—"

"Not that I didn't deserve it," he rushed on. "I realize that I am not the sort of bold rugged man you could admire, the kind of man my grandfather was. But I could change, Kate. I swear it. I would do anything for you."

"Oh, Victor, please," Kate groaned. She hadn't thought it possible to feel any worse about all this than she already did. But Victor was teaching her the true meaning of guilt.

His dark eyes were heart-wrenchingly earnest as he continued, "I know how you adore the sea. My family owns many ships. I could take you sailing clear around the world."

"No, you couldn't. Even getting into a dinghy makes you seasick."

Victor paled at the thought, but he squared his shoulders manfully. "I have heard that even the great admiral Lord Nelson sometimes suffered from sea-sickness, and he managed at Trafalgar. What is a paltry war compared to my love? For you, Kate, I could learn to conquer anything. And there is something else I could do. I could use my St. Leger power on your behalf."

When Kate regarded him blankly, Victor beamed. "You didn't even know I had any, did you?

"I am ashamed to admit I have always taken pains to conceal my special ability, selfishly not wanting to be importuned. But I possess the unique gift to divine what has happened to people who have disappeared. And I would be only too happy to employ my talent to help you."

"Thank you, Victor. I appreciate the offer, but there is no one in my life who has gone missing."

"Not even your mother?" he asked softly.

"Effie? She is in the house, likely taking her afternoon tea."

"I don't mean Effie. I mean your real mother."

"Are you trying to tell me that you—you could—"

"Yes." He gathered both of her hands into his own. "All you would have to do is look deep into my eyes, let me delve into your memory all the way back to the moment of your birth until I saw your mother's face. Then by concen-trating a little more, I could tell you where she is right now, whether still alive or where her headstone lies."

Kate eased away from him, shaken by what he offered. She studied his face, sure he had to be making all this up, seeking yet another way to impress her.

But she read only sincerity in his eyes, the certainty that he could do exactly what he promised. He was, after all, a St. Leger.

But to locate her mother for her, after all these years— Kate felt her heart miss a beat. She tried to remind herself that she had never cared who her real mother was, didn't in the least want to know.

But that was only a lie, another of her fierce denials, her way of thrusting aside anything that had the potential to hurt her. Of course she had wondered about her mother, had ridiculously hoped that one day she might even discover there was a perfectly good reason why she had been left to die in that wretched foundling home.

And now here was Victor St. Leger, of all the unlikely people, offering her the truth.

Kate fretted her lower lip, then reached out to place her fingers back in his. She lost courage at the last minute, snatching her hands away.

"N-no," she said with a shaky laugh. "I really don't want to know. I am sure my mother could not have been a particularly pleasant person."

"If she was your mother, Kate," Victor insisted, "then she had to have been an angel."

"Angels don't abandon their little girls. Nor do they give birth to wicked creatures like me."

"You are not wicked. You are completely wonderful." Victor smiled at her, his eyes glowing with such adoration Kate could bear it no longer. Whatever the consequences, she had to tell him the truth.

"Victor, you are not really in love with me."

"I most certainly am—"

"No, you are not. The truth is . . ." She sighed, then blurted out, "The truth is I cast a spell on you."

"You certainly did. You have bewitched me completely."

"Ohhh!" Kate sighed in pure frustration.

Before she could stop him, he stole his arms about her, drawing her into his embrace. "I adore you, Kate. Please let me prove to you how much. I would willingly die for you."

"That could easily be arranged."

The icy voice came out of nowhere, startling both of them. Kate twisted around, disconcerted by the sight of the man silhouetted in the doorway of the summerhouse, his dark hair swept carelessly back from his face, his black cloak falling to his knees. His shadow seemed to stretch across the stone floor, looming over both of them.

"Good God," Victor said. "Is . . . is that—"

"Val," Kate murmured, feeling a little awed herself. She had never realized that he could appear quite that formidable and overpowering. A strange dark glint in his eyes, he stalked toward them in a slow, deliberate way that sent an inexplicable shiver through Kate. He looked almost . . . *dangerous.*

"Val," she faltered. "What—what a surprise. I was not expecting you."

"That is perfectly evident, my dear."

Kate flushed, suddenly remembering Victor still had his arm about her waist. She scrambled away from him. "Victor was just—that is, he was merely—"

"I can see quite well what he was *merely* doing." Val's gaze narrowed ominously on his cousin.

The young man stood gaping, clearly struggling to take in the startling changes in Val. But he recovered enough to sweep an elegant bow.

"Hullo, Val. You are looking amazingly fit. What have you done with your cane?"

"Smashed it. Into a thousand bits," Val said softly, looking very much as though he wanted to do the same thing to Victor.

Victor gave an uncertain laugh, apparently thinking that Val was jesting. Kate had a sinking feeling he wasn't.

"Uh, Victor was just leaving," she said hastily.

"No, I wasn't."

She shot the young fool a warning glare, but he stubbornly ignored her. "I can guess why you have come, Val. Very likely Lance sent you here to reason with me. But I intend to marry Kate and nothing you can say—"

Victor broke off with a gasp as Val seized him by the front of his cape.

"I am through *talking*," Val snarled.

Kate watched openmouthed as he slammed his cousin back against one of the pillars.

"I've wasted most of my life reasoning with fools like you. So I'll make this plain and simple. You stay away from Kate."

Victor's eyes fairly popped from his head. "But—but, Val," he stammered. "I assure you, my intentions are completely honorable."

"Damn your intentions!" Val gave him a savage shake, banging his head against the stonework. "You ever touch Kate again and I'm going to kill you."

Going to? Kate thought in alarm. Val looked ready to do it right now.

"Val, stop it. Let him go," Kate cried. Never in her worst dreams had she ever thought she would be obliged to protect anyone from Val St. Leger. She rushed forward to tug at his arm.

"Val, please."

He glared at her, but he loosened his grip at least enough for Victor to stagger away from him. Victor rubbed the back of his head, regarding Val with reproach and bewilderment.

"Damnation, Val. What the blazes has come over you?"

"Me? What the devil has gotten into you, *boy*? To ever think I would stand aside and let you have Kate."

"No, Val, please, you don't understand," Kate said. "Victor doesn't really mean any of this. He—"

"Yes, I do," Victor said. "I love you and I fail to see what concern it is of his."

"Because she is mine, damn you. *Mine.* She always has been, always will be."

"*You* are in love with Kate?" Victor asked, incredulous. "But—but you are too old for her."

"Too old, you strutting puppy? Would you care to put that to a test?" Val strode menacingly toward Victor. Victor stumbled back a pace.

"Val, I am warning you. Keep your hands off me. I don't want to hurt you."

"Oh, don't worry about my decrepit old bones." Val gave Victor a rough shove.

"Don't do that, Val, or—"

"Or what?" He shoved Victor again. Harder.

Kate could scarce believe it. It was like Val was trying to force a quarrel on his own cousin.

"Stop it, Val," she pleaded, grabbing for his arm. "Leave him alone."

Her intervention only made everything worse. Val shook her off and drove his fist into Victor's face.

Victor went down hard, sprawling on the stone floor. He lay there, dazed, clutching his eye. With a dismayed cry, Kate rushed to his side.

"Victor, are you all right?" She reached down to help him up, but he struck her hand away.

He struggled to his feet, now as flushed with anger as Val. "Damn you, Val. If you weren't my cousin, I would demand that you meet me for this."

"Don't let that stop you."

"Fine. Name your seconds and choose your weapons. Pistols or swords."

"It makes no odds to me. You choose how you want to die."

"Stop it! Both of you." Her heart thudding with alarm, Kate thrust herself between the two men. They looked ready to fall upon each other like a pair of snarling dogs. This was fast becoming a nightmare. Her spell seemed to be escalating more out of control by the moment.

"Go home," she said to Victor, pointing sternly in the direction of the gate. "Get out of here right now."

Victor's angry eyes flashed toward her in disbelief. "You want me to go? But he is the one who started all this."

"I don't care. It is you I want to leave."

"Then . . . then you are choosing him over me?"

"Yes, of course I am."

Victor paled, looking more hurt than when Val had struck him. Kate felt she could almost see the dreams shattering in his eyes. She had not meant to be that blunt, that cruel, but she was desperate to have him gone before anything worse happened.

Snatching up his hat, she thrust it toward him and said more gently, "Please, Victor, just go home and put a beefsteak on that eye before it completely swells shut. I promise you by tomorrow you will have forgotten all about this."

He regarded her for a long agonized moment. "If I can't have you, I don't give a damn about tomorrow."

He wrenched the hat from her grasp. Victor jammed his hat on his head and strode off down the garden path without another word, his shoulders ramrod stiff, trying to appear dignified and proud. All he succeeded in doing was looking young, hurt, and humiliated.

Kate felt heartsick over what she had done to him, but she reassured herself that Victor would be all right. Just as soon as she found a way to lift the spell from him. She was far more concerned about the man who loomed in the summerhouse behind her.

If she had thought Val edgy yesterday, he seemed ten times worse today. He had taken to pacing, clenching and unclenching his fists in an effort to control his rage. Until that moment, Kate had never realized just how much she relied on Val's quiet strength, his steady presence. She was the one always losing her temper, doing something outrageous.

Seeing him this much out of control made her feel strangely lost, even a little frightened, the way she had been before she had ever met him. She huddled in the doorway of the summerhouse until Val came to an abrupt halt, whipping around to glare at her.

"Stop staring at me as though I've grown another head."

"I—I'm sorry," she faltered. "It is just that I have never seen you so—so—"

"So what? So angry? Oh, yes, heaven forbid that Saint Valentine should ever lose his temper. Even when I find the woman I love dallying with another man."

"But you don't understand. I wasn't. I—"

"Tell me, Kate. What did you do? Rush straight from my embrace to his? Is that why I haven't seen you since yesterday?"

"No!" Kate cried, both wounded and astonished by the sheer injustice of the accusation. "Don't you remember? *You* told me to go away, to wait until you came to me."

"Since when have you ever done what I told you?" He bore down upon her and Kate shrank back instinctively. He seized her by the arms. "I give you fair warning, my girl. If I ever catch you near that young fool again, I will shoot him right between the eyes."

"You can't do that. You don't like pistols and St. Legers aren't supposed to fight each other. Even I know that. *The St. Leger who sheds the blood of his own kin is himself doomed.*"

"I'm already risking one curse by loving you. What the devil does one more matter?"

He hauled her against him, his mouth clamping hard down on hers. Kate had longed for the feel of his arms about her, the sweet pressure of his lips against hers, but not like this. It was a kiss that spoke more of anger and possession than love, his lips breaching hers, invading her with the heat of his tongue.

If any other man had treated her thus, Kate would have boxed his ears, kicked him in the shins. But with Val, she was too shocked to resist, stiffly submitting to the ruthless embrace.

When he drew back at last, the look in his eyes was so wild, her heart thudded, half fearing what he meant to do next. He stared down at her for a long moment, then blinked once, twice like a man snapping out of a trance.

He released her, the terrible light in his eyes replaced by an expression of horror.

"Kate, I—I am so sorry," he said hoarsely. "I didn't mean to— Did I hurt you?"

"N-no, of course not," Kate denied, although she did feel bruised and considerably shaken. "You know I am not that fragile."

He reached out, only to draw his hand back as though he were afraid to touch her again.

"I thought I could control it," he muttered, tugging at the neckline of his cloak almost as if something threatened to strangle him.

Control *it*? What did Val mean by that? His temper? His forbidden passion for her? Kate had no idea. But she found the anguish, the bitter self-reproach that darkened his features nigh unbearable.

Her own fears forgotten, she brushed aside those few stubborn tendrils that tumbled across his eyes.

"It is all right," she murmured.

"No, it isn't." Val caught her hand and put it away from him, refusing to accept her comfort. "I almost hurt you and Victor. Dear God, I felt like I could have killed him and enjoyed doing it. When I found the two of you here together, I was seized by such a demon of jealousy."

"But, Val, you have absolutely no reason to be jealous of Victor."

"Don't I?" His dark eyes searched her face.

"Of course not. How can you even ask such a thing? You know it is you I have always loved."

"Aye, but he's very handsome and certainly a good deal younger than me. Closer to your own age."

"Pooh! I am far older than Victor. I am sure I must be, oh, at least twenty-six."

"More likely not a day over sixteen," Val retorted, but at least she succeeded in coaxing a smile from him, a shadow of his old familiar smile, that wry half quirking of the lips she had always so loved.

He looked once more like her Val, and she melted toward him with a tiny sigh of relief.

"How could you be so foolish?" she chided gently. "As if the years between us have ever mattered. I have never been any dewy-eyed young miss. Sometimes I think I was born old."

"I know that, my dear, and it is something I have always wanted to change for you."

"How? By keeping me a girl forever?"

"No." Val cupped her face between his hands, tracing the tender area beneath her eyes with the pads of his thumbs. "By banishing the shadows, all the bad memories of your youth, those terrible days in London."

Bending down, he pressed a fervent kiss to the top of her head. "Oh, Kate, the last thing I ever want to do is give you more bad memories, more nightmares."

"As if you ever could."

"I wish I was as sure of that." He stared down at her, a brooding expression stealing into his eyes. "I do love you, Kate. But if you had any sense at all, you would run from me, just as fast as you can."

But since he accompanied those extraordinary words by holding her close to his heart, Kate was not unduly alarmed. She burrowed her face against his greatcoat that smelled of fresh salt air and of Val, the ink that frequently stained his fingers, the leather of his books.

"Why would I ever want to run away," she asked, "when I have spent most of my life running to you, shamelessly pursuing you? Why, I even—"

"Even what?" Val prompted when she hesitated.

I even resorted to witchcraft to win you. Kate swallowed hard, knowing she ought to tell him what she'd done. Considering what had almost happened with Victor, her spell had taken a rather dangerous turn.

When she tipped up her head to look at him, his eyes blazed with such love, such passion, her breath caught in her throat. Everything she'd ever wanted from him, ever dreamed of, seemed to shimmer in his gaze. But it was more than that which held her silent.

It was the thought that out of everyone, Val had been the first to believe in her, to find some good in her. If he ever realized how truly wicked and selfish she really was, she might forfeit his regard, his respect, forever. And that would be more unbearable than losing his love.

She swallowed hard and avoided his question by hugging him fiercely and kissing him instead. His arms tightened around her. Val no longer seemed to be making much effort to resist the dark magic she had woven.

His mouth melded to hers until he was kissing her with a passion that amounted to desperation. Kate kissed him back, feeling equally as desperate, burying all her fears, her doubts in the heat of his embrace. His mouth moved hungrily over hers, her lips devoured his.

She clung to him, feeling like they were two lovers hovering on the brink of some violent storm. This love, this passion between them, was supposed to be so wrong, forbidden. Then why did it feel so right?

Val's hands roved over her back, exploring the curve of her hips, the swell of her bottom, cupping her against him. The endless layers of clothing between them proved a frustrating barrier, but she was still aware of the full extent of his arousal. It filled her with a dark excitement.

Her lips parted before his fierce onslaught and she moaned softly when his tongue engaged hers in a wild mating. Val could have tugged her to the floor of the summerhouse and made love to her then and there, and Kate felt as though she would not have been able to resist.

It didn't matter if they ran the risk of being seen from the house, even if the entire world was watching. Just as long as Val kept kissing her, kept holding her this way, Kate felt as if nothing could ever go wrong.

She uttered a faint protest when he broke the heated contact, his ragged breath mingling with hers.

"What a mad, reckless creature you are, Kate Fitzleger," he said with a shaky laugh. "I suppose if you are going to risk being cursed for any St. Leger, it might as well be me."

"There is no curse. And even if there was, I wouldn't care. I'd risk anything to be with you, even my life."

"Don't say that. If something were to happen to you, I believe I would run mad. If I were to ever lose you—"

"You won't."

"Ah, but you don't understand what that stupid Victor has done by going to my brother, insisting he intends to marry you. Lance wants to send you away. To London."

"Oh, Effie has talked about that for years."

"But this time it is serious, Kate. It's going to happen. Lance is providing the money."

Kate's eyes widened in surprise. She had always considered Lance St. Leger her friend, the teasing, often provoking older brother she had never had. And now Lance was willing to pay to be rid of her. She felt a sharp stab of hurt.

"Why would Lance do a thing like that?" she asked.

"To keep you out of harm's way. To protect you and Victor. Prevent you from invoking the St. Leger curse."

The curse. That infernal legend again. Kate stifled a groan, wondering if she was never to be free of it. She firmed her lips into a stubborn line.

"Well, it doesn't matter what Lance is planning. I simply won't go."

"You have no idea how determined my brother can be."

Kate frowned, knowing that was true. Lance St. Leger could be the most playful and easygoing of men. But if he had the notion he was acting for someone's own good, he would be downright ruthless. She had no difficulty imagining Lance abducting her, carrying her off to London by force if he thought it necessary.

She raised troubled eyes to Val. "So what do you suggest I do?"

"To keep you from being sent away? There is only one solution." Val smiled at her. "I will simply have to marry you as soon as possible."

Marry her? Kate's heart skipped a beat. She had waited forever for Val to say those words and she should have been overjoyed. Part of her was. She flung her arms about his neck, exchanging another long, enthusiastic kiss. But she was immediately sobered by the realities of their situation.

"I suppose we shall have to elope," she said.

"Elope?" Val scowled. "No, by God. You shall have a proper wedding, my Kate. With bridesmaids, ribbon favors, and a beautiful gown."

"Oh, Val, you know I have never cared about such things."

"But *I* care that you should have them." His words were tender enough, but the set of his jaw was grim, an almost martial light springing to his eyes. He looked ready to take on his family, the entire village if need be, for the privilege of leading her down the aisle at St. Gothian's.

Usually it was Kate who had always been stubborn, defiant, and Val the calm, sensible one. Kate was beginning to find this reversal of roles more than a little disconcerting. She eased out of his arms, attempting to reason with him.

"Being married here in Torrecombe might prove very difficult. Not without your family's approval and my guardian's consent. I am not even sure we could persuade Reverend Trimble to perform the ceremony."

"Oh, he'll be persuaded."

Something in Val's tone made Kate wary. "You are not planning to give him a black eye, too, are you?" she asked anxiously.

"Not if the man is reasonable."

Kate found Val's quick laugh far from reassuring. But before she had time to argue with him, he seized her by the hand, tugging her down the path toward the house. "Come, we shall begin right now by finding Effie and demanding her consent."

Kate hung back in alarm. Val confront Effie in his present unpredictable humor? He would terrify Kate's poor guardian out of her wits.

"No, Val, please. You must allow me to break the news to Effie alone. You know how she is."

"Aye, a stupid, meddling, foolish wench."

Kate froze, deeply shocked. Granted, Val certainly had reason to feel some anger toward Effie. As the St. Leger Bride Finder, she had completely failed him. But Kate had rarely ever heard Val speak with such bitterness, such harshness toward anyone, not even his great enemy Rafe Mortmain. It disturbed her more than any of Val's erratic behavior thus far.

"I know Effie can be very trying, but she is also the kindest, most tenderhearted creature imaginable. As you yourself have often told me," Kate reminded him. "I have caused her enough worry over the years. I don't want to distress her more than necessary."

Val's lips thinned. He looked annoyed, but he shrugged. "Very well. You may deal with Effie yourself as long as you promise to meet me later."

"Where?"

"By the church. We shall go speak to the vicar. It hardly matters if Effie refuses her consent. You are well above age, by your own accounts. What was it you said you are . . . almost thirty?"

Kate tried to smile at his teasing, but everything suddenly seemed to be moving much too quickly, threatening to slip out of her control. She needed a moment to—

She blinked in pure astonishment at her own thought. Kate Fitzleger trying not to be too impulsive? Wanting time to pause and reflect? Exactly which one of them had been changed by that spell she had cast on All Hallows' Eve?

Val was so adamant, she had little choice but to agree, although she pleaded for a little more time. The missing spell book heavy on her mind, she said, "There is this small matter I need to attend to first."

"Very well." Val paused by the garden gate. Gathering both her hands into his, he kissed first one and then the other. "We shall meet this evening, but don't be late. It grows dark early and I don't want you coming to me after the sun has set."

"There is no problem with that. I have frequently walked through the village after dark. It is certainly safe enough here in Torrecombe—"

"I said *no!*"

The unexpected fierceness of his tone took Kate completely aback.

Val gripped her hands. "Let me make one thing clear to you, Kate. Under no circumstances are you to come near me after the sun has gone down."

"W-what?" Kate stared at him, incredulous. He could not possibly be serious. "And what happens when the sun goes down? Do you turn into some sort of monster?"

But he didn't respond to her jest, his mouth hard and unsmiling, that unnerving intensity in his eyes.

"I mean it, Kate. Until we are married, stay away."

"But—"

"Damn it, girl! For once do as you are told." His grip on her hands tightened almost painfully. When Kate winced, Val relaxed his grasp, moderating his tone.

"Just promise me, Kate."

"A-all right. I promise," Kate said reluctantly, although it still made not the least bit of sense to her.

"Good." Val kissed her one last time, an embrace that left her breathless and trembling. Then he was gone.

Kate clung to the garden gate long after he had vanished, her heart in complete turmoil. She was betrothed, actually betrothed, to Val St. Leger. Her mouth felt bruised and tender from his kisses, her body still flushed with a warm glow. Then why did another part of her feel so cold, even a trifle afraid?

Val was behaving strangely, even for one under the influence of a love spell. His passion was incredible, more than she had ever imagined. But so were his outbursts of temper, his flashes of bitterness. His eyes burned with equal parts desire for her and torment. Like a man who was at war with his own soul.

Perhaps Victor St. Leger was not the only one who needed to be released from her spell.

But the mere thought of surrendering Val filled her with despair, brought a painful lump to her throat. Kate was quick to reject the notion. She couldn't give up now, not when she was this close to becoming Val's bride, to finding some measure of happiness at last, not just for herself, but for both of them. Hadn't Val himself said that he would run mad if he were to lose her?

Aye, of course he did. What did you expect him to say? You have bewitched him as much as you did Victor.

Kate struggled to quell her doubts, the icy voice of her conscience. No, everything would be all right as soon as she and Val were safely married. He would settle down, become more like himself again.

If he was edgy now, a little erratic, it was only because her sorcery had gone slightly awry. She had made him angry and jealous over Victor. Once Victor was released from her spell, all would be well. Or at least so Kate sought to convince herself.

The difficulty now was in finding a way to straighten out the disaster she had created. Unfortunately, with the spell book missing, there was only one person in the world who could help her do that.

Kate shivered. That is, if the great sorcerer didn't reduce her to a pile of ashes first.

CHAPTER ELEVEN

*D*ark clouds hung over the ancient tower, the air heavy with the scent of an impending storm. Even the sun appeared to have wisely hidden itself away as Kate mounted the rough stone stair spiraling upward through the tower's thick walls.

The cold gray light filtered through the arrow slits, rendering the passage full of gloom and shadow, even more forbidding than it had been upon her first visit. Kate picked her way forward with care, wishing she could turn back.

Perhaps if she were fortunate, Prospero would have vanished back to that strange netherworld he inhabited between hauntings. Kate despised herself for the cowardly hope. She needed him to be there, needed his help.

But what the devil was she going to say to him?

"Remember that spell book you forbade me to touch? Well, uh, I sort of borrowed it anyway and—and then I sort of lost it."

Kate cringed. She was stumbling over explanations even in her own mind. When she finally confronted Prospero's enraged stare, no doubt she would be reduced to total incoherence.

But she forced herself to keep going, her heart skittering a nervous beat when she realized a light glowed from the chamber above her. As she cleared the last step, she peered across the threshold.

An eerie fire blazed upon the vast stone hearth. The flames burned with a blue-gold intensity, but they threw out no heat, the room so damp and chill, Kate shivered. The phantom blaze did cast an extraordinary amount of light, illuminating every corner of the circular chamber, the intricately carved bed, the shelves of mysterious vials, the books, the small writing desk. A medieval sanctum that remained suspended in time as much so as the man who hovered by the tower windows did.

Kate's breath snagged in her throat when she caught sight of the sorcerer. Prospero lounged in a reclined position, one elbow bent, his hand propping up his dark head as he perused some ancient text. The firelight bathed him in a golden glow, highlighting the blue-black sheen of his hair and beard, picking out the iridescent threads in his velvet tunic.

He looked for all the world like an idle knight whiling away a gloom-ridden afternoon by engaging in some scholarly pursuit, his swarthy skin, broad shoulders, and muscular legs making him appear as solid and real as any man. Except for one small detail.

Both Prospero and his book were floating in midair.

He did not even trouble to glance up at Kate's entrance, although she was quite certain that he was aware of her presence. She crept forward, feeling as timid as a beggar maid about to approach a mighty king.

"P-prospero?"

Her voice came out in a quaver and Kate had to force herself to speak up. "My lord?"

Prospero glanced up from his book at last, his dark eyes glinting through the thickness of his lashes. "Mistress Kate."

Kate had the curious feeling he had been expecting her all along, that he was not entirely displeased to see her again. She feared that would change fast enough as soon as he discovered the nature of her errand. The sorcerer closed up his book, drifting to his feet to sweep her an elegant bow.

"And to what do I owe the honor of this visit? Have you come for more deportment lessons?"

"N-no. I—I needed to tell you that I—" She broke off, her gaze riveted by the book he clutched, a small, slender volume with a cracked leather binding. A book that looked disconcertingly familiar. She stepped closer, all fear suddenly forgotten. She stared in sheer disbelief at the dragon emblem emblazoned on the cover.

The missing book of spells! It had been neither lost nor stolen. Somehow it had sprouted wings, flown straight back to its master. Kate was so giddy with relief, she almost thought she would faint. Then relief was swiftly replaced by indignation.

She glared accusingly at Prospero. "You took the book from my room. You—you knew I had it all along."

Prospero bowed his head in mocking acknowledgment.

"You might have told me so instead of retrieving the book in that under-handed way, letting me think it had gone missing."

"I sought to recover my stolen property and neglected to inform you? How remiss of me," he drawled. "I do crave your pardon, my dear."

"Do you have any idea how worried I was? How distressed I have been ever since All Hallows' Eve?"

"Aye, it was indeed a distressing night. Strange reports abroad of some half-wild gypsy girl lighting a bonfire near the old standing stone. Then that terrible storm. Enough to give one bad dreams, perhaps of lightning bolts, the village afire, mobs of angry villagers pursuing one through the streets. Brrrr." Prospero gave a mock shudder.

Kate gaped at him, wondering how he could have known about her night-mare. From the wicked gleam in his eye, the answer was far too obvious.

"It was *you*. You were responsible for my dream."

Prospero polished the nails of one hand lightly against the front of his tu-nic. "Just another of my modest talents. The ability to fashion dreams, send them drifting through the night to intrude upon someone else's slumber."

"How could you do such a cruel thing to me?" Kate exclaimed. "That dream you sent me was horrible."

"I had hoped it might teach you a lesson about tampering with the black arts. But apparently not, since here you are again." Prospero rolled his eyes in long-suffering fashion. He noticed that she was taking far too tender of an in-terest in his book and held it well out of her reach.

"Oh, please," Kate said. "I *need* that book, need your help more now than ever."

"As I have already informed you, my dear, I make it a point never to meddle in human concerns."

"You meddle all the time. Whenever it suits *you* to do so." The retort es-caped Kate before she could stop it. The last thing she wanted to do was anger him.

Prospero stiffened for a moment, then relaxed into a reluctant smile. "True enough, but I do try to steer clear of any matters of the heart. So if you have come to plague me yet again for that love spell—"

"No, no! I only need your help to undo the spell I already cast. Or at least part of it."

"The spell you cast?" Prospero looked mightily amused. "I fear you are suf-fering from delusions of grandeur, milady."

"I tell you that I *did*. Using your book."

"Impossible. You couldn't even begin to decipher my secret writings."

"Secret writings? Piffle! Those are Egyptian hieroglyphics and I assure you many scholars have been able to translate them for years."

The sorcerer appeared thunderstruck. His jaw actually fell open. He clamped it closed, looking as though he didn't know whether to be more amazed or affronted that mere mortals now shared in his knowledge.

"So you *were* able to read my book?"

"Easily. Well, not entirely," Kate amended. "I must have misread part of it, or my incantation would not have gone so terribly wrong. I didn't manage to cast my love spell on just one man, but on two of them."

Prospero stared at her, then burst out into a roar of laughter, the rich masculine sound filling the tower chamber. His eyes shone with a mingling of mirth and admiration.

"You managed to bewitch two men with one spell? On your very first try? Brava, milady."

"It is not a matter for congratulations," Kate said. "You have no idea how horrible it is, being pursued by two men, having them threaten to fight a duel over you."

"Most women would find that delightful."

"I am not most women!"

"I am fast coming to realize that." Prospero's eyes gleamed with frank appreciation.

"Now the man I love is jealous, and the other man, the one I didn't want, is quite brokenhearted by my rejection of him," Kate said. "I never wanted to hurt anyone. All I wanted was to be loved."

Prospero must have perceived the full measure of her distress for his mirth faded, his expression softening.

"My dear Kate. Likely you blame yourself over nothing. Casting such a spell would be most difficult even with the aid of my book. Isn't it just possible that these two swains of yours became smitten with you without the aid of any magic?"

Kate sighed. How she would have liked to believe that, not about Victor, of course, but Val. To think that Val had fallen naturally in love with her, truly did adore her so much that he was willing to defy his family traditions, the St. Leger legend itself.

But she shook her head, knowing better. "I fear I am not that charming. Even my own mother did not find me that loveable. She gave me away."

"So did mine."

Startled, Kate's eyes flew to his face. "You? You are a bastard, too?"

"Aye. In more ways than one. Or so some of my former mistresses would have been happy to inform you."

His dry jest could not entirely conceal a rare of flash of vulnerability, some remembered pain similar to her own. His eyes locked with Kate's and for a brief moment, she felt as though they shared some inexplicable bond. Prospero quickly hooded his gaze, stalking away from her.

The phantom firelight played across his handsome face, stroking shadows upon his hawklike profile. He lapsed into silence as though lost in deep reflection, and Kate realized he was actually considering her request, contemplating coming to her aid.

She held her breath, afraid to speak, fearful of tipping the balance against her.

"So exactly what would you like me to do?" he asked.

"Not a great deal. Only help me to undo the spell."

"*Only.*" Prospero gave a dry laugh. He cast her a long, inscrutable look. "Remove the spell from both men?"

"No, of course not. Only the one I bewitched by accident."

"Then you would still pursue this other reluctant swain of yours? You must love him greatly to risk so much, to even consider invoking such dark magic again."

"I do," Kate cried. "I'd risk anything, even life itself, to be with him."

"If I were yet mortal, I could almost envy him," Prospero said softly.

A ghost could not properly be said to sigh, but a sound close to it escaped Prospero's lips. "All right," he conceded at last. "I will see what I can do."

"Oh! Thank you." Kate was so grateful she could have flung her arms about the sorcerer's neck and kissed him. She came close to acting on the impulse and Prospero must have realized it.

"A lovely thought, milady," he said with a wry smile. "But quite impossible."

Kate blushed furiously.

"And please remember that I have promised nothing. I said only that I would try."

"But surely you will succeed. A great sorcerer such as yourself and with all your experience with love spells. What about all those women you seduced?"

"It was not love I ever sought from women, only lust. And I assure you it requires no magic to induce that."

Cracking open the spell book, he proceeded to riffle through the pages. Kate hovered near his shoulder, torn between hope and dread, fearing he would demand to know the names of the men she had bewitched.

If he were yet to discover she had been practicing her dark magic upon St. Legers, Kate doubted the sorcerer would remain so amiable. But to her relief, he asked no questions other than requiring her to point out the exact spell she had used.

Prospero perused it briefly, his brow furrowing in concentration. "Very well," he said. "I think I might know a way to undo the magic. Return to me in one month's time."

"A month!" Kate could not conceal her dismay. "I was hoping you could do something right now. Can you not proceed a little faster?"

Prospero's brows arched upward in a haughty line. "Even I cannot speed up the movement of the heavens. If there is to be any hope at all of altering your spell, it must be done at the same phase of the moon you originally cast it."

"Oh." Kate sought to swallow her disappointment. But an entire month! Anything could happen in that time.

"I will be fortunate if Vict— I mean if my two, er, swains have not killed each other by then," she said.

"You must do your best to keep them apart."

"And just how am I to do that? It is a very small village."

"You are a very resourceful young woman. I am sure you will think of something."

Kate started to protest further, but saw clearly that it would do no good. Prospero closed up the book and drifted over to the hearth. With one graceful gesture of his hand, he caused the fire to flicker and die. No charred wood, no ash remained. The flames had been fueled by a multifaceted chunk of crystal very similar to the one set into the hilt of the St. Leger sword, only much larger.

Even with the blaze gone, the crystal continued to pulse and glow as though possessed of some strange life of its own, sending out fragments of rainbow colored light intense enough it seemed to pierce the very walls.

Her own worries momentarily forgotten, Kate trailed after Prospero to stare down at the glittering stone in awe.

"What is that thing?" she asked.

"Part of an experiment I did when I was yet alive, a little dabbling in alchemy."

Prospero bent down and lifted the crystal from the hearth, cradling it in his long supple fingers. The light it radiated was so brilliant, Kate flung up one hand to shield her eyes.

"This piece was once part of a much larger crystal I had created, but something went awry. There was a terrible explosion and when the smoke cleared, only a few chunks remained. One portion I imbedded in the hilt of my sword to be handed down to my descendants. This one I kept for myself."

He held the stone closer for her inspection and Kate stared at it, half mesmerized, the stone's beauty at once seeming to be so warm, so cold. She stretched out her fingers to touch it.

"Don't do that!"

The sorcerer's sharp warning caused her to snatch her hand back.

"Is it dangerous then?" Kate asked.

"It could be, especially if I were to drop it, causing it to break again. I have noticed that each fragment that snaps off from the whole tends to become more unstable. The smaller the piece, the more unpredictable the magic can become, even deadly."

Kate shivered, taking a wary step away from the sparkling stone. And to think that Prospero had upbraided her for tampering with dark magic.

"Why did you even seek to invent something so dangerous?" she asked. "I suppose like most alchemists you were trying to find a way to transform lead into gold."

"No, I never had any use for gold. I had all the fortune I required, all the power."

"Then what? What were you seeking?"

"Immortality. I wanted to live forever." Prospero's lips pulled back in an ironic smile. "So take great care, my young friend, about using magic to chase your dreams. You might just end up getting what you wished for."

Kate frowned. Was he warning her to abandon her stubborn pursuit of the man she loved? Or were Prospero's words merely meant to be a sad reflection on his own fate?

She was given no opportunity to question him further. He stalked away, waving her off with an imperious gesture of one hand. He clearly considered her visit at an end. Prospero packed the mesmerizing stone away, locking it in the velvet-lined depths of an ancient chest.

With the crystal shut away, the chamber plunged into semidarkness. Was it truly growing that late? Or was the gloom merely owing to the gathering storm clouds outside? Kate remembered her promise to meet Val at the church, his strange words of warning.

"Under no circumstances are you to come near me after the sun has gone down."

Taking a hasty leave of Prospero, she tugged up the hood of her cloak and scurried back down the tower stairs. She managed to steal away from Castle Leger without awkward encounters with any of the servants. Keeping to the shadows, she struck out on the well-worn road that led back to the village, unaware that she was being observed by a phantom figure perched high atop the castle walls.

Prospero drifted along the tower ramparts, peering down from his lordly height, wondering what devil possessed him. He had allowed himself to become involved with few mortals over the centuries he had haunted Castle Leger.

So why now? Why this one? What was it about the girl that so moved him, he who had long ago cleansed himself of any human emotions? Was it her spirit, her courage, her passion? The ruthless fashion she pursued her dreams and damned all costs? So many bitter and sweet reminders of his own folly, the reckless way he had lived his own life.

"I must be quite mad," he murmured. To have ever agreed to help her, especially when he had more pressing worries. That sense of foreboding that had first drawn him back to Castle Leger had not lessened, only deepened with the passing of days.

The nagging presentiment persisted. Only now it seemed to be centered more and more on Kate. Something threatened the girl, something beyond a foolish miscast love spell.

Something evil. Yet try as he might, Prospero could not fathom what it was. It was like a heavy curtain had been drawn before his eyes, refusing to be parted. All he could do was watch as Kate vanished down the darkening road, a small, fragile figure who appeared to be rushing headlong into the eye of the storm.

And for all his vaunted powers, Prospero felt quite helpless to protect her.

CHAPTER TWELVE

*V*al prowled along the low stone fence that surrounded the churchyard, his black cloak snapping at his heels, a sharp wind whipping his hair
across his eyes. He brushed it back impatiently, eyeing the lane behind him,
all but swallowed up in the evening gloom.

The village appeared deserted, everyone having retreated to their own fire-
sides, fastening their shutters tight against the impending storm.

So where the devil was Kate? Blast the girl. She had already forgotten her
promise to meet him before night fell. Dark clouds shifted across the sky,
threatening to steal away what little day remained, and Val could feel the tension in him coil tighter.

He struggled to calm himself, staring up at the church that loomed over
him. It had ever conveyed to Val an aura of gentle peace and strong faith. St.
Gothian's was a simple stone structure erected in the shape of a cross.

But it had also been built over the site of an old druid altar, and it was the
pagan part of the rugged land beneath his feet that called to Val this evening.
The wind tearing through the trees whispered to him of barbaric warriors invading the quiet village. Men who had no need of vicars, who would have
charged in and simply taken the women they wanted.

Val felt his own blood stir, his body growing hard.

Maybe he had no use for a blasted clergyman either. All he needed was the
maiden with gypsy black hair and quicksilver gray eyes, her breasts firm, her

thighs soft and welcoming. She'd challenge him with that teasing smile and he would fling Kate over his shoulder, carry her off to—

Val pressed his hand against his eyes, struggling to check the lust-filled images that flashed through his mind. He tugged at the chain fastened around his neck. It was the crystal prompting these dark desires, rousing the more primitive part of his St. Leger blood.

God knows he should have gotten rid of the thing, especially after what had happened this afternoon, the way he had attacked Victor, been so rough with Kate. The stone was weakening him, breaking down his lifelong barriers of reserve, decency, and honor.

But as his fingers inched beneath his cloak, he was seized by a sensation of defiance. No, damn it! The stone wasn't weakening him. It was making him stronger, more powerful than he had ever been.

His crystal, his magic now, and he could control it. At least as long as some daylight remained. Val moistened his lips, nervously studying the sky. Perhaps it would be wiser if he did not wait for Kate. He would go see the vicar himself, arrange for this marriage while he was still able to keep his thoughts focused more on nuptials and less on simply dragging Kate to bed.

Val vaulted over the low stone wall that surrounded the churchyard, his boots striking the earth with a soft thud. The rectory was positioned in the little lane behind the church, and Val cut across the cemetery to reach it.

Some found the graveyard eerie even in full daylight. But Val had been a doctor for too long, was too familiar with death to have any fear of it. He strode on, barely noticing the memorials to souls long fled until he was struck with the first chill. Like icy fingers grasping him by the nape of the neck.

Val's flesh prickled, his footsteps faltered. The cold seemed to rush up out of the ground, seeping through his boots, chilling him to the marrow of his bones. He glanced around to find himself in the oldest, most neglected part of the cemetery, many of the stones around him so old and broken, it was like being surrounded by a jagged row of dragon's teeth.

Most of the names were worn and faded. He could no longer read them. It didn't matter. Val knew well who owned this part of the graveyard, which rested so unquiet beneath his feet.

The Mortmains, his family's most ancient enemies.

He stumbled back as though he could feel their evil reaching out to infect him even from beyond the grave. When his boot struck up against a headstone newer than the rest, Val let fly a startled oath. Despite the fading light, the name on this marker was still clear.

Evelyn Mortmain
1761–1789

When Val had been a boy, he recalled how indignant he had been that this creature should even be laid to rest upon St. Gothian's holy ground, this evil woman who had schemed to murder both his parents and nearly succeeded. She had come to a violent end and she had deserved it. Like all the Mortmains before her.

Val wanted to stride on, avoid this part of the cemetery as he'd always done. But he found himself unable to move, unable to stop staring at her headstone. It had never occurred to him before, but Evelyn Mortmain had been full young when she died.

Not even thirty. Such a waste of a life, spent on hatred and vengeance, all gentleness set aside, all love forgotten.

Val was completely unprepared for the wave of bitterness and grief that washed over him. It clogged his throat, constricted his chest, and brought a furious stinging to his eyes. He blinked hard, shaken to realize he was all but weeping. Weeping for a Mortmain, wanting to mourn over her grave almost as if she had been his own mother. But it wasn't his pain, his sense of loss he was feeling.

It was Rafe Mortmain's.

How the devil was that possible?

Val stumbled back, sagging against the rough wooden bark of an oak tree. He passed a trembling hand over his face, once more straining to remember what had happened on All Hallows' Eve. A night so much like this one with its wild winds, thunder rumbling in the distance.

Except something dark and terrible had happened that night. Rafe had been ill, dying. Val had tried to help the man, used his power, reached out his hand and—and something had transferred between him and Rafe, something more than that crystal. Something that left Val with the terrified feeling that— He shuddered.

The feeling that his soul was no longer entirely his own.

Val was missing.

Kate paced along the lane, trying not to be unduly alarmed. His new white stallion was tethered to the lych-gate by the churchyard, looking like some phantom horse in the dying light, tossing its silvery mane, pawing restively at the ground.

Val would never have abandoned the horse like that, not with a storm coming on. He had to be around here somewhere, but she had already called in at the parsonage. She was so late, she thought Val might have gone to consult the vicar without her, but Mr. Trimble had merely been astonished by her inquiry.

Dr. St. Leger? No, he had not seen the gentleman all day.

Nor had anyone at the Dragon's Fire Inn. Or at Rosebriar Cottage. She'd hoped to find that Val had grown impatient with waiting for her, had gone to her home to fetch her. But he hadn't.

So where was he? Val couldn't have simply vanished into thin air. He wasn't Prospero.

Kate peered once more down the darkening lane, fretting her lower lip. She wasn't the only one who was worried. Jem Sparkins was out searching for his master, too. It seemed that Val's presence was urgently needed at Slate House by one of his patients.

"And it just isn't like the doctor to go off this way without telling anyone," Jem had told her, his broad brow furrowed with concern. "I don't mind tellin' you, Miss Kate, that Master Val hasn't been acting at all like himself lately."

That was the understatement of the year, Kate thought grimly. She had not even been able to meet Jem's honest eyes, knowing full well who was responsible for the change in Val.

She'd realized that he had been behaving strangely when he'd left her earlier today. She should have never let him go, Kate berated herself. Now Jem was off searching the outlying lanes past the village and Kate needed to do something besides pace in front of St. Gothian's, wringing her hands.

It was then that it occurred to her that she had never looked inside the church, perhaps because it was the last place she would have thought of going herself. She peered dubiously at the small stone building. It looked far too dark and silent for anyone to be inside, but she might as well check. It was better than standing here waiting for Jem to return.

She slipped past the low stone fence and hurried up the few steps to the front door. The massive oak portal creaked in protest when she eased it open, and the interior of the church itself did not seem any more welcoming.

She crept through the tiny vestibule and peeked into the nave. The place looked far different on a storm-ridden evening than it did on those serene Sunday mornings she squirmed on the pew beside Effie. The altar, the pulpit, and the magnificent relief at the back at the church were all but lost in the solemn shadows cast by what little light did still filter through the latticed windows.

"Val?" Kate called in a hushed whisper.

She met with no response other than the heavy silence. Kate half turned to go, and she might have missed him entirely but for the sudden flare of lightning that lit up the nave's interior.

She spotted him huddled over in the very front pew, his head bowed. Kate thought he was lost in earnest prayer until she hurried down the aisle, moving closer. Then she realized that his hands were clenched together more in desperation than devotion and he was trembling.

"Val?" She touched him lightly on the shoulder. He started as though she had struck him.

His head jerked up and even in the dim light, she could see how pale he was, his eyes two dark hollows. He looked almost . . . frightened. But Val had ever been so brave in that calm, quiet way of his. She had never known him to be afraid of anything, and that thought alarmed her more than anything did.

"What is wrong?" she asked. "Are you all right?"

He answered her by hoarsely murmuring her name, flinging his arms about her waist, burying his face against her cloak. He held her so tight, as though he would never let her go, as though she were his last link to sanity.

Kate hugged him fiercely, stroking his hair, trying to murmur soothing words of reassurance although she had not the least idea what was wrong and her own heart clenched with fear.

He released her at last with a deep shudder. Kate sank down on the pew beside him, brushing back the disheveled lengths of dark hair from his face, anxiously studying his countenance.

"My God, Val, what is it? Are you ill?"

"No," he muttered.

She didn't believe him. She pressed her hand to his brow. His skin felt clammy and cold, but he brushed her fingers impatiently aside.

"Don't fret over me, Kate. Remember, I am the doctor. I think I would know if I was unwell."

"Then tell me what is wrong. You look as if you've seen a ghost."

He gave an odd mirthless laugh. "Perhaps I did, but it was not a ghost that belonged to me."

His answer made no sense. He was alarming her more by the minute. He straightened, smoothing back his own hair. Taking in a deep breath, he appeared to make great effort to regain command of himself.

When he turned back to her again, he seemed more himself. He even forced his lips back into a semblance of a smile.

"Stop looking so worried, Kate. I merely grew tired of waiting for you and came in here to rest. Where the blazes have you been?"

"I am sorry I was late. My errand for Effie took longer than I expected."

Errand for Effie? Kate winced, ducking her head. She hated lying to Val. She seemed to be doing far too much of that lately.

He crooked his fingers beneath her chin. His hand was steadier now and he forced her to look up at him, his own eyes narrowing.

"You weren't with *him* again, were you?"

"W-with who?" Kate faltered. Was it possible that Val somehow knew of her meetings with Prospero?

"With that young fool Victor. That's who!"

"Oh. Of course not." Kate relaxed, partly relieved that her secret was safe but dismayed to discover that Val still feared she might betray him with another man.

Val had always trusted her before. He was one of the few people who did. Was this was what being in love did to a man, rendered him so dark and suspicious? Or only a man unfortunate enough to fall in love with Kate Fitzleger?

If Val continued this jealousy, it was going to prove a long, grim month until she was able to get that spell removed from Victor. Kate knew no other way to reassure Val other than to fling her arms around him, pressing her lips to his.

But he thrust her away from him and stood up abruptly.

"You had better go before the storm breaks."

His actions disturbed her as much as his words. She didn't want to leave him, not like this with everything seeming all wrong between them. But she remembered that Jem Sparkins was also scouring the village for Val.

"You have to go, too," she said. "Jem has been looking all over for you. Mrs. McGinty's grandson came to Slate House to fetch you out to her farm. He says his grandmother has taken a very bad turn."

Kate slipped out of the seat, fully expecting Val to go rushing past her, hastening off as he always did when someone needed him. She was surprised when he didn't move. He just stood there.

When he noticed her staring at him, his lips thinned and he hunched his shoulders in a faint shrug. "Mrs. McGinty always claims to be in a bad way. There is nothing wrong with the woman except for a touch of rheumatism and loneliness since her husband died. Neither one of which I can cure."

"But you usually do go out to sit with her for a while, bear her company."

"It is not my company she desires. She wants only what they all want from me."

When Kate regarded him in confusion, he flung up his right hand.

"This!" he said bitterly, splaying his fingers before her eyes. "My cursed power."

Kate was unable to conceal her dismay.

"What? Have I shocked you now, Kate?"

"Yes. I—I mean no," she stammered. "It is just that I have never heard you speak of your power that way. You always seemed to consider it a—a—"

"A gift? A blessing? Maybe at one time I did before—before—" He didn't complete the thought, pacing down the line of pews, running his hand along the worn wood and scowling.

"Do you know how old I was the first time I discovered I possessed such a strange power?"

"No." Kate was surprised to realize she didn't. She thought she knew practically everything about Val St. Leger, but this was something they had never discussed.

"I was only six years old." He slapped the palm of his right hand on top of a pew for emphasis. "Playing at seek and dare with Lance in the gardens at Castle Leger. I never found him but I found one of our butler's children crying beneath the azalea bush.

"Little Sally Sparkins. It seemed she had scraped her elbow and she had these enormous tears spilling down her cheeks. I only wanted to comfort her, get her to stop weeping, so I touched her hand.

"She only cried harder and I didn't know what else to do, so I clutched her hand harder, wishing with all my might I could make her stop hurting, and then something strange happened. My palm began to tingle."

Val flexed his hand, staring down at it as though he was reliving the sensation. "It felt as though my very veins were opening up and then there was this incredible rush of power. The next thing I knew Sally had stopped crying. Of course my own elbow hurt like the very devil for a while, but that didn't seem important.

"That little girl looked up at me, her eyes shining with such gratitude, such awe. And I felt it, too. To possess such a power, Kate, to be strong enough to absorb someone else's pain, to bring such relief to another human being, especially one you care about, one that you love."

Val's face softened, his eyes filling with the wonder he must have once felt. But the expression vanished as quickly as it had come, his mouth turning down.

"I don't know what has gone wrong," he said. "Maybe I am just not strong enough anymore or maybe there have finally been too many butler's daughters, too many Mrs. McGintys, too many hurting people beating a path to my door.

"And always the same cry. 'You must help me, Dr. St. Leger. Please, take the pain away. You are the only one who can do it. The only one.'"

Val pressed his hand against his eyes.

"Lord, Kate," he said. "I am so very tired of being the only one."

Kate started toward him, longing to comfort him, but she hesitated, fearing he might only push her away again.

He lowered his hand, his eyes filled with such despair, it tore at her heart. "I have never admitted that to anyone before. Not even myself. Now I suppose you will realize that I am not quite the hero you have always believed me to be."

Kate's throat constricted. She rushed toward him and flung her arms about his neck. "Oh, Val, how can you say such things?" she choked. "Don't you realize you are quite simply the best man I have ever known? Everything I have ever learned about kindness, goodness I have learned from you."

He held her close, murmuring into her hair, "I haven't felt particularly kind or good lately. I have changed, Kate. Something terrible has happened to me and I don't quite know what it is."

No, but she did, Kate thought, winking back bitter tears of self-reproach. She had done this to him with her reckless pursuit of her own dreams, forcing him to fall in love with her, weaving her dark spells, never stopping to think what the cost might be to Val himself.

She had to release him, let him go, and even now her wicked, selfish heart recoiled at the thought.

"Val . . ." She took a deep gulp. "What if everything could be put back the way it used to be?"

"What do you mean?"

She lifted her head, hardly daring to look up at him. "What if time could be turned back somehow to the way everything was before All Hallows' Eve? Back to when we were just friends."

Val frowned. "You mean back to being crippled, to sacrificing myself to everyone else's needs, to having no hope of ever being able to love you?"

His lips tightened. "I'd rather be dead."

His words should have reassured her. They left her chilled instead. She clung to him and he held her tight. Outside the thunder rumbled, the lightning flashed as the storm moved closer. Rain started to drum against the stained-glass windows.

It was going to be a dark tempest-tossed night, the sort of night that could make any man believe in legends and curses, reminding Val of his heritage. As if he needed any reminders standing in a church where most of his ancestors had been laid to rest beneath the stone floor.

His gaze tracked to the vestibule where he knew the lady Deidre had been buried, or at least her heart, the only part of her that had remained after those villainous Mortmains had finished with her. Val had long felt a kinship with his unfortunate ancestress, and the connection only seemed stronger now.

Both of them healers in their own different ways, both of them falling in love with someone not chosen by the Bride Finder, and both of them murdered by Mortmains. Val could not accuse Rafe of taking a knife or a pistol to him. He could still not recall precisely what Rafe had done.

But he was left with this sense all the same that Rafe had indeed done him in, that some slow poison was spreading through his veins and it was only going to get worse.

Was it merely a Mortmain's vengeance or the St. Leger curse at work? Val had no idea. He longed to protect Kate while he still had some vestige of sanity left. He had heard that the lady Deidre had managed to save her lover by giving the man a potion that had caused him to forget her.

Even if Val had known how to brew up such a potion, could he have brought himself to give it to Kate? Val stared down at her, feeling her warmth, breathing in her light feminine scent. Could he ever bear for his wild girl to simply walk away, forget him forever?

No, he was no longer capable of such a sacrifice, Val thought in despair. He simply wasn't that noble anymore. Maybe he never had been.

He bent to kiss her. He knew the precise moment when day faded for good, plunging them into darkness. He felt the last vestige of his control slip away from him.

"Oh, Kate," he moaned. "You should have kept your promise. You should have stayed away."

Her only answer was to kiss him more fiercely than ever. And he was lost, all remaining thoughts of honor, the legend, and even marriage slipping from his mind. All he wanted to do was get Kate into the nearest bed.

Sweeping her up in his arms, he carried her out into the storm.

CHAPTER THIRTEEN

*R*afe tried to hasten through the narrow streets, the rumbling skies warning him that the rain could break at any moment. But there seemed to be no hurrying the gray gelding. The horse plodded along as though every step was going to be its last.

Rafe had given over riding the poor brute and taken to leading it instead, muttering imprecations under his breath and wondering why he'd spent the better part of his day searching for the wretched beast, why he'd paid almost double to reclaim it.

The horse jobber he'd originally sold it to had wondered that as well.

"You want to buy back this here old bag of bones?" he had chuckled. "Lord, sir, I think you must have pixies playing tricks with your brain."

No, not pixies, Rafe thought dourly. A St. Leger. Whatever madness had induced him to rescue this broken-down horse was the same one that had made him assume protection of a widowed woman and her little boy. Whatever strange magic Val St. Leger had worked upon him on All Hallows' Eve.

The wind whipped fiercely in between the buildings, causing the inn sign to creak, a shutter to bang up against a window. Men clutching their caps, women huddling beneath shawls shoved past Rafe, scurrying for shelter as a loud crack of thunder sounded. The old horse, usually so docile, spooked at all the commotion.

It didn't attempt to rear on its haunches. There wasn't enough spirit left in the animal for that. But it did whinny and pull back on the reins, refusing to move, as stubborn as any mule.

Rafe tugged futilely, wanting to swear and lash out at the recalcitrant beast. He had never been that good with horses. But something about the terror he saw flaring in the gelding's soft liquid eyes brought him up short. He found himself stroking the horse's muzzle, murmuring soothing words.

"Easy old fellow. It's all right—"

What name was it Charley had given to the old brute?

"It's all right, Rufus," Rafe crooned. "Nothing to be afraid of. This little squall isn't going to be anything. Why, you should have seen some of the tempests I sailed through when I came 'round the cape—"

Rafe brought himself up short. He couldn't believe it. He truly had lost his mind. He was actually talking to a horse, and the astonishing thing was that it seemed to be responding. Between his coaxing and petting, he galvanized Rufus into motion again.

The horse trotted obediently after him the rest of the way to the inn yard. It had always been Rafe's custom to hand over the reins of his horse to the nearest ostler without a second look back.

But he felt compelled to linger, make sure the horse was being well cared for. He watched Rufus being rubbed down, fed an extra measure of oats. As he gave the gelding a final pat and turned to walk away, he almost imagined he saw a spark of gratitude in the gray beast's eyes.

It gave him a strange feeling tight in his chest. He had never been the sort of man before to win the trust of a horse, let alone a woman and a little boy. As he strode off through the darkness, his pace quickened as he approached the lodging where he had left Corinne and Charley.

A simple pair of rooms on the topmost floor of the inn. Not the finest place Rafe had ever stayed in his life, but not the worst either. He glanced upward and saw the candle shine flickering through the windows, like the beacon in a lighthouse leading a weary sailor past jagged reefs, guiding him safely home.

Home . . . Rafe frowned over the word, astonished that its use would even occur to him. There had never been any place in his life that he would have called home unless it was the deck of a ship. Why should he apply it now to a pair of dismal rooms in some backstreet inn?

He took the wooden stairs that stretched upward two at a time, trying to dismiss his haste as mere relief to escape the oncoming rain. Not because he was anticipating the look on Charley's face, Corinne's smile, when he told them he had recovered that wretched horse.

Not pausing to knock, he burst into the lodging, realizing belatedly that the door should have been barred until his return. That had been the last thing he had cautioned Corinne to do when he had left. He'd have to scold her for that later, but for right now . . .

Rafe's gaze tracked eagerly around the small threadbare sitting room. A cozy fire blazed on the hearth, filling the room with warmth. There was no sign of Corinne, but Charley sat curled up in a faded wingback chair pulled up to the window. Rafe crossed over to him.

"Charley, I fetched Rufus to the stables. Do you want to come and—" He broke off, noticing that the boy's head lolled to one side, his light-colored eyelashes resting against his smooth flushed cheeks. The child was fast asleep.

Rafe was conscious of a ridiculous feeling of disappointment. He bent down and lightly shook Charley's thin shoulder. The boy's only response was a low mumble. He shifted away from Rafe's hand, curling his body to the other side of the chair.

A low chuckle echoed from the other side of the room. Rafe turned to see Corinne silhouetted in the shadowy recesses of the doorway that led to the bedchamber.

"I am afraid nothing short of cannonfire can rouse Charley," she said. "He's a very sound sleeper."

"So I see." Rafe felt disgruntled and slightly embarrassed that he had been caught even trying to wake the child.

"He's been sitting by that window all afternoon, waiting for you. We were both worried that you would be caught in the storm."

Worried about him? Rafe frowned. He ought to tell her that he wasn't accustomed to concern, nor was it his habit to give an accounting of himself to anyone.

Instead he surprised himself by saying, "I am sorry. My errand took longer than I . . ."

The words died in his throat as Corinne moved closer. She must have used the opportunity of Rafe's absence to wash her hair, for it spilled loose about her shoulders. The tendrils were still damp but the rest of it had dried to a soft sheen, the firelight picking out golden highlights among the warm brown strands.

She had always kept her hair bundled up beneath a cap. He would never have imagined it to be so long or so silken. As his gaze roved over her, he made another startling discovery.

She had a long brown wool shawl flung about her shoulders, but beneath it she was already prepared for bed, attired in no more than her nightgown. Rafe had certainly seen women clad in far less and women a great deal more seductive than Corinne.

Why the sight of her en déshabille should have disturbed him so much, he didn't know. He averted his eyes and muttered, "If the boy is that exhausted, I suppose we should get him to bed."

Corinne nodded. She brushed past him to lift Charley into her arms, but Rafe refused to allow it. The boy was too heavy for her, and carting Charley off to bed would give Rafe something to do other than stand and stare at the boy's mother.

He eased Charley out of the chair. He was like a dead weight in Rafe's arms, the boy's white-blond head flopping against his shoulder. Rafe half envied Charley his deep repose.

Had Rafe ever known such untroubled slumber, even when he had been a boy himself? He doubted it. He'd spent too many nights listening to his mother entertaining her gentleman friends far too near his small cot.

Even after Evelyn had abandoned him at the monastery, Rafe had known little peace. At the age of eight, he'd already been far worldlier than the holy brothers, far more aware of the dangers of the revolution exploding outside their door. The night the red caps had broken into St. Augustine's brandishing their knives, Rafe had been the only one awake.

The memory of that night usually filled him with such horror, he suppressed it. Now thinking about it brought him only a deep sadness that the world could be such a dark and evil place.

His arms tightened protectively about Charley as he lowered the boy onto the bed in the next room, Corinne following them with a candlestick. Rafe was going to ease the child beneath the coverlet when she stopped him, holding up the lad's nightshirt.

It had never even occurred to Rafe that the child would need to be stripped out of his clothes, a task that seemed more daunting than climbing a tall mast to mend a torn sail in a fierce wind.

He was glad enough to step back and allow Corinne to attend to the chore, marveling at how well she managed. The child was as limp as a rag doll and yet Corinne had him disrobed in a trice, her hands efficient and gentle. Charley barely stirred as she tugged the nightshirt over his head.

She eased the boy back against the pillow, brushing a tender kiss against his brow, her long brown hair tumbling forward to mingle with the child's golden curls. There was an innocence, a vulnerability about the pair of them that stirred a chord of fierce protectiveness in Rafe.

The emotion felt as disturbing and unfamiliar to him as borrowing another man's clothes. Rafe started to retreat from the bedchamber when Corinne stretched out one hand to stop him.

"Oh, please, Mr. Moore, I know this will sound foolish to you, but Charley was hoping you would tuck him up tonight."

"The boy's fast asleep. How will he even know?"

"He'll likely ask me in the morning, and I couldn't lie to him."

Of course she couldn't. Rafe doubted that Corinne Brewer had ever lied to anyone in the entire course of her life.

He glanced dubiously from Charley to Corinne waiting by the bed. She had such hopeful trusting eyes, the sort of eyes that could have compelled most men to do any idiotic thing she asked. Rafe was only astonished to discover they could have the same effect on him.

He moved forward reluctantly, his hands feeling awkward as he dragged the coverlet up to the boy's chin. He tucked the blankets around the boy with the same neatness and precision he would have used trimming a sail. He wasn't sure, but he thought he saw Corinne suppress a small smile.

Rafe stared down at the small head slumbering upon the pillow. He'd never particularly liked children, especially not a boy like Charley, so small and fragile. And yet Rafe already sensed a quiet strength in the lad, a generosity of spirit, and a proud determination to take care of his mama. He was a gentle boy who would likely grow up to be a strong man, compassionate, honorable, and good.

A man like Val St. Leger.

Rafe didn't know why thoughts of Val should keep creeping into his mind or filling him with such a sense of guilt. He threaded his fingers clumsily through Charley's babe-fine strands of blond hair until he remembered that Corinne still observed him.

She observed him far too much, Rafe thought, with that honest gaze of hers. He drew away from the child and stumbled from the room.

He paced to the window in the sitting room. The rain bled dark lines of moisture down the pane, flares of lightning illuminating the stable yard below, trees bending in the wind.

Rafe had always liked storms at sea, enjoyed the feel of a deck bucking beneath him, pitting himself against the challenge of the raging waves. But it was a different matter ashore, the relentless rain and the thunder often spiraling him into a black mood, into brooding over the past. Too many grim memories, too many nightmares.

Except not tonight. He was far more conscious of the warm firelight flickering behind him, the soft presence of the woman and boy in the other room.

Rafe stared out into the storm, waiting for the restlessness, the old bitterness to overtake him, but it never came. And he knew whom he had to thank for that.

Val St. Leger and whatever strange healing he had performed on Rafe. With the mere pressure of his hand, he had done more than save Rafe's life. It was almost as though Val had saved his very soul.

But who the devil had asked him to? Rafe wanted to rage. It was deuced unsettling, being indebted to one he had long considered an enemy, and yet he couldn't stop worrying about Val, regretting he'd left him in possession of that cursed crystal.

He tried to reassure himself it would be all right. Rafe had had the crystal locked away in his chest for years. He had even worn it occasionally and it had never proved a danger to him. Not until he had reached the lowest point in his life, when sheer despair and a sense of complete failure had driven him to piracy off the coast of Mexico.

The memory of those days now filled Rafe with shame and self-loathing. He had been a seaman himself since the age of sixteen. He knew how hard the life was without one's vessel being preyed upon by the scum of the earth, the kind of scum he had allowed himself to become.

It had been during those dark days that he had taken to wearing the crystal all the time, allowing it to gain such a hold upon him. It had seemed to reflect back to Rafe tenfold every angry thought, every bitter resentment. But a man as saintly as St. Leger wouldn't have that problem, would never succumb to the crystal's evil power. And even if Val did, Rafe didn't know why he should care.

But he did, to the point that he almost considered risking his own neck, returning to Torrecombe to warn Val. It was as though in some strange way he had absorbed part of Val's nobility, his selfless character.

"Mr. Moore?"

Corinne's low voice roused Rafe from his uneasy reflections. He turned to find her hovering uncertainly behind him. Ever since he had let these lodgings for them, she usually retired discreetly at night with Charley in the next room, leaving Rafe in possession of the sitting room.

It disconcerted him to have her standing so close in her nightgown, with her hair tumbled down that way, the soft clean scent filling his nostrils.

"It is late. You should be abed," he said.

"I know, but I could not retire without thanking you."

Rafe sighed. He was not accustomed to all this gratitude. "Thank me? What the deuce for now?"

"For bringing back Rufus."

"I needed a horse and—"

"You didn't need that one," Corinne interrupted. "And, Mr. Moore, you don't even like horses."

Rafe started, wondering how she had realized that. Even upon their short acquaintance, the woman already understood far too much about him. It was those soft, seeking eyes of hers, seeming to peel back the thick layers of his skin, to strip him clear down to his soul. Only Rafe wasn't sure that it was *his* soul she was seeing.

"I know why you went to fetch Rufus," she said. "You did it for Charley."

Rafe opened his mouth to deny it, found that he couldn't. He shrugged. "It was a small enough matter to buy back the horse, and your son seems attached to that wretched creature."

"I hope Charley didn't badger you about Rufus or—"

"No, no," Rafe was quick to assure her. "He wouldn't do that. He—he's a good boy," he added gruffly.

"And you are a very good man."

"There is nothing in the least good about me, my dear. Don't be imagining I am any sort of hero just because I took this mad whim to help you and your son. If you have found me kind at all, it is only because—because—"

Because of the miraculous change that had been wrought in him by Val. But how could he even begin to explain to Corinne all about the St. Legers and their strange abilities? He couldn't, so he held his tongue, stalking away from her, wishing she would simply leave him alone and go to bed.

But she trailed after him, insisting, "You *are* a remarkable man, Mr. Moore. Very few gentlemen would have burdened themselves with the care of a woman and a child not even their own."

"I told you why I did it," Rafe said impatiently.

"Because a boy should not be abandoned by his mother." Corinne hesitated before asking, "How old were you when your mother left you?"

Rafe tensed. It didn't surprise him that Corinne had been able to guess that much about his past. The woman was far too perceptive.

Evelyn Mortmain was a subject Rafe preferred to leave undiscussed, but he surprised himself by answering Corinne.

"I was around Charley's age when she abandoned me at a monastery in Paris. She died before she could ever return for me."

"Oh, I'm sorry," Corinne said. "Then your mama hoped that one day you would take holy vows yourself?"

Rafe nearly choked at that.

"No," he said dryly. "The members of my family have never been particularly religious. Especially not my mother, and I never had any idea who my father was. I often suspected that he might have been one of the monks at St. Augustine's. My mother was the sort of woman who would have found it amusing to seduce a holy man."

He hoped his reply might daunt Corinne into discontinuing her questions. But she looked more saddened than shocked by his words.

"Then this monastery in Paris—that was where you grew up?"

"I might have done except for the trifling matter of the revolution. Religious establishments were not exactly popular at that time in France. One night the mob broke into St. Augustine's and burned the place to the ground." Rafe shrugged, seeking to brush off the memories of the night that still haunted him, the fire, the blood, the death he had witnessed and barely survived.

But some of those old horrors must have left their trace upon his face. Corinne said nothing, but stroked her hand through his hair, a tender soothing gesture he'd watched her use many times with Charley.

Rafe could not recall any other woman ever touching him that way. His mother had never been that gentle and he'd always been so cold, so distant, no other lady would have dared. Not even the ones he'd taken to his bed.

Corinne's hand was careworn, but surprisingly soft. Rafe stared at her, feeling as tense and wary as any wild animal allowing itself to be lured too close to the human world. She was almost pretty, he realized in some surprise, studying her face. It was those eyes of hers perhaps, large, luminous in the firelight. Or the glossy tumble of her golden brown hair. He had to fight the urge to bury his fingers in the thick, silky strands, her very nearness arousing in him something akin to desire.

Desire for Corinne Brewer? Ridiculous, Rafe thought, but when her fingers caressed the taut line of his cheek, he sucked in his breath.

Catching her hand, he put it roughly away from him. "Don't."

His harsh command caused her to flinch. He didn't want to hurt her feelings. She was only trying to be kind, but damnation, the woman was old enough to have better sense.

"I have tried to make it clear to you that I am not a good man or a particularly honorable one," he growled. "You shouldn't be here alone with me, wearing that flimsy nightgown, touching me, tempting me—"

He broke off as a fiery red blush mounted into her cheeks, her eyes widening. Apparently it hadn't occurred to the woman he might find her desirable, which wasn't astonishing. It had never occurred to Rafe either.

She stammered, "You mean that—that I am—am—"

"Arousing me? Yes." His blunt words should have sent her scurrying for the other room to bolt inside and bar the door.

Instead she fretted the ends of her shawl, her head bowed so that her hair tumbled forward, concealing the bright red flush of her cheeks.

"Mr. Moore, you have been so terribly kind to me and Charley."

"What the devil has that got to do with anything?"

"Only that I have had no idea how I was ever going to repay you unless you truly would want— That is I—I could—"

She was mumbling her words into her hair, and at first Rafe didn't have the least notion what she was talking about until it suddenly dawned upon him.

Corinne was offering herself to him as payment for his aid. This respectable little widow! He should have laughed, should have found the notion damned amusing. But somehow he didn't.

Rafe was on the verge of ordering her sternly to bed when Corinne took a deep breath and dropped her shawl to the floor. She shook back her hair and Rafe felt his mouth go dry.

The nightgown was damned flimsy, old and worn from far too many washings. The light of the fire shone straight through the thin fabric, silhouetting the feminine form beneath. She was a full-figured woman with soft thighs and generous hips, her breasts large and round, her nipples dusky circles pressing up against the bodice of the gown.

Rafe swallowed thickly, made an effort to look away, but Corinne didn't help the situation. She trembled and shyly stole her arms about his neck, moving close enough to give him just a tantalizing taste of her softness, the warmth she was inviting him to share.

He'd done without a woman for a long time, far too long. A shaft of pure arousal shot through him, tightening his groin. He had never been the sort of man to refuse anything a woman was foolish enough to offer. When Corinne melted closer, he groaned and pulled her to him, his mouth claiming hers.

The wind and rain battered at the windows of Slate House, the thick walls muting the sound of the thunder, making Kate feel as though Val had carried her into the very eye of the storm. Shoving back her rain-soaked hood, she tried to adjust her eyes to the darkness, her gaze roving over her unfamiliar surroundings, the shadowy forms of the furniture, the heavy curtains. A flare of lightning illuminated the vast recesses of the bed, and a dark shiver worked through Kate.

She had never been inside Val's bedchamber. He would never have allowed such a thing before. But the Val she had once known seemed in danger of disappearing before her very eyes.

She watched as he moved further into the room, no more than a powerful silhouette of a man, until he struck tinder, lighting one of the candles. The wick flared, casting a glow over his features, his dark, wet hair slicked back except for one stubborn strand falling across his brow, his face ice white except for the burning intensity of his eyes.

Setting the candle atop the bureau, he stripped off his cloak, tossing it aside. His frock coat followed, his waistcoat and damp shirt clinging to him, revealing the muscular strength of his forearms. He almost seemed a stranger to her, this man who had swept her up on his horse and carried her away into the night. A dark seductive stranger . . .

As her gaze locked with his across the expanse of the room, Kate could feel the heat, the power of Val's longing. He intended to make love to her, and she sensed there would be no turning back this time.

It was the moment Kate had awaited forever, and yet as Val stalked toward her, she turned away from him, feeling suddenly uncertain. After his strange behavior at the church, it was getting harder to ignore all the devastating changes she had wrought in him, harder to still her conscience, even harder to continue using her love as an excuse.

Val loomed behind her, his hands coming to rest on her shoulders, his breath warm against her hair. "We should get you out of these wet things," he whispered.

Kate said nothing, her heart hammering so hard, she was scarce able to breathe, let alone speak. Her pulse raced as he reached around her to undo the fastening of her cloak, peeling it off her shoulders, dropping it to the floor. He ran his hands lightly along her arms in a way that sent tingles through her, the heat of his touch penetrating the thin fabric of her sleeves.

Stealing his arm about her waist, he drew her back hard against him. He shifted the damp tangles of her hair aside, pressing his lips to her neck, his mouth warm and rough. A tremulous sigh escaped Kate, the urge to melt against him strong.

But she resisted it, pulling away from him to stand trembling by the bed. Val followed, forcing her to turn and face him.

"What is wrong, Kate?" he asked. "Have you suddenly grown afraid of me?"

Afraid of him? Kate shook her head at the foolish question. How could she even begin to explain to him that it was more herself she was coming to fear, that she could have been ruthless enough to have done this to him, changed him past all recognition.

As he reached up to brush his fingers through her hair, his hand once so strong, so sure, was completely unsteady. And yet beyond the dark emotions in his eyes, she still saw traces of the real Val St. Leger, lost somewhere in the madness of the spell she had woven.

"You can still leave, Kate," he said. "Flee downstairs to Jem. He would find a way to—to keep you away from me tonight, protect you."

"Oh, Val, I don't need protection from you," Kate said. If anything, she thought, it was the other way around. She touched her hand to his cheek.

"I love you," she whispered.

He caught her hand, pressing a searing kiss against the center of her palm, but he gave a strange sad laugh as he echoed her words. "Love me? Kate, I don't think you even know who I am. You believe that I am this—this cross between Sir Galahad and some kind of saint. But I am not like that anymore. I never was. All I am is a man who—who—"

"Who what?" she prompted when he hesitated.

"Who desires you beyond all reason," Val finished huskily, drawing her hard against him. She could feel the heat pouring off his body, his heart pounding in erratic time with hers, as he claimed her lips in a long slow kiss that both stirred her own desire and filled her with despair.

Beyond all reason. Aye, it was an apt description of what she had done with her witchcraft to Val, this good strong man she had known and adored all her life. She had forced him to this, wanting her against his will, even his character, and it threatened to tear him apart.

Before his kiss could steal away what remained of her reason, Kate tried to pull back, peering up at him with troubled eyes.

"But, Val, what if—if the legend is right? What if you should not love me? What if I truly am bad for you?"

"Bad for me? Kate, you have ever been my good angel."

She flushed with shame, shaking her head vehemently at such a description of herself, so ill-deserved. But Val stilled her protest, imprisoning her face between his hands.

"Don't you remember all those nights I sat up in my library, in such pain from my leg I was unable to sleep? And you always came to bear me company, to comfort me."

"Aye." Kate attempted to smile. "I remember how you scolded me for stealing from my bed and roaming abroad at such a hour."

"So I did, but you will never know how glad I was to see you. I spent all my days administering to the aches of this village, taking away pain, but you were the only one who could ever make me forget mine. You always seemed to realize when I needed you the most. How did you know that, Kate?"

"I—I don't know," Kate faltered. It had been something she had never been able to explain even to herself.

"I have no idea how I knew. I just did."

"Then you must realize how much I need you right now. I want you so badly, it hurts. I'll never get through this night without you." Val's eyes blazed with passion, but were shadowed with torment as well.

"Stay with me, Kate," he pleaded, his mouth a whisper away from hers. "Be my midnight angel one more time."

How could any woman resist such an appeal, Kate thought in despair, even knowing it was wrong? His lips closed over hers and she swayed toward him, melting in his arms. What a dark, desperate moment it was to realize that she was going to have to release him from this madness, let him go for all time.

But she could do nothing to break the spell tonight. Would it be truly so wicked if she surrendered, eased his longing? Stole just one night in his arms before she brought an end to this dark magic and condemned them both to a lifetime of being apart?

Perhaps it was, but Kate felt her will to resist slowly dissolve beneath the heated demand of Val's mouth pressed to hers. He kissed her again and again, nipping lightly at her lower lip, teasing her with the thrust of his tongue. She could feel the warmth of his hands as he fumbled with the fastenings of her gown.

"I am sorry I am so deuced awkward at this." He grimaced. "But I have practically lived like a damned monk in this accursed village all these years. God, what a humiliating admission for a man my age to have to make."

"It is all right," Kate said, brushing her lips against his. "We will learn about this as we have done so many other things—together."

She moved to help him with her garments. Her hands were as unsteady as his, but somehow they managed to divest her of the gown. Chemise, stockings, garters all swiftly followed until she stood naked before him.

His gaze roved over her with a boldness that brought the heat flooding to her cheeks. But Kate felt no urge to cover herself. She shook back the heavy fall of her hair, fully exposing the curves of her breasts, a dark tremor of excitement coursing through her at Val's hungry stare.

"You—you have grown into such a beautiful woman, Kate," he said hoarsely. "When did that happen? I turned my head for only a moment and the girl I once knew was gone."

He drew her back into his arms. "I vow I will never take my eyes away from you again."

Beautiful words, beautiful promise. If only it had come from the prompt-ings of Val's heart and not her spell. But Kate thrust such unhappy reflections aside as Val began to caress her back, her hips, cupping her bottom until her body pressed tight to his, making her aware of how hot, how hard he was. Kate trembled, her body quickening with all manner of new sensations, but she felt strangely vulnerable being stripped bare while Val remained nearly fully clothed.

But when she reached for the button at the top of his shirt, he stopped her.

"No!" he said, his voice sounding sharp, almost close to panic. When she peered up at him in surprise, he attempted to smile.

"Not just yet," he said, easing away from her, and she was left with the curi-ous feeling he was hiding something beneath his shirt. But before she could question him any further, he snuffed out the candle, plunging the room into darkness.

Val swept her off her feet, carrying her to the bed. He eased her down onto the mattress and flung himself beside her. His lips found hers in another sear-ing kiss. Kate wrapped her arms around him, feverishly returning the em-brace, but when she tried to explore him as he was doing her, he stopped her once more.

"No, Kate, don't. I am so ready for you, I swear one more touch will finish me," he panted. "Just—just lie still and let me make love to you, arouse you."

Kate tried to do as he asked, settling onto her back. But *lie still?* How was it possible to obey such a command when Val's every touch seemed calculated to fill her with restlessness, coiling the tension ever tighter inside her?

He trapped her arms above her head with one hand, holding her captive to the merciless questing of his other hand, his mouth. Kate moaned softly at each kiss, each caress. For all his claims of inexperience, Val was as passionate a lover as any woman could have desired.

If only it had been real and not the result of witchcraft, of the dark magic she'd woven on All Hallows' Eve. It was strange making love like this in the dark with the rain and thunder rumbling outside, the only sound within the chamber the soft quick mingling of their breath.

Val still had not paused to remove his clothes, only eased down his breeches. It was not at all the romantic and tender way she had once dreamed, but Kate felt more than ready when Val parted her legs, positioning himself above her.

He braced himself on both arms, his mouth taking hers in a hot, hungry kiss as he thrust himself inside of her. Kate felt a fleeting stab of pain, and then nothing but the truly miraculous sensation of his body joined to hers.

"Now you are mine, Kate," Val whispered raggedly in her ear. "And nothing or no one shall ever take you away from me."

If only that were true. Kate felt a sharp stinging behind her eyes because she knew far differently. It was Val himself who would part them once the spell had been removed.

But Kate blinked fiercely, forcing the despairing thought away for now. She wrapped her arms tightly around him as he began to move inside her, faster and faster.

A flare of lightning revealed Val's face poised above her, but she could not make out the expression in his eyes as he drove them ever closer to the culmination of their forbidden desire.

And perhaps it was just as well, Kate thought. Because this way she could give herself up completely to his passion and pretend that he truly loved her.

At least for just one night.

Rafe held Corinne close, savoring the curves of her body pressed against his. Corinne seemed stiff, a little tentative. She wasn't the kind of woman used to expressing her gratitude this way, trading herself to a man in return for the favors he'd done her. But Rafe well knew how to seduce a reluctant female whenever he chose to so exert himself.

He captured her lips, his mouth moving sensually over hers, coaxing her lips to part. Her tongue crept forward, engaging with his in a bashful mating. He suppressed a smile of triumph when he felt her relax against him.

He kissed her long and deep, his hands roaming over her body, finding the old cotton nightgown a nuisance, an unattractive barrier separating him from the womanly form veiled beneath.

Breaking the heated contact of their lips, he began to undo the faded ribbons that laced up the front of her gown. Corinne trembled, a fierce blush staining her cheeks as he eased the nightgown down her pink plump shoulders, but she made no move to stop him.

It was her eyes that did that, gazing up at him, so shy and so vulnerable. He felt himself hesitate, though he was damned if he knew why. His body was already hard for her, pulsing with needs that had gone too long unattended.

And blast it all, she had started this. She had offered herself to him. It was not as though she were any shrinking virgin. She'd been married, gone through the rigors of childbirth. She'd obviously had some experience with the lusts of a man.

Then why did she look so young, so cursed innocent standing there in her worn white nightgown, her hair curling softly about her earnest face? Rafe gritted his teeth, tried to tug the cotton fabric down to expose her breasts. Tried and discovered he just couldn't do it.

Swearing, he pulled the nightgown back up to her neckline and flung himself away from her. For long moments the only sound in the room was the rain drumming against the windows and his own frustrated breathing.

When he dared to glance back at Corinne, she stood exactly where he had left her, looking embarrassed and confused. Rafe didn't blame her. He felt damned confused himself as to why he was allowing himself to burn with thwarted desire when his relief stood only an arm's length away.

But when she tried to approach him again, he flung up one hand to ward her off. "No, don't. Stay the devil away from me."

"Then—then you don't want me?"

Rafe suppressed a groan. Want her? He couldn't ever remember wanting a woman more in his life, but he snarled, "No, damn it. Just go to bed and—and leave me alone."

Corinne ducked her head, but not before he saw her face burn with humiliation, the hurt that flashed in her eyes. "I'm sorry," she said. "I have made a great fool of myself. I am not the sort of woman who would ever tempt a man like you to—to—"

She trailed off, turning toward the bedchamber. If he'd had any sense at all, he would have simply let her go, but somehow he could not bear it, the way she crept away, the dejected slump of her shoulders.

Crossing the room in several long strides, he cut off her retreat, catching hold of her arms. "Damnation, Corinne, of course I was tempted. I think I made that pretty bloody obvious."

She tipped her head to look doubtfully up at him. "Then why did you stop?"

"Because you are not made for a night of casual lust in a man's arms. You are the kind of woman who has forever written in your eyes. And I can't take advantage of your gratitude to me simply because I have been alone for too long."

"And you think I haven't been?" she asked. "Mr. Moore, I have been widowed for over a year, and with my husband away at sea, my bed has gone empty for longer than that."

She flushed, embarrassed by her confession, but her eyes gazed straight into his, shimmering with such wants, such needs, a loneliness far too similar to his own.

He couldn't resist drawing her into his arms, cradling her close. He breathed in the scent of her hair. She smelled like flowers, gentle spring rains, filling his arms with the kind of warmth, the kind of softness he had missed his entire cold life.

And she wanted him as badly as he did her. But that still did not make seducing her any more right. With more self-control than he ever dreamed he possessed, he eased her back out of his embrace.

"It is only the storm, my dear," he murmured, caressing his fingers through the shining length of her hair. "You must trust me on this. I know. The wailing of the wind can play tricks, rousing a melancholy in you, making you think that you want things you should never have."

Her lips curved in a sad smile. "I think you are trying to tell me that I would regret it, come morning."

"No, I am telling you that I would."

His words astonished himself as much as they did her. He pressed a kiss to her brow, then stepped reluctantly away from her.

"And now I think you'd best get to bed."

She regarded him wistfully, but nodded in agreement. "Good night, Mr. Moore."

"Rafe," he said.

"What?"

"My name is Rafe," he repeated, realizing this was perhaps the greatest folly he had committed yet, giving her any part of his real identity. But it suddenly felt ridiculously important to him to hear his name from her lips.

"Good night . . . Rafe," she breathed. And with that gentle parting she slipped into the other bedchamber, closing the door, leaving him filled with confusion and regrets.

What had he done, allowing her to leave him that way? He was going to spend half the night now in torment over needs he could have seen so easily fulfilled. Yet for one of the rare times in his life, he realized he had behaved in an honorable fashion.

And it felt remarkably good.

Tossing down a pillow and a blanket, he stretched out to all the cold comforts of bedding down alone before the dying fire. Despite the rain and wind continuing to batter at the inn window, despite the hardness of the floor beneath him, Rafe rolled on his back, staring up at the ceiling with a faint smile. Thinking about the woman in the next room with the sweet eyes and gentle touch, about the little boy who slept so soundly beside her, Rafe was filled with an unexpected contentment, a sense of peace unlike anything he'd ever known.

Wherever Val St. Leger was tonight, Rafe only hoped that he felt the same.

*   *   *

Val tossed restlessly on his pillow and moaned, caught up in the throes of the worst nightmare he'd ever had.

He was cold, shivering, and alone, lost in the terrible labyrinth that comprised the streets of Paris. Ahead of him he could see his mother, but no matter how hard he ran, he could never catch up to her.

"Maman. Wait. Please don't leave me."

Madeline St. Leger only glanced back at him with a cold, distant smile, then vanished down a mist-spun alley. His heart pumping with fear, Val charged after her. Rounding the corner, he stumbled upon a scene of terrible slaughter.

A church blazed, the flames already licking upward to consume the cross attached to the roof. The hellish fire lit up the street, the shadows of red-capped demons looming large as they hacked away with their swords, cutting down everyone in their path. Gentle-faced men in brown robes, women, children. Their screams rent the air, their blood slick on the pavement beneath Val's feet.

Some of them were still alive and they clutched at him, catching at his cloak, dark desperate eyes all around him, blood-streaked faces pleading.

"Help us, Dr. St. Leger. Please, you must. You are the only one."

But there were too many of them. He whirled about in despair, scarce knowing whom to help first. Then he saw her crumpled at the base of the church steps, her gypsy dark hair spilled about her, her white face turned up toward the firelit sky.

Kate.

Val struck away the grasping hands and rushed toward her, catching her up in his arms. But her eyes were closed, her body so cold, so lifeless. He looked up from Kate's pale face to find Effie Fitzleger standing over him.

"It's the curse," she said, shaking her brassy blond curls at him reproachfully. "You should never have touched her. She wasn't your chosen bride."

"No!" Val shouted at the woman, driving her away from him. He turned desperately back to Kate, certain he could revive her. If only he could take away some of her pain—

He grasped her limp hand in his, grasped it hard, trying with everything in him to invoke his own special brand of the St. Leger magic. But it was useless. His power was gone—

"No," Val groaned again, but this time he was able to snap his eyes open, forcing himself awake. Heart thudding, he struggled upright as though his pillow, or the very sheets would be enough to drag him into slumber and straight back to his nightmare.

He looked wildly about him, taking in the solid familiarity of his bed-chamber. Then he dragged his hand shakily back through his hair, wiping the beads of sweat from his brow.

It had been only a bad dream, but he was unable to comfort himself with that thought because it had not been entirely his dream. He had never been abandoned by his mother, never been to Paris in the entire course of his life.

Now even Rafe Mortmain's nightmares seemed to blend with his, mingling with his own worst fears about Kate, about the St. Leger curse. At least he could console himself that the girl must surely be home safe in her bed.

Except she wasn't. She was in his.

The storm had stopped, moonlight poking from behind the clouds to reveal the slumbering form next to him. Kate lay curled on her side, the sheet tangled around her naked body, looking almost as still and cold as she had been in his dream.

Val reached out a trembling hand to brush back the dark tangle of her hair. He was relieved to catch the slight rise and fall of her breath, but a dark bruise stained the pale skin of her shoulder.

Oh, God, what had he done?

Val recoiled in horror, his chest constricting as remembrance flooded back to him of the way he had taken her, their fierce, passionate lovemaking. It didn't help to remember how warm and willing Kate had been, how eagerly she had responded to his caresses.

The girl had always loved and trusted him too damn much and now he had betrayed her completely. She had already endured so much, the taunts, the sniggers about being born a bastard, a foundling child, abandoned by both her parents.

And now he had dishonored her as well.

It was all the fault of the cursed crystal. He tugged at the chain, drawing the glittering stone from beneath his shirt.

His hand closed over the crystal and he gritted his teeth, trying to summon the strength to wrench it free, get rid of it.

"Val?" Kate's sleepy voice sounded behind him and he froze.

"What—what are you doing? Is anything wrong?" she mumbled. He felt her stirring beside him.

He stared helplessly down at the crystal and then shoved it back into his shirt, knowing that he must never allow her to see it, never be infected by its strange power. He feared it was already too late for him, but he had to protect her somehow before he destroyed them both, before they became one more page in the tragic history of St. Legers who had defied the legend.

He swung his legs over the side of the bed, wanting to put distance between them, but he made the mistake of looking back at her. She had sat up, appearing drowsy and bewildered, the sheets falling away from her naked body.

Val's breath hitched painfully in his throat. He'd always woven stories for Kate about her being the daughter of a selkie, and she very well could have been.

Her long hair clung to her shoulders, the dark tendrils as wildly tangled as a mermaid's tresses, her skin as pale as the moonlight that spilled over it. Her body was as slender and supple as a reed, from the graceful length of her legs to the proud curve of her breasts.

He had no right to touch her again, no right to want her this badly. But the crystal pressed against his skin, thrumming over the region of his heart, pulsing with every desire, every longing he'd ever suppressed.

He was lost. He groaned softly, but he had no choice except to draw Kate back into his arms and make love to her all over again.

CHAPTER FOURTEEN

*D*uring the ensuing weeks Rosebriar Cottage came to resemble the scene of a coaching disaster, half-open trunks and portmanteaus scattered everywhere as Effie kept the entire household in an uproar with her feverish preparations for the journey to London.

Bandboxes had even begun to make their appearance in the parlor; gloves, fans, and other trinkets were piled on the Hepplewhite table. Effie paced the carpet in an agony of indecision, lifting an ormolu clock off the mantel then replacing it as she considered a sturdier timepiece set in a brass casing instead.

Effie's ringlets and the lappets of her lace cap quivered as she clucked her tongue and shook her head.

"Oh dear, oh dear." She turned anxiously toward Kate's still figure, silhouetted in the window seat.

"Kate, my love, you must help me decide. Which one of my precious clocks do you think I should bring?"

Kate stared listlessly out the window, consumed by her own thoughts, none of them pleasant. But she roused herself from her torpor long enough to cast an indifferent glance in Effie's direction.

"You don't need any of them. I am sure they have sufficient clocks in London."

"Yet it is the never the same as having the comfort of one's own familiar timepiece," Effie fretted. "I once heard tell of some duchess or other who could travel nowhere without her own sheets. Well, I am sure I feel quite the same way about my clocks."

Effie decided on the brass, only to change her mind immediately, undoing the wrappings and flinging them on the floor.

Kate sighed and tried to ignore her, wishing Effie and all her infernal clocks to perdition. An ill-natured thought and she was ashamed of it. It was only because the strain of this past month was finally beginning to tell on her. These past weeks had surely been some of the longest of her life.

Rubbing her aching neck, every line of her body seemed fraught with tension and weariness as she peered out the window. The cottages in the village appeared to huddle together beneath a slate gray sky, the wind coming in from the sea, cold and rough. Kate could not remember when she had last seen the sun. Sometimes she feared it was but one more disastrous consequence of her miscast spell, that she had managed to drain all the sunshine out of the world.

Or had she only stolen the light away from the man that she loved?

Val changed more and more with each passing day, his temper more uncertain, his eyes more dark and brooding. The villagers had begun to whisper that Dr. St. Leger had run mad, that he was cursed, and Kate herself feared it was so. Val neglected his patients, avoided his family, and disappeared into the countryside for hours on end, galloping away on that demonic horse of his. Even Kate did not know where he went.

The only times that she herself saw Val these days was when . . . A heated blush stole into Kate's face and she pressed her cheek against the windowpane to cool it.

The only time she saw Val was when they were making love. Or more precisely she didn't actually *see* him for they fondled, caressed, and came together desperately under the cover of darkness. One stolen night in his arms had somehow become two, three, four . . . each time together more heated than the last.

Kate feared that the entire district by now must be aware of their indiscretion. She had caught some of the sly smiles, the whispers behind the hedgerows. No one seemed particularly surprised about Kate. No better had ever been expected of her, the bastard child, the wild gypsy girl. But everyone was astounded that their good doctor could behave in such disreputable fashion.

Kate didn't give a damn what was being said about her. She was used to it. But it hurt deeply to hear Val's honor questioned, his reputation sullied. Yet she could not bring herself to stay away from him. One smoldering look from his eyes, one demanding beckon of his finger, and she was back in his arms, the desire flaming between them.

She had all the passion from Val she had ever craved, but in the process of gaining a lover, she had somehow lost her friend. She missed the quiet times they had once spent together playing at chess, poring over his books, taking long walks, conversing endlessly.

At times during these past days she had felt so lonely, so miserable, she had actually been driven to return to Prospero's tower upon the hill, seeking out the company of a ghost.

But it would all be over by tonight. It was exactly one month to the day since All Hallows' Eve and Prospero had assured her the conditions would now be right. The thought of ending the spell at last filled Kate with equal parts relief, despair, and fear. She was often tormented by the memory of what Val had said when she had proposed to him putting all back as it was before.

"I'd rather be dead."

Kate could only pray that when he was back in his right wits he would think far differently of the matter. Pray as well that he would be able to forgive her when he finally realized what she had done to him. A heavy lump swelled in her throat, tears stinging her eyes.

"Dearest?"

Kate felt Effie's touch upon her shoulder. She dashed the moisture from her eyes before turning to face her guardian. She felt as though she would have greatly welcomed some comfort just now, a bit of motherly advice, but she clearly wasn't going to get it from Effie.

Looking perplexed herself, the older woman held up both of her clocks. "I simply cannot make up my mind, Kate. Which one do you think I should choose?"

Kate gave a ragged laugh. She couldn't believe it. Her heart was clearly breaking in two and the woman was asking her about clocks. Everyone in the entire village seemed to be aware of what was going on between her and Val. Everyone but Effie. Her adoptive mother existed entirely in a world of her own.

Resisting the urge to dash the clocks from Effie's hands, Kate uncurled from the window seat and shot to her feet.

"For heaven's sake, Effie. Take both the damned things if you want. What the devil does it matter?"

Effie backed away from her, looking as wounded as a child that had been slapped. Kate was flooded with instant remorse. Losing one's temper with Effie was like kicking a kitten.

"I am sorry," Kate said wearily, gentling her tone. "Take the ormolu. It is quite your prettiest one."

But the damage had already been done. Her own spirits quite dampened, Effie forlornly replaced both clocks on the mantel. She regarded Kate with a quivering lip. "Do you care nothing about our trip to London, my dear? Are you not the least bit excited?"

No, Kate longed to snap. The truth was that after tonight, it would not matter in the least where she was. Once Val was safely restored to himself, all would become exactly as it once had been. Only it could never be entirely. Her honorable Val would be appalled, ashamed of all those stolen trysts. He would never want her near him again. She would have lost both her lover and her friend.

Beyond tonight, the future was nothing but a bitter void. But for Effie's benefit, Kate forced a brittle smile to her lips. "I am sure London will be quite pleasant."

Rather than appearing reassured, Effie burst into tears. She flung herself at Kate in a fierce hug, her thin body trembling with sobs.

Kate stood stiff and uncomfortable. "Effie, what in the world is the matter now?"

"Ohhh!" Effie clung to Kate, her words coming out in ragged gulps. "I s-simply cannot bear this. Seeing you so—so unhappy."

Kate's eyes widened in astonishment. She didn't believe that Effie had even noticed that much. She hugged the older woman, patting her shoulder, wishing she could cry in that wholehearted fashion, unburdening her woes.

But Kate could just imagine Effie's reaction if she ever disclosed to her guardian all that had been going on this past month. That she had not only bewitched Val St. Leger, but she had been spending night after night in his arms.

Effie would succumb to apoplexy on the spot.

As usual Kate swallowed her own misery and eased Effie away from her.

"Effie, I am not that unhappy. I am merely tired. This getting ready for London has been exhausting."

"A-aye, indeed it has," Effie said groping for her handkerchief. "And—and don't think I don't understand how you feel, my dear. It will be very melancholy for you to leave . . . to leave all our friends. I am sure I will miss that foolish Mr. Trimble myself, but only think of the things we will do and see. The parks, the theatres, the balls."

In short, everything Effie had ever longed for except that it was coming years too late. Kate tried to remind herself of that and sought to infuse some enthusiasm into her voice.

"I am sure it will all be very diverting."

"Oh, it will. It will," Effie agreed. "We shall be so happy, I promise you and—and I will make everything up to you, dearest."

Make everything up to her? What was Effie talking about? She spoke as though she had done Kate some sort of injury. Kate studied her guardian's tear-streaked countenance and suddenly realized that Effie was not the only one who had been blind this past month.

There were lines of strain and exhaustion about Effie's eyes that Kate had failed to notice before. It was as though in her own way Effie was as unhappy about something as Kate was. But before Kate could question her, the little maid Nan bounded into the parlor.

The girl did not look in the least disconcerted to find Effie sniffing into her handkerchief. The household was entirely too accustomed to Miss Fitzleger's megrims.

Nan ducked into a hasty curtsy. "I am sorry to disturb you, Miss Effie. I know as how you said you were not at home to callers. But that Miss Mollie Grey is here, insisting she needs to see you."

Kate felt herself tense at the mention of Victor St. Leger's abandoned bride and Effie let out a cry of dismay.

"Oh, the poor girl. She is probably here to plead with me to do something about that wretched Victor, force him to marry her. Mollie is his chosen bride. I don't know why the scoundrel is resisting her. I don't even know where he has been these past weeks. Do you, Kate?"

"Er, no." Kate winced, ashamed that she had given little thought to Victor of late. She was only too relieved that he had desisted from courting her and was keeping his distance from Val. "I am sure that Victor will come around soon enough to pay his addresses to Mollie."

"Then pray tell the poor girl that, because I am not up to it myself. I quite feel one of my headaches coming on."

"Oh, no, Effie, please," Kate tried to protest. Facing the young woman whose bridegroom she had inadvertently stolen was the last thing Kate wanted to do. But Effie was already darting out of the parlor, making good her escape as she always did when there was anything unpleasant to be faced.

Nan turned to Kate, and she experienced a cowardly urge to tell the maid to send Miss Grey away. Kate quelled it, raising her hand in a wearied gesture.

"Show the girl in," she said.

Kate positioned herself stiffly in front of the fireplace as Mollie entered. The girl crept timidly into the parlor, looking as dismayed to see Kate as Kate was to see her.

Kate had never had any female friends. She had never needed anyone but Val and even if she had, she would never have sought out Mollie's company. The girl had always struck Kate as being particularly insipid. She reminded Kate of a faded flower with her white-blond hair and lackluster eyes.

Even the rose-colored bonnet and pelisse Mollie wore did little to reflect any color to her pale heart-shaped face, although the attire was certainly elegant enough. Mollie was one of five daughters of a prosperous farmer. The rugged land hereabout made it difficult to grow crops, but Squire Thomas Grey had managed to carve out a thriving sheep farm, increasing his holdings through investments in tin mines.

Still, many felt Mollie was aspiring above her station in hoping to wed Victor St. Leger. After all, there was a strain of nobility in the St. Leger blood. But Effie had spoken. She had said that Mollie was fated to be Victor's bride, and no man questioned the decrees of the Bride Finder.

At least not unless that man had fallen victim to her wicked spell, Kate reflected with a sharp twinge.

She fixed a stiff smile upon her lips. "Mollie, how good to see you. I am sorry, Effie is indisposed. But won't you come in and sit down?"

"Thank you." The girl's voice was as soft and colorless as she was. She perched on the edge of the settee like a butterfly ready to take flight at any moment if Kate did the least thing to startle her. "I realize you must be quite busy getting ready for your stay in London. I don't mean to disturb you. I just thought I should return this to Miss Fitzleger before you go."

Mollie handed Kate a small silver plated case. Kate took it from her, recognizing at once what it was, the jewel case that contained Effie's precious pearls, the ones her grandfather Septimus Fitzleger had given Effie on her twenty-first birthday. But what was Mollie Grey doing with them? When Kate regarded her questioningly, Mollie dropped her gaze, staring at the carpet. "Miss Fitzleger is so generous. She was good enough to lend me her pearls, only I no longer have any occasion to wear them."

"Surely you could wear them to the St. Leger masquerade ball tomorrow night?"

"No, I am no longer planning to attend, and in any case, I was going attired as a shepherdess. The pearls are much too fine for that. They were meant for a far more special occasion."

For a moment Kate had no idea what she meant, then the truth dawned on her. Effie had loaned those pearls to Mollie to wear on her wedding day. Kate's heart sank as she stole a glance at Mollie's unhappy face. Would there never be an end to the misery her dabbling in witchcraft had caused?

She sagged down on a chair opposite Mollie. Another woman, Kate reflected, would have known how to reach out to the girl, offer some comfort, or at least how to frame a handsome apology for the mischief she had wrought.

All Kate could do was thrust the box of pearls back into Mollie's hands.

"Mollie, I don't think you should be giving up on that other occasion. Victor may come around sooner than you think."

Mollie colored a little at the mention of his name, but she gave a sad shake of her head. "He used to call at our farm from time to time, but I have not seen him for weeks. He is working very hard to study his family's business. I hear he has been spending a great deal of time at Penryn harbor, learning how to sail, to command a crew, even to climb the rigging."

"Well, there, you see. That must be a sign that he is becoming more serious, making sure he will be able to provide well for you."

"He is not doing it for me, Kate," Mollie said with a look of quiet pain. "He is doing it to impress *you*, to make you think better of him."

"Oh, lord," Kate groaned. "I—I am so sorry, Mollie—"

"Don't be. I am sure it is no fault of yours."

Yes, it was. Entirely, Kate thought, feeling miserable with guilt.

Mollie went on wistfully. "It is no wonder that Victor admires you instead of me. You are so beautiful, so spirited while I . . ." She gave a forlorn shrug. "Even my own papa berates me for being so meek. But Victor was always kind to me.

"We were at an assembly once and all my sisters were dancing, even my youngest. I was as usual busy minding the wall and Victor noticed. He asked me to dance."

A rare spark of animation lit Mollie's eyes, a lovely glow suffusing her face that astonished Kate. She thought it was a pity Victor could not see the girl at that moment. Spell or no spell, he might have remembered who his destined bride was supposed to be.

A soft smile curled Mollie's lips. "He was so handsome in his black frock coat and knee breeches. I think I quite fell in love with him then and there. Very foolish of me, I know."

Mollie's smile waxed more rueful. "I daresay you could not understand what that is like, to be forever yearning for a man who is quite out of your reach."

Kate said nothing, but her throat tightened. She understood far too well.

"I never thought I stood any chance with him until Miss Fitzleger proclaimed me to be his chosen bride. It seemed so incredible, like a dream, and I suppose it was. It would take far more than a legend to ever make Victor St. Leger fall in love with a girl like me."

"Oh, Mollie, no," Kate protested. "If you could just wait a little longer, perhaps—"

But Mollie cut her off with a sad shake of her head. "No, I am certain this one time Effie must be mistaken. It is you Victor adores."

She fixed Kate with pleading, earnest eyes. "Please, Kate, could you not find it in your heart to be kind to him, to try to return his affections?"

"You are asking *me* to love the man you adore?" Kate demanded, incredulous.

"Yes. All I want is what is best for Victor, to see him happy."

Kate gaped at her. The girl was mad. If any other woman had even attempted to take Val from her, Kate would have shot the wench straight between the eyes.

Aye, no matter what Val might have wanted or felt, her conscience chided. She would have behaved as ruthlessly as she already had done, bending his will, his reason, with her terrible spell, no matter what the cost.

Kate felt humbled and ashamed. It would seem this quiet "insipid" girl could have taught her a great deal about the unselfishness of true love.

Impulsively Kate reached out and clasped hold of Mollie's hand. "Listen to me," she said. "You cannot give up on Victor now. Something is going to happen tonight. I cannot explain what, but it will change everything."

"Oh?" Mollie murmured politely, but she cast Kate a dubious glance.

"Think of it as a fairy tale and Victor is your handsome prince who has been under a spell. Only tonight it will be broken."

"Indeed," Mollie said, inching warily back from Kate, trying to free her hand.

Kate only tightened her grasp. "I know this all must sound quite mad. But this is what I want you to do. You should come to the ball tomorrow night. Victor will be there and I think I can safely guarantee he will regard you through different eyes."

"No, Kate, I couldn't possibly—"

"Damn it, Mollie. Just do as I tell you or I swear I will come fetch you myself."

Mollie flinched at the threat. She pulled free of Kate and scrambled to her feet, looking ready to bolt like a frightened doe.

Kate rose also, blocking her path. She softened her tone. "Mollie, please. I know we have not been friends. I have never even been particularly nice to you. But just this once I am begging you to trust me."

Mollie studied her uncertainly. Kate didn't know what swayed the girl in the end, whether it was the forcefulness of her words or that Mollie herself desperately needed something to believe in.

"All right, Kate," she conceded. "I will attend the ball if you truly think that I should."

"Oh, yes, I do." Kate beamed at her and Mollie smiled back tremulously.

By the time Kate ushered the girl out the front door, she noticed a spark of hope had crept back into Mollie's eyes. Kate only hoped that she had not done wrong to put it there.

She had made Mollie a reckless promise, one Kate had no notion whether she would be able to keep. She didn't know what had possessed her to do so except for her need to make some amends for all the wrong she had done, her desire to see some good come out of this disaster for someone.

She paused in the hall to stare at Effie's long case clocks. They seemed to be ticking off the minutes so slowly. So many hours yet remained between now and the time when she would meet Prospero by the standing stone. Kate sent up a fervent prayer that nothing else would go wrong between now and then.

It was a prayer that was not to be answered.

She was halfway up the stairs to the second floor when she heard Nan opening the front door to admit a breathless Jem Sparkins. Before the maid could even demand what he wanted, Val's lanky manservant shoved his way into the hall.

He glanced up the stairs, calling out to Kate in a voice of pure desperation. "Oh, Miss Kate. You have got to come at once. You are the only one with any influence at all over Master Val these days. You have to stop him."

"Stop him from what?" Kate asked, her heart clenching with fear.

"From doing a murder. Master Val is after killing that Reeve Trewithan."

CHAPTER FIFTEEN

Reeve Trewithan crashed through the taproom door, sprawling into the dirt of the stable yard. The big man lay dazed and bleeding. Astonished patrons of the Dragon's Fire Inn poked their heads out of the windows to stare while villagers passing by stopped to gape. Not that they hadn't seen a brawl before. It was simply that no one had ever seen the gentle Dr. St. Leger so enraged.

Val stormed out of the inn, charging after Trewithan. The burly man had managed to regain his feet. He took a wild swing at Val and missed. Val landed a hard right to his jaw, following it with a swift blow straight in Trewithan's soft paunch.

The man doubled over with a low groan, but still Val did not stop. Trewithan's brutish face blurred before his eyes. He pummeled Trewithan again and again, taking a vicious satisfaction each time his fist connected. Trewithan started to sag to his knees, but Val seized him by his shirtfront, raining blows on Reeve's crumpling form.

"Val. Stop it. Can't you see he's had enough?"

The voice seemed to come from a great distance away like someone shouting through a fog. Val scarce heard it, aware of nothing but his own pulsing fury. He seized Trewithan by the hair, his fist cracking into the side of the man's head.

"Damn it, Val. Stop!"

Val felt a strong arm lock around his shoulders, dragging him away from

Trewithan. With a low growl, Val wrenched free, turning on his captor. He drew back his fist only to have his arm caught in an iron grip. Val struggled furiously.

"Val!"

This time the sharp voice penetrated his rage-filled haze. His vision cleared and he found himself staring into his brother's face. The stunned look in Lance's eyes acted on Val like a douse of cold water.

His fury subsided, his arm going slack. Lance released him and Val staggered back, panting. His anger spent, a sudden wave of weakness overtook him.

His knees trembled, a dry cough tearing through his throat. He pressed one shaking hand to his chest, surprised by the degree of burning pain. His head reeled and he was obliged to lean up against the side of the inn. Breathing deeply, he closed his eyes for a minute until the strange pain subsided, until the land steadied beneath his feet.

Then his eyes fluttered open and he gazed with horror at what he had done. Reeve Trewithan sprawled at his feet, moaning, his face disfigured by blood and bruises. Val felt the old instinct stir, the one that had become all but lost to him of late, the urge to reach out, to help, to heal.

But he was thrust aside as Carrie Trewithan rushed forward. With a soft cry, she sank to her knees and wrapped her thin arms around her husband, shifting his head onto her lap. Trewithan peered up at her through his swollen eyes and began to sob, burying his face against her worn shawl.

"Hush," she murmured. "Y-you're going to be all right." She held him close and began to weep herself.

"Carrie . . ." Val tried to rest one hand on her shoulder, but she shrank from him. She lifted her tear-stained face, her eyes glistening with sorrow and bewilderment.

"Oh, Dr. St. Leger, how could *you* do a thing like this?"

How could he? Val drew back in astonishment. This was the same woman whose life he had recently saved, whose pain he had been forced to bear and all because of that great lout she now cradled like a babe. And she was upbraiding *him*, looking at him as though he'd turned into the very devil?

As Val gazed around him, he saw that Carrie wasn't the only one. He seemed surrounded by a sea of faces. Wentworth, the innkeeper. The burly village smith. The grooms from the stables, the kitchen girl and serving maids. All of them regarded Val with stunned disbelief, fear, and confusion. Even his own brother.

Lance was the first to recover. Moving among the crowd, he began rapping out orders. "All right. It's all over. Be about your own affairs, good people.

And you there"—he beckoned imperiously to one of the stablehands—"come and help Mrs. Trewithan get her husband home to his bed."

While the crowd moved to obey, Val stood to one side feeling helpless and awkward, the crystal piercing him with a sharp stab of resentment.

Aye, the good folk of Torrecombe were always quick to heed his brother's bidding. No one would have thought anything of it if Sir Lancelot had been the one to lose his temper and thrash Trewithan senseless. Then it would have been all winks and nudges. Ah, that Master Lance, what a fire-eater and ever handy with his fives.

But it was entirely a different matter for Saint Valentine, Val reflected bitterly. The villagers slunk past him without meeting his eyes, taking care to maintain a wary distance. They melted away from him like frightened shadows, all those people who he'd labored to cure of their petty ailments.

He didn't hear any of them calling out to him now, *Please Dr. St. Leger. Come help us. You are the only one.*

Well, the devil take them all. Val tried to sneer, but his throat constricted with unexpected pain instead. Pivoting on his heel, he strode away, wanting only to put as much distance between himself and this accursed village as possible.

"Val, wait!"

He heard Lance call out to him, but he ignored it. The last person he wanted to face right now was his brother, to be plagued by a load of damned questions he didn't want to answer.

Val quickened his pace, plunging down the worn path that led to the beach, toward home. That is if he knew where that was anymore. Not at Castle Leger, that was for certain, or even Marius's gloom-ridden cottage by the sea.

Val paused to gaze with despair at the dark gray waves breaking against the rocky shore, at this rugged land he'd once loved so well. He didn't seem to fit here any longer, didn't belong. He never had. He'd always been unwanted, an outsider—

No! Val ground his fingers against his brow, trying to crush the thought because it wasn't true. Not of Val St. Leger. It had been true of Rafe Mortmain. But Val was no longer sure where the Mortmain's pain ended and his own began.

"Val?"

He heard Lance directly behind him, his brother slightly out of breath from running to overtake him.

"Val, please," he said, resting one hand on Val's shoulder. "Hold up for a moment. You've got to tell me what happened back there."

Val shook him off. "What did it look like happened? I lost my temper a little."

"A *little*, Saint Valentine?"

"Don't call me that! Don't you ever call me that again."

Lance looked considerably taken aback at his outburst, but he flung up one hand in a placating gesture. "All right. It was naught but an old jest."

"A jest I am mightily tired of. I never did find it that amusing."

Lance frowned. "Val, are you feeling quite all right?"

"Yes, I'm fine," Val snapped. Everyone seemed to be asking him that of late. His servants. His mother. Even Kate. He was getting so damned tired of the question. "Maybe you should go ask Trewithan how he feels. And stop staring at me as if you don't even know who I am."

"Maybe I don't," Lance murmured.

"Just because I got a trifle angry?" Val asked irritably. "It is not as though you've never seen me lose my temper before."

"Aye, but not in that brutal fashion. What did Trewithan do to make you so angry?"

"Nothing," Val muttered. Nothing the man had not done before, lolling about in the taproom when he should have been making some effort to take care of his sickly wife and his babes.

Val didn't know why the sight of Trewithan sitting there guzzling ale should have so enraged him this time. Suddenly Trewithan had seemed like every bully Val had ever tolerated, every miscreant he'd forced himself to forgive, every bastard who'd tried his patience too far. And something had clawed inside of him like a dark demon struggling to get out, a demon he was finding harder and harder to control.

It terrified him, made him fear for his very reason. He felt another ragged cough threaten to tear past his throat and fought hard to suppress it.

"Look, Lance," he said. "I lost my temper with Trewithan, all right? But the man is still alive, so let's just forget about it. I don't want to discuss it any further."

"Damn it, Val, you've got to talk to someone. Tell me what is going on with you these past weeks. You have not come near Castle Leger. All of us are very worried about you."

The concern in Lance's dark eyes should have comforted him, but it only added to Val's irritation. Too little, too late, he thought.

"How touching." He felt his lip curl in an ugly sneer. "You'd have done better to worry about me when I was still limping around like a blasted cripple."

"Naturally I was overjoyed to discover that you found a cure for your leg, but—"

"Oh, I'll wager you were," Val interrupted. "Quite relieved the old guilty conscience, didn't it, brother?"

Lance flinched. "I never thought you wanted me to feel guilty, Val," he said quietly.

"Oh, aye, no indeed. Why should I? Just because I ended up spending most of my life lame and in pain because you chose to play the noble hero, charging about like a fool on that battlefield."

Lance paled, and Val knew he was hurting his brother as expertly as a surgeon wielding his knife, cutting into an old wound, but the bitterness swelled inside him until he thought he would choke if it wasn't released.

"It was your recklessness, your stupidity that resulted in me getting injured. You *should* rejoice to see me well."

Val took a malicious satisfaction in the stricken look that crept into his brother's eyes. Good. It was about bloody damn time that Lance was forced to feel—

No! Val clutched at the chain around his neck, fighting to still the crystal's insistent pulse. He truly was going mad. He didn't want to do this, say such poisonous things, hurt his brother this way. He backed away and groaned. "Oh, God, Lance. Why can't you just leave me the devil alone?"

Despite the pain and confusion darkening his eyes, Lance managed a sad smile. "For the same reason you didn't abandon me that day in Spain, even though you paid a heavy price for it. I am your brother."

Val only shook his head, tried to walk away. To his extreme agitation, Lance stubbornly kept pace by his side. They marched together in grim silence down the same shore where they had often rode together as boys, playing at knights, Sir Lancelot and Sir Galahad.

But the gulf had never seemed so wide between them, as yawning as the vast reaches of the sea, and Val felt as though he were drowning.

"Val," Lance began hesitantly. "Even if you don't want to talk to me, there is something I have to discuss with you."

"Oh?" Something in Lance's tone made Val wary, set him even further on edge. "What the devil is it?"

His brother expelled a deep sigh before going on, "This is truly awkward, but I have been hearing these rumors about you and Kate. Of course, I don't believe it, but—"

"Believe it," Val said tersely. "Every word."

Lance stared at him. "That you would have seduced Kate? No."

"There was very little seducing necessary. I desired her and she desired me."

Lance stumbled to a halt, gaping at Val with such dismay and disbelief that Val found himself longing to hit him. It was all he could do to keep his hands from gnarling into fists.

He faced his brother, clenching his jaw in a taut, hard line. "What is the matter, Sir Lancelot? Oh, I know. You were so dead certain that Kate would run mad for that young fool Victor. Is it that damned difficult to imagine that it is me she wants instead?"

"Of course not, Val, but I never thought that you could—could—"

"Could what? Fall in love? Feel desire like a normal man?"

"But for Kate? I realize she has always been infatuated with you. She is young and impetuous, but you are certainly old enough to know better. She is not—"

"Oh, aye, not my chosen bride according to our family's grand tradition. I'm sick to death of it. I wish I had never been born a bloody St. Leger."

"Val, you can't possibly mean what you're saying."

"Aye, for perhaps the first time in my life, I do. It's been all right for you, hasn't it, Lance? The great romantic legend. You've found your bride, your perfect love. Fairy tale ended, destiny fulfilled. But what about me? What the devil did I ever do to end up condemned to spend my days alone?"

"Nothing, Val. I have never understood Effie's refusal to find you a bride. In fact it angered me. But you . . . you always seemed so resigned."

"Maybe you should have looked a little closer, brother."

"Maybe I should have and I'm sorry for that."

Val dismissed the apology with a furious sweep of his hand and turned to walk away. He felt the crystal give a dangerous pulse when Lance moved to block his path.

"Val, wait. Listen. I swear I'll go to Effie right now and insist—"

But Val cut him off. "Don't you understand? It's too bloody late for that. Even if Effie found me this so-called chosen bride I wouldn't want her. I love Kate and she is in love with me."

"Then God help you both. Because you've studied our family history enough to know what happens to St. Legers who defy the Bride Finder."

"I'm cursed already. So what does it matter?"

"It matters to me. I care a great deal about both you and Kate. I won't stand aside and see you destroyed."

Lance's voice was low and earnest, but Val could see the stubborn resolve forming in his brother's eyes and it infuriated him.

"Damn you!" he grated. "You've interfered more than enough already, help-ing Effie arrange this blasted journey to London. But Kate will never set one foot into that coach. She's not going anywhere."

"Val, you have got to listen to reason—"

Val seized his brother by the front of his cape. "I saved your life once, Lance. Don't make me regret it any more than I already do. I vow I will destroy any man who tries to come between me and Kate, and that includes you."

Lance made no response to the threat or any attempt to release himself. "Val, you are clearly not yourself. Please let me help you. You know I would do anything."

His brother's voice was so full of concern, so unusually gentle.

He's speaking to me as though I've already run mad, Val thought. And per-haps he had. He could feel the black anger growing, swelling inside him, like some dark beast just waiting to be released. It would take so little for him to tear into Lance the same way he had Reeve Trewithan.

He was aware of the wild pounding of his heart, the harsh sound of his own breathing. It took all the will he possessed to release Lance, thrust his brother away from him.

"There's only one thing you can do. Keep the devil away from me."

Pivoting on his heel, Val stormed off down the beach, praying that this time Lance would have the wisdom not to follow. When Val paused to glance back, he saw Lance trudging back up the path, his broad shoulders slumped in a dejected fashion.

The sight filled Val with a mad urge to laugh. So many times Lance had re-jected his help, thrust him away. Now Lance could see exactly how it felt. Now it was his turn to go limping away.

Val experienced a sense of savage triumph . . . a triumph that slowly gave way to an overwhelming despair.

What had he done? He had struggled for years to ease Lance's guilt after that day on the battlefield, to end the estrangement between them. And now he had deliberately driven his brother away from him.

Val watched Lance's retreating figure, struggling with the urge to go after him, call him back, tell him everything. All about what had happened on All Hallows' Eve, Rafe Mortmain, and the crystal. Lance was his brother. He would find a way to help him.

Aye, and the first thing he'll want to do is take away the crystal. A dark voice seemed to warn him, *He'll take away your cure, your power, and he'll take away Kate. And then what will you have to live for?*

"Nothing," Val whispered, his hand closing possessively over the chain fastened about his throat. He watched with desperate eyes as Lance disappeared from view. Feeling more lost and alone than he had ever been, he turned and stumbled on down the beach.

By the time he reached Slate House, he was cold and shivering. Seized by another coughing spasm, he was left feeling so weak, he had to clutch the gate for support.

What the blazes was wrong with him? Anyone else with his symptoms he might have diagnosed with consumption. But somehow he knew better than that. He feared it was no disease that threatened to destroy him, at least no ordinary one.

It was the same darkness that had overtaken Rafe Mortmain.

"Val?"

From a great distance, he heard someone calling his name. For a moment he half dreaded, half hoped that it might be Lance. But when he lifted his head, he saw Kate racing down the beach, far outstripping Jem Sparkins who loped along behind.

Val released his breath in a ragged sob of relief. He managed to straighten away from the gate, holding his arms wide, and Kate flung herself into them. He strained her close, covering her face with kisses.

Kate, his one comfort, his one solace in all this madness. He emitted a hoarse protest when she attempted to draw away to gaze anxiously up at him.

"Val, are you all right? Jem said you were fighting with Reeve—" She broke off, an expression of horror chasing across her delicate features. "Oh, Val! L-look at your hands. Your beautiful hands."

He had no notion what she was talking about until he glanced down himself, for the first time becoming aware that his knuckles were bruised and swollen, the skin split and smeared with blood from the punishment he had dealt to Reeve Trewithan.

He stared at them numbly, the hands that had once been so smooth, so steady, the hands of a healer, a doctor. Now he scarce recognized those trembling fingers as his own. They appeared to belong to someone else, the hands of a coarse, rough-hewn stranger.

He felt something wet strike his knuckle, causing him to wince as it splashed against an open cut. Kate cradled his hand gently in her own and he realized she was weeping over him.

"Don't . . . don't cry, my wild girl," he murmured, barely getting the words out before another wave of weakness washed over him. He would have collapsed beside the gate if not for Kate and the sudden support of Jem Sparkin's strong arm.

*　*　*

Val slumped down in the library chair, his eyes half-closed. Kate felt she should have insisted that Jem take him straight to his bed, but Val had adamantly refused and Kate did not dare to press him.

That in itself was a lowering thought. Kate had never imagined she would have cause to fear Val St. Leger. But even she had learned to be wary of his temper.

She drew up a low stool and perched beside him. Trying to be as gentle as she could, she bathed and treated his hands. His knuckles were so raw, he should have winced when she applied the witch hazel, but Val didn't seem to be feeling much of anything. Beneath the sweep of his lashes, the look in his eyes was terrifyingly vacant, as though he was fast slipping away from her into some dark world she could not begin to imagine.

He did not stir even when Jem slipped into the library to fetch away the basin of water. The servant exchanged a worried look with Kate as he set down a brandy decanter and stole quietly from the room. Kate poured out a glassful and pressed it to Val's lips.

"Here, drink this."

He roused himself enough to take a few sips.

"All of it," she commanded.

Val took a few more swallows, then pushed it away. "Playing doctor now, my Kate?"

He lifted one hand to inspect it. "You do quite well, although it feels most strange. I was always the healer. I am not accustomed to allowing anyone to take care of me."

"Maybe it is time you did."

His lips crooked in a sad semblance of his old smile, a smile that quickly faded. "About what happened back there in the village—"

"I am sure it was not your fault," Kate said quickly. "That Reeve Trewithan has long deserved a thrashing."

"Perhaps that is true. What worries me is how much I enjoyed it. I am not supposed to like hurting people. I am a doctor."

"You are also a man. And a very good, honorable one."

"I used to think so. Now I am no longer sure what I am."

The tormented look in his eyes was almost more than Kate could bear. She tenderly brushed the strands of hair from his brow. Val caught her hand and hauled her down onto his knee, just as he had done so many times during her girlhood when she had been hurting or miserable, needing his comfort.

Kate curled against him, resting her head against his shoulder, trying to recapture the memory of those times, the feel of Val's strong arms around her, his calming presence that promised to make everything all right.

But that all seemed so long ago. Now Val was the one who was hurting and she had caused it. All these frightening changes. There was only one way she could make everything right for him. End the spell. Let him go.

Concealing her aching heart behind a tremulous smile, she caressed his cheek. "Val, please. You are not well. You look purely exhausted. You've been tearing off on that wretched horse of yours every day, riding as hard as the devil. I don't even know where you go."

"To Lostland," he murmured.

"W-what?" Kate straightened abruptly, certain she could not have heard him right.

"I've been riding to Lostland."

It was the grim nickname the locals applied to the old Mortmain estate. Long since abandoned, the manor was no more than a blackened ruin set upon one of the most bleak, dangerous sections of the coast.

"Lostland?" Kate repeated in dismay. "Val, you always warned me to stay away from there. Why ever would you want to go near that terrible place?"

"I—I don't know. Looking for answers, perhaps."

"Answers to what? You already know everything there is to be known about the Mortmains. You were the one who taught me how evil they were, especially Rafe Mortmain. He was the worst of the lot."

"Aye, I suppose he was."

"Val, you *know* he was. He stole the St. Leger sword and nearly got you killed. The man was a pure devil."

"Or else in so much pain he could not help himself. More pain than I could have ever possibly imagined."

Kate regarded him in uneasy astonishment. What was Val talking about? If there was any subject Val had ever been unyielding about, it was his mistrust and condemnation of Rafe Mortmain. She touched one hand to his brow, anxiously testing for signs of a fever.

Val gave a hollow laugh. "Aye, you think I must be delirious to be speaking so of a cursed Mortmain, and perhaps you are right. I seem to be questioning everything of late. Nothing is as certain or as clear to me as it once was. Sometimes I fear I am going a bit mad."

The look he cast Kate wrenched at her heart, his dark eyes full of fear and confusion. She flung her arms about him in a fierce hug.

"Oh, Val, all will be well soon. I promise you. Everything will seem better to you come morning." Or at least so she prayed, that she would be able to undo her terrible spell, all the wrong she had done.

She drew back, cupping her hand to his cheek. "All you need is some rest. You should be in bed."

"With you?" he asked huskily. He brought her hand to his lips, a dark light springing to his eyes, that glint she recognized all too well. Before she could even protest, his hand covered the nape of her neck, drawing her mouth to his. His lips tasted of heat, brandy, and seduction.

When she attempted to draw away, he only deepened the embrace, his kiss powerful, intoxicating, stirring her senses as he never failed to do. Kate pushed against his chest.

"Val, p-please," she murmured as his mouth whispered down her neck in an exploration that caused her to shiver. Kate bit down hard on her lip, fighting to resist the sensations he was arousing. She could not afford to let him lure her into his bed again. Not when her love had already caused him so much harm. Not when she had a far different rendezvous to keep tonight.

With a sorcerer, upon a hillside, near the old standing stone.

As Val's hand crept up to caress her breast, Kate shuddered. With a mighty wrench, she pulled herself free, scrambling off his lap.

"N-no," she said, wishing her voice carried more conviction. She stepped out of his reach, shaking her head.

Val gripped the arms of the chair. Kate emitted a faint protest when he thrust himself to his feet and stalked toward her. She retreated a step, fearing his anger at her rejection. But the pain in his eyes was far worse.

"You, too, my Kate?" he demanded in a voice of haunting sadness. "You intend to shun me, turn against me, just like everyone in this cursed village."

"No, Val. Of course not," she said, horrified that he could even think such a thing. It was all she could do not to rush straight into his arms, reassure him. She hugged herself tightly to stifle the impulse.

"No one is turning against you. Everyone in Torrecombe admires and respects you. More than that, they care a great deal about you."

"They did once. As long as I was the sainted doctor, as long I was perfect. Lord knows I tried to be. Too hard. I can't do it anymore. I am tired, Kate. S-so tired."

"I know, my dearest," she murmured. "That is because you need to—"

"Oh, aye, I know," he said bitterly. "Val, go lie down. Get some rest. Go to bed. But without you."

He tried to draw her into his arms. It took all her will to resist him. The desperation in his eyes was tearing her in two.

"Kate, why won't you stay with me tonight? Do you no longer want me?"

Not want him? If he only knew . . . Kate turned away from him, winking back a sharp sting of tears.

"Of course I want you. It is only that I am afraid."

"Afraid of what?"

Afraid that her cursed spell was destroying him. Kate wracked her mind desperately for another excuse.

"Afraid that—that we are being too reckless. That you might get me with child."

"And you would not want to have my babe?"

Besides Val himself, there was nothing that Kate could imagine wanting more. She swallowed hard and shook her head. "N-no. We are unwed. After what I have been through myself, I would not want my child born a bastard."

"Do you think I would ever allow that to happen?" Val seized her by the shoulders and spun her about to face him. "I would have already married you. It is you who keeps delaying, making excuses."

Only because she realized that as soon as the spell was removed, he would no longer want her. Perhaps not even as his friend. Kate ducked her head, avoiding his eyes to hide her despair.

"Well, I—I had hoped we might obtain your family's blessing first."

"That is never going to happen. My brother is already plotting to take you from me. We nearly came to blows over it."

Val fighting with Lance? And all because of her wicked spell.

"Oh, Val, I am so s-sorry," she quavered. "I never meant for any of this to happen, to set you at odds with your own family."

"Damn my family. The St. Legers are all a parcel of fools. I'll destroy the entire lot of them before I—" Val checked himself, looking as horrified by his angry words as she was.

He pressed his fist against his brow as though to crush the terrible thought. "N-no. I don't mean that. I don't want to fight my brother or anyone else. My father is due home any day and everything will only get worse. He will move heaven and hell to keep us apart and I am afraid that I might do something that I—"

Val shuddered. "God help me. We have got to get the devil out of here. Now. Tonight."

"T-tonight?" Kate faltered.

"Aye. You said that we should elope and you were right."

"But not right now." Kate attempted to smile, conceal her dismay behind a jest. "I don't even have my nightcap or tooth powder."

"I will buy you anything you could possibly need."

"And what about Effie? I have to at least talk to her and—"

"You can leave her a note." Val marched to his desk to fetch her ink and paper. "Now send for Jem and I will give him instructions to have the carriage brought around."

Kate gaped at Val in dismay. He could not possibly be serious. But he clearly was. When she made no move to obey his command, he strode impatiently toward the door to summon Jem himself.

When Kate moved to block his path, he shot her a dark look that caused her to tremble.

"Val, please—" she began.

"No more excuses, Kate."

"I am not going to make any. But you must give me a little more time."

"Time for what?" he demanded. "To change your mind? I warn you, Kate. I would never tolerate that. You are mine now and I don't intend to ever let you go."

Kate's heart thudded as she peered up at him. Was Val actually threatening her? The light glinting in his eyes was hard, dangerous. Her spell had invoked a strain of ruthlessness in him she would never have imagined possible. If she refused to go with him, she realized that he was now fully capable of forcing her. And if he succeeded in dragging her away from Torrecombe tonight, she would never be able to end the spell.

Slipping her arms about his neck, she pleaded, "I need time only to prepare for the journey, to pack a few of my treasured things. Just one more day, Val. Please."

She stretched up on tiptoe to whisper a kiss across his lips. The set of his own mouth was so grim, so unyielding, she trembled, certain he was going to refuse. And then what was she going to do?

But his eyes flickered and to her intense relief, he appeared to relax a trifle. When he gathered her close to him, there was a hint of Val's old gentleness in his arms.

"Very well, my Kate," he murmured. "Another day, but no more. We will leave tomorrow evening."

"But that is the night of the masquerade," she reminded him hesitantly.

"All the better. In all the commotion, it will be some time before we are even missed. I shall have my coach waiting at the crossroads by the castle. You shall come to me no later than eight of the clock."

Kate nodded numbly.

He brushed a light kiss atop her brow. "You won't fail me, Kate."

"N-no."

Kate steadfastly avoided his eyes, but he seized her by her chin, forcing her to look up at him.

"Promise me." His expression was a strange combination of demand and tenderness, the hint of danger never far away.

"I—I promise," Kate said, then promptly buried her face against his shoulder, feeling sick at heart. She was forced to lie to him, deceive him yet again. She had only one consolation.

After tonight, it was not a promise Val would ever want her to keep.

CHAPTER SIXTEEN

*T*he night was brisk and clear, the sky a canopy of brilliant stars, the moon a bright silver crescent shimmering light over the rugged landscape. The sea frothed against the shore, whispering a slow seductive rhythm. A perfect night for romance, for stealing away to find a lover upon the towering hillside.

Except that Kate hadn't come to find the man she loved, only to weave the dark magic that would cause her to lose him forever. Her cloak drawn tight about her, she trudged up the hillside with a heavy heart, her step nowhere near as bold as it had been on All Hallows' Eve. Perhaps because she felt as though she had aged a lifetime since then.

Rather than filling her with a reckless sense of adventure, this time the vast lonely reaches of the night made her feel only small and insignificant. An impudent mortal once more about to meddle with powers far beyond her control, powers that she would have done well to leave alone.

Her footsteps faltered as she approached the ancient standing stone. Etched in moonlight, the massive rock towered above her, more mysterious than ever. Considering the havoc she had wreaked the first time, Kate doubted she would have dared ever to approach this place alone again. But she wasn't alone. *He* was waiting.

Prospero stood at the base of the stone, an imposing shadow of a man. On many of her visits to the tower, Kate had frequently thought he had looked almost human, too real to be a ghost.

But tonight, out here on the moon-spun hill high above the crashing sea, he looked every inch the phantom sorcerer he was reputed to be, a dark-eyed Merlin with his iridescent cape flowing off his broad shoulders, his black hair swept back from the haughty angles of his face.

Kate knew she had no reason to fear him, but she could not repress a shiver. She crept forward to present herself with a tremulous curtsy. A sudden breeze whispered past her face as though cold fingers crooked beneath her chin, compelling her to look up at him.

The sorcerer's narrowed eyes glinted as though he was somewhat amused by her unusually humbled stance.

"Good evening, Mistress Kate. I had begun to fear you might have changed your mind."

"No, I have not. And I hope neither have you." She regarded him anxiously. "Have you?"

"You perceive me here." He swept her a magnificent bow, his spangled cape flashing in the moonlight. "At your service, mistress, although sometimes I doubt whether you truly have need of me. I have wondered whether you might be a bit of a witch after all."

"Why would you think a thing like that?"

"Because you seem to have done a fair job of bewitching me, persuading me to do things I have done for no mortal before."

"You mean like helping me with the spell."

"No, I mean like persuading me to venture beyond Castle Leger. For centuries I have divided my time between those walls and the oblivion of the sky beyond. I do not venture out across the countryside."

"Why not? I thought you could drift wherever you pleased."

Prospero smiled ruefully. "Even a ghost has limits of endurance, my dear. Long ago I realized it best to remain in my tower, cloister myself away from the world. It is far easier on the heart not to gaze upon all you have lost."

His eyes swept past her, seeming to take in hungrily all the beauty of the moonlit hills, the rocky shore, the inky expanse of the sea beckoning toward so many intriguing faraway places. A rare sadness touched Prospero's inscrutable face and Kate realized that it was possible for even a phantom to be haunted.

When she had plagued him for his help, she had never realized what it might cost him to do so. He had ever appeared impervious to any such human emotion as regret. Kate fetched a deep sigh. She seemed to bring nothing but misery to everyone around her these days.

"I—I am sorry," she murmured. "I should never have asked you—"

But he cut her off with an imperious sweep of his hand. Whatever bittersweet memories the sight of the sea-swept coast and darkened hills might have conjured, Prospero was quick to shutter them away again.

" 'Tis no great matter, my dear," he said briskly. "Now shall we set to work?"

Kate nodded, swallowing nervously. She plucked at the hood of her cloak, drawing it as far forward over her face as possible. Prospero bent to peer quizzically at her face now hidden beneath the folds of fabric.

"Er, Kate, I realize the practice of magic calls for a certain amount of panache, but there is really no need for you to try to assume the guise of some ghostly monk."

"I wasn't," she said indignantly. "I am merely bracing myself for the storm."

"Storm? What storm? There is not a cloud in the sky."

"I know. But there was on All Hallows' Eve. Thunder and lightning. I assumed that you are going to have to conjure some."

Prospero essayed a silky laugh. "By my faith, milady, you have a more inflated notion of my powers than I do. Were we within the castle walls, I might conjure for you the *illusion* of lightning, but even I cannot alter the weather."

"Then what are we to do?" Kate asked in dismay. "There was a storm the night I cast—"

"So there should not be one now," Prospero cut in. "Have you already forgotten what I told you? To undo the spell, all must be reversed, the opposite of what took place then. Therefore this fine clear night is perfect."

"Oh." Kate eased back her hood, feeling foolish. She was glad the night concealed the traces of her embarrassed flush, but in any event, Prospero's attention had shifted elsewhere.

He paced before the standing stone, muttering, "However, we still must have our bonfire."

"I'll go gather some wood," Kate said, preparing to dart off at once, but he stayed her with a languid wave of his hand.

"Not necessary, milady. Fire is one minor bit of magic I can provide." Reaching beneath his cloak, Prospero produced his mysterious chunk of crystal. The stone reflected the moonlight with a cold, hard glitter.

Remembering all of Prospero's warnings about how dangerous the crystal could be, Kate took a wary step backward. He set the sparkling stone upon the ground. With a wave of his hand and some muttered words, the crystal vanished, lost in a whoosh of flames licking upward toward the night sky. The eerie ghostlike blaze threw off no heat, but all the same crackled with a fiery intensity, bathing Prospero in a hellish glow until he, too, appeared as ethereal as the dancing firelight.

He extended his open palm toward her. "You have brought what I asked for?"

Kate fished beneath the folds of her cloak and produced a piece of coal that she handed over to him. Prospero held it to the light, examining the markings she had scratched onto the glossy black surface.

"S.V.," he read. "You remembered to reverse the initials as I told you?"

"Yes."

"So the true initials of the men you bewitched would have been V.S."

Kate nodded uncomfortably, averting her eyes.

Prospero continued to study the chunk of coal in frowning silence. "I will try to do as you ask, mistress, but it will not be easy, undoing only half the spell. Removing the hex from one while leaving the other—"

"I no longer want that," Kate spoke up hastily. "You must undo it all, remove the spell from both men."

Prospero's brows arched upward in surprise. "You have now decided to surrender the man you love?"

"Yes." Kate fretted with the lining of her cloak, realizing the moment had come that she had dreaded. She could no longer avoid confessing to Prospero the truth.

"There is something I haven't told you," she said. "About the man that I love, the one I sought to bewitch. His name is—is Val St. Leger."

Kate braced herself for a supernatural explosion of wrath. When moments passed and nothing happened, she risked a glance up at Prospero and was astonished to find his lips curled in an expression of quiet amusement.

"I already knew that, my dear."

"But how could you? Have you been using your sorcery to spy upon me?"

"It took no wizardry to guess your secret, milady. All those charming afternoons you called upon me in my tower, we frequently discussed my descendants."

"But I am certain I never mentioned Val's name. Not even once."

"No, not once. Try more like a hundred times. You scarce seemed able to begin a sentence that did not begin with his name. *Val always says* or *Val thinks that* . . . Only a woman deeply in love could be so tiresome on the subject of a man."

Kate winced, realizing how she must have betrayed herself again and again, and all the while fancying herself so clever. So Prospero had known all along and he wasn't the least angry with her? Perhaps he did not understand quite everything.

"I am not Val's chosen bride, you know," she said gruffly.

"I surmised that as well. Else you would not have resorted to witchcraft."

Kate regarded him in frank amazement. "Are you not angry with me for defying your legend?"

Prospero shrugged. "It is not my legend, Kate. There was no Bride Finder in my day."

"Then how did you choose your wife?"

"In the most mundane and practical way. I found the woman with the most wealth and powerful family connections and married her on the spot. As I told you before, the pursuit of true love held no interest for me then."

"And now?"

"Now?" Prospero's mouth twisted ruefully. "Now I think it is a trifle too late. About five centuries late, to be precise. But I believe we were discussing you.

"Over the years I have had opportunity to observe the legend at work, the happiness of those St. Legers who were joined through the offices of the Bride Finder, the disasters that overtook the ones who were not. Lovers who were obviously mismatched."

"Like me and Val," Kate said unhappily.

"Aye, like you and your quiet scholar. And yet . . ." Prospero studied her through narrowed eyes. "Rarely have I ever witnessed any woman pursue a man with such single-minded devotion."

"It wasn't devotion. It was pure selfishness. I used black magic to get what I wanted, never thinking of what might be best for Val and what it could do to him."

Her throat constricted. "My spell is destroying him. At first I was able to deceive myself that I had done him good, had cured his injured leg. But instead I have thrust him into worse torment, making him love me against his own sense of honor, his reason.

"He has changed so much, become so angry, so bitter I hardly recognize him at times. The kind, gentle man I once knew seems to be fading before my eyes and—"

Kate had to pause to swallow before she finished in a choked voice. "I am terrified that I am killing him."

Prospero's brow knitted in a deep frown. "All that from one spell, milady? I don't think it possible. That incantation you employed was no more than a bit of whimsy I acquired on my travels and set down. I am astonished that it worked at all."

"Well, it did. Or at least enough to make Val love me. Perhaps it is the St. Leger curse that is doing the rest. I don't know, but whatever it is, you must help me to save him."

"I will do my best," Prospero said gravely. "But when I do succeed in ending this spell, what of you?"

Kate shrugged. "Oh, I—I will be fine. Everyone has always told me that all I felt for Val was a silly schoolgirl infatuation, that I would get over it, forget him."

"And do you believe that? I think you must be more in love with him than ever if you are willing to let him go."

"That may be true. But it doesn't matter about me. All that matters is—is Val, that he be restored to himself again." Kate felt a single tear escape to trickle down her cheek.

Prospero's eyes glowed with a rare gentleness. He reached out as though he would comfort her only to check the futile gesture before his fingers passed straight through her. Kate fiercely dashed aside her own tears.

"C-could we please just get on with this? Get it over with."

Prospero nodded, turning slowly back to the fire. "Very well, milady, although I am curious on one point. Who was the other man you bewitched by mistake?"

"Victor St. Leger."

"*Another* St. Leger?" the sorcerer exclaimed. "By God, milady, when you brew up a disaster, you don't do it by halves."

"No, I don't," Kate agreed wretchedly.

"Never mind, child. We shall soon make an end, but you had best stand well clear."

Prospero took up his position before the fire and Kate crept back a safe distance, her heart torn between dread and hope. Despite her feelings of misery, she could not help but be awed by the scene before her, the druid stone, the leaping flames, the sorcerer at his work.

Prospero threw no shadow, but he seemed to loom larger, his face raised to the night. He lifted his arms and flung back his head, his dark mantle rippling from his shoulders.

Low spoken words began to issue from his throat that sounded nothing like the halting syllables Kate had spoken on All Hallows' Eve. The incantation flowed from his lips faster and faster like some terrible dark poetry designed to summon all the powers of hell.

"*Mithrun dineelo,*" Prospero roared. With one mighty flourish of his hand, he flung the chunk of coal into the fire. The flames shot upward in a deafening explosion that caused Kate to cry out, fall to her knees.

The fire flung out sparks like a blaze of skyrockets streaking across the night sky, white-hot comets of blinding flame. Kate cowered down, shielding her eyes.

Another eruption followed, violent enough to rend the earth in two. Kate lay still, her hands clutched over her head. Then suddenly all was silent except for the distant rush of the waves breaking against the rocks far below.

Kate released an unsteady breath and cautiously raised her head. The flames now burned low to the ground like a fire that was about to die. And Prospero . . . Kate's heart lurched. For a moment she feared the sorcerer had simply vanished, left her there alone.

Then she realized that he stood over her, extending one long graceful hand as though he would use his powers to help her to her feet. But Kate felt as though she had had quite enough of magic. Enough to last her to the end of her days.

Although she trembled, she managed to scramble up unaided, brushing dirt and twigs from her cloak with shaking fingers.

"Did it work?" she whispered.

Prospero lifted his head, his exotic dark eyes alert like some strange wild creature searching the night. "I believe so. Whatever spell you may have cast has now been undone."

There was an odd hesitation to his words, but Kate barely noticed. Val was going to be all right. Her spell had been ended. Sometime later, she knew the pain would come, the full realization of what this meant for her, the end of all her dreams. But for now she was flooded with relief. She would have flung her arms about Prospero's neck, embraced him if it had been possible to hug a phantom.

But all she could offer him was her tremulous smile. "Oh, thank you. Thank you."

Prospero acknowledged her words with a somber nod of his head, only wishing he felt he had done something to deserve Kate's shining-eyed gratitude. He had to admit he had put on a dazzling display, had acted to the full limits of his powers.

Why then was he left feeling that he had accomplished nothing except some fire and noise? That the evil that had first summoned him back to Castle Leger still remained, perhaps stronger than ever?

Drifting to the fire, he quelled the flames with one abrupt gesture. Only the glowing crystal remained. Another flick of his hand and even it went dark. He secreted the dangerous object back beneath his cloak, doing his best to suppress his doubts or at least to conceal them from Kate.

The girl had been through enough. Her face looked pale, completely drained of its usual animation.

"The hour waxes late, milady," he said gently. "You should head home for your bed."

"Aye." Kate cast him a hesitant look. "And I should also bid you farewell."

Farewell? The word startled Prospero, but only at first. Of course, he should have been expecting it. All transaction between them was now at an end. Kate would have no reason to return to his tower.

He was astonished by the sudden pang the realization cost him, but he quickly dismissed the wayward emotion. After all, it was not as though he, Prospero, would ever deign to miss the company of a mere mortal.

"I shall be leaving for London soon," Kate said.

"To London," he echoed. "So far away."

"Aye, but it is for the best. Like you, I believe it is far easier on the heart not to be forever gazing upon all that one has lost."

She made a brave effort to smile that was somehow worse than if she had burst into tears. Prospero half raised his hand, only to lower it in frustration. He could never remember longing so much to touch anyone, to offer some warm gesture of consolation.

Instead he stepped back, making her his most magnificent bow. "Fare thee well, milady. And may the good fairies watch over you, see you safely to better days."

Kate nodded and curtsied, apparently not trusting herself to speak. She headed off through the heather toward where she had left her horse tethered at the bottom of the hill, her shoulders squared, her head held as high as any duchess. But Prospero knew well what a great deal of misery and fear could be concealed beneath such a stance. He had marched after the same fashion to his own execution.

"Ah, Kate," he murmured sadly. "If only I was half the sorcerer I claim to be. Then I could surely devise some magic to mend a broken heart."

But all he could do was let her go, her small, valiant figure vanishing into the darkness.

CHAPTER SEVENTEEN

*T*he great hall at Castle Leger had stood silent and unused for many years, but tonight it was as though the great wizard Merlin himself had swept the vast stone chamber back through time, back to the days of Camelot.

A fire blazed on the massive hearth, the medieval banqueting table once again covered with steaming silver platters of food. Ladies in their kirtles and lords in their tunics pranced out the steps of a stately dance while minstrels piped out the tune. Flaming torches and hundreds of candles lit the scene. They cast a glow over the sword thrust through the stone mounted upon the dais, King Arthur's Excalibur waiting to be reclaimed.

Only if one looked too critically could one tell it was all illusion. The tapestries lining the walls were faded, showing centuries of wear. Many of the couples parading down the center of the room giggled and stumbled over the steps of a dance long since forgotten. And the sword Excalibur was merely fashioned of wood, its costly jewels made of paste.

But Effie Fitzleger clapped her hands together and surveyed the chamber with a delighted "ooh." Her horned headdress nearly poked out the eye of some stout knight as she turned excitedly to her companion.

"Oh, Kate, is it not all too wonderful?"

"Wonderful," Kate repeated dully.

"Well, of course, I admit it is nothing compared to the balls we will attend in London. Only imagine what that will be like."

Kate didn't want to imagine. Tonight was hard enough to endure, trying to pretend that nothing was amiss, that her heart was here and not at Slate Cottage. Effie's brow puckered with anxiety as she fussed over Kate, straightening the golden circlet perched upon her head, smoothing out the sleeves of Kate's ruby red velvet kirtle.

"Oh, dear," Effie fretted. "You did promise me you would try to enjoy yourself this evening."

"I am *trying*, Effie," Kate said. But Effie had no notion how difficult it was. The older woman was completely oblivious to the fact that beyond the music, the laughter, there was a tension in the air. Even guests who had traveled here from the more remote parts of the countryside seemed aware that there was something seriously amiss with the St. Leger family and Kate was the cause.

Stares turned in her direction, some cold, some curious. Enough to make Kate wish she had pleaded a headache and stayed home. But that would have devastated Effie, who had been looking forward to this event with all the eager anticipation of a child expecting Christmas.

Kate was relieved when Mr. Trimble claimed her guardian's attention. The plump vicar had attired himself appropriately enough as a medieval friar. Half tripping on her train, Effie peeked at him over the brim of her fan and was soon engaged in a coy flirtation.

Neither of them noticed when Kate slipped quietly away to take up an unobtrusive position against the nearest wall. Studying the brilliant scene before her through listless eyes, her gaze traveled to the tapestry mounted at the end of the hall behind the dais. The faded weaving depicted the St. Leger dragon wreaking havoc upon some hapless villagers, but the tapestry's real purpose was to conceal the door leading up to Prospero's tower.

Kate wondered if all this revelry disturbed the great sorcerer. But more than likely Prospero had already returned to . . . what was it he had called it? *The oblivion of the skies.*

Kate sighed deeply, envying him. She wished herself far away, anywhere but here. Not that she cared that much for the gossip, the disapproval that seemed to surround her. She was accustomed to that. Far worse was how kindly many of the St. Legers were still treating her, especially the lady, Madeline.

Val's mother had greeted her warmly as ever, but Kate had seen the shadows of worry darkening the older woman's clear green eyes. Kate would so have liked to reassure her, all of them. There was no longer any cause to fret over Val St. Leger, but she supposed they would all find that out soon enough.

She had raced to Slate House first thing that morning, but had been intercepted on the path by Jem Sparkins. The haggard-looking servant had informed her that Master Val had passed a bad night. He seemed to be resting

easier this morning, but he had given instructions that he was not up to receiving any callers. Jem feared the doctor's old affliction must be returning to
plague him because he had dispatched Jem to Castle Leger to find the other
cane his master had left there in storage.

That had been all Kate had needed to hear. She had retraced her steps,
heading back home with a heavy heart.

Her spell was undone. All was as it had been before, including his injured
leg. But at least she had managed to save his sanity, his life, Kate reassured
herself. Her gaze traveled wistfully over the throng of milling guests, but she
truly did not expect Val to put in an appearance tonight.

And not just because his leg was plaguing him. She quailed when she
thought of the shock he must be suffering now that he was restored to himself. With what bewilderment and horror he would view these past weeks, all
the times they had made love. And with what self-blame.

Kate knew she would have to find the courage to explain to him exactly
what she had done, that none of what had transpired was his fault. She only
prayed that Val would be able to forgive her in time.

"You are not dancing, milady," a voice murmured from the shadows of a
nearby pillar. Kate raised her head, her first glimpse of lustrous dark hair, that
familiar hawklike profile causing her heart to miss a beat.

But as the man stepped closer, she saw at once that he wasn't Val, only his
twin. Val and Lance had never been identical, but the resemblance between
them was marked enough for Kate to find it painful.

Lance had ever been a dashing rogue and it had been an easy matter for
him to transform himself into his namesake. He made a resplendent Sir
Lancelot in his blue tunic embroidered with silver.

Sweeping her a courtly bow, he extended his hand toward her with that
dazzling smile that had never failed to enchant any lady he'd ever met.

"Mistress Kate, will you do me the honor?"

So even Lance was determined to ignore the rumors and treat her with far
more generosity than she deserved. It was all Kate could do not to burst into
tears.

She summoned up a brittle smile, trying to infuse a lightness into her tone.
"Oh, n-no, thank you. Sir Lancelot should more likely be paying court to his
Guinevere."

"Alas, my queen is fully occupied at the moment." Lance indicated where
his wife was going down the line of the dance. A radiant young woman, Rosalind St. Leger had always borne the appearance of fairy princess with her pe-
tite frame and shimmering blond hair.

She was standing up with a shy colt of a boy who tread upon her dainty toes with every awkward step, but Rosalind merely cast the lad an encouraging smile. Lance's lady had ever been noted for her kindness.

Lance observed his wife for a moment, his eyes shining with an adoration he made no effort to conceal. Then he turned back to Kate, but she sidled away from him, refusing his repeated solicitation for her hand.

"I am afraid I would inflict more damage upon your feet than that boy is doing to poor Rosalind."

"I doubt that," Lance said. "Although as I recollect you always were more fond of fighting than dancing. You and I used to have some mighty sword battles in this very hall when you were still a scrubby brat."

Kate smiled in spite of herself at his teasing. "Aye, with the toy swords your father had fashioned. I recall many rainy afternoons when I wreaked havoc upon the noble Sir Lancelot."

"Only because I allowed you to do so," Lance retorted.

"Pooh! I often managed to get past your guard, even if you did have an unfair advantage with me in my petticoats."

Lance laughed. "Petticoats, milady? I seem to remember you had a shocking penchant for donning breeches."

"I suppose I did," Kate admitted sheepishly. "Much to Val's horror. He always used to scold you for encouraging me to behave like a hoyden. But whenever you were getting the best of me in a duel, he could never resist pulling me aside and whispering advice in my ear so that I could . . ."

But Kate faltered, the mention of Val casting a shadow over both her and Lance's memories. A heavy silence fell that Lance broke at last.

"Kate," he said. "I hope you know that I have ever been your friend, but— but—" He hesitated, floundering for words. Kate came swiftly to his rescue.

"It is all right, Lance. I know what you want to say and you are right. It was foolish of me ever to hope that someday I would defeat your legend, that Val and I could be together. I realize now that is impossible. I will be leaving for London just as you want me to do. I have even begun encouraging Effie to hasten the day. You should be well rid of me before Christmas."

Kate expected that her assurance would fill Lance with relief. Instead he cast her an unhappy look and slapped his palm against the pillar in sheer frustration.

"Damn the legend." He retracted his words almost immediately. "No, I don't mean that. Effie, the Bride Finder, helped to match me with my Rosalind, to find more love and happiness than I ever deserved. I just don't know why she could not have found such a bride for Val, why it could not have been you."

"Me?" Kate said, startled.

"You have obviously done much good for him."

"Good for him? Lance, I have been more of a plague to Val than anything else."

"Aye, you plagued him to abandon many of his quiet, reclusive ways, to laugh, to be less serious. And as for his influence on you, he—he—"

"He gentled me," Kate said softly. "Took a rough, wild girl and convinced her that one day she could grow up to be a remarkable woman."

"And so you have."

When Kate shook her head deprecatingly, he pinched her chin in that playful fashion he'd often used to tease her before. But his eyes were full of sadness. "Oh, Kate. How I wish things could be different for you and Val."

"So do I," she murmured, making a valiant effort to smile.

Lance looked as though he would have liked to say a great deal more, but his attention was diverted by a late arrival, an old friend from his regiment whom he had not seen for years. Obliged to excuse himself to greet his guest, Lance took a reluctant leave of her.

His departure left Kate feeling more bleak than ever. She began desperately to calculate the minutes until this painful affair would be over, when she spied Mollie Grey.

The timid girl had also taken refuge against the wall, a wistful shepherdess clutching her crook while she eyed the dancers. Her silk-striped gown gave her more the look of a Dresden figurine than a peasant girl who seriously tended to the task of minding sheep, but no gentleman present tonight would have found fault with her appearance.

The heightened color in her cheeks, the hope that shone from the girl's eyes rendered her unusually lovely. She anxiously scanned the crowd, and Kate had no doubt whom Mollie looked for so eagerly.

At least the time had come for Kate to right one wrong she had done. Fixing a determined smile on her face, she marched in Mollie's direction.

"Good evening, Mollie."

The girl started at her approach. But before she could even speak, Kate seized her by the wrist and tugged her away from the wall. "Come with me."

Mollie must have read her intentions clearly because the girl's eyes widened with something akin to panic and she attempted to hang back.

"Oh, no, Kate! Pray give me a moment. I—I don't think I am quite ready."

"Of course you are. You are Victor's chosen bride but he is never going to notice you if you keep hiding in corners. Even destiny sometimes needs a little push."

"B-but Kate, do you truly think—"

"Yes, I do," Kate said firmly. She had spied Victor earlier, an earnest young knight clad in a coat and helmet of chain mail. He had seemed indifferent to Kate's arrival, making no effort to approach or foist his attentions upon her. The spell was well and truly over.

Now if the young fool could only be persuaded where his true happiness lay.

Allowing Mollie no chance to protest further, Kate dragged the girl across the great hall. Mollie gripped her crook, stumbling after her, appearing nervous enough to faint.

Kate paused near the banqueting table to scan the crowd. Clad in that ridiculous chain mail and as tall as he was, Victor should not have been that difficult to spot. Surely he could not have left the ball already?

No, but he appeared on the verge of doing so. Kate saw him near the huge arch that led out to the ancient drawbridge. She all but wrenched Mollie off her feet in her efforts to overtake him.

He had nearly disappeared beneath the arch when Kate called after him, "Victor, wait!"

Mollie blushed, cringed, and seemed ready to die on the spot. Victor came slowly around, an arrested expression stealing across his features. He looked almost as though . . . as though he were seeing Mollie Grey for the first time.

Kate rushed up to him, the hapless Mollie in tow.

"Victor, surely you are not planning to abandon us already?"

"Well, yes, I—" His eyes lit up.

"No," he said softly. "Not anymore."

Kate sank into a playful curtsy. "Good knight, may I be so bold as to present a damsel most desirous of dancing with you?"

A slow smile spread across Victor's handsome face. "Aye, indeed you may."

Kate stepped quickly back, all but thrusting Mollie into his arms. The girl cowered behind her crook, looking as though she would have hidden behind the slender staff if she could. She peered shyly up at Victor, her entire heart surfacing in her eyes.

"G-good evening, Mr. St. Leger," she said breathlessly.

Victor blinked. "Good evening, Miss Grey," he replied gravely.

An awkward silence ensued in which the pair of them stood and stared helplessly at each other until Kate's patience gave out.

"You had best make haste," she said. "I believe the next set is already forming." When neither of them stirred, Kate seized Mollie's hand and thrust it toward Victor.

To her astonishment and unease, Victor made no move to take it. "Your pardon, Miss Grey, but I fear I cannot oblige you this evening. It is this deuced chain mail, far—far too heavy for dancing. A most unfortunate choice of costume."

"Oh," Mollie said in a small voice, lowering her eyes. "Of course, I—I understand."

Did she? Kate certainly did not. She glared at Victor. "If the blasted thing is too heavy, then take it off. You have a tunic on underneath."

Victor ignored her suggestion and smiled politely at Mollie instead. "I am sure there are any number of gentlemen here who would be delighted to stand up with you. Do allow me to help find you a more suitable partner."

But Mollie had slipped her hand from Kate's grasp and was backing away. "Oh, n-no. So—so obliging of you, but I am sure my papa—my sisters must be wondering where I . . ."

She trailed off into incoherence. Flushed with hurt and mortification, Mollie spun about and rushed back into the great hall.

"Mollie," Kate cried, and took a hesitant step after her, but judged it best to let her go. The girl was already close to tears. Kate rounded angrily on Victor.

"What a complete blockhead you are. How could you—"

"No, how could you, Kate?" Victor interrupted in a choked voice. "You don't have to return my affections, but don't try to thrust another woman upon me either."

Kate stared at him, stunned. Return his affections? What was he talking about? The spell was over, finished. Then why was Victor regarding her with that expression of desperate longing?

"No," Kate faltered. "It's impossible. You—you cannot still be in love with me."

"What did you think would happen, Kate? That my love was going to fade with the waning of the moon?"

"Yes, I did!"

"I am sorry you should continue to have such a poor opinion of my character. But I assure you my affection for you remains steadfast and unchanged."

"No!" Kate cried, stomping her foot for emphasis. "It is over. You are not supposed to still be in love with me."

"I have made an heroic effort to keep my distance from you, to stop badgering you with my unwanted attentions. I can endure your indifference to me, Kate, but please don't give me the added pain of telling me how I am supposed to feel."

He cast her a final anguished glance before stalking away, leaving Kate trembling with dismay. This could not be happening. Because if Victor was still entangled in her spell, then Val . . . Kate's heart gave a cold clutch of fear.

But, no, Val had sent Jem to fetch his cane. He would never have done that if her spell had not worn off, and she had watched Prospero end it in a magnificent display of fire and dark magic. He was a powerful sorcerer. He could not have failed, could he? She remembered clearly what he had said.

"Whatever spell you may have cast has now been undone."

But what if Prospero had managed to undo only part of the spell? What if something had gone terribly wrong? Only one person could answer that— Prospero himself. Kate prayed that she would be able to summon the wizard back to his tower one last time.

Kate hastened across the great hall, pushing her way through the throng of guests, impervious to the startled looks and affronted glances she received. She supposed she should have been more discreet, but her sense of urgency would not allow for that. Stealing behind the dais, she hurried toward the dragon tapestry that concealed the tower door.

She reached out to thrust the tapestry aside when a heavy hand descended upon her shoulder.

"Going somewhere, my Kate?"

The voice was little more than a whisper, but it chilled Kate to the marrow of her bones. Heart thudding, she spun about to find Val looming behind her. Torchlight flickered over his tall frame clad for traveling in his long black cloak and thick boots. He made a strange contrast to the masqueraders in the great hall beyond garbed in all their fantasy, satins, silks, and shimmering threads.

By comparison Val looked hard, real, and dangerous. Kate raised her eyes fearfully to his face and her heart seemed to stop altogether. Any hope that Prospero had ended even part of the spell died at once.

Val's black hair tumbled wildly about the gaunt contours of his countenance, his skin ice pale, his eyes feverish pools of darkness. He looked more lost to her evil magic than he had ever been.

In one white hand he gripped a silver-tipped cane, but he obviously had no need of it as he stepped closer. Kate backed away until he had her trapped against the hard rough surface of the wall.

"I have been waiting for you for hours." His voice was calm, terrifyingly so, but his gaze pierced her with barely suppressed fury. "You were supposed to meet me at the crossroads. Or have you entirely forgotten?"

"Well, I—I—"

"Oh, don't bother with any explanations. It is all too clear why you failed me tonight. I saw you shamelessly pursuing that young fool."

"No, Val, you don't understand—"

But he pressed his hand to her mouth, his eyes a cold, dark glitter. "No lies, Kate. It would take so little to provoke me. I could go kill Victor right now with scarce a thought."

Kate's heart gave a terrified lurch. She managed to pry his fingers away. "N-no, Val, please."

"Then come with me. Right now."

His hand clamped around her wrist like an iron manacle and he began dragging her toward the unobtrusive side door that connected to the new part of the mansion. Kate hung back, gazing toward the great hall for help, but she was too afraid to cry out. Not because she feared what Val might do to her. She was more terrified of what might happen if someone attempted to intervene.

She saw no trace in his grim features of the gentle man she had once loved. The madness she'd conjured appeared to have overtaken him completely.

He all but hurled her through the heavy wooden door and slammed it closed, shutting out the laughter and music spilling from the chamber beyond. The cloistered hall seemed dark and eerily silent after the revelry of the ball. The only illumination was the moonlight that spilled through the tall, latticed windows, pooling shadows across the floor like the bars of a dungeon.

Val gave her a push, propelling her along in front of him. But Kate dug in her heels, turning to face him.

"Val, you have got to listen to me—" she began, reaching up to cup his face only to gasp in horror at the heated intensity radiating from his skin.

"My God, Val! You—you are burning up."

"I'm fine," he growled, impatiently thrusting her hands away. But his words were belied as he was seized by a savage coughing spell. He lost his grip on his cane, the walking stick falling from his hands to clatter against the stone floor. Val leaned against the wall, drawing in ragged breaths, the moon painting bars of light across his haggard face.

Kate hovered beside him, helplessly running her fingers over his chest. He placed one hand over hers, holding it tight over the region of his heart. Kate could feel how hard it was racing and it terrified her.

"Val, please, you are not well."

"I—I will be well enough when we are gone from here."

"No, you won't be. You don't understand what I have done to you," Kate said, but she realized with despair that Val was paying little heed to her words. He gazed down at her, his eyes fever bright. He released her hand to stroke unsteady fingers through her hair.

"You look beautiful tonight, Kate," he rasped. "Who are you pretending to be? The lady Elaine? Nimue? Or perhaps Morgan le Fey, the lovely enchantress who worked her magic on poor Merlin."

Val's last guess was so close to the truth, Kate's throat knotted with tears.

"Lovely enchantress?" she choked. "Evil witch would be a better description." She seized hold of his hand, squeezing it hard, trying desperately to penetrate beyond the veil of madness clouding his eyes.

"Val, please. *Listen to me!*"

In halting sentences she told him everything, how she had stolen Prospero's book, the dark magic she had woven on All Hallows' Eve, how terribly it had gone awry, her futile attempts to undo it.

Val's lips snaked back in a disconcerting smile.

"Val, do you understand what I am telling you?"

"Aye, you put a spell on me." He flung back his head in such a wild laugh that Kate let go of his hand and recoiled in alarm.

"D-don't you believe me?"

"Oh, I believe you all right. It sounds like the sort of mad, reckless thing you would do."

Then why wasn't he angry with her? Or at least alarmed by what she had told him? She feared her confession had come far too late to do any good, to penetrate through the haze of his madness. His eyes glinted with an unholy amusement that unnerved her.

"My poor Kate," he mocked. "You distress yourself over nothing. Your ghostly sorcerer friend and his so-called book of spells is nothing but a great fraud."

"W-what do you mean?"

"Only that you weren't the only one practicing magic on All Hallows' Eve. I, too, have a secret, my dear. And if you are going to be my wife, I suppose I must share it with you."

His eyes narrowed, his mouth crooking into a sly smile as he beckoned her to come closer. His expression was so strange, it caused her to tingle with fear, but she took a wary step toward him. Val unfastened his cloak and groped at his neck, tugging at a silver length of chain.

Kate had felt the outline of it beneath his shirt many times when they had made love. It was only a holy medal, Val had explained, a historical relic handed down from some ancient St. Leger who'd gone on the Crusades.

But as Val uncovered the length of chain, Kate saw that the object dangling from the end of it was far from holy. It appeared no more than a sliver, an icicle of glass, until it reflected the moonlight spilling through the windows. Then the shard glowed with a strange cold beauty, a glitter that triggered in Kate a disturbing memory.

Prospero's crystal.

"Val," she quavered. "Where did you get that thing?"

"From an old acquaintance . . . Rafe Mortmain."

"Rafe Mortmain," Kate repeated, stunned. "But that villain has been missing for years. Where did you find him?"

"He found me. He came to Slate House on All Hallows' Eve. To give me this." Val dangled the crystal, the tiny prism sparkling with a light that was at once hypnotic and frightening. Kate felt obliged to avert her eyes.

"This is the shard of crystal Rafe stole," Val said. "Chipped away from the stone in the hilt of the St. Leger sword."

Kate had already guessed as much, but there was one thing she did not understand. "Why would Rafe Mortmain risk coming back here to return that to you?"

"He was dying when he landed on my doorstep. In pain . . . so much pain. I couldn't help him, but I tried. I took him by the hand and—and—"

Val faltered, pressing one hand to his brow, seeming unable to continue. But Kate could well guess what he had done. The mere thought of Val using his dangerous power to help someone as evil as a Mortmain made her blood run cold. Only Val St. Leger would have taken such a risk.

"Oh, Val, what happened? What did that horrible man do to you?"

"I—I am not sure. There was—this violent storm, thunder and lightning. Rafe was clutching my hand." Val fixed her with tormented eyes. "God help me, Kate. The—the pain flowing from him to me. N-never felt anything like it and he—he would not let go. The crystal flared and it was as though I—I absorbed the very darkness of his soul."

Val shuddered, trembling violently as though the memory itself was too much for him. Kate flung her arms about him.

"Shh," she whispered. "Never mind, dearest. Everything is going to be all right, I promise you."

Val held her so tight she could scarce breathe. Kate cradled him to her, stroking his hair. So this terrible change in Val had nothing to do with her clumsy efforts at magic. The thought should have given her some relief, but it only deepened her guilt. While she had been prancing around that bonfire like a fool, Val had been left alone in mortal danger. She should have been there, saved him somehow from whatever evil that Mortmain had worked upon him.

But at least there was one thing she could do to protect him now. Kate slid her fingers down his neck, groping for the chain. But Val stiffened and wrenched away from her.

"Val, please. You have got to get rid of that thing."

"No." Clutching the crystal, he backed away from her, looking as wary as a cornered wolf. "The crystal is mine now. Rafe gave it to *me.*"

"I doubt that he did so out of the goodness of his heart. He is trying to destroy you."

"But he is gone, vanished again."

"Aye, because he left that hellish stone to do his work for him. Rafe must have known how dangerous it was."

"For a Mortmain perhaps, but I—I am a St. Leger," Val said desperately, backing even farther away. "I can control its power."

"No, you can't! The crystal is too unpredictable. Prospero himself told me. That shard is part of some terrible magic stone he fashioned, a magic that went beyond his control. The stone exploded. He still has one piece, the other he imbedded in the sword. But each time the crystal is broken, each new fragment becomes even more unstable. There is no telling what that cursed thing is doing to you."

"I know exactly what it is doing. It has cured me, set me free to—to love you."

"No, my dearest," Kate said gently. "It is clouding your mind, confusing you, making you ill. Please give it to me."

She took a cautious step closer, pleading with the full force of her eyes. He stared at her, beads of sweat gathering on his brow, his mouth twisting. Something flickered in Val's eyes as though his reason struggled to reassert itself.

He glanced at her, then uncertainly down at the crystal. He began slowly to pull the chain up over his head. Kate released a tremulous breath and stretched out her hand.

It was a mistake. Val blinked, the darkness descending again as though a door had been suddenly slammed closed. Clutching the crystal more possessively than ever, he snarled at her.

"No! You are only trying to trick me, seize my power so you can escape and run straight back to your precious Victor."

"No, Val, I—"

"Well, it won't work, Kate. The crystal is mine and so are you!" Glaring at her, he hid the stone back beneath his shirt, and her heart sank, realizing that any chance she had of reasoning with him was lost.

Val snatched up the cane he had dropped and seized her arm with his other hand. Ignoring her protests, he propelled her along back toward the main wing of the house. Kate tried to drag her feet, her mind racing as fast as her pulse.

What was she going to do now? Val needed help. He was so desperately ill, sweat trickling down his pallid face, but he still seemed possessed of a ruthless strength. Even when he paused to emit a rasping cough, his iron grip on her arm never wavered.

"Please, Val, you are hurting me," she cried, struggling to pull free.

He didn't even seem to hear her or notice her efforts, marching her determinedly through the silent rooms of the new wing. There was not even a servant about to witness her plight, most of them occupied tending to the guests in the great hall.

Kate glanced up at Val in despair. She could not bring herself to strike out at him, but she had to find some way to escape, summon help for Val before it was too late. Her desperation only increased when Val dragged her out through the tall doors of the breakfast room, out into the night-shadowed garden where he had left Storm tethered to a rhododendron tree far from the bustle of the stable yard.

The ghost white stallion shifted restively in the moonlight as Val approached. Kate tugged with all her might, knowing if Val managed to hoist her onto the back of that demon horse, they'd be away like the wind. And there would be no telling what would happen then.

It almost broke her heart to do it, but Kate gritted her teeth and made a fist. She delivered a sharp clout to his ear. It staggered Val enough that he released her. Kate ran, but not fast enough.

He recaptured her before she had gone many steps. Cursing, he seized her around the waist, half dragging her off her feet.

"Stop." A voice rang out, causing them both to freeze. The tall outline of a man emerged from the house. Kate prayed it would be Lance. He, if anyone, might have a chance of breaking the crystal's insane hold on Val.

But as the man strode closer, the moon glinted off his bright coat of mail and Kate's stomach dipped down to her toes.

Oh, God, no, she thought desperately. Not Victor; anyone but him.

She could feel the tension coil in Val, his grip tightening about her waist, pulling her possessively closer as Victor closed the distance between them.

The young man's brow knit in a puzzled frown. "What is going on? Kate, are you all right?"

Val spoke up before she could answer. "She is fine, if it is any of your concern. Now you will have to excuse us, Sir Knight." He sneered. "Kate and I were just leaving."

"It doesn't look to me as though Kate wants to go."

"No, I am all right," Kate stammered. "Please just go back to the house and tell Lance to come—"

But Victor did not even appear to be listening to her. He spoke in a low voice that he tried to direct at her alone. "Kate, I know you think you are in love with Val. But you shouldn't go anywhere with him. Val has not been himself lately. Some even say that he is—is—"

"Mad?" Val broke in with an icy laugh. He released Kate so abruptly, she staggered to regain her balance. "I'll show you madness, boy."

He grasped the hilt of his cane and to Kate's horror, she suddenly realized its purpose. Val unsheathed a sword stick, the deadly blade gleaming in the moonlight.

"Val, no!" She clutched at his arm, but he shook her off, the gleam in his eyes as dark as any Mortmain's, his smile more terrible.

He stalked toward Victor. The young man stepped back, flinging up his arms. "As you can see, I am unarmed."

Val only laughed. "Rather absurd, isn't it, to pose as a knight and not even think to provide yourself with a weapon?"

"I didn't expect to be fighting a duel at a fancy dress ball."

"This isn't a duel. It's an execution." Val circled him, a cruel predatory light in his eyes. "I always wondered if chain mail was really effective at deflecting a blade. Now we are going to find out."

"Val, stop it!" Kate shouted. As he lunged, she rushed forward, thrusting Victor out of the way. The gleam of the blade was no more than a blur, but she felt its sting, the searing pain that rushed up her arm.

Kate froze, staring down at the tear in her sleeve, the flow of blood that was staining her kirtle an even deeper shade of red. She raised stunned eyes to Val. The realization of what he'd just done seemed to shock him back to sanity. His eyes rounded in horror, the sword dropping from his fingers.

"Kate," he cried hoarsely.

She closed her eyes, swaying on her feet, determined not to faint. But she felt her knees giving way beneath her.

Strong arms caught her, easing her to the ground. For a moment she thought it was Victor until she opened her eyes and found Val bending over her.

Her Val. He seemed to have fought his way back to her, past the darkness, the expression on his face both stricken and tender.

"Kate, my God. What have I done?"

"It's nothing," she murmured. "The m-merest trifle." She attempted to smile, reach out to reassure him, but flinched at the searing pain in her arm. The plea escaped her lips before she could prevent it, just as she had done so many times before, admitting to Val what she never would to anyone else.

"Oh, Val, it—it hurts."

His strong hand closed around hers, preparing to work the age-old magic. But instead of the familiar flood of warmth, something was terribly wrong.

Pain flowed out of Val's fingertips, piercing her veins like a black poison. Pain more excruciating than anything she'd ever endured. Her head fell back, and she screamed, webs of darkness dancing before her eyes.

"What are you doing?" Victor shouted. "Let her go, damn you."

But Victor's command was unnecessary. Val had already released her. Victor elbowed him aside, taking charge of Kate himself. Numbly Val allowed the young man to do so, staring down in pure horror at his own hand before collapsing at Kate's side.

CHAPTER EIGHTEEN

$\mathcal{V}$al St. Leger was dying.

A gloom-filled hush descended over the castle and the surrounding country-side, fear and grief overtaking the village of Torrecombe. The dread lord Anatole was their protector, the dispenser of justice; Master Lance the bringer of new ideas, the breath of the modern world. But few had ever realized the impact of the quiet man who was now slipping away from them.

Val St. Leger had been both healer and comforter, the gentle doctor who had borne the pain of an entire village upon his shoulders. But he had used his great power once too often and now he was paying a terrible price.

Kate paced the floor in Val's old bedchamber at Castle Leger, keeping vigil over the man she loved. No one any longer reminded her that she was not his chosen bride or warned her to stay away from him. Not even Lance had the heart to banish her from Val's side.

He and his mother, Madeline, had kept watch with Kate, but exhaustion had forced the older woman to retire to her bed. Lance, no longer able to endure standing helplessly by, had ridden north to hasten his father's return and that of his cousin Marius as well.

Marius was both a skilled doctor and a St. Leger. If anyone could find a way to end Val's strange malady, surely it was he. If only he did not arrive too late . . .

But Kate bit down hard upon her lip, refusing to allow herself to think that way. Her eyes raw from lack of sleep, she continued to hover over Val's bedside, pressing another damp cloth to his brow in a desperate effort to keep his temperature down. Val had been drifting in and out of consciousness for the past two days, stirring restively beneath her touch.

Kate didn't understand it. The terrible crystal had been taken from him, locked away in a small wooden chest upon his dresser. Surely Val should have shown some sign of recovery. What else had that evil Mortmain done to him?

He appeared all but swallowed up by the vastness of the bed, this quiet, strong man she had depended upon for so much of her life. His black hair was tousled against the pillow, the lines of his face rigid, never seeming able to relax beneath the lash of some inner torment.

As Kate stroked her fingers gently along his beard-roughened jaw, Val writhed beneath her touch, muttering some words she could not understand. Suddenly his eyes flew open wide with a look of terror, like a man roused from a violent dream.

"Oh, God!" he cried. He startled Kate by attempting to sit bolt upright.

She caught him by the shoulders. "No, Val. Please, you must lie still."

He regarded her wildly for a moment before recognition set in.

"K-Kate?"

"Aye, I am here, love. Everything is all right."

He was so weak, it was an easy matter to ease him back against the pillow although he remained tense beneath her touch. His gaze traveled past her, clearly bewildered.

"Where—where am I?"

"You are home," she said, tucking the coverlet around him. "Safe in your old room back at Castle Leger."

He released a long breath, appearing to relax although he continued to study his surroundings. He flung one hand across his eyes as though even the pale light penetrating the chamber was too much for him.

Kate rose from the edge of the bed, intending to close the curtains.

"No," Val said in a panicked voice. "Don't leave me." His fingers closed around her injured arm and Kate stifled a small gasp of pain.

He released her at once, staring. "I had this terrible dream that I hurt you. That I—" With trembling fingers, he touched her arm, the thickness of the bandage evident beneath her sleeve.

"Oh, God, it wasn't a nightmare," he said hoarsely. "I really did cut you with my sword."

"Hush, Val, it was nothing. The merest scratch. Your mother fast set me to rights." Kate attempted to reassure him. "Just a few quick stitches as tiny and neat as any of her embroidery."

"Mama is—is good at such things." A faint smile curled his lips. "She should have been a doctor herself with—with the number of wounds she bandaged for Lance and me."

"Just as you always did for me."

"But I wasn't able to take care of you this time."

"You soon will be well enough to do so again."

Val shook his head weakly, his eyes dark and empty with despair. "No, not anymore. I've lost my healing gift, Kate. I can't take away pain. All I can do is inflict it."

"That isn't true. None of this has been your fault. Everything that has happened is because of that evil Mortmain and that cursed crystal."

"No, not everything." Val managed to lift his hand, tenderly touching her cheek. "I love you, Kate. I always did. It has nothing to do with any spell book or magic crystal. You—you must always remember that and not weep for me."

His words both moved and alarmed her. She clutched at his hand. "Stop talking as though you are going to die."

"But it's the only way . . . only way to protect people I love."

"We don't need protecting. Not from you. You are going to get well, be yourself again. You are rid of that damned crystal."

"It makes no difference now. Don't you understand, Kate?" he murmured. "The darkness is in me . . . was there all the time."

His words made no sense to her. As his eyes fluttered closed, she realized he was drifting away from her again. But he seemed to be breathing easier, the rigid lines of his face relaxing. Kate touched his brow and was heartened to feel his skin no longer so warm.

Perhaps all Val needed was some rest, a long uninterrupted repose. She thought she saw him shiver and hastened to add more wood to the bedroom grate. Fetching another blanket, she tucked it carefully around him.

She tested his forehead again. He seemed much cooler now. In fact . . .

Kate anxiously pressed the back of her hand to his temple, his cheek, and his jaw. He was almost ice cold. He lay perfectly still, no warm rush of breath stirring, the rise and fall of his chest imperceptible.

With trembling fingers she felt for his pulse and could hardly find it. A bolt of sheer panic shot through her and Kate had to force herself to remain calm.

No, this wasn't what it seemed, the abrupt change in Val's condition. She checked her alarm, reminding herself that he had done something very like this once before when he had taken a pistol ball in the back.

Val had reduced himself to a deathlike trance, not moving, barely breathing for days. It was but another aspect of his strange St. Leger power, this ability to close down, to heal himself. That had to be what he was doing now.

All the same, Kate thought, she had best summon Val's mother, tell Madeline what was happening. Kate turned away from the bed, preparing to race for the door. She almost hurled herself into the shadowy figure behind her.

Kate bit back a startled shriek, stopping just inches from walking straight through Prospero's ghost. She clutched her thudding heart, but for once she was not even tempted to scold the sorcerer for creeping up on her that way. She was far too relieved to see him.

"Oh, thank heaven. You—you have come back."

"I doubt heaven has anything to do with it," he drawled. "You seem quite determined, Mistress Kate, to never allow me to rest in peace."

Despite his complaint, the sorcerer smiled at her with a rare softness. Prospero appeared different in the fading twilight of Val's bedchamber, somehow more subdued, even the iridescent folds of his cloak lacking some of its sparkle.

He drifted past her to peer down at the man resting so still upon the bed. Kate hovered anxiously beside him.

"It—it's Val," she explained. "He—he's very ill."

"He's dying, Kate," Prospero told her gently.

"No!"

"I can tell whenever a St. Leger is about to pass from this world. It's a dark, empty sensation that always pulls me straight back to the castle."

"This time you are mistaken," she insisted. "You don't know how strong, how unusual Val's power is. He's done this before, shut himself down to heal."

"But not this time. He is willing himself to die."

Kate glared at the sorcerer, her eyes burning with fierce tears because in her heart she feared that he was right, Val's words returning to haunt her.

"The only way to protect the people I love."

Bending over the bed, Kate seized hold of Val and shook him hard, frantically calling his name, attempting to rouse him.

"Damn you, Val. Don't you do this."

But her efforts were futile. She turned desperately to Prospero.

"Bring him out of his trance. Make him stop it!"

Prospero stood over the bed, his eyes narrowing. He seemed to pierce Val with his gaze as though he would strip through the layers of his consciousness, summon him back. Long moments passed and Kate waited breathlessly.

But Prospero slowly shook his head. "I am sorry, my dear. He has a will of iron, this gentle scholar of yours. I have no power over him."

"Then what exactly do you have power over?" Kate demanded, her fear sharpening to anger. "All that nonsense you recited on the hill that night, all your fancy tricks with the fire. It undid nothing."

"Then it was because you never succeeded in casting any spell. Just as I once thought. None of this was your fault."

"No, because it was yours. You and your damned crystals."

Prospero's brows rose in haughty surprise at her accusation. Kate marched over to the dresser and picked up the wooden chest, thrusting it at him.

Lance St. Leger had the key, but it was no great matter for Prospero to unseal the coffer. With one long stare and a slight movement of his hand, the lid flicked open.

The sorcerer's eyes widened at the contents. Kate stepped warily back, shielding her eyes as he lifted the chain, the shard of crystal winking evilly.

"The missing piece of the St. Leger sword," he murmured. "I warned young Lance St. Leger years ago that this should be recovered or it might be capable of doing great harm."

"And so it has." Kate told Prospero all that had happened or at least as much of it as she understood.

"And—and when Val tried to help that wretched Mortmain, something terrible happened. It is as though he absorbed some part of that bastard's black soul."

"That may be exactly what he did. I sensed some great evil approaching, but its nature was unclear to me. That, however, is not surprising." He frowned, holding the glittering stone aloft. "It is the power of these crystals. They have ever distorted my judgment, clouded my extraordinary perceptions."

"Then why did you ever seek to invent such a vile thing?"

"I told you. I was questing after power, immortality. I admit I was a great fool and I paid a high price for it."

"And now so is Val," Kate cried.

"Not necessarily."

"What do you mean?"

"There might yet be a way to save your Valentine. That is, if I am right about the nature of this." Prospero studied the tiny prism of glass intently. "I believe this particular piece of crystal is acting like a magnifying glass. At first it seduces with surges of power, augmenting one's strength, one's vitality. That is why young St. Leger felt his leg was cured.

"But it also heightens one's darker emotions as well, jealousy, anger, bitterness, until they become all consuming."

"Val is a kind, gentle man. He has no dark emotions."

"We all have a dark side, Kate. But I fear his was increased tenfold by whatever black emotions he absorbed from the Mortmain, which is why Val's condition may be reversed."

"How?" Kate asked eagerly. "Tell me."

"Rafe Mortmain must be found, fetched back here. If he dons the crystal, takes Val by the hand, reclaims his own misery, then perhaps all may be set right."

"I'll find the villain," Kate vowed fiercely. "I'll drag him back here even if I have to shoot him and—"

"No, Kate," Prospero said. "There is one thing you must understand. This will work only if Rafe consents to the transference. He must willingly make the same sacrifice that Val did for him."

The sorcerer concluded gravely, "And that may be a great deal too much to expect from any Mortmain."

Kate hastened downstairs to the library, a path she had taken so often during her girlhood, she could have found her way blindfolded. Whenever she had arrived at Castle Leger, she had scarce paused to greet anyone else, bounding straight for the book-lined chamber at the back of the house where she had known she would find Val.

She'd burst into the room to spy him lost in some volume, head bent in deep concentration, dark hair spilling across his brow. But he'd glance up at her entrance, his eyes lighting at the sight of her.

"Ah, Kate," he'd exclaim. "You've come just in time. You must come and see this fascinating new book I ordered from London."

And he would hold out one strong hand, his lips crooking in his gentle half-smile, her wizard waiting to transport her to some faraway land with just his touch, the rich timbre of his voice.

The memories that assailed Kate were so bittersweet and strong, she had to swallow hard before she could bring herself to turn the knob and enter the library. It was not Val who awaited her this time, but a far different gentleman.

Victor St. Leger slumped down in a chair before the dying fire, the young man fast asleep, his head lolling to one side. Most of the guests who'd attended the masquerade had departed days ago. Only Victor had lingered, watching and waiting like a forlorn hound. Once when emerging from Val's bedchamber, Kate had nearly tripped over him. Weary and tense herself, she had snapped at him to go home.

Kate felt guilty about that, especially now when she needed Victor's help.

She tiptoed across the room to peer down at the sleeping man. Usually so dapper, Victor's breeches and waistcoat were rumpled. He hadn't even made any effort to don a cravat, his shirt left open at the neckline. Nor had he shaved, a faint stubble shadowing his jaw, curiously at odds with the boyish way his dark lashes rested against his cheeks. He looked as exhausted and strained as they all were.

Kate rarely experienced any motherly impulses, but she wished she could have tucked a shawl about Victor's shoulders, allowed the young man to continue his repose. Instead she was obliged to shake him awake.

"Victor? Victor!"

"Mmmf?" His eyes fluttered open to peek groggily up at her. "Kate? Is it morning yet?"

"No, but you have to wake up."

Victor blinked hard, rubbing his hand across his face. "What—what time is it?"

"I don't have the least idea."

Victor slumped back, showing an alarming tendency to nod off again. Kate shook him more vigorously. "Victor, please! Stay awake. I need your help."

The urgency in her voice seemed to penetrate his sleepy haze. He gave himself a mighty shake and struggled awkwardly to his feet. His eyes cleared as he peered down at her with concern and alarm.

"What is it, Kate? Is it Val? Has there been any change?"

"None for the better. Which is why I need you to do something for me. Something very important."

"Anything," Victor said eagerly. "You have but to name it."

"You told me once that you have a special ability to locate missing persons. Is that true?"

"Aye," Victor said, although he appeared rather nonplussed by Kate's abrupt question. "You have decided you want me to find out who your mother was after all?"

"No, the devil with her. I need you to locate a man who used to live in this village. Do you remember Rafe Mortmain?"

Victor gave an incredulous laugh. "I should say I do. I am a St. Leger, Kate. We don't tend to forget any Mortmain."

"Good. Then focus his image in your mind and tell me where Rafe is. He is the one responsible for what has happened to Val and the only one who can undo it. I have to go find Rafe Mortmain and bring him back here. So get on with your conjuring and tell me where the villain is hiding."

To her dismay, Victor only frowned and locked his arms across his chest. "I don't think I should do that, Kate."

Kate stared at him in disbelief. He was actually refusing to help?

"Damnation," she growled. "I know you consider Val your rival, but he is your kinsman as well. You cannot allow him to die because you are jealous of him."

Victor stiffened indignantly, flushing at her accusation. "Of course I don't intend to let Val die. But I am not going to give you information that will only lead you into danger. I'd never forgive myself if I did."

"And I'll never forgive you if you don't," Kate said fiercely.

Victor firmed his lips into such a stubborn line, Kate longed to shake him. But she curbed her fear and frustration, resting her hand upon his sleeve instead.

"Oh, Victor, please. You talk about danger for me, but don't you understand? If anything happens to Val, my life is over."

"It certainly will be if you try to go after Rafe Mortmain."

"I don't care! I would risk anything to save Val."

"You—you love him that much?"

"Yes! I would willingly die for him."

Victor flinched at her passionate words. Kate supposed she should have remembered that Victor still fancied himself in love with her, made some effort to spare his feelings. She took his hand, squeezing it gently.

"Victor, I am so sorry—" she began, but he cut her off with a shake of his head. Disengaging his hand, he stepped away from her.

"No, don't apologize, Kate. I guess I have finally realized that I have been making a great fool of myself over you."

Kate gave a guilty wince. "That may not be entirely your fault. At one time I actually thought I had cast a spell over you. A love charm that I tried to work upon Val on All Hallows' Eve. When you suddenly began pursuing me, I feared my magic had gone somehow awry. And perhaps it really did."

Victor smiled ruefully. "There is only one problem with that notion, Kate. I had made up my mind to be in love with you well before All Hallows' Eve."

Made up his mind? What a strange way of putting it. Kate frowned over the words.

"You *decided* to be in love with me? I didn't think love was an emotion that could be so well regulated. And even if it could be, what in the world ever made you settle upon me?"

Kate's words seemed to throw Victor momentarily for a loss.

"Well, because," he faltered. "Because you are very beautiful."

"So are a good many other women. Even more so."

"Aye, but you are also so strong willed, so sure of yourself, something I have always admired." Victor grimaced. "Perhaps because that makes you very different from me. Most of my St. Leger cousins, even my own grandfather, scorned me for being this weak dandy, this good-for-nothing fellow.

"But I always dreamed that someday I would show them all they were wrong. I would turn out to be this remarkable, powerful man who accomplished something great."

Victor turned to her, his eyes growing wistful. "And part of that dream, Kate, was to lead this beautiful woman to the altar, some sweet, kind lady who would love me despite all my flaws, whom I would cherish and protect forever."

"Sweet and kind lady?" Kate echoed. "Oh, Victor, don't you see? That isn't me you are describing. It's Mollie Grey."

Victor's mouth set in a mulish line. "Don't start that again, Kate. I have been bullied most of my life by the St. Legers. I won't be told whom I am to marry as well. I realize that as soon as the Bride Finder declared Mollie to be my chosen bride, I was expected to rush her straight to the church, but whenever I look at Mollie, all I want to do is turn tail and run. I suppose that makes me very different from the other St. Legers."

"No," Kate said dryly. "It makes you exactly like the rest of them."

Victor shot her a look of such astonishment, Kate was obliged to smile.

"It is obvious that I know far more of your family history than you do, thanks to Val. Most of you St. Leger men do seem to balk when first presented with your chosen brides. I believe that Lord Anatole was ready to send Madeline straight back to London. And as for Lance, he put up a mighty resistance to Rosalind when they first met."

"He—he did?"

"Aye," Kate assured him. In fact there had been only one St. Leger male Kate had ever known who had been eager to locate his chosen bride, and that had been her poor Val. She remembered his cruel disappointment when Effie had refused to help him. Kate also recalled with shame her own secret rejoicing that Val would never belong to another.

If he survived this . . . no, when he survived, Kate amended quickly, she vowed she would somehow find him his destined love, the kind of lovely gentle lady Val had always deserved. Kate would see him made happy in the arms of his chosen bride even if it killed her.

Kate stole a glance at Victor. She didn't know if anything she had said had convinced him or changed the young man's mind about Mollie, but she believed she had at least given him pause.

His brow was furrowed in a thoughtful frown. "I always believed that when a St. Leger found his chosen bride, it was supposed to be love at first sight."

"Not even a legend can guarantee that," Kate said. "The Bride Finder can only point out the right lady. After that it is all up to you, to get to know her mind and heart. I really do think you should give yourself a chance to become better acquainted with Mollie and then see what happens.

"Perhaps from living with Effie for so long, some of her bride finding talent has worn off on me. Even I can picture you and Mollie someday living happily ever after together."

"And if I was to begin courting Mollie," Victor retorted, "it would certainly get me out of your hair."

"I don't want you out of my hair. In time, I even hope we can be friends." Kate tentatively held out her hand to him.

"Especially the kind of friends who help each other, eh?" Victor said with a suspicious lift of his brows. But he took her hand, lapsing into a reluctant grin. "Very well, Kate. I will locate Rafe Mortmain for you, but only under one condition."

"What is that?"

"That I be the one to go after him."

"What!" Kate struggled to contain her scorn for such a proposal. She had no wish to insult Victor, but sending him to fetch Rafe Mortmain would be like sending a lamb to herd a wolf into a pen.

Victor must have clearly read her thoughts for he added, "Oh, don't worry. I don't intend to go alone. If Lance were here, I would turn this matter over to him. But since he isn't, I will ask Caleb and some of my other cousins to accompany me. We will hunt Rafe Mortmain down, but you must promise to remain here, Kate. Agreed?"

Kate fetched a deep sigh. "Oh, very well. But we have no time to lose, so get on with it. Use your power and reveal where he is."

Victor nodded. Rubbing his temples as though to clear his mind, he turned and focused his gaze intently on the dying embers of the fire. Kate stepped to one side, trying to curb her impatience and remain as quiet as possible.

She didn't quite know what to expect when Victor exercised his St. Leger gift, but certainly something a little more than this. He simply stood there staring into the fire as though he were falling into a trance.

Or maybe he was merely falling back asleep. As the endless moments ticked by, Kate could bear it no longer.

"Blast it all, Victor. Is anything happening? Can you see anything yet?" she demanded.

"I see . . . water," Victor said slowly. "Rolling waves. A vast stretch of—of ocean."

Kate's heart sank. "Damn the villain," she muttered. "He's fled across the sea. I should have guessed as much. He's had plenty of time to be long gone from England. We'll never fetch him back in time."

"No. I sense that he is not that far away. He—he is residing at an inn in a town near the sea."

Victor blinked hard, and then his entire face lit up. He whirled toward Kate with a triumphant grin. "Falmouth, Kate. He is in Falmouth."

Kate let out a glad cry and flung her arms about Victor. "Oh, thank you, thank you. We can have the rogue back here before tomorrow eve."

Victor eased her away from him. "Aye, but remember your promise, Kate. You agreed to remain quietly here with Val, to let me handle this."

"Oh—oh, yes, of course." Kate folded her hands in front of her, staring down at the carpet. Her manner of meek acquiescence would never have fooled Val, but it satisfied Victor.

Only after the young man had bolted from the library did Kate look up. She supposed she should have warned Victor, told him what Prospero had said. That Rafe Mortmain needed to be persuaded, not captured by force. But it scarce mattered.

Let Victor assemble the other St. Legers, Kate thought grimly. Before the men had even saddled their horses, Kate intended to be long gone.

Chapter Nineteen

*K*ate flung articles of clothing out of the wardrobe onto the floor of her bedchamber until she found what she was looking for. Breeches, an old frock coat, and a pair of masculine riding boots. She had not worn them for years, trying so hard to learn to act the lady for Val.

But it was not a lady he needed now, Kate thought grimly. She scrambled into the breeches, coat, and boots. Moving the candle closer to the wardrobe, she groped until she found the final object of her search, the pistol Lance had given her for her birthday.

"Kate?" a small breathless voice called just outside her bedchamber, followed by a light knock. Kate straightened abruptly, whirling about to find her door easing open. She cursed herself for forgetting to lock it.

Kate stifled a groan as Effie slipped into the room. She had never known her guardian to rise before noon. Why did she have to pick today of all days to be up and stirring before dawn?

Effie crept closer, a small ghostlike figure in her white nightgown and lace cap, a pale pink shawl fastened about her shoulders, her bare toes peeking out from beneath her hem. She appeared at once more childlike and older than Kate had ever seen her, the light from the candle she carried flickering over the haggard lines of her face.

"I did not realize you had returned home," she said. "But I heard you rustling about and as I could not sleep either . . ."

Effie's words faltered to silence as she held up her candle, her horrified gaze taking in Kate's strange attire, the pistol she gripped in her hand.

"Oh, Kate," Effie squeaked. "Whatever are you up to now?"

"Nothing," Kate began only to stop herself. The present situation was far too urgent, and she was far too wearied for her usual prevarication and denials. She tucked the pistol beneath her frock coat.

"I am sorry, Effie," she said. "I planned to leave you a note after I had gone. Please, don't worry. Try to forget you ever saw me and—and just go back to bed."

Taking Effie by the elbow, Kate propelled her toward the door. But Effie dug in her heels, her eyes widening with trepidation.

"Gone?" she shrilled. "Gone where?"

Kate sighed. She had little time to be offering explanations or soothing Effie. She tried to speak as reassuringly and simply as she would have done to a small child. "I know this is going to sound alarming to you, Effie dear, but I—I have to go away for a while. Val is dying. There is only one way I can save him and that is to find the man who has brought this curse upon him."

Effie's mouth puckered with fear and bewilderment. "What man?"

Kate hesitated, then confessed reluctantly, "I have to find Rafe Mortmain."

"M-Mortmain?" Effie's reaction was even worse than Kate might have imagined. The older woman's face blanched as white as her nightgown. Her hand trembled so badly she was in danger of setting Kate's bedcurtains afire. Kate hastily plucked the candle from Effie's grasp, setting it safely down on the bedside table.

For a moment, Kate almost feared Effie was about to faint. But the woman seized the front of Kate's frock coat with a surprising strength.

"No, Kate! I absolutely forbid it, do you hear me?"

Kate regarded her in surprise. In all the years she had known Effie, her timid guardian had never outright forbidden her to do anything.

"You must not go anywhere near that wicked man," she cried. "Promise me."

"I promise that I will be careful." Kate tried to disentangle her coat from Effie's clutching fingers. "But I must—"

"No!" Effie's mouth quivered. "If—if that villain must be fetched back here, then you let someone else do it. Lance or—or one of the other St. Leger men."

Kate managed to ease Effie away from her, shaking her head. "This will be hard for you to understand, Effie, but if anyone is going to take the risk of going after Rafe Mortmain, it has to be me."

"B-but why?"

"Because so much of this disaster is my fault. I have always known Val better than anyone else. I should have realized sooner what was wrong with him, found a way to help him. But I didn't even realize he was in trouble. I was too caught up in my own selfish schemes to defy the Bride Finder legend and force him to marry me."

Kate swallowed past a hard knot that formed in her throat. "He was my dearest friend, and I let him down, failed him when he needed me the most. Perhaps I even brought the St. Leger curse down on his head."

"Oh, no, Kate, you couldn't have. You—" Effie checked herself abruptly, taking a desperate turn around the room, wringing her hands. She gave a soft moan. "Oh, if anyone is to blame, it is me. This is all my fault, all mine."

Kate caught her by the shoulders to stop her agitated pacing. "Don't be foolish, Effie. How could any of this be your fault? You always warned me to stop chasing after Val, that I was not his chosen bride."

"I know." Effie moaned again. "I lied."

"What?" Kate eyed her sharply, certain she could not have understood properly. Effie ducked her head, staring fixedly at the carpet.

"Effie?" Kate gripped her shoulders hard, trying to peer into her face, but Effie's eyes slid guiltily away from her.

"I—I lied," Effie said in a small voice. "I have been lying to you and Valentine for years. I realized from the first moment I saw you together, even when you were still a little girl, that you were meant to be his bride."

Kate released her, stepping back, too stunned to say anything.

"I am Val's chosen bride?" she demanded at last. "I always have been?"

Effie gave a jerky nod.

Kate released a long, shaky breath, struggling to absorb the full impact of Effie's words. She was destined to be Val's bride, his forever love, just as she had always dreamed of being. Her lips curved momentarily in a tremulous smile.

Kate had known it. Somehow in her heart, she had always known. If only Effie had not always been so adamant that—

Kate's smile faded, the fleeting joy she felt at the discovery displaced by a sense of outrage, a hurt and anger unlike anything she had ever known. She bore down upon Effie.

"You *knew*?" she grated. "All these years you knew and yet you tried to keep Val and me apart? You let him believe that he had to remain alone forever. And as for me, you saw that my heart was breaking and still you—you—"

Kate choked off, glowering at her. "Damn you, Effie. How could you do a thing like that?"

Effie shrank back from her anger, cowering against the bedpost. "I kept hoping that I was wrong."

"In God's name, why?" Kate cried. "Am I that much of a pariah? Oh, I realize that I am not the sort of proper born lady as most St. Leger brides. Only a foundling brat from the stews of London. I cannot even begin to imagine what sort of wicked woman my mother must have been—"

"I can," Effie interrupted her in a broken whisper, tears cascading down her cheeks. "The w-wicked woman was . . . is me."

"Are you trying to tell me that—that—"

"I am really your mother. Yes." Effie buried her face in her hands. Sagging down on the edge of the bed, she began to weep in earnest.

Kate could only stare at her in total disbelief. No, all these strange confessions had to be but more of Effie's melodramatics, her usual flare for creating a scene out of nothing at all.

But despite Effie's sniffling, the woman did not appear to be indulging in her familiar hysterics. When she lifted her head to risk a glance at Kate, the older woman's face was shadowed with a quiet despair, a genuine misery she appeared to have been suppressing for years.

"Oh, Kate, I—I am so s-sorry." She attempted to reach out to Kate, but Kate recoiled from her, crossing the room to sink down upon the chair at her dressing table, her mind reeling.

Effie . . . Effie Fitzleger, her mother. Kate had spent so many years refusing to even think about the woman who could have given birth to her, then abandoned her. It would have been better to discover that her mother was a harlot, the cheap kind of doxy Kate had always imagined her to be.

But Effie, despite her flighty ways, had always seemed so kind, so caring. Effie was even now regarding Kate so wistfully, as though measuring the distance Kate had put between them.

A terrible silence ensued, finally broken by Effie's plea.

"Please s-say something, Kate."

"What do you expect me to say? First you tell me that you lied for years about my being Val's chosen bride, and now I also find out you are my mother. You are the woman who left me to die in that terrible orphanage."

"No, I never meant that to happen. Kate, I swear it. I gave you into the care of my cousin. She promised to find some good family far off in the country to look after you."

"To keep me hidden away, you mean. So obviously there was little hope of you marrying my father. Who the blazes was he? Some groom from the local stables? Some wandering gypsy lad?"

"N-no. Far worse than that."

"What could possibly be worse?" Kate sneered. "Unless you slept with the very devil."

Effie flinched at her words, an odd expression flitting across her face almost as though Kate's accusation carried some element of truth. Kate frowned. The very devil? There were not very many men who had passed through Torrecombe who fit that description. In fact, Kate could think of only one . . .

Rafe Mortmain.

But no. Effie and Rafe? The notion was at once too ludicrous and too horrible to contemplate. And yet Kate eyed her guardian uneasily, remembering what seemed to have triggered all these startling revelations from Effie after so many years. Kate's announcement that she intended to go after Rafe Mortmain.

Kate averted her gaze, suddenly feeling as though she had heard quite enough of Effie's secrets. She didn't want to know any more. But like the lid ripped off Pandora's box, the suspicion refused to be ignored or go away.

"Who was he, Effie?" Kate asked hoarsely, her heart hammering in trepidation. "Tell me my father's name."

Effie merely cast her a piteous glance.

"Answer me!" Kate snapped.

Effie shrank down until it seemed she would disappear altogether.

"R-rafe. Rafe M-m—" Effie choked on a flood of tears as though she could not even bring herself to speak the name.

"No!" Kate breathed, her stomach taking a sickened dive. She pressed her hand to her mouth, feeling she truly might be ill. All her life she had feared she might be possessed of bad blood, but never anything like this. Never that she might have been spawned from a family infamous for its evil and madness.

She was a Mortmain. A God-cursed Mortmain.

Kate staggered to her feet, desperately seeking her reflection in the mirror, half fearing she would find herself transformed into some sort of monster. All she saw was her own face, pale, shadowed with fatigue, and stroked with a wide-eyed vulnerability that reminded her strangely of the woman weeping on the bed.

"No," Kate murmured. "Rafe Mortmain, my father? I don't believe it. It isn't true."

"I w-wish it wasn't," Effie wept.

Kate stormed across the room to tower over the cowering woman. "How is this possible? Did he rape you?"

Effie shook her head miserably.

"Then you went *willingly* to his bed?"

"I th-thought I was in love with him."

"With a Mortmain? Were you completely mad?"

Effie gave a deep sob and began to tremble. But before she could dissolve into complete incoherence, Kate seized her by the shoulders and gave her a brisk shake.

"No, Effie. Not this time. No hysterics, no megrims. And most of all no more lies. You are going to cease sniveling and tell me everything. Right now."

Kate didn't know if it was her own fierce demeanor or if Effie herself had finally reached a point beyond tears. The woman drew in a shuddering breath and composed herself with a loud sniff.

Kate rummaged in her drawer and produced a handkerchief, which she silently extended toward her. Effie accepted it gratefully, mopping at her red, swollen eyes.

"Th-thank you." She attempted to smile up at Kate, but Kate turned away from her. Arms folded, she stared out her bedchamber window, feeling as cold as the gray light of morning, which was breaking over the village rooftops.

Shoulders slumping, Effie fetched a deep, mournful sigh as she commenced her tale.

"Well, it—it all began in Portsmouth." She paused to correct herself. "No, that isn't right. I fear it started long before that when Rafe first came to Torrecombe. He was the last of the Mortmains, abandoned in Paris by his mother. She was indeed a wicked woman who plotted to destroy every last one of the St. Legers. She did nearly succeed in killing Lord Anatole.

"But Anatole and Madeline St. Leger are remarkable people, so forgiving. They felt sorry for the boy, orphaned, destitute. They brought him to Castle Leger when he was but a lad of sixteen to live with their own family."

"I know all that," Kate interrupted impatiently. "Val long ago taught me the black history of the Mortmains."

"But there is one thing Val could not know. He was only eight years old at the time. He would have never realized the impact Rafe made upon all the girls in the village. He set all the local maids into a foolish flutter, including me. I was little more than sixteen myself at the time and Rafe was quite unlike any boy I'd ever seen. He was so dark, handsome and—and wild."

Kate shot Effie a scornful look. She had recollections herself of seeing Rafe Mortmain during her own childhood. But as the St. Leger's enemy, the villain who had nearly destroyed her beloved Val, Kate couldn't think of the man as anything but vile. It was very difficult to listen to Effie ranting on about how handsome the Mortmain had been, but Kate compressed her lips together, managing to hold her tongue and allow Effie to continue.

"Well, after a while, a terrible thing happened. Lance St. Leger nearly drowned and there was strong suspicion that it was not an accident, that Rafe was responsible. Nothing was ever proved, but for the safety of his own family, Lord Anatole decided Rafe must be sent away. My own grandfather concurred.

"He was the vicar of St. Gothian's at that time and Lord Anatole set great store by his opinion. Rafe was found a position as apprentice seaman on a merchant ship bound for the West Indies. That should have been the last I ever saw of Rafe Mortmain. But our paths crossed again five years later."

Effie fretted with the handkerchief, twisting it into knots. "I was past twenty and still unwed. Even my grandpapa was becoming concerned. He wanted me to marry a local lad, remain in Torrecombe. Partly to remain near him and partly because I was destined to be the next Bride Finder.

"Ah, but Kate." Effie sighed. "I had dreams of my own. I wanted romance, adventure, excitement."

Kate was unable to refrain from gaping at her, and a slightly rueful smile tugged at Effie's lips. "You stare at me, Kate. I suppose the idea of someone as nervous as I longing for excitement strikes you as ridiculous. But I wasn't always quite such a goose."

Effie's voice took a dreamy tone as she went on, "How I longed to travel, to see the world beyond Torrecombe. More than anything I wanted to go to London for the season, but my grandpapa had a great mistrust and fear of large cities. However, he did offer to take me to Portsmouth."

Effie pulled a wry face. "Portsmouth! It was a city, to be sure, but it certainly wasn't London. It did have the advantage that one of my aunts lived there, and Grandpapa had not seen Aunt Lucy for years. So off we went. After the initial amusement of being in a new place, I was soon as bored there as I had been in Torrecombe. At least until the day the *Meridian* docked in Portsmouth and brought him back into my life.

"Rafe Mortmain," Effie murmured. "If he had been handsome at sixteen, the man was devastating at twenty-one, with that hard, rugged look of all seamen. Only Rafe had something more, this air of mystery about him, dark, brooding, dangerous. I was always a bit of fool, but even I possessed enough common sense to know I should stay away from such a man."

"Then why didn't you?" Kate demanded.

Effie gave a helpless shrug. "I—I don't know. One chance meeting in the street outside of a shop and the next I knew I was stealing off to meet him on the sly. I had never deceived my grandpapa before, but I could not seem to stay away from the man. Rafe could be so—so utterly charming."

A Mortmain charming? Kate could not refrain from a contemptuous snort.

"He *was*, Kate," Effie insisted. "Or—or at least I thought so. I began to perceive him as this wronged hero, maligned and misunderstood. He made me forget everything, all my dreams of a season, a grand match. I was besotted with him, believing he would eventually marry me."

Effie folded her hands, staring glumly down at her lap. "To make a wretched story short, one morning I woke up to discover his ship had sailed. He was gone without a word of farewell and shortly thereafter I discovered I was with child.

"I could not bear for my grandpapa to find out how foolish and wicked I had been. I badgered him unmercifully until he did finally allow me to go to my cousin in London and I confided my plight to her. She was very kind, helped me to take care of everything."

"Everything being me," Kate said bitterly.

"Aye. I thought I would hate the sight of you because you were his daughter. But you were so beautiful, Kate. It nigh broke my heart to part with you. I held you for only a few hours and—and then you were gone."

A single tear escaped to trickle down the older woman's cheek, the most genuine tear Effie had ever shed. Kate was almost moved to pity except for one thing.

"I was gone, all right," she said. "Taken straight to one of the worst foundling homes in London, straight to the portals of hell."

"I didn't know that. Please, you must believe me. I thought you had been taken to a kind and loving home."

"You should have—" Kate checked her angry words. What should Effie have done? A young woman seduced, abandoned, left with child. What would Kate have done herself in those circumstances?

"Go on," Kate said gruffly. "Finish your story."

"There was not much else to tell. I recovered and returned home to my quiet life in Torrecombe. I was strangely glad of it. In time I even learned to appreciate the attentions of my old suitors, although I never married any of them."

"Because they were not good enough for you."

"No, I only pretended that was the reason for rejecting any offers that came my way. The truth was that I never considered myself good enough for any decent man. I was a fallen woman now, despoiled by Rafe Mortmain."

"Oh, Effie," Kate murmured, shaking her head.

"I remained quietly in Torrecombe until my grandpapa died. But I was never able to stop thinking of you, Kate, remembering my little girl. I thought if I could just see you one more time, assure myself you were happy and well cared for, everything would be all right. So I journeyed back to London and forced my cousin to show me where she had sent you.

"You cannot imagine what I felt when I found you in that—that foundling home. That terrible place. God knows how you survived. I had only one thought: to get you away from there as quickly as possible.

"So I brought you back to Torrecombe as my adopted daughter. To everyone it seemed like a foolish thing I would do, just another of Effie's silly whims. No one ever suspected the truth, not even you. I had you back, another chance to take good care of you this time.

"All seemed wonderful until I realized the truth about you and Valentine. Val already showed signs of being so fond of you, but I lived in dread that someone would discover that you were descended from a Mortmain."

Aye, Kate could understand that. Legend or no legend, it was the one heritage that no St. Leger would ever be able to forgive or accept, not even her gentle Val.

"Everything seemed even worse when Rafe Mortmain turned up back in Torrecombe for a time," Effie went on. "He was a customs officer now, assigned to this part of the country. He often rode past my cottage. He didn't even give me a second glance, as though he had entirely forgotten me, which was just as well."

"He was too busy creating other havoc," Kate said. "Stealing the St. Leger sword, almost killing Val."

"Aye, he certainly did little to raise anyone's opinions hereabouts of the Mortmains. I was quite relieved when he disappeared again except that I saw your love for Val growing stronger every day. I should have sent you away, but the thought of parting with you was unbearable."

Effie finished her story at last, turning to Kate with a sorrowful plea, "Oh, Kate, can you ever forgive me? You must completely despise me now."

Despise Effie? Perhaps Kate should have felt more anger with the woman, but she didn't. Her hatred was entirely reserved for the villain who had brought both her and Effie to this pass.

Crossing the room, Kate wrapped her arms around the older woman, murmuring, "Hush now. Everything is going to be all right."

"Kate, I am s-so sorry. But at least you do understand now why you have to stay away from that evil man."

Kate averted her face. There was no sense telling Effie that she had given

Kate only more reason for tracking Rafe down. After she hauled him back here to save Val, she intended to see that the villain finally answered for his crimes, even if she had to be the one to put a bullet through his black Mortmain heart.

Another question suddenly struck Kate. The answer truly should not have mattered to her now, but she had wondered about it for so much of her life.

"When *was* I born, Effie?"

"Well, strangely enough, Valentine was not far off when he gave you your birth date. You were born on All Hallows' Eve."

"All Hallows' Eve?" Kate's mouth twisted wryly. "The devil's night. I might have known. And exactly how old am I?"

"Nineteen, dearest."

"Only nineteen," Kate marveled sadly. "How odd. I have always felt so much older."

Chapter Twenty

The gulls wheeled overhead, emitting their strident cries, while the sea lapped quietly against the shingled beach. Sunlight glistened on the water and the wet slick stones. Despite the crisp bite to the air, it was a gentle day for this early in December, a soft breeze blowing toward shore.

Rafe perched on the trunk of gnarled driftwood, debris cast up by some recent storm. He breathed in the salt air and watched the slow rhythmic break of the waves. Usually the sight of the sea stirred in him a restlessness, an eagerness to be gone. But as his gaze shifted from the boy at his side to the woman in the distance, he was filled with a quiet contentment.

Charley sat nestled close to him, his small face all but swallowed up beneath the brim of a large cap as the boy struggled to fashion a half hitch knot in a short length of rope. Corinne strolled some distance away, her worn brown cloak folded about her shoulders, tendrils of hair escaping from her neat chignon as she turned her face out to sea.

Like Rafe, she appeared to be enjoying this respite from their cramped quarters back at the inn. Those two rooms had begun to seem mighty small to him, Rafe thought, especially since the night he and Corinne had almost become lovers.

Living together after that should have become deuced awkward for both of them. That it wasn't, Rafe realized, was more owing to Corinne than him. She was such a sensible woman, carrying on with a brisk cheerfulness as though nothing had happened. And he should have been able to pretend the same.

But more and more often Rafe caught himself studying her gentle features with a longing he couldn't explain. He still wanted her, yes, and badly. But the past month had taught him something he had never known before, that there were pleasures to be found in a woman's company other than carnal ones. Pleasures as simple as the quiet way she bent over her needlework, the lilt of her voice, the shy turn of her smile.

Shielding his eyes from the sun, Rafe tracked Corinne's slow progress down the beach until he felt Charley tug at his sleeve, drawing his attention back to the boy.

"How is this, Mr. Moore?" Charley held up the gnarled rope for his inspection.

"Er, good, but you made one wee mistake, lad." Rafe took the rope from the child and undid Charley's tangled efforts with a patience he would never have imagined himself capable of.

"Now try again." This time Rafe bent over the boy, guiding Charley's stubby fingers. "Take that end there up and over and loop it through."

Tongue held determinedly between his teeth, Charley struggled to follow Rafe's instruction. He completed the knot, his face flushing with triumph.

"I did it, Mr. Moore. I did it."

"So you did and a finer half hitch I never saw."

Charley beamed from ear to ear at the praise, the tip of his nose turning pink with pleasure. Rafe had seen cabin boys, many younger than Charley, master the art of rope tying. It was quite absurd, the surge of pride he felt in the lad's accomplishment, but Rafe found himself grinning back.

Charley immediately undid the knot, tackling the rope again.

"Just to see if I really learned how to do it, Mr. Moore." But as he started to twist the ends again, he stopped, angling a hesitant glance up at Rafe.

"What it is, lad?" Rafe teased. "Forget how to do it already?"

Charley shook his head. "No, I was just wondering if—if . . . Would it be all right if I started calling you Uncle Rafe?"

After nearly a month in Charley's company, Rafe thought he had become accustomed to the multitude of peculiar questions that a small boy could ask. But Charley still managed to catch him off guard.

"Well," Rafe said hesitantly. "I suppose you may call me whatever you please."

"Truly?" Charley asked, his eyes large and solemn. "Then what I would really like to call you is Papa."

Charley's hopeful face touched Rafe in a way that caused his throat to constrict. The boy's wistful look was one Rafe understood all too well. He must have once appeared much the same, studying the face of every man Evelyn Mortmain had ever brought home, wondering if this might be the one, the father he had never known, the father he would never have.

"No, Charley," Rafe said at last, as gently as he could. "That would not be a good idea."

Refusing the boy was one of the hardest things Rafe had ever had to do. Charley's face fell, but he nodded with a solemn air of understanding.

"I 'spect it's 'cause you're not going to be my new father, are you? Mama says you are a sailor like my real papa was and you'll want to be going back to sea soon."

"Yes, I suppose that is true," Rafe said.

Charley ducked his head, but not before Rafe saw the slight quiver of the child's lip, and damned if he didn't feel like lapsing into a strange fit of melancholy himself.

"Well, that is something neither one of us has to think about right now," Rafe said briskly. "So let's get back to practicing our knots, shall we?"

He soon had Charley absorbed again with the rope, but Rafe found it more difficult to distract himself. As Charley practiced his knots, Rafe feigned deep interest, doing his best to conceal his own troubled frown.

He was no more near to making some sort of provision for Corinne and Charley than he had been weeks ago. But he had to think of something and soon. They could not go on as they were, lodging at the inn. And yet the prospect of settling them somewhere, leaving them, seemed to grow a little harder each day.

Rafe remembered how often he had sneered at the seamen with families, the ones who had made such tearful partings at each sailing, who had all but fallen over the rails in their eagerness to disembark upon the return home. Rafe had never understood what could possibly tie a man's heart that much to the land . . . until now.

Charley soon grew tired of his efforts with the rope and tore off down the beach to inspect a large leatherback turtle that had crept ashore. Other boys would have poked and prodded, but Charley maintained a respectful distance. He kept clear of the turtle's path, angling his head to one side to study the reptile's slow movements with an intent curiosity that caused Rafe to smile.

Damn, but he had to admit he'd grown fond of the lad. He could not have been more so than if he truly had been the boy's father. Rafe's smile faded and he sobered immediately, realizing that was a dangerous thought for him to be having.

But no more dangerous than some of his thoughts regarding the woman who approached him. Corinne bent to pick up the rope Charley had abandoned and dangled it before Rafe with a look of laughing accusation.

"And what is this, Rafe Moore? Have you been trying to make a sailor of my son again?"

Rafe rose to his feet with a wry smile. "There's little danger of that, madam. Far more likely he'll run off to take up work as an ostler. He has a real way with horses and he's deuced fond of the brutes, though I can't begin to fathom why."

"I am rather fond of the 'brutes' myself. Perhaps I could disguise myself as a lad and Charley and I both could become grooms at some grand stable."

Rafe attempted to laugh, but he hated to hear her talk of seeking employment, even in jest, and he realized the possibility was more and more on Corinne's mind of late. She huddled her cloak tightly about her shoulders and appeared to shiver a little.

"Are you cold?" he asked.

"Oh, no," she said.

And even if she were, she'd never admit it, Rafe thought. Corinne never complained. He wished he could replace that worn wreck of a cloak with one of soft wool, well lined. A deep forest green would become her. But although Corinne was grateful for anything he might do for her son, her pride had drawn the line at allowing Rafe to buy clothing for her. He respected her for that, but found it a bitter irony when he reflected on all the expensive baubles he'd carelessly bestowed on other women over the years. He would have given all he possessed for the right to bestow even a pair of warm gloves on this one small, gentle lady.

But all he could do was position himself to block some of the breeze coming off the sea. He longed to be able to draw her close, shelter her within the warmth of his arms. A dangerous impulse, one of many he had learned to curb these past days. He locked his hands stiffly behind him to resist the temptation.

"Likely this outing was a foolish idea," he said. "It is far too chilly. Perhaps we should go back."

"No, not yet," Corinne protested. "It is a fine afternoon. Charley and I have enjoyed it immensely. And who knows how many days we have left before— before—"

She lowered her eyes and didn't finish. But she didn't have to. Rafe knew full well what she meant. Before it was time for them to separate, for him to move on. But it was a prospect Rafe did not care to dwell on and he shoved it aside once more.

Charley had wandered some distance down the beach in his pursuit of the turtle and Corinne prepared to start after him. Rafe offered his arm to escort her, and after a small hesitation, she accepted.

It was the most touching either had allowed ever since the night that they had shared such passionate kisses. Rafe found the soft pressure of her fingers against his sleeve very sweet and he was acutely aware of her warm presence so close to his side.

As they set off to follow Charley, Rafe moderated his pace. It wasn't the first time he and Corinne had strolled along the beach this way and he had learned to match his longer strides to her much shorter steps.

They moved together in perfect accord and Rafe could only marvel at how comfortable, how right it felt just being with her. He, who had always been too edgy to be comfortable with anyone for long. He pointed out to her a schooner skimming along the horizon, the sight of the billowing sails filling him with a quiet pleasure.

Corinne attempted to share his enthusiasm, but her own smile was pensive.

"You must miss it greatly, don't you? Being at sea."

Rafe shrugged, "Well, not necessarily. I—"

"Oh, don't try to deny it. I know what you sailors are like. I was married to one, remember? I vow you have salt water in your veins."

"Perhaps I do," Rafe conceded. "But as long as I am at least within view of the sea, I can be content."

"No, you can't. Not indefinitely." Corinne's face clouded over. "Rafe, you have been very good to Charley and me, but we cannot keep trespassing on your kindness—"

"Damn it, Corinne," Rafe growled. "Don't start this again. We have had this discussion too many times."

"And it is never resolved." She tugged at his arm, forcing him to stop while she gazed up at him, her brown eyes sad but determined. "Charley and I have already kept you here in Falmouth far too long. We cannot go on this way forever."

Rafe compressed his lips in a stubborn line, but he realized she was right.

"Well, I have had this one notion," he said. "And don't refuse until you have entirely heard me out," he added hurriedly, anticipating her reaction.

"I thought I might rent a house for you and Charley at one of these small villages up the coast. A little cottage right near the sea. Charley would like that and the fresh salt air would be good for both of you. Then even after I had gone, I could continue to send money and . . ."

But Rafe trailed off in frustration because Corinne was already shaking her head.

"Rafe, you cannot burden yourself with our care forever."

"It is no burden and it wouldn't be forever. Only until Charley is old enough to support you both."

"That will be a good many years."

"What the blazes does that matter? What else do I have to do with my money?"

"I am sure you could think of something." Corinne attempted to smile, but her lip trembled instead. "And—and besides . . ."

"Besides what?"

She ducked her head and he had to bend closer in order to hear her above the breaking waves. "It would be very lonely in this cottage of yours by the sea after . . . after you had gone."

No more lonely than he was going to feel, strolling the deck of some ship, far away from both of them. It was strange, Rafe thought. That was what he'd hungered for most of his life, to be master of his own vessel, to live upon the sea. He had never minded being alone, or so he'd always convinced himself. Now the mere thought of it left a great aching void in his chest.

It was a damn fool thing to admit to himself, let alone to her, but Rafe seemed unable to help himself. He gathered both of her hands into his own.

"There is nothing that I want more than to be able to stay with you and Charley, but there is so much you don't know about me, Corinne, about the kind of man that I have been."

"I know the kind of man you are now. Surely that is all that matters."

"I wish that were true. But I have done a great many wicked things in my life, things I am now heartily ashamed of. Even you must remember what a miserable wretch I was the day I first met you."

"I remember only how ill you were," she said. "I was so afraid for you the night you rode away on Rufus. I feared you would die before you even left my farm."

"I should have died. The only reason I didn't is because something very strange happened to me on All Hallows' Eve. Something so strange I can't even explain it to myself. But I was healed, changed by the touch of a very good man."

"And you don't think this change is permanent?"

"Lord, I hope it is. Whenever I look it at you, I believe it is." He gazed down at her. The sunlight seemed to reflect off her face, emphasizing the sweet expression of her eyes, the gentle curve of her lips.

"I love you, Corinne." It was the last thing Rafe had ever meant to say. The words escaped him in a shaky breath.

"I . . . I love you," he repeated again in an even more awed tone. "My God, Corinne, you don't even know what a miracle it is that I can say that. I never imagined that I could love anyone, let alone feel as though I could love just one woman until the end of my life.

"And I have barely known you one month," he marveled. "Am I quite mad?"

"Then I must be, too," she said with a tremulous smile. "Because I think I fell in love with you from the moment I first watched you lift my son into your arms."

They simply stood and stared at each other for a long moment, clutching hands.

"Then . . . then it seems the sensible thing for me to do is marry you," Rafe said.

"Oh, yes, very sensible," Corinne agreed, smiling tenderly up at him, her eyes misting over.

Rafe bent toward her slowly and touched his mouth to hers. One brief sweet kiss but it was all they were allowed before a shout from Charley interrupted them. They drew guiltily apart, realizing they had all but forgotten the boy.

He didn't appear to have noticed their kiss, waving his hand and calling for them to come look at the hermit crab he had just discovered. Corinne gave a rueful laugh, but went to her son. Rafe remained where he was, still a little stunned by what he'd just done.

Was he quite insane to be declaring his love, proposing marriage to this woman? A man with his grim past, his dark heritage, an accursed Mortmain. And yet what better way to atone for the wrongs he had done than by cherishing Corinne and her child forever? He could take them far from these shores, carve a new life, a fresh beginning for all of them.

Corinne . . . his wife, Charley, his son. The thought was so incredible, it flooded his heart with a strong emotion unlike any he'd ever known. An emotion so different, so strange, it took him a moment to understand what it was.

Happiness. For perhaps the first time in his life, he knew what it was to be truly happy. He watched Corinne bend over Charley, smooth her hand gently over the boy's brow as she whispered something in his ear. Charley glanced back at Rafe, his small face lighting up with joy. The boy came racing toward him pell-mell and Rafe hunkered down, opening his arms wide.

"Rafe! Rafe Mortmain."

The sharp cry seemed to come out of nowhere. Rafe tensed, hoping, nay, praying that he'd only imagined it. But Charley stumbled to a halt, peering fearfully at something or someone beyond Rafe's shoulder. Corinne did likewise, a worried frown creasing her brow.

And the hoarse voice called again, "Damn you, Mortmain. Don't even think of pretending it isn't you. I know you full well."

Rafe felt his blood turn to ice, realizing the moment he'd long dreaded was hard upon him. He'd been recognized, identified, marked for the villain he'd once been. But not now, he wanted to plead. Why did it have to happen now when all he had to do was reach out to take Charley's hand, to draw Corinne into the circle of his arms? All the happiness any man could dream of and it seemed about to end before it had even fully begun.

He straightened slowly, his heart thudding with fear, but not for himself. For Corinne and Charley. What would become of them if he were taken, imprisoned, hanged? Turning about, he positioned himself protectively in front of them, prepared to resist as best he could, even if he was confronted with an entire posse of armed men.

But there was no posse, no mob of outraged citizens. Only one slight figure bundled in a cloak, the hood obscuring his features. But he looked to be neither some overzealous constable nor one of Rafe's burly old mates eager to turn him in for the reward.

As the figure stalked closer, flinging back the hood, Rafe saw that it wasn't a man at all. He gaped in astonishment. It was merely a young slip of a girl clad in breeches, her masses of disheveled hair as coal black as his own.

But she had the most angry gray eyes Rafe had ever seen.

Kate followed Rafe Mortmain into the chamber at the inn, but her steps were slower, more wary. She hadn't tracked this villain down to allow herself to be led into some trap. But the Mortmain seemed more concerned with urging the strange woman and little boy into the next room, speaking in a voice so gentle it astonished Kate.

She wasn't prepared for that or the cozy domesticity of the sitting room, the fire burning low on the hearth, a woman's workbasket perched on a small table, a little boy's newly mended and washed stockings left drying over a chair. It was not exactly the den of iniquity where Kate had expected to find Rafe gone to ground.

It made it difficult for Kate to view him as the villain she knew he was, especially when she observed how he tousled the boy's hair, smiled tenderly at the woman.

But never trust a Mortmain, Val had always warned her. For all she knew, Rafe could be planning to steal into the adjoining room with the woman and child, then escape out some back window.

Kate started forward to prevent that, but Rafe had finally persuaded the woman to take her son into the other room and was already closing the door behind them. He came about before Kate was ready for him to do so, looming over her.

Kate tensed, groping for the pistol beneath her cloak, but the Mortmain only peered down at her with a strange sad sort of look and stalked past her without saying a word. He bent and began to heap more logs on the fire as though he were cold. He well might have been. He looked very pale.

Kate crept closer, intrigued in spite of herself. He wasn't at all what she had expected, the monster she had ridden so far to find. Neither the devil of her childhood imaginings nor the cold, arrogant customs officer who had once galloped so heedlessly through their village.

Instead she saw a man of quiet bearing, his rich black hair threaded through with silver at the temples. The corners of his dark gray eyes were creased with lines that might have been the product of wind and sun or a hard lifetime of bitter experience.

Kate regarded him with a tangle of confused emotions, anger, mistrust, and a sense of longing she hadn't anticipated. This tall distinguished-looking man was her father. *Her father.* Under other circumstances she might almost have been glad.

But Kate backed away, fiercely reminding herself of who and what he was. A cursed Mortmain, the blackguard who'd all but ruined poor Effie, the demon who even now was destroying the man Kate loved.

Rafe applied the bellows to the fire and then turned at last to face her.

"Would you care to sit down?" he asked with such grave courtesy Kate snorted in disbelief.

"No! What the devil are you going to do next? Offer me a bloody cup of tea?"

"If you like." His lips twitched with a faint smile and Kate thought she understood the reason for his calm. He didn't perceive her as a threat. Well, she would fast disabuse him of that comforting notion.

Reaching beneath her cloak, Kate produced the pistol with a dramatic flourish and leveled it at him.

The Mortmain's dark brows arched upward, but more in surprise than fear.

"I give you fair warning," she said. "This pistol is loaded and I know how to use it."

"I am sure you do," Rafe murmured.

To Kate's complete dismay, he settled himself comfortably into a wingback chair. She braced herself, moving her fingers to cock the pistol when he reached for a knife.

But it was only to take up a piece of wood that he had obviously been whittling. Kate saw that he was fashioning it into the hull of a small boat. No doubt for that little boy in the next room. She wondered about his relationship to Rafe. Perhaps he was like herself, another of the Mortmain's by-blows, but at least he had chosen to claim the boy.

Kate was surprised to feel a prickle of something close to envy, but she was quick to shrug the emotion off. She hadn't traveled here looking for a father, only the devil that had brought such devastation to her Val.

"I have come to take you back to Torrecombe to answer for your crimes, Rafe Mortmain," she announced.

"Indeed?" Rafe carefully shaved off a strip of wood from the toy boat's hull. He didn't even bother to look up. "You look full young to remember any of my crimes. When I lived in Torrecombe, I daresay you were one of those charming urchins who used to hide in the hedgerows and fling mud at my horse while chanting 'Devil Mortmain.' "

"I never threw mud. I threw rocks," Kate said fiercely. "And I wish now I had managed to hit you, knock you dead."

Rafe did lift his head at that, but he looked more saddened than surprised by her vehemence. "I suppose I must have given you some cause to hate me so much, Miss . . . er, Miss . . ."

"Fitzleger," Kate supplied, watching him closer for his reaction. "Kate Fitzleger."

Rafe's face stilled, some hidden emotion flickering beneath his eyelids.

"Don't try to pretend you are unfamiliar with the surname," Kate growled.

"No," he said quietly. "I remember the name well enough."

"You should. You seduced and abandoned my mother."

"Your mother?"

"Effie Fitzleger."

He set aside his carving, his eyes narrowing on her face. "Yes, I do seem to remember hearing something about Effie adopting some foundling child from London."

"*Hearing* something? I was right there under your nose. You must have rode past our cottage a hundred times when you made your rounds as customs officer, indifferent to both Effie and me. But I wasn't merely Effie's adopted child. It turns out that I was her natural daughter as well, conceived, it would seem, nineteen years ago in Portsmouth."

Rafe stiffened, staring at her, and Kate could almost feel the intensity of his gaze, saw him flinch as the realization struck him. He lurched to his feet and she shrank instinctively away, trying to keep the pistol steady.

But he advanced closer. It was as though he didn't even see the weapon, his eyes devouring her, his face looking torn between incredulity and wonder. His gaze flicked from her to some point on the wall and back again.

Although it was unwise to take her eyes off the villain, Kate could not help shifting a little to see what he had glanced at. It was a mirror mounted on the inn wall, crude and unframed.

But she and Rafe Mortmain were reflected back in its polished surface. Kate peered at herself, biting down hard to still the sudden tremor of her lip. Her diminutive stature, the delicacy of her features, those were Effie's. But the mass of jet black hair, the stubborn strength of her chin, and most of all her storm-ridden gray eyes, those were all pure Mortmain.

They stood shoulder to shoulder in silence for a long moment, simply staring at the grim truth reflected back from that mirror.

"My God," he breathed. "You—you are—"

"Your daughter? Unfortunately so it would appear," Kate said bitterly. She was trembling so badly, he could have easily disarmed her. But he made no move to do so. He gazed at her in awe, reaching up as though he meant to caress her hair.

Kate shied away from him. "Don't touch me. Don't you *ever* touch me," she said through clenched teeth.

Rafe lowered his hand immediately. "Of—of course I won't. I am sorry."

Kate sucked in a deep breath to steady herself. "I didn't come here for your damned apologies. Or any tender reunion.

"I don't cherish particularly tender feelings toward you, *Papa*." She sneered. "Especially since I spent my childhood abandoned in the worst part of London, struggling to survive, fighting for every crust of bread."

"Oh, Kate," he murmured. The depth of sorrow in his eyes astonished her. She really hadn't expected him to care.

"I didn't tell you that to make you pity me," she said, lifting her chin proudly. "Only that you should understand. I learned to be tough, to be utterly ruthless about getting what I want."

"And what do you want from me, Kate?" he asked quietly. "Money or—or some sort of acknowledgment?"

"Good God, no!" She gave a harsh laugh. "The last thing I want is to be claimed by you, branded as being a Mortmain.

"Though I should not have been so terribly surprised to discover that's what I am," she added with a slight catch in her voice. "I always knew I had bad blood, that there was something wicked about me."

"Don't say that, Kate. It might once have been true of me, but surely not you. The Fitzlegers were good people. Your great-grandfather was a vicar and—and Effie was a sweet young woman."

"Is that why you seduced her?" Kate asked scornfully. "Or was it merely another part of your Mortmain scheming to try to get revenge on the St. Legers?"

"I don't know. Maybe a little of both. That winter when I docked at Portsmouth, I was bitter at the St. Legers, at the wrongful accusations that had forced me to leave Torrecombe. And the old man, Reverend Fitzleger, had had as much of a hand in it as the dread Lord Anatole."

"So you took out your anger on poor Effie."

"She didn't exactly run from my advances."

"Because she was a foolish girl. She thought you something wonderful, dark, handsome, and dangerous."

"I wasn't all that dangerous then, Kate. Just lonely and unhappy. I found comfort for a brief sweet spell in a young girl's arms."

"You took advantage of Effie's infatuation for you, her innocence."

"So I did and I am not particularly proud of that."

This was not all what Kate had expected, any sign of remorse coming from this villain. But it was there in Rafe's darkened gray eyes, in the wearied set of his mouth. Kate tightened her grip on the pistol, steeling herself against the look he cast her way, a look that seemed to plead for her forgiveness and understanding.

"I can't change the past, Kate. God knows I wish I could. But if there is any small way I can make some amends to you or Effie, then please . . . tell me what it is."

"There is one thing."

"Name it."

"You can restore to me the man that I love."

Rafe's brow furrowed in confusion. "I am afraid I don't understand."

"Val St. Leger. You have all but killed him."

Rafe flinched. "Oh, God," he said hoarsely. "The crystal."

"Aye, the damned crystal you gave him on All Hallows' Eve. Val has changed past all recognition since then. So angry, so bitter, in so much torment. It—it is like it is burning him up inside."

"Then you have to ride back to him at once. Get the blasted crystal away from him. Make him stop wearing it."

"It's too late for that," Kate cried. "Because it is more than the cursed stone destroying him. It was what happened during the storm when he took your hand and tried to heal you. It's as though he absorbed all your poison, all your evil into himself."

"I know," Rafe said softly. "Damnation, I never meant to hurt him—" He paused, grimacing. "Well, I suppose at one time I did mean to do just that, but not anymore. You have to believe me, Kate. I wish him no ill. The man saved my life. He did more than that. He gave me a new one, one I never dreamed possible."

"Then you've got to help him now," she urged.

"How? I would willingly do anything."

"There is only one chance. You have to return to Torrecombe, put the crystal back on, and take hold of Val's hand. Touch him until all is put right, transferred back as it was."

The eagerness died out of Rafe's face. "I would do anything," he said flatly. "Anything but that."

Kate's heart sank. He was refusing. She should not have been surprised or even especially disappointed but somehow she was. So what did she do now? Jam the pistol into his back? Bash him over the head and try to drag him out of here by his heels?

The words of Prospero's warning drifted back to her.

"Remember, Kate. The Mortmain has to play his part willingly or there is no hope at all the magic will work."

It took all of Kate's will to curb her desperation, her anger against Rafe Mortmain, to lower her pistol and plead with him instead.

"Please! You have got to help him. You are the only one who can."

Rafe regarded her sadly. "You don't know what you are asking me, Kate. Val cured more than my sickness. He took away a lifetime of anger and pain. For the first time I have a chance at real happiness. I feel more at peace with myself than I have ever been."

"Because it's his peace you have stolen! His kindness, his gentleness. You've taken away his very soul and you have to give it back."

Rafe paced away from her, raking his hands through his hair in an agitated gesture. His eyes reflected such turmoil, such agony of indecision, that Kate held her breath, waiting. Perhaps there was enough of Val in the villain, she would manage to sway him after all.

But then he slowly shook his head. "No, I'm sorry. I can't."

Kate's last hope flickered and died. Prospero's words forgotten, she brought the pistol to bear, leveling it straight at the Mortmain's heart.

"I am no longer asking you," she said. "I am telling you. Come with me to save Val or I swear I will shoot you right now."

But Rafe made no move to comply. "Then that is what you must do, Kate. Go ahead and fire. Because I would rather be dead than go back to what I was before."

Damn the villain! Did he not think she would actually do it? Obviously Rafe Mortmain had no notion how badly she hated him. And if he intended to let Val die, then he would die, too.

Clenching her jaw, Kate pulled the hammer back, her eyes blazing with angry tears. The Mortmain simply stood there, quietly waiting like a prisoner resigned to his execution.

Kate's breath came quick and shallow. Her hands trembled and she braced herself once, twice, for the loud retort of the pistol. But try as she might she could not seem to release the hammer.

She stared fiercely at Rafe Mortmain, trying to tell herself how much she loathed him, how much he deserved to die. But all she could see was Val's gentle eyes and melancholy smile, Val as he had once been, her quiet steady friend who had taught her so much of kindness and forgiveness, who would have expected so much better of her than this.

With a sob of defeat, Kate slowly eased the hammer back into place and lowered the pistol. She turned away from Rafe Mortmain, a hail of hot tears coursing down her cheeks.

"Kate . . ." The villain actually had the temerity to reach out to her to try to comfort her.

Kate wrenched away from him. "Leave me alone, damn you! I would kill you in a heartbeat but it would do Val no good. And I will find a way to save him, with or without you. After all, you are not the only cursed Mortmain here."

"What—what do you mean by that?"

Kate raised one hand to fiercely dash her tears aside. She hadn't meant anything really, just angry bitter words. And yet . . .

Not the only cursed Mortmain. The words echoed through her head, a desperate plan forming in her mind.

"Maybe you aren't the only one who can save him," she murmured, speaking more to herself than to Rafe. "It was a Mortmain who brought his curse on Val, but perhaps another one could release him. If I were to wear the crystal—"

"No!" Rafe Mortmain caught her by the shoulders. The man had actually gone pale. "Listen to me, Kate. You have to leave that crystal alone. You have no idea what it can do, how dangerous the cursed thing is."

Kate shoved him away from her, shooting the man a contemptuous glare. "Trying to offer me some fatherly advice and concern? Spare me. You are years too late. I am going back to Torrecombe to save the man I love and you . . . you can march straight to hell."

Before Rafe could prevent her, she whirled away from him and hurled herself out the door. He charged after her, shouting her name, but Kate ignored him. She fled down the inn steps, vanishing into the twilight.

Rafe stared after her, his heart thudding with trepidation. He had no doubt Kate would do exactly as she'd said. She was reckless enough for anything. The poor girl would have been far better off if she had more of Effie in her and less of him. She was obviously far too much his daughter.

His daughter . . .

Rafe released an unsteady breath, still stunned by the revelation. He heard someone stir in the doorway and realized that Corinne had come to stand quietly behind him.

"Rafe?"

He turned to face her, finding her gentle eyes full of trouble and confusion.

"I am sorry," she murmured. "But I heard her leave and could wait no longer."

Rafe said nothing, merely reached out to draw Corinne in his arms. "Then you must have overheard some of what Kate was saying?"

She nodded. "She sounded so angry, spoke so loud. Is she truly your child?"

"Aye. It would seem I found a daughter and lost her in the space of one afternoon."

"But is she—" Corinne tipped back her head to peer up at him with a worried look. "Forgive me, but do you think the poor girl is entirely in her right mind? Some of what I overheard, some of things she said made absolutely no sense. It—it almost sounded as though she was asking for your soul."

"Far worse than that, my dear." Rafe smiled sadly. "She wants to give it back to me."

He stroked his fingers through Corinne's hair, wanting to beg her to forget Kate's intrusion into their lives, longing to be able to do so himself. He held Corinne close, trying to recapture the happiness he'd felt earlier down on the beach, trying desperately to envision the future that shimmered before them.

He stared past Corinne into the deepening twilight, the light that was casting a final blaze over the rooftops. A sun that was setting, not rising, and all Rafe seemed able to see was Kate's dark, despairing eyes.

CHAPTER TWENTY-ONE

*T*he storm laid siege to Castle Leger, hurling rain and cannonades of thunder at the thick stone walls. Cold, wet, and tired, Kate straggled into the main hall like the sole survivor from a shipwreck. It was well past midnight and no one else was stirring. It was as though the entire household had fallen under a spell, the mansion encased in an eerie silence.

Exhausted footmen slumped over in their chairs, the ancient butler nodding off at his post. Even the mistress of the house had fallen asleep perched in a chair positioned before the parlor window, the better to keep watch of the road, lines of strain streaking Madeline St. Leger's beautiful countenance.

Just like in some fairy tale, they all kept their sleep-ridden vigil, waiting for a miracle, the knight to come riding to break the enchantment, the warrior to capture the dragon. Only Kate had never felt less like any valiant warrior and she had certainly failed to fetch home the dragon.

Weary and defeated, she crept upstairs, taking care to make no noise. If anyone guessed what she was about to attempt, she feared they might try to stop her. Most of all she dreaded the interference of Prospero. But she sensed no hint of the great sorcerer's presence as she slipped inside Val's bedchamber. A fire blazed on the hearth as though someone had hoped the warmth, the glow would be enough to draw Val back to the light.

It hadn't been. He looked exactly as he had when Kate had left. His dark head rested upon the pillow, his hands folded on the coverlet as pale and unmoving as an effigy carved in wax. Kate's heart clenched, fearing she might already be too late.

Anxiously she pressed her head to his chest, breathing a small sigh of relief when she heard the faint thud of his heart. Val was not dead and one look at his face should have been enough to have told her that. His gentle countenance had not settled into that repose of eternal sleep. The set of his mouth was grim, deep furrows creasing his brow as though even lost in his deep slumber he found no release from the inner darkness tormenting him.

Kate stood over him, heart aching as she stroked the hair back from his brow.

"Everything is going to be all right," she said. "I am here now and I know what I have to do to save you. Even though I am quite sure you would not approve."

Her lips curved in a sad smile. "You would give me a thunderous scold, tell me to leave the crystal alone, that it is too dangerous, and as usual, you would be right. If this transference works, I have no idea what I will be like after— after—"

Kate trembled, but she was quick to hide her trepidation behind a shaky laugh. "Hellfire! I am already so wicked, I daresay the crystal won't have any effect on me at all. But if it does, if I am changed past all recognition, there is one thing I want you to know.

"I love you, Val. I always will. There is no dark magic in the world that can ever alter that."

She stared down at him, seeking some sign that he could hear, that he understood. But there was no response at all in those cold, still features. She forced herself to turn away and marched over to the dresser where the small wooden jewel case was waiting with its deadly object tucked inside.

Kate released a tremulous breath as she lifted the box into her hands. A shiver of dread coursed through her, but she fought to suppress it, sending up a fervent prayer.

"Please, God. I don't care what happens to me. Just let me save him," she whispered.

Prospero had sealed the casket again, but it took Kate little effort to pick the lock open with one of her hairpins. She felt the catch give and then, steeling herself, she flung back the lid.

The silver chain nestled against the velvet lining, the shard of crystal looking insignificant and harmless until lightning flared just outside the bedchamber window. The crystal blazed with a sudden intensity that blinded Kate, dazzling her eyes. Don't stare at it; don't look at it too long, she adjured herself. She couldn't afford to fall under its power, not until she had done what she needed to do.

But she couldn't seem to tear her gaze away. The crystal sparkled and gleamed with a beauty that mesmerized. Scarce able to breathe, Kate reached to lift the hypnotic stone into her hand.

She fastened the chain around her neck, feeling at once a strange surge of power and an overwhelming despair.

You will never be able to do this, an icy voice seemed to taunt. *Who are you to tamper with such magic? A foundling wretch, a bastard child. And even if you can, why take such a risk for Val St. Leger? You'll never be anything to him now, only another cursed Mortmain.*

Kate closed her eyes. It was the crystal, trying to work on her already, magnifying her every bitter thought and despair. She forced herself to stifle such black emotions, thrusting them away.

Rushing over to the bed, she bent and pressed her lips to Val's, stealing one last desperate kiss. Then bracing herself, she reached for his hand. . . .

Lightning illuminated the imposing front door to Castle Leger, making Rafe Mortmain feel like a beggar huddled on the doorstep. Soaking him to the skin, the rain poured down his face, icy rivulets trickling past the collar of his greatcoat. But he scarce felt the chill. It was nothing compared to the cold dread that gripped his heart.

He must be quite mad to have come back here to this place, the very bastion of his enemies. The stone manor loomed above him, flooding him with painful memories of the brief time during his youth when he'd actually been welcomed behind these doors, offered kindness and friendship.

It hadn't lasted long before he been driven away by the suspicion and mistrust that seemed to be his legacy, the curse of bearing the infamous name of Mortmain. He'd finally managed to escape all that, find love and happiness for an all too brief, sweet time.

Why was he risking that, preparing to surrender it? Rafe backed away from the door, wishing he'd been able to overtake Kate long before she reached the castle. But he had been fortunate that old Rufus had performed as well as he had. Kate had been far better mounted and the girl rode like the very devil.

But then why not? Rafe thought grimly. She was the devil's own daughter, poor child. Likely he was too late to stop her from pursuing her reckless attempt to save Val St. Leger. He should turn and ride away while he still could.

But somehow he could not bring himself to do that. Bad enough he had un-wittingly cursed the girl with his own infamous heritage, his mad Mortmain blood. He couldn't allow her to be cursed yet again with the power of that damned crystal. If there was anyone who deserved to be cursed, it was him.

He approached the front door and started to reach for the knocker, when the heavy portal suddenly creaked open, almost as though someone had ex-pected him. Yet there was no one there, the hall beyond dark, silent, and empty.

Rafe stepped inside, further unnerved when the door slammed shut be-hind him as though pulled by the wind.

"H-hello?" Rafe rasped. He braced himself, expecting at any moment to be discovered, pounced upon by several burly St. Leger retainers. But the entire house seemed curiously deserted.

He paced toward the stairs, the only place he could see any light glowing. He thought he detected a movement on the landing above.

"Is anyone there?" Rafe called.

There was no response, but Rafe felt a chill sweep through him, a strange compulsion that beckoned him upward to follow the mysterious light. He moved forward cautiously, mounting the stairs until he emerged in the upper hall.

It had been many years since he had been inside Castle Leger and his memory of the layout of the new wing was not good. He saw doors leading to what he knew were the family bedchambers, all closed, except one.

Light spilled across the threshold into the hallway, and Rafe scarce fath-omed how, but somehow he knew that was where he was meant to go. He crept toward the light, entering the bedchamber that seemed eerily silent, re-moved from the force of the storm brewing outside.

A fire blazed on the hearth, casting a flickering light over the curtains and the dark-haired girl. Kate knelt by the bed, clutching Val's hand, her head bowed. Her shoulders shook with suppressed sobs, and Rafe caught the glint of that hellish crystal fastened around her neck.

"No!" he cried hoarsely. Flinging himself across the room, he seized hold of Kate and wrenched her away from Val. Hauling her to her feet, he spun her around to face him.

The crystal glinted evilly. Kate's face was death white, streaked with tears, her eyes dark empty pools.

"My God, Kate. What have you done?" Rafe demanded. She shuddered and seemed unable to answer him. Gripped by his own terror, Rafe gave her a brisk shake.

She blinked, staring up at him like a lost child.

"It—it didn't work," she said despairingly. "I—I couldn't make the crystal work."

"Oh, thank God," Rafe breathed, flooded with relief. Instinctively he tried to draw Kate into his arms, comfort her, but the movement seemed to snap her out of her grief.

Striking out at him like a wild thing, she wrenched herself free. Backing away from him, she glowered through her tears.

"What—what the devil are you doing here?"

Rafe wished he had a sane answer to that question. "I suppose I came to stop you from doing something stupid."

"What I do is none of your concern. N-now you just get away from Val before I scream for the servants."

Rafe gave a tired sigh. "Don't be foolish, Kate. I mean him no harm. I only want to help him."

"Help him?" Kate sniffed, eyeing Rafe with suspicion and mistrust. He didn't blame her. The words he'd just spoken surprised even him.

"Why?" she demanded fiercely. "You refused before. You said you would rather die. Why did you change your mind?"

Rafe slicked back the damp ends of rain-wet hair from his eyes. Why? Damned if he knew himself. Perhaps it was because of the man lying on the bed, so still and silent. Val St. Leger had sacrificed a great deal to give Rafe back his life; more than that, to give him a new life that Rafe had never dreamed possible.

Or perhaps it was because of Kate, the child he had unwittingly abandoned to danger and hardship, just as his own mother had done to him. Kate, his daughter, who obviously loved Val St. Leger, valued him more than her own life.

"What does the reason matter?" Rafe asked wearily. "I am here, so let's get this blasted thing over with. Give me the crystal, Kate, while you still can."

Kate's hand closed protectively over the shard, and he could see that the devilish stone had already had some effect on her. It obviously took a great deal of her will to be able to remove it, hand it to him.

Rafe shuddered as his fingers closed over the stone. He felt like a prisoner who had known an all too brief taste of freedom consenting to be shackled back in the cold darkness of his cell. He flung the chain over his head and felt the crystal settle like an icy weight over the region of his heart.

Rafe stumbled past Kate over to the bed to peer down at Val, the man's quiet features shadowed by a torment Rafe knew all too well.

Val St. Leger, his enemy, but also the man who had given him his greatest gift. One month free of his own evil and darkness, one month to find love, happiness. Rafe supposed it was more than many men were ever granted.

He closed his eyes briefly, conjuring up Corinne's wistful face, Charley's solemn eyes. Then he forced himself to banish the image, knowing if he didn't, he would never be able to go through with this.

He bent down, taking hold of Val's hand. The man felt so cold and lifeless, for one moment Rafe was ashamed to feel himself hope that he was too late. But he wasn't. He could already sense a strange shift in the atmosphere of the room, and his heartbeat quickened.

It was growing colder, darker, the fire suddenly dying. The storm seemed to rage closer, lighting the room with intermittent flashes of lightning. Rafe was dimly aware of Kate hovering anxiously at the foot of the bed, but his gaze never wavered from Val.

Of a sudden, the window casement flew open, causing Kate to cry out. Wind and rain invaded the room, but Rafe ignored it, focusing intently on the man before him. Had he imagined it or had he felt the faintest stirring in Val's fingers?

Another flare of lightning illuminated the bed and Val jerked. His eyes flew wide, staring straight up at Rafe.

"M-mortmain," he whispered hoarsely.

"It is all right, St. Leger," Rafe said. "You know why I'm here."

Val shuddered and tried to withdraw his hand. Incredible, Rafe thought. Even infected with Rafe's own villainy and damnable pain, Saint Valentine was still trying not to hurt him.

"Damn you, St. Leger," Rafe growled. "No more blasted heroics. Give me my pain. Give it back to me."

He clutched down so hard, his knuckles turned white. Val groaned, twisting back toward Rafe with an agony too great to resist, to contain. He had to release it.

Val's fingers convulsed and Rafe gave a sharp gasp. It was as though razors were tearing through his flesh, slicing through his veins. The poison was flowing back to him, all the darkness, bitterness, and despair.

Rafe cried out, wanting to break the contact, but he forced himself to hang on. He felt the crystal sway about his neck, and then there was a blinding flash of light, a deafening explosion.

Rafe felt himself flung away from the bed and tumbled to the carpet, rolling in agony. He panted, closing his eyes, surrendering himself at last to merciful oblivion.

A terrible silence settled over the room. Kate crouched down behind the bed, covering her eyes. She finally dared move. Trembling, she lifted her head, half fearing she would find the entire bedchamber reduced to rubble. But all seemed returned to normal, even the fire crackling on the hearth. The storm sounded as though it had receded.

Seizing hold of the bedpost, Kate pulled herself up, peeking over the side of the bed. Val had fallen back against the pillows, his head tumbled to one side and eyes fast closed. Heart thudding with trepidation, Kate rushed to his side. His face had relaxed, gentled into an expression of such repose that for a moment Kate feared the worst. The transference had gone terribly wrong, killed him. But then she saw the even rise and fall of his chest, the color starting to steal back into his cheeks.

She touched trembling fingers to his brow. Warm, he was so warm and very much alive. Kate pressed a fervent kiss against his cheek, tears of relief streaming down her face. Val was going to be all right now. She felt certain of it. For long moments she was so caught up in her joy, she almost forgot about the other man.

Kate glanced around sharply, discovering Rafe crumpled beneath the windows as though the force of the explosion had flung him across the room. The casement was still open, rain blowing in on his unconscious form.

Kate hastened to close the window, then crept closer to Rafe as cautiously as she would have approached an injured wolf. Rafe Mortmain. Her father. She would never be able to think of him that way, but neither could she think of him with her former loathing.

Whether he had been reluctant to do so or not, he had saved Val's life and she could not help but be grateful to him for that. He had done so at considerable cost. Val might appear eased into a gentle, restoring sleep, but it was obvious Rafe was locked in a nightmare. The set of his mouth was grim, his brow contracted with torment as though he once more wrestled with his inner demons.

It may be no more than he deserved, but Kate could not help feeling compassion for the man. There was nothing she could do for Rafe, except perhaps relieve him from the terrible influence of the crystal fastened around his neck.

She was afraid to touch the cursed stone again but steeled herself to do so. Kate reached for the chain, only to draw back with a sharp gasp. The crystal . . . Either she was going completely mad or the stone had moved by itself.

Her pulse gave a frightened leap as she watched the shard rise up, taking the chain with it, snapping it free of Rafe's neck. She scrambled fearfully back, watching with stunned eyes as the crystal floated across the room toward the fireside.

And straight into Prospero's outstretched hand. The wizard materialized by the hearth, his hooded eyes regarding Kate with that familiar inscrutable expression.

Kate released a long breath of relief. At least one mystery was now solved for her, the reason behind Rafe Mortmain's sudden appearance, his dramatic change of heart. She beamed at Prospero. "It was you all along. I might have known. You used your magic on Rafe. It was you who brought him back here."

Prospero secreted the crystal away, coming to stand over the inert man with a bemused frown. "Certainly I used my powers to ease his entry into the castle, but as for fetching him here . . . No, my dear. I told you the Mortmain had to surrender of his own free will and that was what he did."

"But he sacrificed everything to save Val—his happiness, his freedom. Why did he do it?"

"I have no idea. You will have to ask him, although I doubt he will ever be able to tell you."

"Why?" Kate glanced at Rafe, surprised to feel a stab of anxiety. "Isn't he going to be all right?"

"Oh, he'll do well enough, especially since I have taken the crystal. Both Rafe and your Val will be essentially the men they were before, which means you had better summon your servants to have the Mortmain restrained before he regains consciousness."

"Restrained?" Kate faltered.

"Aye, Rafe Mortmain is completely restored to his old self. When he awakes, he will be as dangerous as he ever was."

"Oh, aye, of course," Kate murmured. But somehow Rafe did not look dangerous, merely broken and defeated. Yet she was unwilling to take any risks, especially when Val's life might be prove to be the one at stake.

She hurried to do Prospero's bidding while the sorcerer himself took steps to make sure the dangerous crystal was sealed away for all time. Neither of them saw Rafe Mortmain's lashes flutter or the single tear that slid down his cheek.

CHAPTER TWENTY-TWO

*V*al braced himself on the wooden cane Jem had carved for him and slipped quietly out the library door into the garden. The gloom-ridden silence that had hung over the house for days was dispelled by the chatter of excited voices. Not only had Lance returned with his father and Marius, but the grim report of Val's illness had reached his sisters as well.

Mariah, Phoebe, and Leonie had descended upon Castle Leger with their families and the manor was now full of rejoicing women, women who had feared to attend Val's funeral and were now happily planning his wedding.

Val appreciated all the outpouring of love and congratulations from his family, but he was finding it a bit overwhelming. He stole out into the relative quiet of the sunlit garden with a grateful sigh. To the rest of the St. Legers, it was as though this last dark month had never been.

Val wished he could as easily forget some of it, the violent outbursts of his temper, the ruthless things he'd said and done. He had a good many fences to mend with many people: his brother, Lance; his cousin Victor; Carrie Tre-withan; her husband, Reeve. Well, no, Val was obliged to admit. He still felt no compulsion to apologize to Reeve.

But there was one person more than any other whom Val did long to see and crave her pardon. Kate. His lady, now his chosen bride. Val smiled softly, his heart flooding with a quiet joy at the mere thought of that.

Effie had stunned everyone by appearing early at the castle that morning, not with her usual flood of tears, but with a courage and sad dignity that had been astonishing. But no more astonishing than her revelation, the secret that she had kept hidden for years that she was Kate's natural mother and Rafe Mortmain was Kate's father.

Effie and Rafe . . . that still seemed to Val too incredible for belief. But he had scarce taken as much heed of that confession as Effie finally admitting that Kate had always been Val's destined bride.

The revelation had astounded Val and yet somehow it hadn't. In some corner of his St. Leger heart, he felt he had always known. He was surprised only that Kate had not come with Effie to tell him the truth. With Effie? Damnation! Val would have expected Kate to turn up on his doorstep with the vicar and the ring.

But his wild girl had seemed oddly subdued since his recovery and even more strangely absent from his side. Kate was exhausted, Effie had explained, worn out by the events of the past few days and Val could scarce blame Kate for that. He had put his love through a terrible ordeal this past month and he intended to spend the rest of his life making up for that.

Leaning on his cane, Val ignored the familiar twinge in his knee and headed down the worn path leading toward the stables. He met his brother coming from the opposite direction. Val froze at the sight of Lance, feeling stiff and awkward, remembering the last time they had exchanged words alone, the grim quarrel that day on the beach.

But Lance did not appear to suffer from any such constraint. He grinned at Val, giving him a hearty clap on the shoulder.

"Aha, what's this, Sir Galahad? Attempting to flee from the ladies? Not very chivalrous."

Val sighed. "I fear they are apt to drown me with their tea and solicitude. Even Mama is not showing her customary restraint."

Lance chuckled, but as his gaze raked over Val, his eyes grew uncomfortably misty for a moment. "Damn, Val," he murmured. "But it is good to see you up and about, looking like your old self again, although I would have preferred that it be without—without this." Lance gestured awkwardly toward the cane.

Val smoothed his hand over the rough wooden knob. "Actually I think Jem did a remarkable job carving this on such short notice. I am sure you will understand I have no desire ever to set eyes again on my silver one with the sword stick."

"I daresay Victor doesn't either."

Val attempted to smile, but some remembrances, such as the night when he had attacked Victor and injured Kate, were still too raw for jesting about.

"Lance," he began hesitantly. "This past month I discovered that there are far worse things that can afflict a man than an injured knee. About the quarrel we had that day after my fight with Trewithan—"

But Lance was already shaking his head, attempting to cut him off. "Good God, Val, you don't have to try to explain to me. I know you were under the influence of that crystal."

"The crystal might have exacerbated my temper, but it didn't put the words in my mouth. All those things that I said to you—"

"Were things that likely finally needed saying. I know that what you did for me on that battlefield, you did willingly. You are my brother. I would just as quickly have made the same sacrifice for you, if I could. But that is not to say that I wouldn't have felt some regrets afterward when I had to live with the consequences."

Lance regarded him earnestly. "I think you always felt guilty for your regrets, tried to deny you ever had them. But you are only human, Val."

"Aye," Val agreed with a grimace. "If this past month has taught me nothing else, it has taught me that."

"Then perhaps some good will come of this yet because you always did strive to be too perfect, Saint—" Lance checked himself, looking so abashed, Val had to smile.

"Saint Valentine. Go ahead and say it, Sir Lancelot."

Lance grinned. "No, because then we will have to start cuffing each other and end up wrestling through the garden. Not only are we getting too old for such behavior, I would not want to end up blackening your eye before your wedding day."

"You could try to do so," Val retorted. He added anxiously, "You will stand up with me, won't you, Lance?"

"Lord, haven't I been waiting forever to do so? And speaking of weddings and your blushing bride, where is the little hellion?"

"Kate is at Rosebriar. I was just on my way to fetch her."

To Val's surprise, an uneasy expression settled over Lance's face. He cut an odd glance back in the direction of the stables.

"Uh . . . Val, there is one other matter we have to discuss. It's about Rafe."

"What of him?" Val asked. "When I woke up from the transference, he had disappeared again. I assume he is long gone."

Lance scratched his jaw, looking uncomfortable. "Er, no, actually when I returned to the castle, I discovered that Jem and one of the grooms had shackled Rafe in the old dungeon beneath the keep. I—I let him go."

Lance angled a glance at Val that was both guilty and defiant. "Damn it, Val,

I know you have long despised and mistrusted the man, but I always believed there was much good to be found in Rafe and he did return of his own accord to save your life. And like it or not, he is Kate's father and—and—"

"Lance!" Val held up one hand to halt his brother's breathless flow of words. "You did the right thing. I am glad you released him."

"You are?" Lance stared at him in astonishment. "Well, that is a mighty good thing because Rafe is down at the stables even now saddling up to leave, except that he insists upon speaking to you before he goes."

Val tensed a little at the prospect, but nodded solemnly. He headed off in the direction of the stables, Lance trailing anxiously behind. Val paused long enough to thrust out his cane, halting his brother.

"Lance, if you don't mind, I would prefer to speak to Rafe alone."

When a look of alarm sprung to Lance's eyes, Val said with a dry laugh, "Don't worry. I promise you that Rafe and I will not be trying to kill each other this time."

Lance did not appear completely reassured, but he hung back while Val continued on. As Val approached the stable door, he noticed grooms and stable hands scattering as though they too feared some sort of grim confrontation, like two rival knights about to collide.

Gripping his cane, Val stumped inside the stables, his eyes adjusting to the shadows of the interior, his nostrils filling with the sweet scent of hay, leather, and horses. He peered down the long row of stalls to where Rafe stood adjusting the bridle on an old gelding even more disreputable looking than Val's Vulcan.

Rafe appeared much as Val had always remembered, cold, distant, and arrogant. Except he now knew all too well the pain and despair Rafe concealed behind his hard exterior.

He glanced up from his task, perceiving Val's entrance, and the two men measured each other in silence for a long moment. It was most strange, Val thought, staring into the eyes of one who had long been his enemy and realizing that he now understood the man, almost better than he did his own brother.

Rafe was the first to speak, gruffly clearing his throat. "I am glad you are up and about, St. Leger. Your brother has given me permission to leave. But I didn't feel as though the decision should rest with Lance. You are the one I wronged, the one who should say whether I go or stay."

"You are entirely free to leave, Rafe," Val said. "As soon as you answer me one question."

"And what would that be?"

"I lived with your nightmares and your pain for only a month and it was nearly enough to drive me mad. I don't think I could have willingly taken on such a burden again. You didn't have to come back here to save me. Why did you do it?"

Rafe shrugged. "You forget I have lived with a part of you, too, St. Leger. You seem to have made for a brief time some sort of God-cursed hero out of me who rescues widows and orphans."

A shadow passed over Rafe's face. He lowered his eyes, concealing his expression as he continued, "There is a woman and her son I left back in Falmouth. Corinne and Charley Brewer. I realize I have no right to ask any favors of you, St. Leger, but—but I would be grateful if you would find them, see that they both remain safe, well cared for."

"Aye, I would be happy to do so, but why will you no longer be looking out for them?"

"Have you forgotten?" Rafe said bitterly. "The crystal has restored me to my old self. I am nobody's hero now."

He led his horse out of the stall, but Val caught his arm, gently restraining him.

"Rafe, before you leave, there is one thing you have to understand. The transformation that came over me wasn't merely owing to whatever bitterness I absorbed from you. I have my own darkness."

Rafe frowned. "Why are you telling me this?"

"Because I don't think that the change that came over you was entirely due to me either. All these years, Lance tried to tell me that I was wrong about you and I should have listened to him, given you a chance. I am sorry."

Rafe gave a mirthless laugh. "Now you are starting to believe that beneath my evil Mortmain hide, you might actually find traces of a decent man. Is that why you have decided to let me go?"

"Partly. And also because it would seem rather ill-mannered to hang the father of my prospective bride."

"You intend to marry Kate?"

"Aye."

"Even knowing she is my daughter?"

"Aye, what difference could that possibly make to me? I love her."

Rafe's eyes widened. "It is only that for a St. Leger and a Mortmain to marry . . ." He let out a long low whistle. "That will be enough to send all of our ancestors spinning in their graves."

"Or perhaps it will finally be a fitting an end to this senseless feud."

Rafe's mouth creased into a reluctant smile. "Perhaps."

Val held out his hand and after a brief hesitation, Rafe took it. As their palms met Val felt the stirring of the old urge. To reach out to Rafe, to ease some of the pain he saw shadowed in the other man's eyes.

But it was not his responsibility to try to save the entire world. Rafe would have to find his own healing. Val withdrew his hand.

He followed Rafe out into the sunlight. As Rafe swung up into the saddle, he said, "You will tell Kate good-bye for me?"

"You have no wish to see her yourself?"

Rafe shook his head. "She has no need of a father now. It is a husband she'll be wanting. But I wish you could make her understand one thing. I may be a thorough scoundrel, but if I had known about Kate, I would never have left. I would never have abandoned her."

"I know you wouldn't have," Val said softly. "And I will make sure Kate does, too."

Rafe gave a grateful nod. Then with a brief salute, he wheeled his mount about and rode away. Val watched him until he was out of sight and then headed back into the stable himself, preparing for the one thing he felt he had waited a lifetime to do. He was going to claim his chosen bride.

A short while later, Val knocked at the door to Rosebriar Cottage, trying to contain his eagerness and impatience. When seconds ticked by and no one answered his summons, he raised his cane to rap again.

But even as he did so, the door was flung open, not by one of the servants, but by the mistress of the house herself. Effie took one look at Val and promptly burst into tears.

"Oh, please, Effie," Val said hastily. "It is all right. I told you this morning that I forgive you so there is no need—"

"I—I am not weeping about that," Effie sobbed. "It's Kate."

"What about her?" Val demanded. "Is she ill?"

When Effie appeared unable to answer him, Val pressed anxiously past her into the hall. "Where is Kate? Let me speak to her."

"I c-can't."

"Why the devil not?"

"Be-because I don't know where she is," Effie wailed. "Kate is gone."

Val marched up the worn stone stairs, scarce feeling the throb in his knee as sharper emotions overrode any physical discomfort. Kate had been missing for hours. No one had seen her anywhere at Castle Leger or in Torrecombe. Val had been making desperate inquiries of every living soul in the village when it had suddenly occurred to him he was seeking answers in the wrong place, that he shouldn't have been asking the *living* at all.

His mouth set in a taut line of worry and fear, Val emerged into the tower chamber, the mysterious room as silent as though it had been abandoned for centuries. His own senses heightened by his apprehension for Kate, Val wasn't fooled.

"Prospero?" he called.

There was no answer. The sorcerer had materialized to many members of the St. Leger family, but he had never deigned to put in an appearance for Val before. That was going to have to change right now, Val thought, clenching his jaw.

"Prospero!" he roared, striking the tip of his cane loudly against the stone floor.

"I heard you the first time," a silken voice replied. "I happen to be dead, not deaf."

The response, quiet as it was, startled Val, the sudden chill in the room causing the back of his neck to prickle. He came about slowly to find the sorcerer standing behind him, leaning up against the bedpost, studying Val through narrowed eyes.

At any other time, Val might have been filled with a sensation of amazement and wonder. Once he would have given anything to encounter Prospero, to ply the shade of his ancestor with a hundred questions about the St. Legers' history. But now there was only one thing he needed to know.

"Where is Kate? Where has she gone? What have you done with her?" he demanded.

Instead of replying, Prospero eyed him with an amusement Val found infuriating. "By St. George, first you invade my tower bellowing and now you rap out questions like a grand inquisitor. And I thought you were supposed to be the quiet one."

"I'll show you quiet," Val growled. "If you don't tell me where Kate is, I'll raise enough of an uproar to bring this tower crashing down about your ears."

Prospero yawned, looking singularly unimpressed by the threat. "So you have lost your lady? Careless of you. What makes you think I would know where she is?"

"Because from what I have gleaned, you and Kate have been thick as thieves of late. During the past month, I have a feeling it is you she has been coming to for—for—"

"The comfort and friendship she once had from you? Aye, she has. Jealous?" Prospero taunted. "I confess, were our situations reversed, if Kate were my lady, it would make me so."

He gave a deprecating cough and added quickly, "Of course, always presuming that I am prey to such petty mortal emotions, which I am not."

"Well, I fear I am prey to a good many of them." Val sighed. "I do envy you for every moment of Kate's company you have had, every smile she bestowed upon you. But at the moment, I am far more worried than jealous so will you please tell me where she has gone?"

Prospero locked his arms across his chest and frowned. "Why do you want to find her?"

"Why do you think?" Val asked impatiently. "I love her and I want to marry her."

"Even though she is a Mortmain, the daughter of your great enemy?"

"Aye, what does that matter?"

"Kate seems to feel that it would matter a great deal to you."

Val stared at Prospero, at first stunned by the sorcerer's words, then stricken with remorse. Of course, now it began to make sense, Kate's subdued manner, why she had been avoiding him since his recovery.

Val gripped the knob of his cane, silently cursing his own stupidity. What a thickheaded insensitive clod he had been, so caught up in his own rejoicing to discover Kate was his chosen bride. He had given little thought to what she must be feeling, be going through as she struggled to deal with the shock of learning her father's identity.

"My God," Val murmured. "So is that why Kate ran away? Because she learned that she is descended from the Mortmains? How could she possibly think that would make any difference to me?"

"Oh, I don't know. Let me see," Prospero drawled, stroking his beard. "Perhaps it is the history you wrote, meticulously recording every black deed of her family. Or perhaps it is the way you taught her to curse all Mortmains as evil, especially the man who turned out to be her own father."

Val flinched. "Aye, I fear that I did. I was mistaken about Rafe, mistaken about a good many things in the past, but never about my feelings for Kate."

"So you would not now look into her eyes and see the reflection of your enemy?"

"Of course not."

"Never be tempted to regard her with suspicion and mistrust?"

"No, damn it," Val insisted. "I would not care if Kate were descended from the devil himself. It would not change who she is, a warm, wonderful, courageous woman."

"I trust you are clear on that point, Dr. St. Leger, because if you harbor even the whisper of a doubt, you need to stay away from her. Kate has been through enough hurt and rejection in her life. I won't see her subjected to any more."

Prospero's unexpected fierceness astonished Val. "By God," he said softly. "I do believe you have half fallen in love with Kate yourself."

Prospero at first looked taken aback by the suggestion, and then he drew himself up indignantly. "What a complete fool you are. I told you I am not subject to any such idiotic human failings."

He stalked past Val, the picture of such regal outrage, Val was forced to bite back a smile. "I do crave your pardon, my lord."

"So you should," Prospero snapped. He stormed over to the arrow slit and stood staring outward for a long time. At last he said reluctantly, "You will find your lady where you would expect to find a Mortmain."

The sorcerer's cryptic words puzzled Val at first. Then understanding dawned on him along with a jolt of alarm.

"Lostland!" Val breathed. "You permitted Kate to go to that bleak forsaken place?"

"You should be familiar enough with your Kate to realize that no one ever permits her to do anything," Prospero said dryly.

Heart thudding with renewed alarm, Val barely took the time to thank Prospero for the information. Tightly gripping his cane, he bolted for the tower stairs.

CHAPTER TWENTY-THREE

*R*afe Mortmain trudged down the narrow cobblestone street that led to the wharf, his collar turned up against the bite of the wind, his battered portmanteau clutched in his hand. He calculated that he had just enough money left to take the packet boat to France. From there he could find a berth on some oceangoing vessel as a first mate, a bosun, even an ordinary seaman; the employment scarce mattered.

The crystal was gone. His health and vitality were restored. At least he had come away from Castle Leger with that much. As for the rest, the bitterness and despair that had always dogged his footsteps— Rafe fetched a wearied sigh. He'd survive. He always had. He was good at that.

He focused on the harbor ahead of him, the masts wreathed in the early morning mist. Rafe tried to summon up his old eagerness for setting sail, but the sight of all those ships riding at anchor left him feeling strangely as cold and gray as the water lapping against the pier.

Against his will, his thoughts kept drifting back to the cozy chamber above the inn. The woman and boy had been still asleep when he had stolen away. But Corinne would rise soon to find his letter of farewell. It would come as no surprise to her. Since his return from Torrecombe yesterday, she had to have noticed the change in him, the icy distance and the surly withdrawal from both her and the boy.

He supposed he should have had the decency to bid her good-bye to her face, tell her he was going. But a farewell note was more than most of his mistresses had ever received from him.

Except Corinne had never been his mistress. Whatever she had been, whatever he had imagined that he'd felt for her, it was gone. All part of the madness induced by the crystal on All Hallows' Eve. After he left Falmouth, he doubted that he would even remember her face.

As though to hasten the process of forgetting, he quickened his pace. He scarce heard the woman rushing after him until she called out his name.

"Rafe! Please . . . wait!"

Rafe froze at the sound of Corinne's voice. He came about slowly, grimacing to find her racing down the street toward him. He'd planned to make good his escape before Corinne realized he was gone, or barring that, he'd hoped she would have enough sense not to come after him. But he knew how to handle the situation. His icy disdain and cold glare had always been enough to send any female packing.

He drew himself up to his full height, attempting to fix his mouth into his familiar hard sneer. But the expression wavered as soon as he realized Corinne had scarce taken time to dress herself properly. The worn black shawl she had flung over her thin cotton dress made poor protection against the damp, morning air.

"Damnation, Corinne," he growled as she overtook him. "What are you trying to do? Catch your death?"

Corinne said nothing, too out of breath to reply. She shivered, the sharp wind tangling strands of brown hair across her eyes.

"Have you no sense at all, woman? Coming out here half-naked and not even wearing a bloody bonnet!" He plunked down his portmanteau. Seizing hold of her shoulders, he dragged her ruthlessly behind the shelter of some crates stacked near a dockside warehouse.

Rafe positioned himself in front of her, glaring as she struggled to brush the hair back from her face. Her nose was already nipped red although her eyes remained remarkably clear. She obviously hadn't been weeping, which was a relief. But the wistful expression she turned upon him was almost worse.

"What are you doing here, chasing after me?" Rafe growled. "Didn't you read my letter?"

"Y-yes," she faltered. "Although I didn't quite understand all of it."

"What was there not to understand? I think I left you an accurate and lengthy accounting of all the crimes I've ever committed. I am a thoroughly bad lot and you and your son are well rid of me. I am a wanted man."

"But I always knew that, Rafe."

Rafe was doing his best to recover his icy, remote bearing but her soft admission caught him off guard.

"You knew? How?" he demanded.

Corinne shrugged, trying to drag the meager warmth of her shawl more closely about her shoulders. "You have this way sometimes of looking over your shoulder as though you were expecting trouble, even when you were at your most carefree, playing with Charley on the beach. And whenever there was a constable about, you always took great care to steer us to the opposite side of the street."

Rafe stared at her. He hadn't thought she had ever noticed, but knowing Corinne, it didn't surprise him that she had. But one fact did fill him with astonishment.

"You guessed that I might be a criminal, a man with a price on my head, and yet you never did anything about it?"

"What would you have me do, Rafe?"

"You should have summoned the constable yourself, turned me in. If not for the reward, at least to protect yourself and your son."

"Charley and I were never in any danger from you."

"No, but only because of what happened to me on All Hallows' Eve."

"Aye, the piece of crystal and that St. Leger doctor with his unusual healing power. You explained all that in your letter, too."

"But of course it sounds completely mad to you and you don't believe me."

"Oh, I believe you," Corinne said. "There is only one thing that confuses me."

Rafe rolled his eyes. After his insane account of St. Legers, crystals, sorcerers, and changes wrought by dark magic, there was only *one* thing Corinne didn't understand?

"And just what would that be?" he demanded.

Corinne fixed him with her clear honest gaze. "I was wondering what spell you were under this morning that caused you to leave me and Charley nearly all your money."

"Well, I—I—" Rafe scowled at her and blustered. "I told you before money does not mean that much to me."

"And what spell are you under right now," Corinne continued inexorably, "that is making you be so kind to me?"

"Kind to you? In case you haven't noticed, madam, I have been growling and swearing at you ever since you caught up to me."

"Aye," Corinne said softly. "But, Rafe . . . you are also standing between me and the wind."

Rafe opened his mouth to refute her words, but was discomfited to find that he couldn't, because she was right. He was still trying to protect Corinne, would have done so with his last breath.

No matter how hard and distant he struggled to appear, it didn't stop her from smiling up at him, nor raising herself up on tiptoe to brush her lips against the grim set of his mouth.

He should have prevented her from doing so, but he felt as though he was the one frozen, vulnerable to the icy blast of the wind. But it was a cold that started to crack and melt with the first touch of her lips.

What a fool he was, Rafe thought desperately, to have ever imagined he was going to be able to forget this woman. Her sweet lips, her gentle touch, her soft brown eyes were going to haunt him until the end of his days.

With a low groan, he caught Corinne hard against him, crushing her mouth with a fierce kiss. He strained her close, whispering harshly into her ear.

"Damn you, Corinne. Why did you have to do this? Don't you understand I was trying to do the decent thing by leaving and I no longer have St. Leger's magic to help me?"

"I am glad," she said, clinging to him, kissing him just as fiercely, his chin, his lips, his cheeks, any part of his face she could reach. "I don't want you trying to be that noble. I love you the way that you are."

"The way that I am?" Rafe gave a bitter, despairing laugh. "A pirate, a thief, a damned Mortmain. What kind of husband would I make for you? What kind of father for Charley?"

"I don't know. Why don't you ask him?" Corinne shifted in Rafe's arms to peer at the street beyond him. Rafe twisted around himself and groaned aloud at the sight of the small figure standing but a few feet away.

Oh, God, not the boy, too. Charley stared up at Rafe with wide solemn eyes that were already filling with tears. Rafe peeled himself away from Corinne, trying to regain some control of the situation, groping for his icy mask.

But it was too late. Charley had already launched himself at Rafe, wrapping his thin arms tightly about his legs, nearly sending Rafe staggering back.

"Oh, Rafe. P-please don't go."

Rafe swore under his breath, attempting to stiffen. But it was quite impossible to strike a pose of icy hauteur, not with a small boy wrapped sobbing around one's legs. Rafe bent and lifted the child into his arms.

Large tears streaked down the boy's freckled cheeks. "You—you don't have to leave, Rafe. No matter what you did. I—I've done plenty of bad things, but Mama always forgives me."

He melted against Rafe, burrowing his face against Rafe's shoulder. Rafe patted his back, giving over any attempt to be cold and stern. He sought to reason with the boy, but found his own throat strangely too constricted to say a word.

Rafe turned toward Corinne, shooting her a look that appealed for her to be sensible, to help him to do the right thing. But the woman offered him no quarter.

Her own eyes now luminous with unshed tears, she murmured, "A boy shouldn't be abandoned by his father either, Rafe Mortmain."

Rafe regarded her helplessly, wondering what had become of his cold Mortmain heart, the one that was supposed to have been restored to him. Perhaps there were other forms of magic to be found in the world that didn't come from crystals and St. Legers.

Healing magic as simple as the love of a small boy and the faith to be found shining in one woman's honest brown eyes. But would it be enough to change him, to banish his bitterness and darkness?

Rafe prayed that it would because he didn't have the strength to put the boy down, turn his back on Corinne, and walk away.

Bracing Charley with one arm, he used his other hand to reach out to Corinne and brush aside the single tear that had escaped to trickle down her cheek. Swallowing hard, he said, "You are a madwoman, Corinne Brewer. But if you are stubborn enough to persist in this, if you are crazed enough to wed me, I—I vow to both you and the boy, I will never give you cause to regret it."

"I know you will not." Corinne smiled mistily up at him.

Rafe pulled her into the circle of his arm, catching her against him in a fierce hug. For a moment the three of them were lost in their own world, hovering somewhere between laughter and tears.

Rafe was the first to recover, setting Charley on his feet and saying brusquely, "All right. Enough of all this—this sentiment. We have a decision to reach." Rafe cast Corinne a glance full of love, apology, and regret.

"You know I cannot stay here in England. The St. Legers have been remarkably forgiving, but I doubt the local authorities will be as pardoning if I am caught."

"I realize that and it doesn't matter, Rafe," Corinne said. "As long as we are together, I can make a home wherever we go."

Rafe felt Charley tug at his coat sleeve. The boy dashed aside what remained of his tears and peered hopefully up at him. "What about Africa, Rafe? I've always wanted to see a lion."

"Er, ah, well, I had some place a little tamer in mind. America, perhaps."

Charley beamed. "Oh, America would be fine. And can we bring Rufus, too?"

Drag that broken down old horse on a long sea voyage? Rafe looked over the boy's head and met Corinne's laughing eyes.

"What the devil," he said with a resigned sigh and a grin. "Why not?"

Charley let out a whoop of joy, slipping his hand into Rafe's. Rafe stole his other arm about Corinne and began herding them back to the inn, to claim their belongings, to book passage for his family to a new world, a new life.

Corinne and Charley, his *family*, Rafe thought, his heart swelling with love and pride. He very much liked the sound of the word.

CHAPTER TWENTY-FOUR

*T*he wind blew in from the sea, whistling mournfully through the barren branches of some blighted oak trees. Kate shrank deeper beneath the hood of her cloak and picked her way carefully through the blackened ruins of what had once been an elegant manor house.

The few stone walls that remained looked ready to totter and crash down at any moment, their windows blasted out, rotting beams littering the ground. The grim aspect of the house seemed to match the land that surrounded it, an isolated valley stretching down to a narrow cove.

Normally Kate would have been drawn toward the sea, straight to the water's edge. But she hung back, shivering, finding the beach with its dunes and sparse tufts of sea grass bleak and uninviting. The waves breaking against the shore appeared cold and melancholy, the jagged reef beyond said to have brought more than one ship to grief.

So this was Lostland, once home to the proud and villainous Mortmains, her ancestors. Kate had trudged the property for hours, trying to feel some connection to the place. But all she felt was cold, tired, and sore at heart.

Turning away from the beach, she prepared to head back to where she had left her horse tethered when she spied the rider galloping over the hill. Kate tensed, knowing most honest folk avoided this deserted spot like the plague. She was considering the advisability of concealing herself until this stranger had galloped past when she stiffened.

Kate shielded her eyes from the pale stream of sunlight, squinting in disbelief. It was no stranger approaching. It was Val. Or at least that was whom she thought it was, his dark hair tangled across his pale face, his worn cloak flowing out from his shoulders. Her heart gave a painful leap. She might have known he would seek to come after her. He had been protecting her for most of her life. He would not stop now no matter how repulsive he found her ancestry. The man was far too noble for that.

Kate felt the old longing to rush forward to greet him, cast herself into his arms. But the blackened ruins of the house seemed to cast a long shadow over her, reminding her of what she now was . . . a Mortmain.

She remained where she was, her eyes widening when she realized that Val was still riding his demon of a white horse. Kate watched anxiously as Val drew rein and prepared to dismount. He swung out of the saddle, favoring his good leg, flinching only a little as his feet struck the ground.

Despite his limp, he moved nimbly enough to tether the stallion's reins to a branch of the oak tree. Kate hurried forward to free his cane from the saddle and hand it to him.

"Thank you," he said as calmly as though she were meeting him in the stable yard of Castle Leger instead of this wild, desolate place.

"Val, what are you doing here?" Kate asked in dismay. "And riding Storm. I thought you would have gotten rid of him."

"I planned to do so, but we seem to have reached an understanding." Val stroked the stallion's velvety muzzle. "He now agrees it would be bad manners to try to throw the man who pays for his oats."

"But—but the strain of riding him. Your leg—"

"Is just fine." Val shrugged. "Oh, perhaps my knee will exact a price from me later, but it will be worth it. I gave up on my riding far too easily. Besides, I will have need of a swift horse if you persist in running away from me."

"I—I wasn't running away," Kate was quick to deny.

"No? Then you do a fine imitation of it, my dear. Disappearing without a trace, worrying me half to death."

"I'm sorry. I didn't mean to distress you."

"Then next time leave word of your whereabouts with someone other than a recalcitrant ghost. Except that there isn't going to be a next time. I much doubt that I will ever let you out of my sight again."

Val crooked his fingers beneath her chin, forcing her to look up. His touch was as gentle as his familiar half smile, but there was something different in his eyes. Not the feverish light of the past month, but not the resigned patience of the old Val either. His gaze held hers, strong, steady, and determined. The look of a man who knew what he wanted and had come to claim it.

Kate felt her heart miss a beat.

"Now, my dear, what is all this nonsense?" he demanded tenderly. "Why have you been avoiding me?"

"I am sure you know why I have stayed away and it isn't nonsense, Val," Kate said miserably. "I—I am a Mortmain."

"If that is all that is troubling you, dear heart, it is a situation easily remedied. You once asked me to share my name with you and I am more than willing to do so."

He bent to kiss her and it was all that Kate could do to pull away, resist him. He was as usual trying to be far too kind.

"N-no, Val."

Val folded his arms, staring down at her with a slight frown. "So what are you planning to do, Kate? Leave me and set up housekeeping here?"

"No, I—I don't know," Kate faltered. She was not sure herself what she had hoped to accomplish by fleeing to Lostland. "I have always heard that this place is evil, as evil as the Mortmains themselves. I suppose I just wanted to see for myself."

"And have you seen anything evil?"

Kate glanced uncertainly around her at the blackened ruins of the house, at the bleak aspect of the cove. "No," she was obliged to admit. "This place seems more sad and neglected than anything else, lonely and deserted."

"Aye," Val astonished her by agreeing. "I had the same feeling myself when I seemed compelled to ride over here all those afternoons. If there is anything haunting Lostland, it is the tragedy of so many lives wasted in frustration and bitterness."

Val smiled tenderly at her. "The same thing that would have happened to me, but for you, Kate."

"Oh, no, Val," she said. "It was only the crystal that made you that way and—"

But Val cut her off with a firm shake of his head. "No, Kate. You have always wanted to imagine me this perfect being, but I have the same weaknesses as other men. I fear I would long ago have become a recluse, shut away with my books and my pain, except for you."

"Pestering and plaguing you," Kate said ruefully.

"Making me laugh, forcing me to remain in the sunlight." Val sighed. "Oh, Kate, I have made so many mistakes, one of the worst being the way I taught you to despise Rafe Mortmain. He was not a total villain any more than I was a perfect hero.

"I can tell you one thing about the man. I lived with his nightmares and pain enough to know. If he had known about you, Kate, he would have cared for you and loved you. He would never have deserted you. You have to believe that."

Val stared down at her, his eyes dark and earnest.

"I—I believe you," Kate said, her own eyes filling with sudden tears she had to blink fiercely away. It should not have mattered so much to her, hearing this about Rafe, but somehow it did. The one thought more than any other that had always given her pain had been believing that she had been rejected, abandoned by both her parents to die.

"I never gave Rafe a chance simply because his last name happened to be Mortmain," Val continued. "It took one strange All Hallows' Eve and a dangerous shard of crystal to make me able to understand him, to understand myself as well.

"I am no saint, Kate. I never was."

"Oh, Val." Kate could not stop herself from reaching up to tenderly touch his cheek. "I never wanted you to be."

"Good." He stole his arm about her waist, seeking to draw her close, but Kate braced her hands against his chest, wanting so desperately to believe in this miracle, but still unsure.

She searched his face anxiously. "Val, are—are you truly sure you still want me? That you are not just being kind and—and doing your duty. You must feel obliged to marry me now that Effie says I am your chosen bride."

"Obliged?" Val laughed. He gave her a look rife with both tenderness and exasperation. "My dear Kate, you still don't comprehend my family's legend, do you? It has nothing to do with duty or obligation, only the magic of two hearts being brought together. Two people destined to find each other, to love forever. Just like you and I."

"Like you and I," Kate repeated, held fast, mesmerized by the love she saw shining from his dark eyes.

He swept her hands impatiently aside, drawing her close and claiming her mouth in a way that left her no room for any more doubts. His kiss was long, slow, and tender, rendering Kate breathless and trembling.

"And now will you cease all this foolishness and consent to be my wife?" he demanded with mock sternness.

"Oh, yes, Val," Kate whispered, agreeing more meekly than she had ever done to anything in her life.

He flung down his cane and seized her with both arms, hauling her hard against him. He kissed her in earnest this time, tenderness melding with heat, with a fierce passion that Kate had never expected to experience from her gentle Val again.

She broke off to stare at him, dazed and panting. "Val, you are not still under the influence of some kind of spell, are you?"

He gave a hearty laugh. "Not unless you have been dabbling in witchcraft again."

Kate shook her head.

"Then I reckon it must be purely me responsible for all these wicked thoughts that are springing into my head." Val caressed the back of his fingers down her cheek, his eyes blazing with such love and desire, it robbed Kate of what little breath she had left.

"Considering the scandal we have already created, I suppose we should attempt to behave with some sort of propriety until we are married."

"I suppose we should," Kate agreed. But her sigh was as regretful as his own.

Their resolve lasted only until their eyes chanced to meet. Then they were immediately back in each other's arms.

They spent the rest of the afternoon in Val's great bed, the tangled sheets bearing mute testimony to the heat of their passion. Kate curled up close to Val, nestling her head against his shoulder, savoring the fact that there were no longer any barriers between them.

Val lay completely naked beside her. Sated as she was, she could not seem to stop touching him, running her fingers over the muscular contours of his chest, the dark matting of hair. Val cuddled her close, brushing a kiss against the top of her head with a contented sigh.

"I don't think I ever fully understood how uncontrollable it is, the St. Leger urge to mate with one's chosen bride." Val gave a rueful chuckle. "At some point, my dear, we are going to have to get dressed and go find the vicar."

Kate's only response was to roll on top of him, playfully pinning him beneath her. She smiled lazily down at him, lightly tracing her fingers along his beard-roughened jaw.

"Don't worry. No one will blame our wickedness on you. They will say it is all the fault of that horrid Kate Fitzleger, the foundling brat.

"It is so strange," Kate mused softly. "All my life I have been called a foundling. But I never truly felt 'found' until that day you took me in your arms."

Val returned her kiss and her smile, but his expression turned immediately serious. "Kate, I know the people in Torrecombe have not always been kind to you. If you like, once we are wed, we could move away from here, make a fresh start."

Kate shook her head stubbornly. "No, this is my home as well as yours. Besides, there is Effie to consider."

"Aye, she will doubtless be quite lonely once you have moved from Rosebriar. We—we could have her live with us," Val said, but Kate laughed at the dismay she saw filling his eyes at the prospect.

"That is very generous of you, my love. And you claim you are not heroic. But, no, I have far different plans for Effie. I am determined to see her wed to her adoring Mr. Trimble."

"Turning matchmaker, my Kate?" Val teased.

"Perhaps. You realize, as Effie's daughter, I am likely destined to be the next Bride Finder. Look how well I have already done with Victor. This morning before I left Torrecombe, I saw him heading out toward Mollie Grey's farm.

"I believe I may have inherited Effie's gift, only I will never be as tame about it as she was," Kate said, steeling her jaw. "Just let me catch any St. Leger balking at the bride I choose and see what happens."

"Heaven help us all." Val chuckled.

"Except for you, sir. There is no one to save you now." And Kate proved it to him by claiming his mouth in a fierce kiss.

Val's arms tightened around her immediately, rolling her onto her back, touching, stroking, and caressing, fire melding with tenderness, passion with love.

"Oh, Kate," he murmured. "My wild g— No." Val stopped to correct himself with a loving glance.

"My lady. My sweet wild lady," Val said huskily before kissing her again.

They had known each other forever, first as friends, then lovers. But there still seemed so much to learn about each other, so much left to discover. But they had all the time in the world now to do so.

Forever, in fact.

EPILOGUE

*I*t was on a crisp sunny December morning that the wedding of Kate and Val finally took place much to the relief of the entire St. Leger family and the village of Torrecombe. Stories were still told of Lord Anatole's grandfather, a scandalous rake so consumed by passion for his chosen bride, he kept his lady a week between the sheets before the couple ever made it to the altar.

No one had ever expected that record to be broken, leastwise not by the respectable Dr. Val St. Leger. But the older and wiser heads in the village clucked their tongues knowingly and murmured. Wasn't it always the way with the quiet ones?

As Kate and Val emerged from the church, all of Torrecombe turned out to cheer, the children waving ribbon favors and tossing flower petals. It was noted that Miss Kate made a lovely bride, for once looking surprising demure and ladylike. Her bridegroom clearly had eyes for no one but her. The good doctor swooped his wife into his arms for a passionate kiss right there on the steps of St. Gothian's, both delighting the crowd and shocking the vicar.

No one took note of the tall man watching from a distance, a rare look of wistfulness stealing into the lord Prospero's inscrutable eyes as he observed the radiant bride.

"Take care of our wild girl, St. Leger," he murmured. Then with a soft smile, the great sorcerer turned and vanished in a stream of mist.